JOHNNY APOCALYPSE

BOOK 1:
Johnny Apocalypse
and the Nuclear Wasteland

BOOK 2:
Johnny Apocalypse
and the Fight for a New World

BOOK 3:
Johnny Apocalypse
and the Battle for Freedom

BOOK 4:
Johnny Apocalypse
and the King of New York

BOOK 5:
Johnny Apocalypse
and the Sky People

Join the Johnny Apocalypse Discord:

ymBcADDZFR

JOHNNY APOCALYPSE

AND THE BATTLE FOR NEW YORK

MARK ROBIJN

BLUE FORGE PRESS

Port Orchard ⚙ Washington

Dedicated to all my fellow readers and writers of science fiction and adventure. The Nuclear Wasteland is vast. What new creatures and dangers exist in its massive expanse waiting to be discovered? The only limit is your imagination.

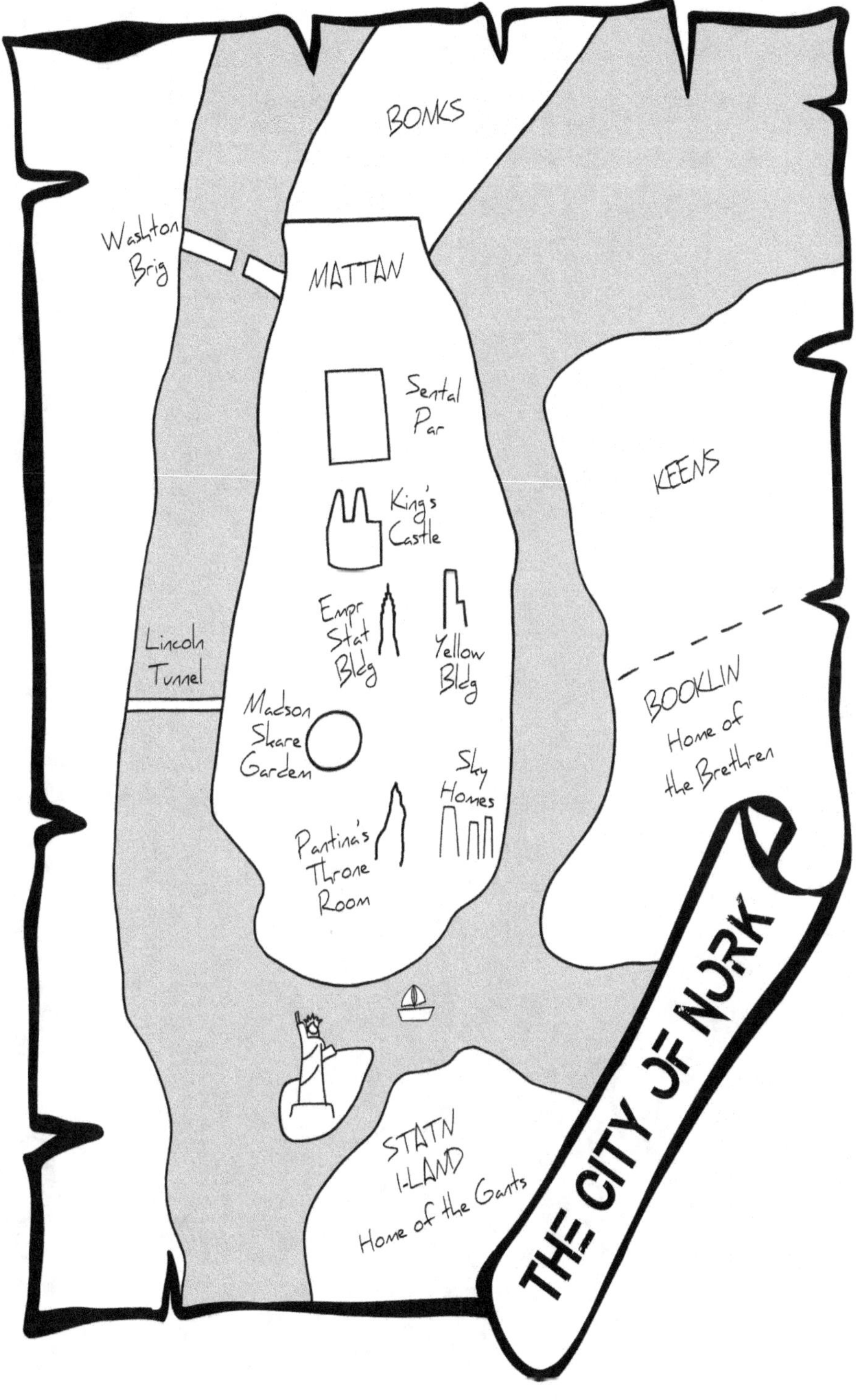

BONKS
Washton Brig
MATTAN
Sental Par
King's Castle
Empr Stat Bldg
Yellow Bldg
Lincoln Tunnel
Madson Skare Garden
Sky Homes
Pantina's Throne Room
KEENS
BOOKLIN
Home of the Brethren
STATN I-LAND
Home of the Gants
THE CITY OF NURK

JOHNNY APOCALYPSE

AND THE BATTLE FOR NEW YORK

MARK ROBIJN

WHAT HAS HAPPENED SO FAR
IN THE WASTELAND

Johnny Apocalypse, his mate Deb, their two friends Starbucks and Super and Johnny's dog-beastie Deecee take off for new adventures. An old friend named Lady Stabs follows them. Lady Stabs used to be a member of the evil gang called the Doomsday Prophecy Johnny's sworn enemies.

But Lady Stabs never really wanting to be part of the evil gang, so she asked Johnny if she could join his tribe and she was welcomed with open arms. Now a member, she secretly follows Johnny and his friends, unsure if they would want her along on their adventures, but desperate to join them.

Lady Stabs is not the only one following them, however. An old foe, another member of the gang Doomsday Prophecy, is pursuing them as well. His name is Monsta, and he fought in the battle between Johnny's tribe and the gang. He watched Johnny kill Ripper. Monsta vowed revenge to kill Johnny and his friends and take Deb, Johnny's girl, as his own.

Johnny and his friends, not knowing they are being followed, travel to the old city of Bosson where they run into horrible spider-like creatures called the Kraken. Trapped in an old building, things look grim, but it is then that Lady Stabs makes her appearance. Distracting the Kraken so Johnny, Deb and their friends escape, Lady Stabs makes her escape as well. But then Lady Stabs runs into Monsta. Monsta, who thinks Lady Stabs is still loyal to the Doomsday Prophecy, forces her to join him in following after Johnny, thinking that she too would like to see him dead. Lady Stabs plays along, looking for her chance to escape.

Johnny, Deb, Deecee, Starbucks, and Super come upon the old city of Pill-a-delpia, where their original Sanctuary was located, only to find a new society has sprung up in the city the newcomers call Pelpia. Johnny and his friends quickly find the new people to be friendly and kind, and interested in creating the old 'mocracy that existed before, just like Johnny's people. They call themselves Letfreedomring. Johnny quickly decides to introduce the newcomers to Johnny's tribe in Washington Deecee.

But before Johnny and his new friends can solidify their plans, the city of Pelpia is attacked. The army of an evil king from the city of Nork, what used to be New York City in the north, arrive at the city at Pelpia's northern gate. They ride huge, evil rat-beasties and demand the people of Pelpia pay tribute. When the leader of Pelpia, Restaria, tells the leader of the Nork army, Moxie, that they don't have the requested tribute, the Nork army attacks!

Soon the city is under siege. At just that moment, monsters from the South, the Kraken, who have followed Johnny and his friends, come running toward the city. The Kraken, running on their spider-like legs with their tentacles waving in the air, plan to kill and eat everything in their path!

Johnny sees a chance to turn the tide of the battle. He leads the Kraken to the north side of the city, where, just as Johnny hoped, the Kraken attack the army of Nork. But soon the Kraken make their way into the city of Pelpia and attack everyone! As battle rages, Deecee becomes lost. Johnny and Deb become separated, and so do Starbucks and Super.

When the battle is over, most of the Kraken are defeated and scatter, but the army of Nork is victorious. They take the people of Pelpia prisoner, and Moxie captures Deb, too!

Moxie and the army of Nork round up the people of Pelpia and march them and Deb northward to the city of Nork as their slaves. Moxie fancies Deb and decides he's going to make her his girl. Johnny and Starbucks pursue the fleeing army. Johnny desperately hoping to find a way to rescue Deb from Moxie, even though the chances of stealing her away from the middle of the Nork army camp seems impossible.

Starbucks turns back to look for Super, and Johnny goes on alone. Meanwhile, Super has allied with the genral of the Pelpia army, Lightpole. Together they ride a Harley south to try and get help from Misterwizard and Johnny's tribe.

Moxie, the Nork army and their prisoners arrive at three tunnels known as the Lincolm Tunnel that lead to the huge wall that stands at the entrance into Nork. Moxie decides to rest there before taking one of the tunnels to the gate. They don't know that inside the tunnel, undead monsters called Lurkers have escaped from the Nork subway where they were trapped through an opening in the tunnel wall. The Lurkers roam around inside the dark tunnels, waiting for victims.

Johnny manages to rescue Deb and escape with her into the middle of the three dark tunnels ahead, unaware Lurkers wait in the darkness. Clancy and his clan pursue them, but when they hear the Lurkers ahead, they quickly turn back and give up the chase. Johnny and Deb are almost caught by the Lurkers, but Deecee finds them again just in time, allowing them to escape on the other side of the tunnel.

Monsta and Lady Stabs are captured by Moxie and the Nork army. Moxie tells two of his soldiers to take them to the king, and so Monsta and Lady Stabs ride along ahead with their captors.

Super and Lightpole contact Johnny's tribe and Misterwizard, and the tribe is eager to help rescue the people of Pelpia. A small army of soldiers from the tribe is gathered up, led by Misterwizard. They head north to help their newfound allies.

Meanwhile, the Lurkers pour out of the tunnels. In a panic, Moxie leads everyone into one of the tunnels in a desperate rush to get to the gate of Nork before the

Lurkers can kill them. In the dark tunnels full of Lurkers, Moxie is bitten by one.

Johnny, Deb and Deecee arrive at the gate of Nork. As they try to figure out what to do, since the army they came to rescue is not behind them on the other side of the tunnels, somewhere amazing happens. Beings with giant white wings descend from the sky, grab them and carry them away!

Moxie and the army arrive at the gate to Nork after Johnny, Deb and Deecee are gone. They manage to get in, but Moxie is turning into a Lurker. They lead their prisoners from Pelpia to an old stadium inside the city, where they keep them prisoner until the king of Nork decides what to do with them.

Monsta, Lady Stabs and their two guards are attacked by the winged men. Lady Stabs is captured by the winged beings, one of the guards is killed, but the other guard and Monsta manage to get away. Later, Monsta is recaptured by two more Nork soldiers, who bring him to the king.

Johnny, Deb and Deecee are taken to the top of one of the tallest buildings in Nork. There they are introduced to the winged people who call themselves the Sky. They have a happy reunion with Lady Stabs. The people of Sky and Johnny and his friends soon become good friends. Johnny and Deb make a new friend, a young man Johnny's age named Mantayo. Mantayo explains that the Sky are constantly under attack by the army of Nork, for the king of Nork wants to destroy them. Johnny and Deb also learn that the Sky worship a young winged woman with red hair they consider a goddess named Pantina.

Moxie and his second-in-command meet with the king of Nork. They tell the king about their prisoners. The king is upset, for he didn't want more mouths to feed, he wanted food to give to his starving people. Moxie also gives him the bad news about the Lurkers.

Moxie also tells the king about Johnny Apocalypse and how his friends are trying to rescue the prisoners.

As the king ponders all this information, Moxie turns into a Lurker. The king quickly has him restrained before he can bite and infect anyone. But the king doesn't have him killed, thinking that Moxie might be useful.

Misterwizard and the Tribe head north with Starbucks and Super, unaware they are heading for the Lurkers. And Monsta meets the king of Nork. Realizing that the king is just the type of person Monsta wants to serve, Monsta pledges his undying devotion to the king. The king accepts, if Monsta is able to do one thing for him. Monsta must find a way to ascend the building where the Sky goddess lives, kill her and bring the king back her head. If Monsta does that, the king will make him an important man in the kingdom. Monsta sets off to do what the king asks.

The story continues in *Johnny Apocalypse and the Battle of New York...*

CHAPTER 1

The king of Nork sat on his throne, a glum frown on his face. His hands drooped on his lap and his chin rested on his chest. And strangest of all, a look of fear shone on his face and danced at the back of his eyes.

The throne room stood empty, with not even his guards there, strange as if being empty was an unnatural occurrence. Even the women, his ladies in waiting that the king used to cheer himself up with weren't there, which showed how worried the king was, for he never went anywhere without his pretty girls.

The king wore his new outfit, green leotards, a green felt shirt with a brown belt at his waist, and a green pointed hat with a feather, for he had decided they would all stop being gangsters and be characters from a book he'd read called Robin Hood. But even the new outfit didn't cheer him up. The weight of being king bore heavily on his mind, pressing down on him like a boulder on his heart.

He talked to himself, letting his fear have full reign.

"What should I do, Daddy?" he asked, as if hoping his father would appear and give him advice. "Lurkers are at our gates. Enemies surround me on all sides. I don't want to worry about things; I only want to have fun."

As the king spoke and heard his own words, he became more and more agitated, and soon his fear shown plainly on his face. "Clancy and his horrible clan of dirty savages are just waiting for me to make a mistake, so they can kill me and take over my throne. And the people of Nork do nothing but complain for food and fight each other. And then there's this Johnny Apocalypse fellow, who sounds terrifying. I'm supposed to appear strong and without fear. And it was fun being king before all these problems decided to spoil everything. I don't know what to do!"

"Perhaps if you took your counselor's advice more often…"

The king jumped and turned his head, to see Ferdinand standing on his left, slightly behind the throne peering at him.

Anger boiled up inside of the king along with even more fear and his lip curled. "How dare you sneak up on me, enter my presence without telling me first! I should have you fed to the Lurkers!"

The king hoped Ferdinand would wilt in fear, but was not surprised but very dismayed when Ferdinand didn't. Instead, Ferdinand grinned darkly, in a most frightening way. Ferdinand stood in a long, green felt robe tied with a gold sash. He leaned on a black cane with a small black skull at the top. The cane was one he often walked around with, and it had frightened the king since childhood, for he'd seen Ferdinand hit children, and even adults with the end when they displeased him.

"You are only king because your father was. He was a ruthless and cunning man. You, on the other hand are nothing but a weak, childish fool, playing games and pretending to be characters from your books. If you threaten or insult me again, I will leave, and then you can solve all your problems on your own."

The king's heart leapt with fear at the thought, and his stomach felt queasy. "No, don't do that. I'm sorry."

The king stood up and turned to face Ferdinand. Wishing he hadn't dismissed all his guards and ladies in waiting, the king felt cold and all alone. He also regretted wearing the green outfit, for now it made him feel silly and childish in front of Ferdinand. Still, the king tried his best to look fierce and strong.

"You know I am only acting as I should, like a king," the king said, trying to sound brave, but sounding weak and afraid instead. "You have always been my friend and adviser, Ferdinand. But we are in such a mess right now. What do we do?"

Ferdinand grinned, making the king wonder what he was up to. Then Ferdinand put a comforting hand on the king's shoulder.

"This is all too much for you. How could you be

expected to deal with so many problems? Wouldn't you rather be lying in your bed, eating delicious food and partying with your ladies?"

The king smiled, thinking about what Ferdinand said. Then he nodded.

"Why don't you go to your room now. I will come up with the answers to all our problems, and when I do, I'll tell you. Then you can say you thought them up, and impress the people with your wisdom!"

The king relaxed and felt happy. Everything was going to be all right. The last thing he needed now, with all the problems of the kingdom, to lose his old mentor and aide. He didn't know what he'd do if that happened. And Ferdinand was going to fix everything! The king nodded as Ferdinand put an arm around his shoulders and led him behind the throne towards the king's bedchamber.

"I am tired. I haven't slept well lately," the king admitted. "And there is one new girl, with cute yellow hair..."

"I will fetch her for you, Your Majesty!" Ferdinand walked the king over a purple door on the back wall with a rounded top and gold edging. He opened to door and led the king inside.

The king's bedchamber was vast, a large space with marble floors and long white columns. The floor was covered with beastie furs, most with the heads still attached. Two fireplaces, one on either side of the room, crackled merrily with fire, throwing out orange glows and a cheery warmth. The cold stone walls were made warmer by long velvet curtains covering them.

The room was full of toys, wooden horses, and dolls and stuffed animals. At the back of the room, lay a huge bed covered with furs and pillows under a huge canopy. Tables held the remains of food and drink, and the floor was covered with trash and bits of food, for the king was a messy person who didn't care.

The king, suddenly wanting nothing more than to get in his bed and cover his head, ran towards it and flopped himself down. Without meaning to, he started sobbing, for the weight of everything came crushing down on him.

Ferdinand just stood by the bed and watched, grinning slyly. "I will send in your ladies and maybe a jester or two. Have fun, Your Majesty! After all, that's what being a king means! Get into bed, and don't worry about a thing."

The king wiped his eyes and looked up at Ferdinand, still unsure if the man could be fully trusted. "You won't tell anyone about this, will you? How I appeared…"

"Of course not. Remember, Your Majesty, I'm your friend. I always have been."

The king nodded. "I do remember, Ferdinand. You have always been loyal to us. I won't forget it, either."

Ferdinand helped the king out of his green clothes and into his pajamas. Then when the king was in bed, Ferdinand pulled the covers up over him.

"Take a rest, Your Majesty. I will do all the work,

while you just rest."

The king nodded and smiled happily, glad to not have to think anymore. "Make sure you keep me up to date. I won't sleep long."

Ferdinand walked back to the door at the other end of the room. He turned and looked at the king. "Sleep for as long as you like, Your Majesty. Sleep forever."

Ferdinand walked out and closed the door behind him.

The king frowned. What did Ferdinand mean by that last remark? He shook his head. Sleep overcame him, and he dismissed the question. He was too tired to care just then. He'd figure it out, after he'd had a nice sleep.

The king closed his eyes and lay his head down. He smiled, just about to drift off into a nice, long sleep.

He heard something from near a wall on the right of the room. He opened his eyes. Someone was standing there, just behind the curtain! The person was peeking out and staring at the king! The king sat up and pulled the covers up to his chin? Who was it?

All he could see were the whites of the person's eyes, watching him.

Then he heard the shuffling of feet. From behind the curtain, Moxie walked out.

Johnny held Deb's hand and gazed into her eyes. She gazed back at him, love and devotion shining on her face. They sat on a couch in front of a huge opening in the wall of the tall building in Nork where the Sky had given them a room. Deecee lay next to them on the floor. Outside Nork was blanketed in a white fog, and only the tops of the skyscrapers peeked out at the top of the clouds.

Johnny, with his short yellow hair sticking up in all directions and strong features, wore his usual outfit of black leather pants, a cloth shirt, black leather vest, and black boots. He leaned forward and pressed his lips against Deb's. She kissed him back passionately. But then she pulled her hands away and glared at him, fear and unhappiness on her face.

Deb, her long blond hair blowing in the slight breeze from the opening in the wall, gazed at Johnny with her vibrant blue eyes. Her blue jeans, pink fuzzy sweater and white tennis shoes with pink socks did little to keep the chill out, and she shivered.

"I don't like you going down there alone, back to where those monsters are. Leaving me alone again. I like the Sky, but the horrible spider-beasties that cling to the buildings, they scare me. They say their goddess Pantina controls them, but how can she? And I'm tired of us being separated all the time."

Johnny took her hands in his. "You won't be alone. You'll have Deecee. And Lady Stabs. And what can I do, Deb? I have to warn our Tribe and Misterwizard before it's too late."

Deb stood up, walked over to the large hole in the wall and stared out. It was a day when the clouds came down and hugged the world. Misterwizard called it a strange name: "fog." Deecee stood up and padded over to stand next to her.

After being with the Sky for a few days now, Johnny and Deb had learned a little about the city of Nork. The building they were in was one of a collection of buildings on the south side of the i-land of Mattan, the main i-land of Nork. To the west another i-land sat, one broken up into two areas, Keens to the north, occupied by the people of Nork, and Booklin to the south, an area protected by a large wall. Mantayo told Johnny that area was owned by a people called The Brethren. They kept to themselves, and attacked anyone who tried to enter their land.

Through the opening in the wall, Deb could another building across the street. This was the main meeting place of the Sky, and where they conducted most of their business. As Deb gazed at it, the fog swirled around it, making it look like a ghost. Spider-beasties webbing interlaced with rope a floor below her crossed over to the other building, and also to the building on the right which Lord Flaggalon kept as his own private residence.

A little distance away, just visible if Deb peeked her head out the opening, she could see the top of the tall building where Pantina's throne was located. It looked as if it was made of black glass, for all the sides were made up of it. Across the street Pantina's throne building, another tall building stood where people went to prepare to see Pantina. From that building they flew or were flown to her throne room when they were invited, for no webbing touched the building where Pantina's throne room was.

As Deb gazed out, she could just see the dark shapes of some of the spider-beasties through the fog, a horrible sight. As a cool wind blew her soft, yellow hair back and her face lost color because of the cold, she shivered. "I'm just afraid, Johnny. If we keep tempting fate, one of these times we may lose."

Johnny wrapped his arms around her waist from behind and rubbed his cheek against her hair. "One of these times, we will finally be done fighting, and have peace. And then you and I can settle down and be boring old people, just like our parents."

Deb couldn't help but laugh, a smile springing to her face. She turned around and looked at Johnny. They laughed together, and Deb felt better.

Mantayo and his mother Layla walked in. Mantayo, a strong youth of sixteen seasons with huge white wings, strode confidently over to Johnny and Deb and stood beside them. Deecee barked and walked over to him, and Mantayo petted his head. Layla, with soft shoulder-length brown hair, did not have wings like her son. She stopped at the doorway and watched them from a distance.

"Are you ready, Johnny? We should go now!"

Johnny let go of Deb, who sat down and watched the two boys, frowning unhappily.

"What kind of weapons do you have, Mantayo?" Johnny asked.

"We have fire," Mantayo said. "And swords. We will set the Lurkers ablaze, or cut them to ribbons with our swords. And we will shoot arrows at them. We will concentrate on the ones on the edges, so the others are trapped in the middle."

Johnny nodded. "Have you thought of commanding the spider-beasties to attack the Lurkers? How do you control them? "

Mantayo rubbed his chin. "Pantina controls them with her thoughts. But she is only willing to do that when there is danger to our home. And we have no way of getting the spider-beasties, as you call them, to where we are going."

Johnny nodded, understanding. "I guess it's just up to us, then. How many of your men are coming with us?"

"Twenty," Mantayo said. "That is the most we dare take, or Lord Flaggalon will find out. Then we will have to get his permission, and we don't have time for that."

"Johnny," Layla said from the doorway. "Do your people have a way to fight?"

"Yes, Layla. I'm sure they have many weapons. After all, they are coming to help free the people of Letfreedomring."

"Good," Layla said, nodding somberly. "If you don't make it before they meet the Lurkers, at least they'll have a way to defend themselves."

"All right, let's go!" Johnny said.

Lord Flaggalon, the high priest of the Sky, an old man with a long, white beard and long, wrinkled face came in. Mantayo and Layla both frowned in surprise and disappointment, afraid his presence meant he knew their plans. They usually frowned when Lord Flaggalon was present, for never brought good news, just complaints and more orders for people to follow. Deecee growled low in his throat, and Johnny quickly walked over and put an arm around Deecee's neck, calming him.

Lord Flaggalon stomped up to Layla with a look of anger, after eyeing Deecee suspiciously. "What is this I hear; you are planning attacks and ordering soldiers to fight without even consulting me?"

Lord Flaggalon realized his mistake, but not before both Layla and Mantayo, and Johnny, caught it. "I mean without Pantina's blessing?"

"We had no time!" Mantayo burst out. "Johnny's people are in danger!"

Lord Flaggalon spun on Mantayo. "Insolent boy!" He turned back to Layla. "Haven't you taught this boy any discipline? To interrupt like this when adults are talking?"

"He means no insult, Lord Flaggalon, and he is right," Layla stated firmly. "There was no time for a consultation. Even now, Johnny's tribe might be walking right into the Lurkers. They will not even know what is facing them. "There are only a small group going, and all they are going to do is warn Johnny's people. They don't plan to fight anyone," she lied.

"I forbid it!" Lord Flaggalon thundered, shaking his fist. "We have to think of our own people!"

"Please," Johnny said, stepping forward. "My friends don't know what's coming towards them. We want to be your allies. But if you let my people be ambushed by these monsters, I don't see how we could be. If you allow us to be harmed, you are no real friends."

"Lord Flaggalon, I will pay any penalty you ask," Layla said. "Let us help Johnny's people. We need all the allies we can get against the Groundworms."

Lord Flaggalon scowled grumpily, hating to give in and lose face, but he had to admit their argument had merit. Still, he had to turn the circumstances somehow so he retained his power.

"I have consulted Pantina about this," though they all knew he hadn't. "She will allow our people to warn Johnny's people, and that is all. They are to call down from above. They are not to land or to interfere in any way with what happens. Do you understand? If you disobey me, er, Pantina, she will be very angry."

"We will do exactly as you say!" Mantayo said, his voice full of relief and joy. "Johnny, let's go!"

Mantayo walked to the opening in the wall. Johnny followed, then turned to Deb. "I'll be back before you know it. Take care of Deecee for me!"

Deb's eyes grew moist with tears, but she held her face emotionless. She knelt down and put her face into Deecee's neck, trying to hide her dismay.

Johnny wanted to run over and hold Deb, tell her it was going to be okay, but instead he stepped in front of Mantayo. Mantayo placed a harness on Johnny that he had made up. The harness connected to one Mantayo wore.

Mantayo flapped his wings and rose in the air. Slowly Johnny, in the harness, rose up off the ground as well. Then Mantayo leapt out. He plummeted out of view, but in a few seconds could be seen rising, flying away at a quick speed, with Johnny hanging just below him.

From other buildings, other members of the Sky joined them, and soon there was a whole group, looking like strange giant bird-beasties.

Lord Flaggalon, Deb, and Layla watched them disappear into the fog. Lord Flaggalon's eyes were the only thing which showed his jealousy of Mantayo's flying ability, though it ate at him like a cancer. Deb's face was a mask of worry and sadness, seeing Johnny once again leaving her. Layla smiled quietly, simply glad that Mantayo had been allowed to go, though she knew there would be consequences to both her and Mantayo later.

CHAPTER 2

Monsta moved slowly, gazing warily down the street in all directions. A big man, standing six feet tall, with a scraggly black beard, long black hair and a scar on his cheek, he didn't look like the type who would be afraid of anything. There was a time when he thought he never would be. Then he met the little scrabbler girl here in Nork who bit him. Now, in this place, he was afraid of his own shadow. The people here were waksy, desperate. And hungry.

Monsta spied an empty storefront and hid himself in the doorway. He peered out at the street. It seemed like this area of Nork must have been an important place once, for the street was wider than most. Buildings crowded in on every side, all shapes and sizes. Piles of rusted old cars dotted the street, one pile so high it rose into the sky and Monsta had to crane his neck to see the top. It looked like it would fall over and crush people below at any second. He wondered how so many cars could have all rode around the city at the same time. Didn't they run into each other?

The buildings here had big posters on their sides, almost covering the whole buildings. The posters were all tattered and faded, some turned into mulch which flapped in the wind. Some buildings had big, black, rectangular glass panels on them. Monsta wondered what they'd been for. Some of the panels were cracked or broken and Monsta could see wires behind the glass. Others were just so dirty he couldn't see the glass through the dirt and grime.

Many of the buildings were broken at the top, leaving jagged edges that looked like the ends of pieces of metal Monsta found sometimes to make weapons out of. It looked like the mushroom monster had not hit the city directly, but still managed to do a lot of damage. He could see inside the buildings where the outside walls were gone, or where the windows had broken. Inside the rooms there was nothing but piles of rotting garbage or rubble. The whole world seemed to be made up of rotting old junk. No wonder the people were all starving!

People moved about in the streets, some dressed in dirty rags, others in the strange gangster clothes that seemed to be the rule. Most simply wore one or two pieces of old gangster costume on over their dirty rags. The people looked normal, except for the look of hunger in their eyes. Monsta knew if he got too close to any of them, they would recognize him as a stranger and all attack. Monsta had never been afraid of ordinary people before, but there was something creepy here.

Every now and then, a soldier rode down the street on a ratty. These guards held big sticks with sharp ends. They watched the crowd, looking bored. They had the power though, and Monsta wished he was one of them, riding around, handing out pain wherever he wanted, making people run in fear, his ratty nipping at people and snarling. Maybe if he pleased the king, he could be one soon. But what he really wanted was something even greater, a position of true power in the kingdom. If the king didn't give it to him, he'd find a way to take it.

Monsta grew hungry again and his stomach rumbled. He wondered why he was so waksy as to agree to do the impossible task for the king of Nork. How was he going to get up into the top of one of the buildings where the Sky were and kill their goddess? He might as well sprout wings himself and try to fly there. Agreeing had helped him escape, and that was good. Now, he could just run away. The king would never know. The thought was very tempting. But where would he run to? He really like this king, he was cruel, just like Ripper. Monsta decided he would try to do what the king asked, and if it proved too hard, he could always give up and sneak back to Pelpia, his old home. But then what of his revenge on Johnny? And what would he do? Spend his days knowing he was a coward, he thought. And wander the wasteland, alone. No, he was going to kill the goddess and earn the king's favor. It was really his only choice.

Monsta nodded to himself. But the first order of

business was to find some food and water. Then when his belly was full, find a way to climb one of the buildings.

Monsta walked out from the doorway. Trying to look waksy so they would think he was just another citizen of Nork, he looked at the sidewalk, not making eye contact with anyone. He weaved a little, tried to look hungry, and walked fast. He glanced up every few seconds, looking for something interesting that might mean a place where there was food, and to make sure he wasn't drawing too much interest.

Monsta wandered into the street, right next to a pile of cars, orange from rust with nothing but metal shells left. The people stayed on the sidewalks, shuffling along as if they had no real purpose, eyes staring blankly forward. As far as Monsta could tell, this was what most people in Nork did, nothing. They simply wandered around looking for food or getting in fights. They were really the type just begging for a dictator to take charge, one like Ripper. Ripper would have scoffed at all the weak, waksy people. Ripper would have known what to do. And Ripper wouldn't have been afraid at all.

Suddenly Monsta saw something high in the sky which made his heart leap with excitement. More winged beings flew towards them! There were so many of them they seemed to fill the sky, and a sense of amazement and wonder mixed with excitement made Monsta shiver. He knew an attack was coming, for the creatures held flaming balls in metal boxes. The balls of fire looked like living orange monsters, ready to wreak destruction.

Monsta looked at the people of Nork. None had noticed the flying attackers yet. Monsta grinned, for despite the coming danger, he loved a good fight, and he knew the next few minutes were going to be filled with scenes of death and carnage he would want to remember.

Monsta ran to the pile of cars and climbed inside one at the bottom through a glassless window. The car had a small, silver piece of metal with of five circles on the trunk, hanging vertical, held by one remaining screw. Monsta nestled down on the hard metal seat on the front passenger side, for any padding in the car had rotted away a long time ago. Monsta lowered his head so he could see out the front window and waited with a thrill of excitement for the show.

Then it came! A flaming fireball tore down from the sky, exploding on the ground not ten feet from him. Screams and shouts filled the air, and he saw the people of Nork look up in fright and run in all directions.

Monsta giggled. It was an amazing sight, as fireball after fireball exploded on the ground, sending plumes of smoke and flames into the sky. Screams of pain filled the air and Monsta looked with dark glee to see a man on fire, writhing around in agony before falling to the ground.

Why did the strange flying creatures hate the people of Nork so much? Monsta could now understand why the king of Nork wanted to get their goddess so much, and it made him feel strangely warm, thinking what the king planned to do to the winged people after their goddess was dead. The heat from the fireballs warmed Monsta's face, somehow pleasant, for it came with the smell of burning flesh. The streets grew empty as everyone hid inside the buildings, only the burning bodies of victims laying on the streets, burning and smoking.

Then a Nork soldier with a Tommy Gun ran out of a building, his face twisted in hatred and anger. He pointed the gun towards up at one of the attackers and pressed the trigger. A rat-a-tat-tat filled the air, echoing off the surrounding buildings. The man turned the gun back and forth the spraying the sky with deadly bullets. It was an awesome battle, all for Monsta's enjoyment!

Restaria rose from her sleep and gazed about. She lay on the hard ground in the middle of the strange round arena. She shivered, for none of the guards gave her people any kind of blankets or way to warm themselves. The people of Letfreedomring, lay sleeping or milling about. Restaria looked up at the sky and saw the red eye was high in the sky, hidden by clouds. It did not give much warmth. A slight mist rolled along the ground, and the grass they sat on was wet with dew.

How long had they been in this strange, empty, lonely prison? It seemed like an eternity, but she knew it was only a few days. How much longer could her people survive before they starved, or at least gave up all hope?

They were trapped in some kind of giant round building, with rows of seats that sloped backwards from the ground all about them. It looked like some kind of arena where people in the days before the Mushroom Monsters sat and watched something. She wondered if the Mushroom Monsters froze the ghosts of the people where they died, and if people from the old world were all sitting in the seats, watching them right now. What would the people from before think of the new world?

Restaria turned her head and studied the guards positioned on all sides of them. The guards seemed to take special precaution to watch the openings between the rows of seats, so no one could sneak by them. The guards looked half-asleep themselves, however, and the guns in their hands drooped. But what good was it? Most of her people were too weak from hunger and too tired to mount an attack, and half were women and scrabblers. She only had a small handful of fighting men. Some of the women would fight too of course, but still, the guards were on all sides of them. Once they made a move, the guards would wake up and be on the alert. How could they fight them all at the same time?

Restaria's second-in-command, Johnthebaptist walked up. He held out his hand and helped Restaria to stand. They glanced about to make sure no one was watching them, then spoke in hushed tones.

"Johnthebaptist, I don't like the look of our people. They grow weaker by the moment. I'm afraid they will begin to get sick from lack of food and warmth."

Johnthebaptist was a brown man with black hair who might have been referred to as latino in the old days. He looked strong, a man who had spent many years working hard under the sun. He was in his mid-thirties, still young but old enough to have seen the world, and be able to learn from it. Restaria liked him, for he was an even tempered and intelligent man who had a good heart. He often advised her on problems that arose at Pelpia, and if she was younger instead of in her late fifties, Restaria might have had romantic notions about him. She doubted he would be interested in a woman of her age, but it didn't keep her from musing about it.

Johnthebaptist glared sullenly at the guards. "Those animals don't care if we die. Just less mouths to feed." He turned to Restaria. "We can't just sit here and wait until this king decides what gruesome fate he has for us. I have a plan."

Restaria turned to look at him with surprise and renewed interest, and a glimmer of desperate hope. "What is it?"

Johnthebaptist sat down on the ground, and Restaria sat next to him. "It's going to be dangerous, and we might be worse off than we are now," he started, talking in a low voice. "We may all die. But it's better than sitting around here, waiting, doing nothing."

Restaria nodded. "Tell me the plan. Then we can discuss whether it is worth doing."

"Okay," Johnthebaptist said. "I've been able to wander about, behind the guards, into those covered areas under the stairs around the sides of the stadium. If you're careful, the guards don't even take notice of you at night. There are many old food booths of wood there, full of rotting food and machines."

"Yes, go on," Restaria said, as she chewed on a piece of bread, her eyes tightly fastened on Johnthebaptist's face.

"All of the entrances going to the outside are held closed by heavy chains and some kind of locking devices. However, there is one entrance that is not chained. A set of heavy wooden planks hold the doors shut, held in place by rows of old benches. That entrance may be our way out."

Restaria stopped chewing on the bread and put her hands out in confusion. "What good will it do us to get outside? The people of Nork will see us and give the alarm."

Johnthebaptist looked grave, but smiled. "This entrance does not go outside. It goes down."

Restaria took this new information in. "Where does it lead to?"

"I suspect Nork is a lot like Pelpia. It has underground tunnels, where the old long metal tubes that ran on the metal bars lay. I suspect the tunnels run underneath the whole city. We can go through those doors and escape by running down these tunnels."

Restaria looked uncertain. "But didn't that soldier Moxie say that is where those evil monsters came from? And how do we know where these tunnels lead?"

"We don't have much choice. It is either take our

chances in the tunnels, or die here."

Restaria shook her head. "It sounds like suicide. Those creatures, if they bite us will kill us and make us undead, like them. We could be trapped down there and surrounded by those things. And there may be no other openings out of the tunnel that are not barred and sealed. It could be a deathtrap."

Johnthebaptist nodded. "There are a lot of reasons to say no. But our only alternative is to wait here, until we are led off like cow-beasties to the slaughter. Or fight our way out onto the streets of this city, which will be almost as suicidal."

Restaria put a hand on Johnthebaptist's shoulder. "We will have to knock out all of the guards at once, and in a way where our people are not killed."

Johnthebaptist nodded. "There are a lot of reasons to say no. And not many to say yes."

They sat for a moment, contemplating their terrible choices. Restaria looked around at the people sitting in little circles, huddled against the cold of the night near fires. They looked sad, dejected, and defeated. Something had to happen soon.

"When would we put this plan in place?"

Johnthebaptist looked up at the night sky. "Tonight, when the yellow eye is high in the night sky so we can see well to fight."

Restaria looked up as well. "All right. It looks to be our only choice, though it is a terrible one. Pass the word."

As the strange caravan trundled down the gray strip of highway with loud creaks from the vehicles' old shocks and explosions and coughing from their engines, the mood inside was one of excited cheerfulness. They headed out on a quest, and none of them thought about the possibility of dying or being hurt, just the thrill of going to the rescue of a people they didn't know, in a strange new land.

In the front bus, everyone quietly laughed and pointed at the strange oriental man in his odd outfit, his sword strapped to his side who stood by the driver. Lightpole knew he seemed strange to the people of Johnny's tribe, but he smiled, not offended. He knew the people meant no harm, and had already accepted him as one of their own.

Sephie and Wheaties got up and walked up to Lightpole. He turned and smiled at them.

"You're from the city where we used to live, is that right?" Sephie asked.

Lightpole nodded. "Yes. We call it Pelpia now."

"We left there for a better place," Wheaties said, a somber expression on his brown face. "Washington Deecee is the captol. It has lots of white buildings with long sticks in front. It's where the people used to live, who were important and ran the whole world."

Lightpole thought about this, rubbing his chin. "I had never heard of this Washington Deecee, until Johnny mentioned it to us. I am sure it is very special. Pelpia is a nice place now too. We have made a nice home there.”

Sephie pointed at Lightpole's sword. “Johnny has a sword too, but yours is different. Yours is thinner, and curved.”

“Swords come in many different shapes and sizes,” Lightpole said. “This one was passed down from my ancestors to me. It is very special to me. It is called a Katana. And it will never leave my side.”

Outside, Misterwizard stopped his moped and raised a hand in the air. Starbucks stopped too, and then the rest of the caravan. Misterwizard hopped off his moped and walked over to Starbucks and Super, who looked at him with curiosity.

“The time has come, my stalwart companions, to take a brief interval and solidify our preparations for our coming engagement. We must formulate a battle plan for engaging our antagonists and rescuing our wayward companions.”

“Yep, we got to figure out what to do next,” Super agreed. Starbucks chuckled.

“Precisely, my courageous heroine! You put it very succinctly.”

Starbucks looked up at the sky, which darkened with the oncoming of the yellow eye and nighttime. “Why don't we make camp here, then after we eat, we can sit down and come up with a plan.”

“A most excellent suggestion Starbucks. It will give us time to do an inventory of our current weaponry and manpower as well. We will be ready in the morning to sally forth with courage and confidence on our mission, and a much higher percentage of chance for success!"

"Yeah, it will let us be more ready too," Super said, this time just to be funny.

Misterwizard put an arm around Super. "I will inform our contingent to prepare to bivouac. Meanwhile, Starbucks, you and Super can engage in a hunting expedition to acquire any provender in the local area."

"We'll scout for some food," Starbucks said, getting in on the game. Starbucks and Super laughed and headed towards one of the nearby walls on the side of the road, as Misterwizard trundled off towards the buses.

Neither Starbucks, Super or Misterwizard heard the soft groaning coming from the darkness ahead.

CHAPTER 3

Clancy, Alasdair, Gavin and the rest of the Clan tramped on, following the edge of the large river that flowed between Mattan, where the Norkers and the king of Nork lived, and the west side, a place called Nu Jersi, where Clancy's clan had their homes. Weary and tired, they still felt the heavy sorrow of losing Angus to the Lurkers. They walked silently, feeling defeated. Their time with the army of Nork was supposed to provide them with food and treasure to bring back home, but instead it had only given them grief and the loss of a companion.

They passed by deserted houses as they tramped down a two-lane concrete road next to the river. On their right, the river stretched on for what seemed like miles, quiet and cold. In the distance beyond it, they could see the tall buildings of Nork, looking like silent black ghosts in the morning mist.

Alasdair glanced over at Clancy. Clancy stared forward, his face dark, his steps plodding.

"I don't much like coming home with nothin' to show for it, Clancy," Alasdair said. "No treasure, and no prisoners. We don't even have much food to show for our efforts."

Clancy didn't answer, simply nodded, his face holding an unhappy grimace.

"That king promised us some of the food and bounty from the fight," Gavin said, his axe laying heavy on the shoulder of his fur coat. "Instead, he ends up with a whole city of prisoners. What do we end up with? Angus dead, and empty bellies."

Clancy finally spoke. "Don't be too angry with Moxie and his men, mates. They're all likely Lurkers by now. And the prisoners be Lurkers as well. We're lucky this time to escape without dying."

Ahead they saw the trees grasslands of home and smiled with weary relief. The Clan were the only people living in the area next to a huge, broken bridge that spanned across the river. The Clan killed or drove away any wildies or crazies in the area, and eaten most of the game. They lived on a patch of land which had once been called, "Flat Rock Brook." The Clan didn't know how to read the old words of writing so they called it Clanshame. It was here they set up their tents and houses made of logs, among the trees and small streams and rocky terrain.

"Aye, thank the makers," Gavin said. "I can't wait to sleep, maybe for a thousand year."

"It will be nice to see our families again," Clancy muttered, without emotion.

Clancy stopped and raised a hand. The rest of his men stopped and looked at him.

"Hold it, fellas. What Alasdair said is true. Our people are expecting us to return with food and riches. I know we're all tired, but we need to go hunting before we enter Clanshame. We should at least bring home some food for our people."

The rest all nodded wearily. "Where are we going to find it, Clancy?" Gavin asked. "We've hunted all the game around Clanshame. There be nothing left. 'Twas why we join up with the Norker scum at all."

"Aye," Clancy said, "most of the game is gone, but we're going to have to look until we find some, even if it takes us all night. Then, we have another job to do."

Clancy walked over and looked at the huge, broken bridge that stretched out into the river. It seemed to soar up into the sky like giant metal fingers that arched over the water. Near the middle of the river the bridge stopped, broken, and pieces lay sticking up out of the water. After an open area, the other side of the bridge could be seen in the distance, as if reaching out to touch the first half, but unable to reach it.

"After we've had a wee bit of rest, we're going to gather all our men, every last one who has the spirit to fight. We'll cross over to Mattan on that there Washton Brig."

"But Clancy!" Alasdair said. "It's dangerous crossing there. The brig only goes half way, and then we'll have to swim for it. The current is strong, and we'll have to climb up and down to get to the top of the brig.

And even if we make it, we'll have to climb the wall of Nork."

"And won't the king of Nork hear of it? He'll declare us his enemy," Gavin asked.

"I twould not concern meeself about that. I suspect he be busy with his own problems right now, if you know what I mean. Which is why this is the time to act."

They all grinned and nodded.

Alasdair said, "Aye," Alasdair said. "His army is far to the south, fighting Lurkers. He's got that Johnny character, a minor fly-beastie in his soup, but a pain nonetheless. And he's got all them prisoners to deal with."

Clancy put a hand on Alasdair's shoulder. "This be our best chance to storm his castle. If the gods be with us, we will force him to make me king of Nork. Then it will be the Clan who tells the people of Nork what to do."

They all smiled with dark hope. It gave them renewed energy.

"Let's hurry then and find some food," Alasdair said. "We don't have much time. Too long has the king of Nork had his foot upon our necks. And," Alasdair said, looking at Clancy with a smile, "you might even find that pretty maid you fancied again, and still make her your own."

That thought made Clancy smile. "Soon, I'll have my foot on the neck of their king. And then I'll chop it off for all his people to see. I'll find this Johnny and my bonny lass. And she will sit beside me, king and queen of Nork."

They all laughed began their search for game, their minds full of lofty thoughts of death and conquest.

Ferdinand lounged in his long black robe on the king's throne, a smile of dark satisfaction on his long, wrinkled face. His bony hands grasped the carved lion-beasties on the throne's arms, feeling their contours with pleasure, taking in every sensation, especially the feeling of power that coursed through him.

He looked over the room, imagining all the people of Nork cowering on their knees before him. Soon he would be king! Then the wretched, annoying rabble who constantly begged for food would look to him for help. But he wouldn't give them any. He hated the dirty, stupid people, who wandered the streets eating small rattys and bugs for food, and drinking from pools of filthy rain water. Once he was king, they would cower in fear of him, and he would kill them for his pleasure.

To stand behind the old king, that little fool as he sat in it with his stupid, giggling concubines, laughing like a hyena and making ridiculous laws for the people to follow. "Dress like old gangsters today, and talk like they do in the old book," the king would say, and all the fools wandering the streets obeyed, like stupid cows.

"And now, I want you to all act like you're from the time of Robin Hood." How Ferdinand hated helping the spoiled little fool, doing all the real work and making all the real decisions, so he could sit around and have fun. He was a spoiled, immature waksy little boy, and he never deserved such a seat of power.

But now, finally, things were going to change. The king had a nice visitor, and unless something had gone terribly wrong, the king was now joining the genral of his army Moxie in the dark underworld.

From behind the curtain which hid the front doors, Alcapoon appeared, summoned by Ferdinand to appear. Alcapoon walked up respectfully, but wearing a frown of confusion. He wondered what was Ferdinand was doing sitting on the king's throne.

When Alcapoon reached the throne, he knelt and bowed his head, for he had no idea what was going on, and it was best to act contrite until he knew the play. "Hello, Lord Ferdinand. Where is the king?"

Ferdinand wore a dark sneer, and his eyes smoldered with an angry fire. "King Richard, as he wanted to be called now, has unfortunately taken gravely ill."

Alcapoon's eyes widened with alarm and worry. He looked up at Ferdinand with concern, the wheels behind his eyes turning, for Alcapoon could tell Ferdinand had something to do with the king's condition. Ferdinand noticed the look in Alcapoon's eyes, and saw that he understood what was happening.

Ferdinand smiled with malice.

"No one is to know this. It would cause panic and unrest among the foolish rabble. For now, just tell everyone the king has put me in charge until such time as he feels better and can resume his kingly duties."

"Whatza matter with him, Ferdie?" Alcapoon asked, forgetting himself.

"You will call me Your Majesty, from now on! I am now King Ferdinand!"

Alcapoon knew how things went when one boss rubbed another out, and took over. He knew that the old king wasn't coming back, period.

"I'm so sorry, Your Majesty. Shall I make an announcement to the people?"

"For now, tell the genrals of the army and those who help run the kingdom. The rabble of the streets don't really care anyway. They are too busy simply trying to survive to care who rules them."

Alcapoon stood up. "So, what are we supposed to talk and dress like? Are we supposed to be like gangsters, or like this Robin Hood guy the king was talking about next?"

Ferdinand stood up and stood in front of Alcapoon. Ferdinand was tall and thin, and always sent a thrill of fear through everyone, for they all knew how devious he was.

"Forget all the foolishness the idiot king imposed," Ferdinand said. "I don't care how everyone dresses or talks. Only that they obey me, and live in fear." Ferdinand walked over to the table and poured himself a glass of wine. "I want you to round up all the girls and fools the king kept to entertain himself. I will find a new way for them to entertain me, one which involves much darker sport. Then I want you to gather the army, so I can talk to them in front of the castle."

"Yes, Your Majesty," Alcapoon said. He looked up at Ferdinand with a look of hope. "Who is to be the leader of the army now?"

Ferdinand grabbed a chicken-beastie leg and idly munched on it. Then he pointed it at Alcapoon as if it was a royal scepter. "You are, Genral Alcapoon, For the time being, as long as you prove yourself loyal, and ruthless."

Alcapoon smiled with joy, and stood up a little taller. "You can always count on me, Your Majesty. I will die in your service."

Ferdinand grinned in an amused fashion. "I'm glad to hear that, genral. Ferdinand grabbed a glass of wine and took a long drink. Then he gazed at Alcapoon again. "We have many pressing issues, ones the idiot was too busy to deal. It is time we dealt with Nork's many enemies. That annoying Clan to our North, who the king was too stupid to see were planning a foolish coup against us. The freaks in Booklin cursed by the mushroom monsters to become blackened or their eyes changed. It's time they ceased to exist. The Gants on Statn I-land, who are huge but slow, who the king placated by giving them people to feed on so they wouldn't attack us. And those infernal Angels, living in our buildings just out of reach because they have those horrid spiders protecting them, like flying bugs you can't reach. All these enemies should have been dealt with years ago, but the king was too occupied with foolishness. He was a fool, but he is king no more."

Alcapoon stared at Ferdinand. "Is the king dead?"

Ferdinand grinned darkly, realizing his own slip of the tongue. "You heard what happened to Moxie, haven't you?"

"Yes, Your Majesty," Alcapoon said. "He became a Lurker."

King Ferdinand laughed. "It seems Moxie had a private audience with the king, and it didn't go well for him."

Alcapoon's eyes opened wide with horror and dismay. "The poor king!"

"Yes, but a fitting end for him." King Ferdinand stared at Alcapoon. "Things are going to be different around here now, and men who prove their loyalty will find themselves richly rewarded."

Alcapoon nodded, but he looked grim.

Ferdinand continued. "We also have an army at our borders, led by this strange fellow Johnny Apocalypse, who everyone talks about as if he is a modern day, Robin Hood. We also have Lurkers outside the gates. But they may turn out to be very useful."

Alcapoon stood and walked over to Ferdinand.

"Gather the army. Tell them to get their weapons ready. Soon there will be death and war, if we are lucky."

CHAPTER 4

Monsta watched with glee as the Nork soldier sprayed the air with bullets aimed at the winged attackers. A bullet hit one of the winged men in the chest! Like a wounded bird, he fluttered to the ground. As soon as he landed, a mob descended on him. Monsta watched with evil pleasure as they beat him to death and ripped him apart. It was the best battle Monsta had ever seen, and he tried to capture everything in his mind, knowing he'd be reliving it forever.

The winged men and women flew away as the bullets filled the sky. "Cowards!" Monsta yelled, chuckling darkly.

Suddenly something happened that when Monsta saw it, he hopped up and down in excitement. One of the winged creatures, a beautiful girl with long dark hair who appeared to be about seventeen seasons, was hit by bullet fire! As Monsta watched with fascination, she fluttered in the air like a wounded butterfly, up and down, looking as if she was going to drop at any second.

The Nork soldier saw it too, and he smiled with dark glee. He aimed at her again to finish the job. Suddenly a fireball hit the man! He burst into flame, screaming in agony, dropping his gun. Monsta crawled out of the old, rusted car as fast as he could, scraping his back on the hard, steel frame. He scraped his knees too, but due to his excitement, he barely even felt it.

For now, Monsta's attention was fixed on the winged girl. A plan was forming in his dark mind. If he managed to capture her, she just might be his way into the lofty towers of the winged assailants.

Monsta frantically searched the sky, looking for her. Then he saw her. She was only a few feet above the buildings, but she was at least a block away! Monsta, ignoring everything around him, ran as fast as he could in the direction where she was falling.

Suddenly she was out of sight behind a building. Panic gripped Monsta's heart in a vise-like grip as he saw his opportunity quickly disappearing. He forced his legs to move, feeling pain shoot through them from the effort. He pumped his arms back and forth, barely taking time to breathe.

He reached a corner and sprinted around the building on his right. He looked right beyond it down the street. To his despair, he didn't see her anywhere! Was he too late?

He ran down the street, glancing into the buildings on either side of the street, trying to get a glimpse of the dark-haired winged girl. As he reached the other end of the block, he hadn't spotted her, and gloom filled his dark mind. He stopped and bent over, wheezing from the effort, sweat breaking all over his body and dripping from his forehead. What an idiot he was? Why couldn't he have run faster, he thought to himself.

Then he heard a soft, melodic voice crying out from a building down the street. It sounded like the tinkling of little bells, and Monsta knew in an instant, it had to be the girl. He grinned evilly, and forced his tired body to run towards the sound.

The sweet voice cried out again, and Monsta could tell it was a cry for help mixed with pain. An evil warmth filled him, for he loved the sound of people suffering, and it naturally gave him a good feeling. She was going to be helpless before him! He grew close to the sound. Excitement gripped him, giving him extra energy.

He glanced around and saw something very useful. A jagged piece of shiny metal lay on the ground. It was the length of his arm, shaped just like a sword and had a very sharp point at the end. He picked it up with pleasure and held it up in front of himself to inspect. It looked like some part of the building that had fallen off, and it was crude, but it would make a nice sticking weapon. He held it in front of himself and ran into the building where the sound came from.

The building was three-story brick, and had at once time been one of storefronts along the block, with doors into each one and living spaces on the upper floors. The roof was gone on most of the building, having fallen into the interior, and half of the upper floor had collapsed. Glaring light from the red eye shone down from the sky, filling the room with garish white light.

There on a pile of bricks lay the girl. Monsta stopped and gazed at her. She was a thing of beauty, with huge golden wings, dark black hair, and long legs. Her face was soft and lovely, with high cheekbones and a pointed chin. Monsta could tell she was young, maybe seventeen or eighteen seasons. What was someone so young doing in such a fierce battle, he wondered? Served them right for getting her hurt, the fools, Monsta thought, making such a pretty girl risk danger and death.

As he walked in, he saw the girl held her side with both hands. She lay on her back, nestled up against the remnant of the wall. Blood seeped from between her fingers, and Monsta wondered if her wound was bad enough that she would die soon.

As soon as she saw Monsta, the girl screamed in fright and terror. The sight of a six-foot tall man with long black hair, a black beard and a scar on his face, who was also dirty and unkempt from a day wandering about in the city half-starved, coming toward her with a jagged piece of metal would terrify anyone, let alone a helpless, wounded teen girl. Her scream filled Monsta with a thrill of pleasure.

Monsta grinned widely, showing yellow teeth, thrilled at the reaction he caused. It made him feel like a ganger again, back in the Doomsday Prophecy, causing terror and mayhem. For a brief moment, it was almost like being back home again, when Ripper and the gang were kings of the city, and everything was wonderful.

Monsta advanced on her, bloodlust flowing through his veins. She was young, and weak from blood loss and helpless, the perfect victim, and Monsta could do anything he wanted to her. It was like a dream come true!

Monsta stopped in front of her. Her eyes were open wide, staring at him with fright. "Get away from me! They are going to come looking for me, and they will kill you if you touch me!"

Monsta burst into loud laughter. He tilted his head back, having the best laugh he'd had in a long time. His eyes twinkled with evil pleasure, for he was finally in a moment he could totally understand and feel comfortable about.

Monsta relaxed, for it was obvious she was in no position to flee or do anything to fight him. He smiled at her, showing compassion. "I only want to help you. You're wounded. Let me find something to bind your wound."

Her pale face contorted in pain, and Monsta could tell she didn't believe him. Monsta didn't know how much blood she'd lost, but he hoped she wasn't about to pass out.

Still, she pretended she did trust him. "Thank you, kind stranger. Please hurry. I think the bullet passed through me, but I'm weak. I can't move."

Her words peeked Monsta's interest, for he

sensed she was lying, and maybe not as wounded as he thought. He suspected as soon as he turned to look for something to help her, she might attempt to fly away.

Monsta gazed around, looking for something to help. Then he came up with a plan. He put his metal stick down and carefully picked the girl up.

"What are you doing?" she cried weakly, but Monsta ignored her.

He carried out the back of the building and into another one nearby, one with a broken door and a dark interior. He carried her through the building to an interior doorway leading to an inner room. Looking around inside, he saw an old metal bed, perfect for his needs. The mattress had long ago disintegrated, but the bed frame still remained.

Monsta carried her over and laid her down.

"Rest here," Monsta said, smiling darkly, "while I find you something to bind your wound, and some medicine."

The girl looked up at him fearfully, not trusting him. "Listen, if you tell my people where I am, they can fix me. All you have to do is stand on the street, wave your arms towards the sky and yell my name, Dallanda. They will come and take me home. Then they will pay you well!"

Monsta didn't believe anything she said. They would take her away all right, but then they would probably kill him. Monsta searched the room and found an old piece of rotted cloth. He carried it over and as she watched in dismay, he tied her legs to the bed frame.

"What are you doing? Stop! You're hurting me!"

Monsta laughed. "I'm just making sure you won't try to fly away while I get you medicine! You might hurt yourself worse!"

The young woman tried to pull her feet out of the bindings, but then Monsta grabbed one of her wrists and started tying it to the bed frame as well.

"Please listen!" she pled as she struggled weakly. "My people will give you food, clothing, pretty colored rocks, whatever you want if you let them know I'm here! You can be rich! They will even take you away from here, wherever you want to go!"

"None of those things are what I want," Monsta said. "What I want is to meet your goddess, Pantina."

Dallanda stared at Monsta, suspicious. "What do you want with Pantina?"

"Only to worship her!"

Dallanda knew that was a lie, and fear played across her face, as she suspected Monsta of having plans to hurt Pantina somehow.

Monsta saw something else he liked in the corner. He strode over to a huge piece of concrete with metal rods sticking out. With extreme effort, picked the chunk of rock up. Carrying it over to the girl, he raised it up over her legs.

She looked at him with dismay and raised her hand in defense. "Stop! Don't kill me!"

Monsta grinned as he laid the chunk of rock on top of her legs. He positioned it so it was resting on the bed frame and not actually touching her, but because it was so heavy, he knew she would never be able to lift it.

"Let me go! I'm wounded; I won't survive!" she yelled shrilly, struggling against the bindings and the rock.

Monsta stood up and smiled with satisfaction at his accomplishment. "You will be fine, I'm sure. Now you won't leave, until I can contact your friends."

"The stone is crushing me!" she screamed. "You will pay for this! When they find me, they will kill you!"

Monsta chuckled, for he knew she was lying, only trying to get him to remove the rock so she could fly away.

"Be quiet now, or I may decide you'd make a good dinner. I'll start with your legs, and then your arms, and then your wings. Then at the end, I'll eat your head. But, if you cooperate, I will find some clean cloth to bind your wound. Then we will talk about what you're going to do for me."

Monsta went back to the first building and grabbed his makeshift weapon, and just in time. There in doorway stood a winged young man with a sharp sword in his hand. He stared at Monsta with suspicion.

"Who are you?" the young man said.

"No one you need to concern yourself with, winged freak."

"Have you seen a young girl with wings like me? You haven't done anything to her? If you have hurt her, I will make you regret the day you were born!"

Monsta grinned with humor and chuckled. "Bold

talk for a boy barely older than a scrabbler. Come over here, and try to fight me. I'm in the mood for killing someone."

"I don't want to fight you," the young man said, his voice full of sadness. "I only want to know where Dallanda is."

"Now, now," Monsta said. "I haven't hurt your flying angel, but she is wounded. I suspect if she doesn't get help soon, she will die."

The boy's face filled with worry. "Where is she?"

"I've hidden her where you'll never find her."

"What do you want?"

Monsta scowled, and his eyes filled with darkness.

"Let's talk about that."

CHAPTER 5

The strange collection of vehicles were parked close to each other, almost as if trying to huddle together in the dark night. In front the two buses were parked crossways on the road to make a protective wall. Behind them, the other cars were lined up.

Inside the buses, the people of Johnny's tribe tried to sleep as comfortably as they could, but the space was crowded and the seats were not very soft. The floor was even harder, and the aisle was lined with people side by side on blankets, trying their best to rest for the exciting day ahead. In the cars other members slept on the seats. No one in any of the vehicles looked like they were having a good night's sleep.

Misterwizard sat in front of the buses on a wooden chair and smoked a cigar. His little Moped stood next to him on its kickstand. He stared ahead at the three dark tunnels in the far distance, lined up like three somehow sinister open mouths, waiting to consume them. Misterwizard's brow furrowed as he sat, deep in thought.

Misterwizard brought the people of the tribe here to this strange new place to help the new friends Super and Starbucks had told them about, the people of Pelpia called Letfreedomring. He had been so excited at the thought of making new allies, he had rallied the men and women willing to fight and created a moving armada. He left Foodcourt, the sitting presdent, a group of men and most of the women and scrabbles behind to protect the home front. Now Misterwizard wondered if he had been foolish and overeager bringing the small army here, so far away from their home, and had overestimated his makeshift army's ability to fight. Was he simply leading them into death and danger?

Misterwizard had known they were arriving blindly, with no knowledge of what they would face. He had counted on meeting Johnny who would tell him what they were up against. Now, since they had not found Johnny, he was aware they would be facing an unknown quantity of enemies, and would have to do serious reconnoitering to assess the danger.

Misterwizard looked to his left, and smiled at what he saw. Young love, he thought. There, sitting on the ground in front of their Harley, Starbucks and Super held each other and talked in soft whispers, gazing at each other's faces and smiling. Misterwizard felt a pang of jealousy, wishing that somewhere in the Wasteland, he could find a suitable companion to travel life's journey with. He did have to admit to suffering the pangs of loneliness at times, and though he enjoyed the companionship of his friends, they didn't fill the emptiness that only a lover would bring. But how to find someone in the Wasteland who shared Misterwizard's passions and intellect? That seemed to be a monumental task, and the thought of how difficult it might be made Misterwizard feel sad. He turned away from looking at Starbucks and Super, and tried to think more pleasant thoughts, though it wasn't easy to dispel the gloom that now filled his heart. Soon sleepiness overtook him, and his eyes began to close. He lay back in the chair, and soon was fast asleep.

In the bus on the right near the back, seven-year-old Sephie raised her head and looked forward at all the sleeping bodies. The soft sound of snoring filled the bus, a comforting sound that normally put her to sleep, but right now she was wide awake. She was tired of doing nothing. It had been a long, boring ride. It was time for an adventure.

As quietly as she could, Sephie grabbed onto the seat in front of her with her hand and pulled herself up. With her heart in her throat for fear of waking anyone, she ever so slowly stepped over the bodies on the floor and made her way towards the front of the bus, careful not to step on anyone's body and alert them.

Sephie's heart beat wildly, and a big, dark smile shone on her face, for she was once again acting like her hero, Johnny. While everyone slept, she was sneaking off on an adventure, just like he used to do. The thought of danger didn't enter her mind, for nothing bad ever happened to Johnny when he went on adventures, only fun and excitement.

After what seemed like forever, she finally reached the front of the bus. The weird glass doors were shut! She looked at the silver handle which she knew opened them. Could she operate it quietly enough so no one would hear?

"Hey!" A whispered voice erupted in the darkness, scaring Sephie to bits and almost making her fall down. Had she been discovered?

"Where do you think you're going?" the voice whispered. It was male voice, and Sephie grinned. It was just Wheaties! Hearing his voice made her feel happy, for Sephie really liked Wheaties a lot, and she wouldn't mind him being her companion in adventure.

"Be quiet!" Sephie scolded in a whisper, in as stern a tone as she could muster.

Wheatie's face appeared out of the darkness, a sly grin on his face. Sephie couldn't help but grin back, thinking how handsome the older boy was, and how much she liked him. Then she quickly wiped the smile off her face and frowned, but Wheaties had already seen it, and his smile remained and his eyes twinkled.

"None of your business!" Sephie said, but secretly hoping he wouldn't listen.

"You're going out to explore, aren't you?" Wheaties said. "You can't go alone. You need me along to protect you."

"I don't need your protection!" Sephie said, real anger flaring up inside her. "I can take care of myself. Don't you know about my adventures?"

Wheaties frowned, contrite. "I know. I'm sorry, I didn't mean you weren't brave. I just meant I could come along and help keep you safe."

Sephie smiled again, mollified. "Okay." She motioned with her hand, then pointed to the handle. "We have to open this so no one hears."

Wheaties nodded. He tiptoed over, and looking at Sephie, put both hands on the handle. As both Sephie and Wheaties held their breath, Wheaties pushed the handle slowly, slowly, trying his best to not make any sound.

Slowly the doors began to budge open. Sephie hurried down the steps and grabbed the doors, hoping to help keep them quiet.

Then with a soft clunk, the long, vertical doors parted and swung open. Both Sephie and Wheaties glanced over at the sleepers in the bus, looks of panic on their faces. But no one moved! They had done it!

They grinned at each other with devilish glee, their eyes shining with triumph and adventure. Then Sephie slowly walked down the steps one at a time, careful to hold the railing. When she reached the last one, she hopped out onto the ground. Wheaties hurried to follow and soon they both stood outside in the dark, cold night.

They glanced around to see if they would be spotted. They both saw Misterwizard sitting in his chair not far away, his back to them. In the darkness smoke curled in the air from his cigar, and the embers at the end of it glowed like a firefly in the night sky.

Sephie put a finger to her mouth in a shushing motion and Wheaties nodded. She looked up at the yellow eye, high in the sky, and the stars which looked like a million lanterns lit against a dark blue carpet. Since they'd left Sanctuary, Sephie had come to love the night time, and she would often come outside back home at Washington Deecee at night and sit on one of the stone benches, just to gaze up at the beauty.

Right now, she wasn't thinking about the stars, though, she was thinking about where to go for their adventure. She and Wheaties both gazed around. Sephie grabbed his arm and pointed to the dark half-oval shapes of the tunnels. There was where they had to go, of course! But how? Misterwizard was sitting right in the way!

Suddenly they heard a sound, and it made Sephie grin. It was snoring. Misterwizard had fallen asleep! Perfect timing!

This time Wheaties took the lead. He tiptoed towards Misterwizard, but at a safe distance. Sephie hurried to follow, her heart beating with fright but her mind racing with excitement. They were going to see the tunnels before anyone else! How far did they dare go?

As Sephie reached Wheaties he stopped and turned to her. He held out his hand. "Maybe you should take my hand," he whispered, "just so we don't get separated."

Sephie smiled, and as her heart fluttered, she held out her hand. She felt Wheaties take it in his firm strong one. They smiled at each other with affection.

Then they started walking quietly, towards the tunnels, and their adventure.

Ahead of them unseen, dark shapes appeared, shuffling in their direction.

Lady Stabs lounged in a soft, green leather chair in a common room in one of the buildings. She didn't know which one it was, but it was not the tallest, and it was made from gray stone. Outside on the ledges, stone creatures that looked like bats, but had very cruel expressions stared out at the world.

In the room where she sat, a giant metal stove with a pipe leading out the wall for exhaust sat on a floor of bricks by the far wall. This was one of the places where the Sky all came to take their turns cooking their food. There was no 'lectricity, so each room had a makeshift fireplace or firepit to keep the people of Sky warm. It was essential, since a lot of the buildings had missing walls or open places where windows had once been.

A flurry of activity happened all the time, with Sky people flying in to the buildings with loads of wood, food or treasures they'd found, and them flying out again, much like the bird-beasties Lady Stabs remembered seeing above their new sanctuary in Washington Deecee. She could understand how the people of Nork could find the Sky annoying, for they were always flying down to the ground, grabbing things and flying away. Others who couldn't fly were lowered to the ground in the baskets, mostly at night, to forage. Some of them never made it back, so it was only done when there was a desperate need for supplies.

She also understood why the Sky hated the people of Nork so much, for since Lady Stabs had been there, she'd seen many attempts by Norkers to break into the Sky's domain from below in the buildings or shoot up at them with guns and arrows to try and kill someone. If it wasn't for the spider-beasties, Lady Stabs knew the people of Nork would easily break down the barriers the Sky had placed in the stairways of the buildings to keep them out. Then their superior numbers would quickly overwhelm the Sky.

Lady Stabs knew the Sky were good people, who didn't really want to fight unless they had to. Lady Stabs, even with her strange appearance and way of dressing, was welcomed and liked by everyone among the Sky. With her long hair on one side of her head and the other half shaved, the ring in the side of her nose, her tattoos on her arms that everyone in the Gangers was forced to get, and her black leather outfit, she thought that she would be shunned, like she was everywhere else. But maybe it was because the Sky were strange in appearance themselves, with their wings that the people accepted her as a kindred spirit. Or maybe it was just because they were such nice people. All she knew was that in a strange way, she felt more at home and happy among them than anywhere else she'd been before, even among Johnny's tribe.

Lady Stabs had learned how to navigate the strange, weblike walkways that connected the buildings. She found that the holes between the webbing were so small that there was little chance of falling through, and the tough, thick material seemed strong enough to carry the weight of anyone who might walk on it. The only building that didn't have webbing to it was the one in which the goddess, Pantina resided in. The only way to access that sacred place was by having someone fly you there.

Once Lady Stabs had sat on the top floor of a building across from Pantina's building, and waited, hoping to get a glimpse of the goddess. The window was gone in the building where she sat, so there was only a big, open hole she gazed out of. In the building which housed Pantina's temple, Lady Stabs saw a large window which looked onto a room full of golden statues, soft pillows and fabrics on the floor and a table full of delicious looking food.

Lady Stab sat there for a long time, until the red eye dipped over the horizon disappeared and the yellow eye rose in the night sky. She had nothing else to do, it was peaceful watching night slowly envelop the world, and she was eager to see what this strange goddess looked like that no one ever got to see. The thought of being one of the only ones to know what she looked like gave Lady Stabs a secret thrill. Even Johnny had never seen her, and if Lady Stabs did, he could tell Johnny what she looked like.

And then it happened! Pantina crossed in front of the window. Lady Stabs quickly pulled back into the shadows, so the goddess wouldn't see her. Lady Stabs gazed at Pantina, drinking in her appearance with guilty pleasure.

Pantina appeared to be a girl of about twenty seasons. Her hair was frizzy, and of a color Lady Stabs had never seen before, a fiery orange. She had large, golden wings which were tucked against her body. Lady Stabs knew Johnny and Deb really didn't think Pantina was a goddess at all, but looking at her, Lady Stabs thought she was the most beautiful girl she'd ever seen, and she began to wonder if she really could be a higher being.

Pantina wore a green, flowing nightgown of silk. She walked slowly, with elegant steps, and as she walked, her wings rustled and opened and closed, as if trying to get comfortable. Lady Stabs thought how regal and quietly elegant Pantina looked. But the expression on Pantina's face made Lady Stabs concerned, for there was sadness, and loneliness. Pantina mouth turned downwards in a melancholy frown. Pantina seemed to mill about, as if she had no real purpose, nothing really to do. As Lady Stabs watched, Pantina walked over and picked up a piece of fruit. She held it in her hand, stared at it, took a bite, and then dropped it, as if it held no pleasure for her.

Pantina's expression turned to one of such sadness, and a tear fell from her eye. Deep sorrow stabbed Lady Stabs' heart, for she began to realize that

Pantina was all alone in her temple, with no one to talk to or care for her. It made Lady Stabs angry, thinking how this "goddess" was made to live alone. She wondered if Pantina had any choice to be their goddess, or if she was a prisoner, kept there by the evil Lord Flaggalon. Lady Stabs began to realize Johnny was right. Pantina was not a goddess at all, just a girl who Lord Flaggalon was using to keep the people in line. It made Lady Stabs furious, and hatred filled her heart for Lord Flaggalon. He was just like Ripper, a cold-hearted monster who only cared about himself. How many horrible men like them existed in the world? Why couldn't they finally weed them all out, and have a good world? The thought of how impossible a task this was, depressed Lady Stabs. Then she thought of how Johnny and Misterwizard were making a better place, where good and kind people could live, cheered her up again.

Suddenly Pantina turned and looked right at Lady Stabs! Lady Stabs had no choice but to walk out in the light of the yellow eye so Pantina could see she was not there to harm her.

The two gazed at each other for a few moments, both mesmerized by the appearance of the other. Lady Stabs smiled at Pantina and waved her hand. Pantina smiled back and waved back. Lady Stabs grinned widely, happy to have given Pantina someone to talk to. On the other side, Pantina gazed at Lady Stabs with intense curiosity. She'd never seen anyone like Lady Stabs, and in the light of the yellow eye, Lady Stabs appeared even stranger and more bizarre than normal. Still, Pantina didn't look scared, just intrigued.

Lady Stabs had heard someone coming behind her, so she quickly hurried into the shadows. Pantina stared after her for a few seconds. Then Pantina walked away before she was spotted.

As Lady Stab hurried away, she vowed to see Pantina again, hoping the two would become friends. As she hurried across the nearest webbing to the next building, the memory of the beautiful red-haired maiden with the golden wings stayed in her mind.

CHAPTER 6

King Ferdinand lounged on his new throne, enjoying a dark, evil joy he never thought possible. He sipped on a glass of dark red wine, enjoying the sensation of it trickling down his throat, meanwhile planning who he was going to kill and how he was going to totally seize power.

The people of Nork didn't care who was in power; they were too busy simply foraging for food and trying to stay warm. The only real problem came when the king needed more soldiers or men to keep the peace. Force and cruelty had kept the people in line so far, but every day, they seemed to get angrier, more waksy and more ready to riot. Ferdinand had been trying to come up with a solution for a long time, just in case the people did suddenly turn violent. He had a plan now, though. He couldn't wait to rid the city of the useless rabble.

King Ferdinand stood up and walked casually to the back of the room, towards the old king's bedroom. Opening the door, he walked into the bedchamber, a dark, evil smile on his face.

The room was decorated sumptuously, with red velvet cloth on all the walls and heavy purple curtains on the windows at the far end of the room. Paintings of naked women and wild beasties decorated the walls, along with ones related to the king's idiotic interests, such as pictures of old gangsters with their tommy guns. Lately, a new painting had been added, one of a man with a beard in a green outfit with a green pointed hat. The king had called the man in the painting Robin Hood, and it was all the king talked about lately. King Ferdinand had grown increasingly tired of the king's childish, foolish nonsense, and feared the king was becoming more and more out of touch with reality.

But now, King Ferdinand thought with delight, he had solved the problem of the foolish king, once and for all.

A huge bed filled the middle of the room, covered with soft, red blankets and with silk pillows at the top. This was the king's favorite place to be, and Ferdinand had more trouble every day simply convincing the king to get out of bed and attend to his duties.

King Ferdinand walked to the bed and gazed down at the king sleeping. King Ferdinand glanced with satisfaction at the chains he had attached to the king's wrists and ankles, which then attached to the legs of the bed. The king's hair and face were wet with sweat, and the king tossed and turned fitfully, moaning in fright.

King Ferdinand chuckled. It wouldn't be long now. He glanced over to the corner of the room. There, with a chain around his waist attached to the wall, stood what was left of Moxie. Now just a shadow of the man he once was, his skin was shriveled and shrunk, and his eyes were black like raisins. His skin was blue, and his lips had disappeared into thin lines. It was apparent to Ferdinand that Moxie was dead and decaying, and yet some force inside kept him on his feet and moving. Ferdinand knew if he turned out the light, he would see a faint green glow emanating from Moxie's eyes, and he warned himself not to get too close.

King Ferdinand turned to the former king again. He looked at the bite mark on the king's neck, where Moxie had left his mark. Ferdinand knew the former king would never assume his throne again and would soon join Moxie in the land of the walking dead as a Lurker. He had to be careful however, for even though most of the people couldn't care less who was king, there were some who were loyal to the fool lying in the bed, and if Ferdinand moved too quickly, he might face fierce opposition. There might even be some who would try to kill him and take over the throne themselves. Ferdinand had to find a core of loyal supporters, ones with power and control of the army to cement his new position. Then no one would dare oppose him.

But for now, more pressing matters needed to be attended to. There were the prisoners of Pelpia. Ferdinand already had some dark ideas what he would use them for. There were the Lurkers free outside the main gate to deal with. If they stayed outside the city, King Ferdinand thought, it didn't matter where they went, even if they infected the whole world. Inside the city, King Ferdinand had plans.

There were the people of Booklin, and the minor problem of Ticktock. Another sign to Ferdinand of how the king was slowly getting more waksy every day was allowing Moxie to talk him into letting a man with black skin from Booklin to become a soldier in the army. Ferdinand had time and again told the king how those people living there were dangerous, that their different skin colors and odd looks, such as slanted eyes proved they had been affected by the bombs.

Ferdinand tried to explain to the king that the same thing which was affecting the people of Nork had caused the people in Booklin to be born different. If they were allowed to enter Nork, Ferdinand explained, they would infect everyone! He had managed to get the king to banish anyone who was different to Booklin a few seasons ago, but Ticktock had joined the army before that, and Ferdinand couldn't convince the king Ticktock was dangerous. One of Ferdinand's biggest goals was to wipe out everyone in Booklin, down to the last freak, purge the land of anyone who looked different, for safety reasons. And the fact that the people of Booklin occupied land that should belong to Nork was even more reason to eradicate them.

Of more immediate concern, however, was the army at their southern border, and this person everyone kept talking about, this Johnny Apocalypse. There was hope the Lurkers would take care of them, but Ferdinand couldn't take the chance. He had to make sure the threat of this invading army was taken care of.

Ferdinand smiled, for the beginnings of a plan had formed in his mind. Ferdinand looked down with mock pity at the king. The king looked up at him, mouth open, his eyes not comprehending.

"Yes, Your Majesty, you are dying," Ferdinand said with an evil grin. "You'll be joining your father soon. And I will be king. Do you understand?"

The king stared blankly, drool dripping from his mouth. Finally, he managed a weak, "Ferdie?"

Ferdinand leaned over slightly, as if listening intently to the king's wish.

"Yes, Your Majesty? Would you like a drink of wine? A piece of fruit? One of your girls to attend you?"

"It hurt," the king said, his voice full of pain and fright. "Please, make it stop."

Ferdinand stood up again and grinned. "It will stop soon, Your Majesty. Simply give it time."

As night descended, Mantayo soared high above Nork, so high the buildings looked like toys beneath him. Since it seemed as if they would be carrying Johnny and his friends often, Mantayo and the other Sky youth had designed a harness. The harness attached to them and had a second harness hanging below for a passenger. This made it easier for the people of Sky to fly freely while carrying the extra weight.

Below Mantayo in the harness, Johnny Apocalypse held onto the straps and gazed at the world far below. Johnny was getting more used to being in the air with Mantayo carrying him, but he maintained a slight unease, despite his best efforts to dispel it.

As they flew through the dark night, the yellow eye seemed so close Johnny felt almost as if he could reach out and touch it. He'd never seen it so close, and looking at it, he saw it didn't look like an eye at all, but a giant rock with a craggy surface. Quiet amazement filled him, and a sense of wonder, as he realized how little his tribe and he knew about the real world, and how much they were learning about it. He felt a strange sense of elation at the thought of how much more interesting and exciting things he had yet to learn and see as he continued his adventures.

The buildings passed underneath him, dark shadows, and far below them the street looked like a gray ribbon crisscrossing the world. A cold breeze blew Johnny's hair back, and a quiet glee filled him. He had met so many new and strange people since he and his friends had ventured out from Sanctuary, seemingly a million seasons ago. What would the world have been like if they had stayed? They probably would have been conquered by Ripper and his gangers, and all been killed or enslaved.

Johnny's thoughts turned to his tribe and Misterwizard. Quiet alarm filled Johnny's heart as he wondered if they would be too late, and the Lurkers would have already reached his friends. Would they simply arrive to see Misterwizard and even Starbucks and Super dead, shuffling around, Lurkers?

"How much further?" Johnny yelled over the wind.

"Not long now!" Mantayo yelled back. Mantayo pointed his finger ahead. "See, there is the wall and the gate. Beyond it are the tunnels, and then we should see your friends."

Johnny peered down at the street in front of the metal gate. The street seemed to stretch off in both directions forever. Something seemed odd, and he tried to think what it was. Then he did.

"Where are the Lurkers?"

Mantayo looked down at the ground too, a look of concern on his face. He stopped flying forwards and hovered for a moment so they could study the land below. The other Sky stopped flying forward too, for Mantayo was the leader. They flapped their wings and waited for him to proceed.

"I don't know," Mantayo said. "There should be a lot of them. I hope that doesn't mean they are all on the other side of the tunnels. Or have managed to climb out off the road and are spreading around the land."

"They're already attacking my tribe!" Johnny said with alarm. "Hurry!"

Mantayo nodded grimly. Then he flapped his wings harder, sending them forward at a fast speed.

Johnny's heart sunk, and a sick feeling filled him. He dreaded the thought of what he might see ahead, knowing he had no choice but to keep going until he did.

He braced himself for the sorrow and horror he might have to witness soon.

Johnthebaptist walked through the camp, from fire to fire, studying the groups of people huddled close to stay warm. As he passed, some of the men would look up at him, dark smiles of understanding on their faces. Johnthebaptist would smile back, for they were all part of the plan, and just waited for his signal.

Johnthebaptist finished his tour of floor of the stadium, satisfied all the men were ready. He decided to do a quick tour of the guards around the outer edges of the arena one more time, to make sure there was nothing new which might make them have to put their plan on hold.

He passed by two guards. They followed him warily with their eyes, frowning. Johnthebaptist had a moment of doubt. Could they really pull it off without all being killed? As he walked on, not looking too close at the guards, he thought how they had little choice. The people of Letfreedomring grew weaker by the day, for the meager food they were given barely kept them alive. The water was somehow tainted as well, and Restaria was worried it might be full of the bad sickness caused by the mushroom monsters. Another reason they had to leave soon.

After he passed the two guards and was out of

their sight, he stopped and studied the arena. With a large grassy area in the middle, the concrete seats rose up on all sides in a circle. He saw the dark openings where the players who had once competed here would exit. Then he looked at the one which led to the underground, and possible freedom, or death. It was time.

Johnthebaptist walked over to the closest fire. The men there turned and looked at him. He nodded and they smiled. Johnthebaptist took the end of the long stick he carried with a rag at the top and lowered it into the fire. The rag caught immediately and soon the end of the stick was ablaze.

Johnthebaptist held his breath. The next few moments would bring freedom, or death. He held the end of the burning stick in the air. Men from every campfire rose up and prepared themselves.

The battle for their freedom had begun.

CHAPTER 7

Sephie and Wheaties walked slowly through the darkness, peering ahead, holding hands, their hearts pounding but with big smiles on their faces. They were being brave and disobeying the rules, both things which gave them a secret thrill.

"How far are we going to go?" Wheaties asked, as he tried to see Sephie's face in the darkness.

"Just to the start of the tunnel," Sephie said. "We'll look inside just a little way, then head back before they miss us."

Wheaties nodded, grinning. He was happy to be doing something special with Sephie, for he'd had a crush on her for a long time. She was beautiful, with long brown hair and blue eyes. And she was courageous and smart. He only hoped she thought he was good enough for her. Her going on this adventure with him must have meant she liked him! He hoped she'd agree to be his girlfriend soon, and then, who knew, maybe her mate someday! He hoped on this adventure, maybe she'd let him kiss her. He wondered if he dared try now, since they were all alone. Would she maybe even tell him she loved him? Wheaties breath quickened at the thought, that he might be heading for a moment of romance with the girl he loved.

Sephie looked over at him and squinted, wondering what he was thinking, for he'd become suddenly very quiet. "You, okay?" she whispered.

Wheaties, feeling embarrassed at being caught, shrugged and said in a squeaky voice, "I'm fine!"

His response made Sephie laugh. She grinned pretty sure she knew what Wheaties was thinking. She was thinking along the same lines, and the fact was, she found his brown skin, black hair and dark eyes handsome, and she really liked him too. Even more now that he seemed brave and adventurous, like Johnny. She wondered secretly if Wheaties was going to be her Johnny someday, and they'd fall in love and run off on their own adventures.

Suddenly Sephie saw something frightening and stopped. Since she was holding onto Wheaties' hand, he was forced to come to a jarring halt as well. He looked at her with alarm. "What's wrong?"

Sephie saw a shadow ahead. The shadow of a man. Somehow, she knew the man wasn't from their tribe, for there was something sinister, creepy about him. The man's shadow was hunched over and he shuffled towards them, dragging his feet in a very scary way.

"Somebody's here!" Sephie shouted in

a whisper.

Wheaties saw the shadow then too. Both stood still in fright, staring at the dark shadow. The real danger of what they were doing came to them then, and the real possibility of getting hurt or even killed.

"Let's go back, quick!" Wheaties whispered.

Sephie nodded and turned around, still holding Wheaties' hand. He had to let go of her hand to turn around as well. As soon as he did, he felt the air, trying to grab it again.

Sephie screamed. Wheaties saw why. He grabbed her hand again. In front of them now two more shadows, heading right for them! One was tall and thin, the other looked like the outline of a woman.

"Who are they?" Sephie asked in a high voice. They turned without a word ran to the left, hopefully away from all three shadows.

Wheaties didn't answer. He just knew they had to get back to safety fast. He pulled Sephie's hand, making her run faster. Then he realized something with dread: he wasn't sure which was led back to the buses!

He didn't have time to think about it, only run, for then came a sound more terrifying than even the sight of the shadows. One of the shadows moaned in a gruesome way. Both Sephie's and Wheatie's hearts jumped and they felt sick inside. Sephie squeaked in fright. Wheaties knew they were in real danger now. He had to be a man now and help Sephie get back to safety, even if it meant his life. All his thoughts of love disappeared. His mind turned now simply to the thought of survival.

They ran into deeper darkness as the two shadows which had been behind them and the one in front joined up. The three terrifying shadows turned in their direction and shuffled towards them. All three made horrible sounds and it became clear they were not normal people. They were some kind of monsters.

Wheaties and Sephie ran, their minds blank with fear, simply trying to put distance between them and the terrors in the dark. Suddenly they reached a wall! The edge of the road!

Another shadow appeared on their left, in the direction of the tunnel. This one cried out in what seemed like pain. It was another woman, her head covered by a dirty shawl, her voice crying out, as if for help.

"Which way?" Sephie said, in full panic mode.

Wheaties pulled her the direction away from the new woman shadow, for in the corner of his eye he saw the other three still heading for them. He wished he'd made better note of where the buses were, for he couldn't tell which direction to go.

Then Wheaties saw something more terrifying than anything they'd see so far. In front of them stood not one, not two but a whole group of shadows! The dark creatures milled about, as if without purpose, shuffling back and forth. But Wheaties had no doubt if one of them caught Wheaties and Sephie, they would do terrible things to them.

"Help!" Sephie screamed, hoping to be heard by

the tribe. Wheaties stopped and looked around. There was only one option. He pulled Sephie again. They ran past the woman on the left, towards the dark tunnels in the distance. As Wheaties suspected, the woman reached out a hand and tried to grab them. In the light of the yellow eye her hand became visible. It was shriveled and bony. In fact, Wheaties could see the bones in her hand, for some of the flesh was gone!

Wheaties didn't know what these things were, but he knew at that moment they were very horrible and dangerous. He pulled Sephie along and they ran silently for a few moments. Then when it seemed like they were alone again, they stopped, panting.

They peered around, trying to figure out where they were. The dark hulks of cars surrounded them, making it hard to see in any direction. They couldn't even tell in which direction the tunnels were now, for neither could see over the cars.

Sephie turned to Wheaties and spoke in a serious but calm voice. "What do you think we should do, Wheaties? We don't know where the buses are."

They gazed at each other. Wheaties could see Sephie was scared. On impulse, he hugged her, holding her close. "I won't let anything happen to you, I promise."

They parted, and Sephie smiled at him tentatively. "I know."

Wheaties had an idea. "Let's climb into one of these cars and hide. Then when the red eye appears in the morning, we can see which way to go, and maybe those things will be gone!"

Sephie grinned, impressed. "That's a smart idea!"

Wheaties felt pride swell in his chest, and the love for Sephie blossom again. He'd just impressed his girl! He nodded happily.

They found a larger car, one that looked like a small bus. Carefully so they didn't get cut or scraped, they climbed inside. Wheaties closed the door, unhappy that it made a creaking sound. Then they laid down as best as they could, so none of the monsters could see them. They held each other's hand, cuddled close together for warmth, and waited, eyes open, listening for the monsters.

Deb stood at the jagged edge of the wall where a window had once been, on a floor high above the ground, and gazed out towards where she had seen Johnny and Mantayo fly away. Deecee lay on the couch, dozing. A melancholy feeling of dread lay on Deb's heart, like a dead bird-beastie lying on her chest.

The room was forty floors high from the ground, and a cold wind whistled through the opening, blowing her soft, blond hair back and chilling her, but she didn't want to move. Something bad was going to happen, she knew it, and she felt helpless to stop it, so far away from Johnny's side.

The room was the one the Sky had given her and Johnny to sleep in, and it was decorated beautifully in rich red velvet curtains and rugs. A four-poster bed sat by the wall to her right, and on a table on her left sat her very delicious dinner, mostly untouched. Still, the large opening in the wall kept the room chilly, despite the large fireplace on the interior wall. The Sky had tried to make them comfortable and show them hospitality, and Lady Stabs as well, who had a room nearby. Deb was jealous of Lady Stabs. Even though Lady Stabs had a smaller room without a fireplace and nothing but a cot and a few rugs, it was not on the outside wall with a large opening in it. It didn't matter anyway, all Deb could think about was Johnny.

The cold forced Deb to move from the opening. She pulled the large drape down to cover the open hole, and though the drape flapped in the breeze, the cold was reduced. The fire in the large fireplace crackled merrily and radiated heat, and now that the opening was covered, the room warmed up a little.

She sat down on the red velvet couch where Deecee lay and stroked his fur, but she didn't relax, just sat still stiffly. What was she doing, she thought? She should have insisted on going with Johnny. She should find a way to the ground, through all the barriers the Sky put up to keep the Norkers out. Then she should run all the way to the gate. She would find a way out of the city, make her way through the Lurkers outside and find Johnny and Mantayo and help them. She smiled grimly, knowing how silly and impossible the whole plan was. All she could do was wait, and it was miserable.

The door to the hallway opened. Lady Stabs walked in. She saw the look of worry on Deb's face and hurried over to sit next to her. Deecee raised his head and wagged his tail. Lady Stabs smiled at him and petted his head.

"Hi, Deecee." She studied Deb's face. "You're worried, aren't you?" She placed a hand on Deb's hand.

Deb nodded, and her face grim. Deb's throat tightened, and tears fell from her eyes. "Lady Stabs, something bad is going to happen to Johnny, I just know it."

Lady Stabs smiled reassuringly. "No, it's not! Johnny is still Johnny. He's tougher than a lion-beastie. No matter what he faces, you know he always finds a way to win."

Deb smiled, humor in her eyes. "I hope you're right."

"Let's put our minds on other things. Guess who I just saw?"

Deb, mildly curious, asked, "who?"

Lady Stabs' eyes widened with excitement. "Their goddess Pantina."

Deb's eyes opened with surprise and interest. "How?"

Lady Stabs described her experience, and what Pantina looked like. "She's just a girl, like you and me. She has strange red hair, and golden wings. But she seems very lonely. I don't think it's her choice to be kept apart from everyone and worshiped. I think it's that evil

Flaggalon who has made her out to be a god so he can use her to keep control of the Sky."

Deb nodded, Lady Stabs' words interesting enough to take her mind off Johnny for a moment. Deb shrugged. "There's really nothing we can do about it, Lady Stabs. It's their society. If we interfere, we may get ourselves kicked out." The thought of taking on another peoples' fight made Deb feel tired and grumpy. It seemed like they were always helping other people fix things, and there was never an end to people with problems.

"We have to do something!" Lady Stabs said, her face scrunched up with concern. "Surely Layla and some of the other good people of Sky see what is going on. We can't just leave Pantina trapped like that!"

Deb looked at Lady Stabs and smiled, realizing somehow that this fight was personal to Lady Stabs. It made Deb curious. "What do you think we should do?"

"We should talk to Layla in private. I can't believe she and the other smarter people of the Sky really believe she is a goddess." Lady Stabs frowned.

Deb shook her head and smiled sadly. "So, in the middle of our fight against the Lurkers, and trying to save the people of Pelpia, we're going to start a rebellion among the Sky, and free their goddess? Don't you think we have enough to deal with right now, without adding that on top?"

Lady Stabs and Deb looked at each other and both laughed.

"I suppose," Lady Stabs said. "But I won't rest

until Pantina is free, even if it's a fight I have to do all by myself."

Deb felt more cheerful now, even though nothing had really changed. "You won't have to. But you might have to wait just a little while, until we've taken care of a few other things first."

Lady Stabs nodded.

Lord Flaggalon walked in the room, and Deb and Lady Stabs glanced at each other with concern then turned towards him. He wore a dark scowl, and both girls knew something unpleasant was about to happen. Deecee growled, and Deb put a hand on him, to quiet him.

Lord Flaggalon walked up and stood in front of the velvet couch where the girls sat. The girls both tried to look innocent and friendly, though neither of them could stand the old, creepy man.

"Hello, ladies," Lord Flaggalon said, his voice dripping with poison-laced honey. "Are you enjoying your stay with us?"

He looked at Lady Stabs. "You've been with us quite a while, haven't you, Lady Stabs?"

Lady Stabs scowled, showing her dislike of Lord Flaggalon. "Yes. The Sky have been very generous to me."

Lord Flaggalon grinned darkly, for he sensed he had just made another enemy. He turned to Deb.

"Be careful not to get too close to the wall, or walk the webs when the yellow eye is not shining. The spiders might mistake you for food, and eat you."

Both Deb and Lady Stabs looked queasy, which made Lord Flaggalon smile.

"What do the spider-beasties, or spiders as you call them, normally eat?" Lady Stabs asked.

"Why, Groundworms, of course. Ones foolish enough to try and climb up and get caught in their webs, or ones we capture and feed to them. Our amazing goddess is able to control the mind not only of the spiders, but weaker Groundworms as well. Sometimes, she convinces them to offer themselves as dinner."

"So that's how you control them? Pantina does it?" Deb asked.

"She alone makes them obey."

Deb and Lady Stabs looked at each other then back at Lord Flaggalon.

"Is all that stuff," Deb asked, "we walk on from building to building, is that all spider web?

"Not all of it, some of it has been reinforced with rope and wire to make it stronger, and keep us from sticking to it. But let's talk of something else."

Lord Flaggalon walked over and stood in front of them. Deb grabbed Deecee around the neck, afraid he might lunge at the old man.

"If you and your people are to stay with us much longer, it is time you started earning your keep."

Deb and Lady Stabs looked at each other, not liking the sound of what he said. Then they looked back at Lord Flaggalon.

"You will begin helping the Sky hunt for food and supplies. From now on, when a party goes out to forage, you ladies will go along. Everyone who benefits from our hard work should have to join in the labor."

Except you, Lady Stabs thought, but she knew better than to say it.

"How will we do that, Lord Flaggalon?" Deb asked.

"You will be lowered down in the baskets, or carried by one of the Sky. We may even ask you to join us in a fight."

Deb frowned. "I think we should wait for Johnny to get back to discuss this," she said.

Lord Flaggalon's face filled with dark humor. "We don't know when that will be, do we? If you are not willing to contribute, maybe we should just take you both and drop you off in Nork, to see how you fare amongst the Groundworms."

"You lousy—" Lady Stabs stopped herself, but just barely. "You waited until Johnny left to pull this, didn't you? Knowing there was no one to stop you."

Lord Flaggalon walked to the door and turned back. "I will only ask you to go on foraging trips, for now. Be ready to join the next one tomorrow morning,"

Lord Flaggalon walked out. Deb and Lady Stabs looked at each other with worry. "What do you think he's up to, Deb?" Lady Stabs said.

"I think he's hoping something will happen to us," Deb said unhappily. "I just hope Johnny gets back, and soon."

CHAPTER 8

Ferdinand sat on the throne and studied the Nork genrals who stood in a semi-circle in front of him. Alcapoon stood in front, with his curly black hair and a chin full of black stubble. Alcapoon was of average height. He wore a green coat with colorful ribbons on the upper left. He still wore the pants with the stripes from his old gangster uniform and ragged tennis shoes, making him look ridiculous to Ferdinand. The outfit made King Ferdinand chuckle, for it was Alcapoon's attempt to look like head of the army.

The other genrals still wore the old striped suits and looked uncomfortable, as if not sure just what was happening. Suspicion shown in their eyes, but carefully veiled. The king was no longer there, and many of them had secret alliances with him. If Ferdinand had seized control, what would happen to them?

Ferdinand took a sip of the glass of wine he held in his hand, and then looked at the men intently. "As you may have surmised, there has been a change. The king is no longer able to rule. He will never be king again, for he was bitten by a Lurker and is now one of the undead."

The men's eyes all opened wide with surprise, alarm and dismay. They looked at each other, not sure what to think.

Ferdinand smiled. "He will not be joining us for the rest of his life. The king had no heirs. From now, on, I am king of Nork. You will address me as King Ferdinand."

The genrals remained silent, thinking their own thoughts. King Ferdinand stared darkly at them. "As king, I will accept nothing but complete loyalty. Anyone found disloyal will soon join the king in his grisly fate. Am I making myself understood?"

The genrals all nodded vigorously. King Ferdinand continued. "I know that some of you had strong loyalty for the old king."

King Ferdinand glanced at certain genrals who knew he was talking specifically about them. "And many of you hated me as well. But don't concern yourselves that I might be planning revenge," King Ferdinand lied. "There are many problems the former king did not address, being too busy playing games and acting a fool. I have no time for reprisals. As long as you are loyal to me, the past will be forgotten."

All the genrals nodded and smiled, but some frowned secretly, knowing King Ferdinand was only making a speech, and there wasn't much truth in it.

King Ferdinand spoke again. "There are captured enemies in our city, and new enemies at our southern border. There are also Lurkers roaming just outside the city. We must deal with these problems at once. We will inform the people of the king's demise when we are once again in a state of peace."

King Ferdinand looked at Alcapoon.

"Genral Alcapoon, new leader of the army, lead your genrals and ready the army. It is time they fought for me."

All the men turned to leave, all except Alcapoon, who waited until the others were gone, then walked up to King Ferdinand.

"What will happen to the old king, and Moxie?" Alcapoon asked.

King Ferdinand put an arm around Alcapoon's shoulder and led him over to the table full of food. "They are key to my new plan. And you are my new trusted friend, Alcapoon. Eat, leader of my army."

Alcapoon didn't need a second invitation. He quickly grabbed some food and stuffed it in his mouth. Then he poured himself a glass of wine. King Ferdinand watched with amusement.

"We have had a powerful weapon which we have never utilized. All of this time, we have had them roaming around just below us in the subways. It is time we put them to use against our enemies. With their help, we will rid this city of all the garbage, and create a clean, orderly society with only people we want."

Alcapoon, realizing what King Ferdinand meant, froze in mid-bite, his eyes full of terror. "You don't mean..."

King Ferdinand nodded his eyes full of malice.

"Like any other weapon, if controlled and used correctly, the Lurkers can destroy our enemies and make us powerful and invincible. When we are finished, no one will dare oppose us."

Alcapoon went back to eating, but he seemed worried. "Can you really control them? What if they escape and start killing the people?"

Lord Ferdinand smiled. "Don't worry. If a few of the rabble die, it is of no real concern. And the Lurkers are like dumb beasties, easy to control. But our Lurker army is small now, and it needs to grow. And I know just where to find a whole stadium full of volunteers to join it."

Alcapoon smiled knowing just what King Ferdinand meant. "In a place called Madson Skar Gardem."

King Ferdinand chuckled. "Precisely."

As soon as Johnthebaptist raised the torch, two men started a fight in the middle of the camp, just as planned. One man, a strong, strapping brown man with curly black hair and bulging muscles strode up to a much shorter man with short, stiff black hair which stood up like a brush and white skin black from soot. The shorter white man held a chicken-beastie leg in his hand which he had just cooked and was about to bite.

The tall brown man pushed the short man's

shoulder. "You took my food! I'm going to kill you for that!"

The other man snarled and threw the leg down, just as rehearsed. The two men grabbed each other's arms and struggled with fierce grimaces, yelling at each other and dancing around the nearby campfire. People nearby started shouting and ran to get out of the way. Little scrabblers sitting by the fire jumped up and screamed, running for their parents. The men fighting stumbled into the fire, kicking burning pieces of wood and sparks everywhere. Others started yelling in anger for them to stop, but their fight just grew more intense and violent as they began punching each other and kicking.

Johnthebaptist glanced over at the guards around the outside of the stadium. Just as he'd hoped, their eyes were all drawn to the ruckus. Some of the guards pointed and laughed with each other. Others simply watched with bored grins. A few began wandering towards the commotion.

The fight continued, and now a few others joined in. Two sets of two guards headed towards the commotion from different directions to break it up.

What none of the guards on watch noticed were the groups of prisoners, both men and women, who had slowly wandered close to each guard post, just waiting for the signal.

Johnthebaptist raised the torch again, the signal they were waiting for. The prisoners all jumped the guards at the same time. Using clubs, sticks and their bare hands, the prisoners beat the guards and grabbed at their weapons. The Nork guards realized what was happening, but too late. They tried to aim their guns and swing their swords but they were outnumbered two to one. Some managed to shoot in the air, shattering the quiet with the loud explosion of gunfire.

"Help them!" Restaria shouted to the rest of the people. Quickly all the people of Letfreedomring ran towards the nearest guards to join the fight, even the scrabblers.

A guard managed to pull his tommy gun down and he fired at an old man holding his arms. The old man flew backwards with a cry, then lay on the ground, dead. The others attacking the guard became even more furious and beat him with their fists. They kicked him in the legs until the guard fell. He was quickly smothered by people beating him until he finally slumped, beaten unconscious.

It was over quickly, for the guards had been caught completely by surprise, and they were mostly half asleep before the attack began. Most had been up guarding the prisoners for hours, and could barely keep themselves on their feet.

As the last guard fell to the ground out cold, the people of Letfreedomring shouted with victory, raising their swords and clubs in the air. One fired a guard's rifle in the air in celebration.

Restaria and Johnthebaptist found each other and smiled, relieved and happy to have the battle over so quickly.

One of the men, an old one with white hair and wrinkled skin, wearing an old tattered green army shirt and pants, walked up to Restaria. His teeth were set in anger and he scowled. "Let's kill them all!"

The people all heard and cheered, their voices tinged in hate.

Restaria raised a hand. Then she spoke firmly but softly. "No. We are not like them. We do not kill for revenge. Tie them up, and we will leave them in the tunnel under the rows of seats. Then gather all your things and be ready to move!"

Some of the people grumbled with disappointment. The old man glared at Restaria and spat on the ground to show his displeasure. Then he spun around and tramped away. Restaria and Johnthebaptist looked at each other and chuckled about the old man. Then they set off in opposite directions to help the people get ready.

Soon the guards were all tied up.

"Put the guards behind the old wooden booths in the tunnels under the seats, out of sight," Restaria directed. "Make sure you gag them, so they can't make too much noise."

"Are you sure we shouldn't just kill them?" another man asked. "They're just going to die anyway of starvation or thirst."

Restaria shook her head. "Someone will surely come when the red eye rises to check on us, and will find them. We have to be long gone before that happens."

The man nodded reluctantly. Soon all the guards

were laid on the floor behind the counters of the old food booths, tied up tightly with cloth in their mouths so they couldn't be too loud. They lay on the floor struggling against their bonds.

Restaria walked out into the arena and met Johnthebaptist again. "All right. Lead us to this way out."

Johnthebaptist nodded and walked away. Restaria followed him, and all the people fell in behind them. Johnthebaptist led the whole group to the archway he had seen before. He walked into the dark interior, holding the torch up high to see.

Here, just as before, he saw the words above a high archway with huge wooden doors. Benches lay one on top of the other in front of the doors, all the way to the ceiling. Other objects were placed there as well, chunks of old concrete, old pieces of equipment and rows of seats. It was clear the people of Nork didn't want whatever was inside to get out. And they were going to go there intentionally. Johnthebaptist once again wondered if they were only walking from one danger into a worse one.

He turned to Restaria. "Here it is. We need to clear the doors as quickly as possible. We don't have a lot of time."

Restaria, looking uncomfortable and reluctant, nodded.

Together they directed the strongest men and anyone else who was not too weak to take the old debris and benches from in front of the doors. It took time, and it was growing uncomfortably close to morning when they finally finished.

When the opening was clear, everyone looked at Johnthebaptist. He smiled grimly, walked up to the doors and pulled them open as Restaria and the people watched.

As the doors swung wide, a cold breeze blew up from below. They all peered in to see what was there. They saw a set of stone steps, leading down into a black void.

The people of Pelpia looked at each other in fright and murmured. Restaria turned to Johnthebaptist. "Do you mind going first, and seeing what's down there?"

Johnthebaptist nodded. "We have to hurry. The red eye is about to rise."

Restaria nodded back. As everyone watched in silent excitement, Johnthebaptist walked down the stone steps, holding the torch high, until he disappeared below.

Ticktock, totally exhausted and with his purple suit rumpled and dirty, approached the huge area with trees and grass. He passed under the big sign which said, "Central Park," though he never bothered to look at it, for he couldn't read. People just called the place Sental Par, or just the Par.

All he knew was where the cages were and beasties of all types had once lived, was where they trained and kept the rattys. And not far away from there was the place where the army lived. Set up in tents on the grass in one of the areas without trees the king called "Sheep Meadow," the army trained and gathered until they were needed to fight or scavenge food.

Ticktock figured Moxie should have been back with the prisoners by now. After Moxie had shown them to the king, and if he was still alive after the king found out Moxie didn't bring back any food, this is where Moxie would be, hanging out with the troops.

Ticktock liked it here, for it was the only place in the city with trees and grass, and it felt safe, for the army had leveled all the tall buildings nearby so no angels could bomb them from above. Even in his old home of Booklin they didn't have a nice place like this. Ticktock liked evenings hanging out with the army here, looking up at the yellow eye and the points of light above, and feeling the cool breeze. It was one of the only times he felt like he was really a member of the Nork army.

Ticktock was eager to find out if Moxie and the army had arrived yet, and wanted to make sure to square things with Moxie. After all, it wasn't his fault they been attacked. He tried for hours and hours to find the missing prisoners, but they had vanished. Nork was such a big place, with old buildings everywhere, it was like trying to find one little bug in a million of them. Ticktock suspected they'd been captured by the Angels, and he sure hoped so, but he had no way to prove it. If they had escaped and were wandering around the city, Ticktock would be in big trouble.

Ticktock, despite being a big black, strong black man, looked beaten down and scared. He had wandered through the city, his heart full of fright and pounding, starving and thirsty, for hours. Ticktock always knew he was an outsider in Nork, being from what Ferdinand called the Cursed in Booklin. Ticktock, was once like all the other Brethren in Booklin, someone who hated the Norkers. But in the old days, he liked to swim across the big water and steal things then hurry back. Once in a while, he would even fight a Norker or beat one up, just for fun. Then one day, Moxie and the army caught him. Ticktock thought they'd kill him right away, but instead Moxie put Ticktock in a cage with a sick ratty. To Moxie's surprise, Ticktock killed the ratty with his bare hands. Moxie was so impressed, he brought Ticktock to the king and convinced him to let Moxie use him as a soldier. The king didn't seem to hate the people of Booklin as bad as Ferdinand, which was a lucky thing for Ticktock.

Now he had risked everything by pulling a dumb move like running away. But what was he supposed to do; let the Angels kill him with fire and arrows? It didn't make him look very tough though. Maybe he would have been better just going back to Booklin. That would have been the smart move. He still could do it, but he really didn't want to. He had a good deal here with the Nork army, and Booklin was crowded and had little opportunity to get rich. Ticktock knew it was only a matter of time before the Norkers conquered Booklin anyway, and then he'd be smart to be on the winning side.

Booklin was almost as big as Keens to the north, and it was packed with people of all different kinds, black people like him, brown people, people with the slanted eyes and yellow skin; the only type who was not there were white people like those from Nork or Pelpia. Ever since Ferdinand, that evil creep, had convinced the king they were cursed by the mushroom monster, there had been a war between them. The people of Booklin now hated all white people, which Ticktock thought was unfair, but they'd been treated so badly, he understood. When Nork finally attacked Booklin, it would be a terrible fight, but Ticktock was pretty sure Booklin would lose.

As he wandered his way through the trees, he heard the screeching of the rattys. He really hated those things, disgusting and horrible. He stopped to brush off the dirt on his suit and straighten it out. As he started walking past the ratty cages, he kept his eyes open, looking for soldiers from the army. All he saw so far were the trainers, leaning on the cages or sitting down on the ground by them, the men who whipped and beat the rattys into submission.

Ticktock wondered just what happened when Moxie arrived. Where had he put the prisoners from Pelpia? What did the king say to Moxie when he returned with no food? Did Moxie wonder why the two prisoners Ticktock and Charly were bringing back weren't there?

So many questions Ticktock wanted answers to, and the answers would determine his fate.

Ticktock passed a cage with a huge, ugly, ratty with mangy black fur. It looked like it had been in a fight, for it had a big scar on its side which was still healing. As Ticktock passed, it hissed at him. Ticktock was in a mood, so he walked over and hit it on the snout with his fist. It squealed and pulled its head back inside the cage. Ticktock grinned. It felt good to take his frustrations out on something.

He reached the end of the cages and entered into a small area of trees. Beyond them was the open grass area where the army was. Ticktock's stomach grumbled, and his mouth watered at the thought of the pots over the fires at the army camp full of hot food. Most of it was mystery meat, a mix of whatever the men could catch, but it was filling, and that's all Ticktock cared about at the moment.

As he grew close to the edge of the trees and the grassy area, he heard a voice behind him.

"Hey."

Ticktock turned to see Lary, a tall, lanky but strong soldier with dirty brown hair. Lary was a jerk, who liked to steal anything you left lying around, and he complained all the time. But he also had a quirky sense of humor, and he and Ticktock had become friendly, if not friends.

"Hey, Lary. What's cookin'?" Ticktock said, fully meaning in the pots.

"You, is what." Lary walked towards Ticktock

with a big, dark grin.

"What chu mean?" Ticktock said, irritated. He was in no mood for a riddle.

"Ain't you heard? You're gonna be in one the them cooking pots soon."

Ticktock walked up to Lary, wondering what kind of game he was playing. Ticktock scowled and looked dangerous.

"You better tell me what you talkin' about, real soon. I'm here to see Moxie."

Lary chuckled and scratched his dirty brown hair. "You don't want to see Moxie, no you don't."

Ticktock felt a sudden urge to knock Lary on his behind, and he balled up his fists. Lary saw it and he backed away hastily.

"Hey! I'm tryin' to help you, buddy. Moxie ain't among the livin' anymore. And you ain't gonna be, unless you high tail it outta here, and fast."

Ticktock opened his fists, and once again looked confused.

"Look," Lary said, putting a hand on Ticktock's shoulder. "Your days are numbered here, Bud. The king is not in charge anymore, that old creep Ferdinand is. And Moxie got turned into a Lurker. They escaped from subways and is running around outside the city. The king ain't been seen for a while, and there's rumors Ferdinand fed him to Moxie, making him a Lurker now too."

All this information was almost too much for Ticktock. He stood still, dumbfounded, trying to take it all in.

"Lurkers?"

"Yeah," Larry said. "When Moxie and the army got to the tunnels, Lurkers attacked 'em. Moxie got bit. Then he turned into one, right in front of the king, so I hear."

Ticktock frowned, full of dismay. All his hopes to be part of the Nork army seemed to be crumbling in front of him.

Ticktock nodded, feeling grateful to Lary, and thankful he was helping him.

"What happened to the prisoners?"

"They're all being guarded at Madson Skar Gardem. But it ain't them you got to worry about. What you give me to tell you what you really got to be afraid of?"

Ticktock had a feeling he needed to know what Lary knew, but he had nothing, nothing but his suit. He looked around at himself, felt inside his pockets.

Lary smiled. "I always liked that purple suit you got on. And I bet it'll fit me better than it fits you."

"What am I supposed to wear?" Ticktock said glumly.

Lary shrugged. Ticktock stared at him for a moment, then started to take his jacket off. "What you got to say better be good."

As Lary stared with hunger at the suit, Ticktock said, "Okay, but no double cross."

Ticktock took off his pants and Lary shucked his clothes and dropped them in the dirt. Ticktock picked them up and struggled into them.

When they were both dressed, Lary looked good, even though the suit was dirty. Ticktock looked totally miserable in clothes two sizes too small. Ticktock snarled, "Okay, give."

As Lary turned to walk away he said, "King Ferdinand put out contract on you. He even put up a reward. Whoever kills you gets to live like a king for a week. You know how much he hates people like you. You better high tail it back to Booklin. Your life ain't worth a plugged nickel here no more."

Ticktock's heart fell. His mind filled with unhappiness and disappointment. If everything Lary said was true, there was no way he was going to get to stay in the army. In fact, he had better run, and fast.

Ticktock studied Lary, and something told him Lary wasn't lying. He turned and started running the way he'd came, fast.

"Remember," Lary said. "If things go sour here, and I gotta come to Booklin, you vouch for me!"

Ticktock was running too fast to answer. The idea Lary, a white guy, could even take two steps into Booklin without getting killed was funny, but it didn't really matter right then. Ticktock just hoped he made it back home himself with his skin intact. It was a long way from the trees and cages to the edge of the city, and a long swim after that. He had a long way to go. And he had a feeling he would be passing a lot of people who wanted him dead.

CHAPTER 9

Sephie and Wheaties lay in the small van, trying to be quiet. Wheaties took a chance and peered over the edge of the window fame. He saw two dark shapes approaching them.

"What is it?" Sephie whispered in a nervous voice.

"More of those things," Wheaties whispered back. "Be quiet."

At first, Wheaties saw one dark shape, the outline of a man silhouetted by the light of the yellow eye behind him. His hair seemed ragged and there was something strange about the way he seemed hunched over. His movements were jerky too, as if he was having trouble walking. Then more shadows appeared behind him, two, three, then many more. It was a whole crowd of people.

Suddenly the children heard a tortured moan from one of the people in the back. They began to hear a scraping on the ground, the shuffling of feet. Their hearts leapt to their throats, and they instantly knew whoever it was approaching them, they were not normal, and something horrible.

Wheaties turned to Sephie and looked at her. He could see the whites of her eyes in the darkness. "I hope they don't find us here!"

Sephie nodded quickly, afraid. Both of them peered out the window frame.

The woman, for that's what it was, came into the light of the yellow eye. Sephie and Wheaties gazed on her with horror, for she looked dead. The flesh on her face over her right eye sagged, exposing the shriveled eyeball inside and the skull beneath. Her clothes hung in rags, exposing her rotting skin and bones underneath. She moved mechanically, as if she couldn't see where she was going, her hands in front of her as if trying to feel what was ahead. She headed right for their hiding place!

Then she was right next to them! They could smell her; she smelled like rotten meat and dirt. She looked as if she was going to shuffle right past them, and they held their breath. But then at the last moment, she turned towards them. She moaned loudly and reached into the van. She'd spotted them!

"Back to the buses!" Wheatie yelled, pulling Sephie out the other side of the van. But once again, they had no clue which direction to go. The monsters were everywhere. Wheaties pulled Sephie in the only direction which seemed to have no monsters, and they weaved between cars, out of breath with fear.

Even though the yellow eye shone above, the

hulks of the cars rose above them, creating a maze which they had to navigate through. Sephie's head began to spin, and she felt as if the buses were a million miles away. The sound of moans drifted softly on the breeze, and now it was hard to tell from which direction they came from. A slight mist rose up from the ground, and the air was chilly. Sephie began to see how foolish it was for them to wander out on their own.

Wheaties, wanting to show himself to be the man who would protect Sephie, kept leading her around, but every time they came around another car, all he saw was more cars. Wheaties realized in the darkness, they had wandered into the middle tunnel, and darkness surrounded them.

Suddenly moans seemed to come from every direction! And they seemed really close! Wheaties made a decision. He looked around and saw an archway in the side of the tunnel, and all he could see was darkness ahead.

"This way!" Wheaties said, dragging Sephie along.

"Where are we going?" Sephie asked, her voice full of panic.

"Shh, quiet," Wheaties said. He led them to the van. "In here."

Sephie followed Wheaties into the dark archway. They ran down a small set of stone steps, and reached a metal door. It was closed shut, but they were hidden in the small alcove from the main tunnel.

"Get down!" Wheaties said.

They scrunched down on the concrete. Wheaties looked at Sephie, whose wide eyes showed fear. "We'll hide here until morning. They won't find us here."

"But what if they come down here? We'll be trapped!"

Wheaties thought about what she said. He stood up and pulled on the metal door. With happiness, Wheaties watched it slowly groan and open slightly.

"We go in here, and close the door."

Sephie looked more scared but nodded. Wheaties squeezed her hand. "Don't worry. I won't let them touch you!"

Sephie smiled weakly, but with pleasure. Wheaties was trying to be her hero. She wanted to be Johnny herself, but she realized then she was happy to be Deb and let Wheaties be her Johnny. Despite the danger, she felt a warm happiness fill her. She was with her boyfriend, on an adventure.

They sat down as best as they could. It was cold, so Wheaties put his arms around Sephie to warm her. Sephie smiled and forgot about the monsters, and just enjoyed being in Wheaties' arms.

King Ferdinand stood with the two soldiers at the door to the king's bedchamber. Ferdinand wore a dark, evil grin, but the two men looked terrified, their eyes wide open as they held poles in their hands with loops at the top.

"Now, remember, your former king is no longer, himself," Ferdinand said. Ferdinand stood behind the men, his old, wrinkled face grave with tension. He wore a silk purple outfit with gold dragons; one he had recently found in the king's wardrobe. He had enjoyed going through the former king's possessions, finding gold rings for his fingers and necklaces of silver and jade. It was like a holiday, made even more special by knowing the former king was only a room away, now dead, turned into a Lurker.

"What if he is waiting inside the door?" one of the men asked nervously. "He'll bite us."

"Better he bites you, than what I will do to you if you don't obey me," Ferdinand snarled. "Stop wasting time! Open the door now!"

With reluctance, the closest man opened the door, which swung inward. There was silence. They could see the bed straight ahead, on the far side of the room. It was empty. All three gazed about, trying to find the Lurker king.

After a few seconds, Ferdinand grew impatient. He put his hand on the soldier closest to the door and gave him a violent shove. The man yelled and fell into the room, on his face on the floor. As the man struggled to get up, the other soldier and Ferdinand waited, searching the room with their eyes, wondering where the Lurker king could be.

Suddenly from the right the king appeared. His face was purple and distorted, and had already started to swell and rot. He still wore his silk pajamas, which somehow made him look even more horrible. As Ferdinand and the other soldier watched, the king leapt on top of the first guard and bit at him.

The man screamed and struggled, trying to reach his hand around behind himself to ward the king off, but the former king was rabid and fast and he sunk his teeth into the man's neck.

Both Ferdinand and the other soldier grinned with dark delight. Then Ferdinand pushed the other soldier into the room. "Quickly! Put the rope around his neck!"

But just then Moxie stumbled out from the king's powder room. The second soldier yelled and tried to run backwards, but Ferdinand pushed him back in.

"There are two of them now!" the soldier yelled in terror.

"Get the rope around the king's throat and lead him out, before Moxie catches you!" Ferdinand said, chuckling.

The second soldier hurried to the king and with clumsy motions, looped the rope attached to a pole around the king's neck. The king, lifted his head, taking a grisly chunk out of the dying soldier's neck with him. The king turned towards the other soldier; his eyes black with death. Moxie stumbled towards them from the side of the room.

"*Aaah!*" yelled the soldier, and he almost dropped the pole.

From the doorway, Ferdinand yelled, "Hold him

at arm's length! Keep hold of the pole! Bring him this way, quickly!"

The soldier gripped the pole hard as the dead king rose up and put his hands out, grasping in the air for the other soldier. But the dead king couldn't reach him for the soldier held the pole tight. Moxie reached the bed and fell on it, becoming entangled in the covers. The soldier quickly pulled the dead king towards the door.

"Good! Good!" Ferdinand smiled, nodding. "We shall control them all this way. Then, when the time is right," he stroked his pointed chin. "We will release them on our enemies."

The soldier managed to pull the king outside of the room. King Ferdinand slammed the door, leaving Moxie and the now dead soldier inside.

"Poor king," the soldier said, gazing at the former king with a look of pity as the king writhed and moaned, reaching out his hands towards them. "You wasn't a bad king."

The king continued to paw at the air, his mouth bloody and with bits of skin still in his teeth. The king was so strong, the soldier almost fell backwards and had to stumble to his feet. Then he held the king tight, eyeing him nervously.

"What's going to happen to Ralph?" the other man asked, gazing at the closed door with pity.

"He will become a much better soldier," King Ferdinand chuckled, "for he will join our Lurker army. That makes an army of three, so far."

"Where you gonna get the rest?" the soldier

asked, looking at King Ferdinand suspiciously. "You're not going to kill some of our people, are you?" The soldier's voice made it clear he wouldn't like that.

"Of course not," Ferdinand lied. "Why should I? When we have a whole building full of prisoners, who at present are totally useless, but soon will be of immense value. They don't know it yet, but coming to Nork was the worst thing that could have possibly happened to them."

The soldier laughed evilly, and Ferdinand joined him.

The early morning rays of the red eye warmed Misterwizard's face as he lay uncomfortable in his chair in front of the buses. His back ached from sleeping on the chair all night. Despite Misterwizard's short round body, the chair was stiff material called in the old days "plastic" and it didn't make for a comfortable bed.

Misterwizard stood up without opening his eyes, yawned, and stretched his arms. He let out a happy groan. He noted it was approaching the time called "fall" in ancient times, and the morning was chilly. Wearing nothing but a pair of green cotton shorts, a sweatshirt with stains from his many meals and ragged holes all over it with the words, "Cleveland Browns" on the front, whatever that meant, and a pair of bunny slippers, Misterwizard wasn't protected very well from the cold.

Before he opened his eyes, his mind was already going at high speed. He thought of how they would get through the tunnels. They would have to leave the buses and other vehicles behind, for the tunnels were choked with old cars and trash. This meant traveling on foot to the gate of Nork, not an ideal way to confront an enemy. But then, they really couldn't just walk up and knock on the door anyway, could they? They would have to find a secret way into the city, one Misterwizard had not discovered yet.

The thought of walking up, knocking and asking the Norkers if they could please have the people of Pelpia back made Misterwizard laugh. *If only everyone were civilized, and reasonable,* he mused.

Misterwizard finally opened his eyes and looked around. He saw someone curious. A man stood in front of him, twenty feet away, near the entrances to the tunnels. Misterwizard realized it was not a normal man, but appeared to be what was left of a man. The man's skin was green and sagging off his bones, exposing his ribs and spots on his legs. His rotted clothes hund off him, dirty and torn. The man's eyes were sunken in and rotted. His teeth were exposed, for his lips had long since rotted away.

"Mother of Murgatroyd!" Misterwizard said in a fervent voice of fascination. "I appear to be looking at a dead man walking!"

The man gurgled something and raised its hands. It moved towards Misterwizard, looking like it meant to grab him. Misterwizard, fell backwards into the chair again as the horrid creature advanced. The dead man moved closer, only a few feet away!

Misterwizard yelled, "Leaping Lizards!" and stuck out his foot to halt the creature's advance. His foot came in contact with the dead man's chest, and as the man continued to press forward, Misterwizard was tipped over backwards.

A woman's scream sounded behind Misterwizard. From where he lay on the ground, he turned his head backwards to see who it was. One of the women from the tribe had seen the monster, but she was pointing ahead in a different direction. Misterwizard turned his head from his position sitting in the chair, his back on the ground, and looked where she was pointing to see something even more distressing. More dead creatures advancing on them! A veritable horde!

Misterwizard's realized something very dangerous and totally unnatural was occurring, and imminent death awaited them if they didn't react to the crisis fast. Just as he was thinking these thoughts, the creature in front of him bent down and reached for him again.

Misterwizard rolled to his left and scrabbled away on all fours. The man, losing his prey, moaned in disappointment and turned to follow. Misterwizard finally managed to get far enough away to leap to his feet. He saw many members of the tribe outside the buses now, staring and pointing at the advancing creatures.

There was not a moment to lose!

"Everyone, retreat to the buses!" Misterwizard yelled as he put a hand on the woman's back and pushed her towards the nearest bus.

Some stood, petrified in fear. Others ran towards the buses. Super and Starbucks ran up to Misterwizard.

"What are they, Misterwizard?" Super asked, her voice full of excitement and fright.

"It seems the dead have been re-animated and are looking for a snack!" Misterwizard said. "Hurry! Our only solution is to find refuge in the buses! Help me secure all our companions in our steel shelters before they become undead sustenance!"

Super and Starbucks turned and ran to comply. They grabbed the people frozen in fright or amazement and dragged them towards the buses. Misterwizard did the same. Confusion reigned, as everyone screamed in panic and ran in all directions. A mad rush to the doors of the buses caused a log jam and people fell to the ground and stared at the oncoming horde, pointing and yelling. Misterwizard realized there was no way everyone outside could get safely on the buses before the strange undead host was upon them. He would need to create a distraction.

Searching around, he found an old car hubcap. Then he found an old stick. He picked them up and ran towards the undead creature. He banged the hubcap with the stick, making a loud sound which echoed in the air.

"Over here, foul escapees from the graveyard!

Come eat me! I'm round and fat and very delectable. There is enough of me to feed you all and then some!"

The undead did turn towards the sound, and saw Misterwizard, just as he'd hoped. He was closer, and short, round body did indeed look like a tasty morsel. They turned and shuffled towards him, dragging their feet on the concrete and staring at him hungrily with dead eyes.

Misterwizard led the undead chorus towards the tunnels, away from the buses. He glanced back, happy to see the log jam was clearing and people were getting on the vehicles. Then he looked forward again and almost fainted. The creatures were only a few feet away!

He turned to run, but happened to look up at the sky. Despite his danger, he couldn't help but freeze in place, in total amazement. His mouth opened wide and his mind blanked for a second. He wondered briefly if he was actually still asleep and having some kind of strange, bizarre dream. Misterwizard knew of certain substances which when inhaled or smoked, could cause the mind to go on strange journeys, devoid of any touch with reality. Though in the past in his castle he had experimented with them, for research purposes only of course, he was fairly certain he had not imbibed in any of those substances lately. Could he have eaten a bad piece of meat, or drunken something that didn't react well with his body? For what he now saw was so bizarre, so strange, he couldn't believe it could be real.

There in the sky he saw men with wings! They flew towards him high in the sky. Some of them held other men beneath them in harnesses. Most of them held swords or bows and arrows, and a few carried smoking pots, which looked as if they held fire.

"What strange new creatures has this world created now?" Misterwizard said to himself, smiling with pleasure and excitement.

Misterwizard looked back at the undead monsters, then up at the sky again, then back at the monsters. He slapped himself on the cheek, and it hurt. Could he actually be awake? Could the world have changed so much, that now nothing was too strange or bizarre to be reality?

Suddenly as Misterwizard watched in pleasant fascination, the flying men dove down and began pouring the fire out of the pots onto the undead monsters. Others swooped down and with swords in their hands, struck the creatures, lopping their heads off or making them fall to the ground and flew back up.

Joy and happiness filled Misterwizard's heart, for it appeared as if these creatures were there to help them! He chuckled, then he laughed out loud. If this was some kind of dream, it was mighty entertaining!

As the fire hit some of the creatures, they burst into fire and became undead torches. This didn't seem to stop them from moving about, but as the fire burned their bodies, eventually the ones on fire began to fall to the ground. The ones whose heads were lopped off continued to walk about, as if looking for their missing body part.

Then Misterwizard saw something that made

him forget all about the winged men or the monsters, for his heart filled with joy to the point where tears came to his eyes. As he watched, one of the winged men dropped to the ground and deposited his passenger. With total elation, Misterwizard saw it was none other than Johnny Apocalypse!

Johnny looked just like he always did, in his black leather pants, black vest and boots, his yellow hair sticking up in all directions but somehow making him look handsome and roguish, and a sword strapped to his side. Misterwizard's heart hurt with emotion, and he realized just how much he had missed his good friend. Misterwizard realized how emotional he had become and grew angry with himself. Not very scientific of him! He wiped his eyes and determined to have a more stoic demeanor when he spoke to Johnny.

"Old fool," he said to himself, but it didn't help. He was just so happy to see Johnny and know he was in good health; it was all he could do to stop from crying.

Misterwizard stumbled towards Johnny, still trying to get his emotions under control. Johnny, Misterwizard could see, was just as full of emotion, for his face was contorted with joy and Johnny was fighting his feelings too. Johnny ran to Misterwizard and put his arms around him.

"Misterwizard!" Johnny yelled, and then both of them lost control and let the tears flow. Johnny let go of Misterwizard and they gazed into each other's eyes, both knowing what the other was feeling.

Finally, Misterwizard patted Johnny on the arm

and choked out, "Salutations, my boy."

A monster lurched toward them. Johnny grimaced with anger, whipped out his sword and hacked at the undead creature. Misterwizard, finally getting control of his emotions, began to feel his scientific curiosity begin to arise. He watched with fascination as Johnny hacked the creature's head off. The head fell to the ground but the mouth continued to open and close, like a flopping fish-beastie. Misterwizard bent over the head and studied it.

"How scientifically improbable and medically impossible this is, and yet, if my mind is not having hallucinations, it appears to be substantiated by the visual evidence. Men who have expired, still showing signs of animation and decisive decision making."

"Lurkers is what they call them," Johnny said, grinning, his dripping sword draped over his shoulder. "They came out of the subway from Nork. They were created by water tainted by the mushroom monsters. If they bite you, they spread the green water to you and you become one of them. We have to kill them all and find out where they escaped from, before they get off the road and start spreading their disease."

Misterwizard stood up and tried to assess how many Lurkers were still at large. There seemed to be at least twenty, maybe more, still pouring out of the tunnels.

"Indubitably," Misterwizard said. "I ascertain their bite is worse than their bark, as it were. This must be a mutation caused by radiation from the bombs, er, mushroom monsters. One bite from them causes their saliva to enter your bloodstream, I suspect, and..."

"And you become one of them!" Johnny said.

Misterwizard grinned darkly. "Glad to see you back, my boy, but our happy reunion will have to wait to be fully consummated. I'll rally the other men from the tribe to assist in the Lurker elimination!"

Misterwizard turned and ran towards the buses. Johnny nodded and turned to look for another Lurker to disable.

CHAPTER 10

As they descended down the cold stone steps into the utter blackness, Restaria, Johnthebaptist and the people of Pelpia gazed ahead with wide eyes full of fright. The only light came from the flickering torches held by Restaria and Johnthebaptist at the front, and two more men at the back of the group. The torches danced, creating shadows on the cold marble walls. Old, tattered and rotted posters covered the walls, though some, preserved in the dry darkness, had not faded as badly as ones above in the open air. Images of men and women from ages long past stared at them with cold, dead eyes. The images seemed to dance in the flickering light of the torch, watching them as if they were intruders to their peaceful, empty tomb.

"Do we even know where we're going?" The voice of a man somewhere in the middle asked in a wavery voice which echoed off the stone walls.

Restaria found the question irritating, for of course they didn't, and the man asking the question only added to everyone's fear. She ignored it and hoped the man stopped talking.

"How much further?" a little girl asked, her voice high and full of fright. Another question they had no answer to, in fact, Restaria suspected their journey had just begun, and where it ended, there was no way of telling. Once again, Restaria didn't answer, for if she started answering questions like that, she would never get to stop. They would all just have to wait and find out.

Down, down, down they went, one step after another, descending into who knew what. Each step seemed more dangerous, less close to what they knew above, and further away from safety, but down, down, down they went.

Finally, after what seemed an eternity, Restaria and Johnthebaptist stopped. In front of them stood a series of metal poles about three feet high, with spikes of poles in a star pattern on top of them. Beyond the poles, only more darkness.

"What do we do now?" Restaria asked.

"Go over them, I suppose," Johnthebaptist said. He walked forward as the rest watched. He tried to turn one of the poles on top, for it looked as if it rotated, and it budged for a second then stopped, held by something.

"Hold my torch," Johnthebaptist said, handing his torch to a man close by. Then he walked back to the poles and with a grimace, raised his foot and kicked the closest one. It moved slightly, then stopped. He did it again and again, as everyone watched. Finally, they heard a clunk somewhere inside the mechanism. A tinny sound was something small and metal falling to the ground. Johnthebaptist grabbed the closest bar again, and smiled as he saw that now the bar turned. They could pass through it. He turned and smiled at Restaria, who smiled back gratefully.

Johnthebaptist grabbed his torch and passed through the metal star. Unnoticed to him, a little number counter on the front of the mechanism turned from 505 to 506.

Johnthebaptist raised his torch over his head to try and see what was around. He saw only a large platform that ran in both directions, and a lower area three feet below which did the same thing. In the distance, he could just make out some giant shadow hulks in the lower area, like giant dead beasts. He could only see a few feet down the platform, and nothing but empty space.

He turned to speak to Restaria. Somewhere in the darkness behind him, someone groaned. Everyone froze in fear and stared towards the sound. Johnthebaptist froze as well, then he turned, raised his torch and peered into the darkness, trying to figure out where the sound came from.

"Oh, no!" Restaria whispered, her face a mask of concern. "Please tell me that's not one of those things that attacked us before."

"I don't know," Johnthebaptist said softly. "Perhaps, or it might just be a wildie who lives in the dark."

Restaria studied Johnthebaptist's face. "What if

this place is filled with those things? Should we continue?"

Johnthebaptist turned to look at her. "We have no choice. We can't go back."

"We could leave the building above from one of the doors."

"We discussed that," Johnthebaptist said. "We would surely be caught by the guards again. We're just going to have to be ready to fight."

"But if those things are all over down here, what are we going to do?"

Johnthebaptist looked grim and thought. "We will go to the next place where there are stairs, and find another opening. Hopefully, we won't encounter too many of those things until then."

Restaria nodded reluctantly, unhappy. She hated putting her people in such danger, but it seemed there was no choice. She turned to address the people.

"Listen. Everyone, keep your weapons ready. We're not sure what we are going to face ahead." She didn't want to tell them what she and Johnthebaptist were worried about, because it might have created a panic. "We must stay together and follow the person in front of you. Watch the torches. We will need to move fast, so don't stop and look at anything. And if you see something moving toward us in the dark, stay quiet!"

"Hello," an old man with a wrinkled face and long white hair said, his back bowed with age. "Can you tell us where we are going, Your Mayorness?"

Restaria smiled at him, finally relenting and

answering the question. "We don't know. We are going to try the next opening, and see where it leads us. With any luck, we will find a passage to another building where we can hide and make plans to escape. That is all I can tell you."

The old man nodded, smiling with satisfaction. "Thank you for answering me. At least I'll know why I died!"

Everybody chuckled, and it seemed to lighten the mood slightly. Restaria turned to Johnthebaptist. He moved backwards, and she motioned for the people to start going through the metal pole stars. Slowly they all walked through and joined Johnthebaptist on the other side. The little clicker counted them, one by one.

Monsta strolled leisurely over to a pile of rock and sat down. He placed his jagged piece of steel next to himself, close enough he could grab it if he wanted. The young man watched Monsta from the doorway warily, unsure who he was.

"You don't look like a Groundworm," the young man said.

Monsta leaned back against the cold concrete wall and grimaced. "They are called Norkers, and if you want to get along with me, you will not insult my friends. But you are right I am not one of them. I am a member of the Doomsday Prophecy."

The young man's brow furrowed with confusion, for he had never heard of the group Monsta spoke of. Then he forgot, for he really didn't care, and pleaded, "If it's shiny metal you want, we have lots of it. Pretty yellow and silver and white. And stones, beautiful stones. Bright red, and green, and blue, some set in rings of yellow metal, and others in necklaces. I'll get you all you want enough so you can't carry it all. If it's food, you want, we have yummy meat, and leafy greens, and even fruit. All you can eat. Or a nice weapon. I can give you a really fine sword that will slice through anything."

Monsta chuckled at the boy's frantic attempts. Then he yawned, looking bored. "Maybe I will take all that from you later. Right now, there is only one thing I desire. Do it for me, and I will tell you where to find your precious Dallanda."

"What?" the boy asked eagerly, glad there was something he could do to save Dallanda, and desperate to find her before she died.

Monsta gazed up at the sky and tried to look sincere, but he wasn't very good at it. "I hear you worship a beautiful goddess. I understand she is the most powerful, wonderful being in the world. I wish to worship her also, so she will give me her blessing. I have wanted to worship a goddess for so long!"

The young man was not as simple-minded as Monsta had hoped, and he saw through Monsta's deception immediately. He wrinkled his lip and brown in disdain. "Pantina is the goddess of the Sky. She has no interest in the worship of mere mortals. Especially mortals who are evil and lie."

Monsta became furious, and he leapt to his feet. He wanted to ram his steel stick right through the young man's heart, and moved towards the boy to do it. The young man leapt a step backwards and raised his own sword, a scowl of anger and a look of bravado on his face. At the last moment with a supreme effort, Monsta was able to restrain himself. He forced himself to calm down. "You hurt my feelings. Even mortals have feelings, you know."

The young man knew he was being toyed with, and began to feel uneasy, realizing how much bigger Monsta was then he, and how easily Monsta could beat him.

"I am sorry. I was inconsiderate. But you must know, Pantina is only the god of the Sky. There must be other gods here on the ground you can worship."

Monsta grew tired of the verbal battle, and his fingers twitched on his steel stick. He wanted so much to see the boy suffer and die, and vowed it would happen someday, but for now he had to play the game, no matter how much it irritated him.

"Oh, we have gods," Monsta said, trying to keep his breathing steady, "but they are small and weak, compared to your Pantina." Monsta was lying. To the members of the Doomsday Prophecy, only fools worshipped gods.

"I could not take you to see Pantina. I would be cursed and banished."

"Listen to me, boy," Monsta said through

clenched teeth. "Enough of the games. You take me to see Pantina, or your girlfriend dies. You have a few moments to decide. Then I'm going to go to your Dallanda and stick this steel right into her heart. Do we understand each other?"

The boy frowned glumly, not really certain what he should do. All he did know was Monsta was pure evil, and there was no way he was taking Monsta to Pantina.

"I will not take you to Pantina, but I will take you to Lord Flaggalon. If he is willing, he will take you to Pantina so you can worship her."

Monsta smiled. It was not the solution he wanted, but it was one he could work with. A lot of things could happen before they arrived to this Lord Flaggalon, and Monsta knew he could outwit this boy easily. All he needed was a way to get up to the tops of the buildings, and if he had to, he could find his own way to this goddess. Then when he was done, they would need a new one, for she would be missing her head. And somewhere along the way, this boy would die, no matter what.

Monsta chuckled to himself and felt warm inside at that thought. He nodded to the boy. "Hurry, let me ride on your back!"

"No, you are too big!" the boy said. "I will tie a rope around you, and carry you beneath me. I just hope I can carry your giant weight."

The boy turned and walked out. Monsta picked up his piece of steel and hid it under his shirt. Things were working out very well. It wouldn't be long before he could return with Pantina's head, and make the king of Nork very happy.

Lady Stabs made her way across the strange, sticky web between the buildings again until she was in the one closest to Pantina's home. She had purposefully waited until it was almost dark again, so most of the people would be sleeping or settling down, and she wouldn't be noticed.

As she entered the floor from the webbing through a large window frame, she walked over to the large opening which looked onto Pantina's temple. Even on this side the opening was decorated with flowers. Excitement and a strange feeling of elation washed over Lady Stabs as she anticipated talking to Pantina again. What she was doing was dangerous and unwise, for if Lord Flaggalon caught her, he would surely banish her. Then she would lose contact with Johnny and Deb and be forced onto the streets of Nork. And that would surely mean a beastie existence, fighting for food and trying to keep from being eaten herself.

The danger, rather than scaring her, filled her with a secret thrill of excitement. She was on a mission to help the trapped goddess, and the possibility of being caught was worth the risk. She began to realize she had more than just a desire to help Pantina. She could tell she was beginning to fall in love with the red-haired, golden winged goddess, and was becoming entranced by Pantina's smile.

The room had been turned into a worshiping chamber, full of elegant gold silk blankets, shiny rocks of different colors, and shiny yellow metal. Here and there around the room lay piles of food or other gifts for the goddess. At the end of the room, facing Pantina's home, a carpet of rich red fabric lay next to the opening, so worshippers could kneel and pray to Pantina.

Lady Stabs placed a small gold covered chair on the carpet and sat down facing Pantina's home. It was cold, and she shivered for her leather pants, light pink cotton shirt and black leather vest didn't hold much heat. The half of her head which was shaved was exposed to the cold as well, and she felt her whole body grow chill. She looked around and saw a silk blanket. She walked over, grabbed it and wrapped it around herself. Then she sat on the chair again.

"Pantina!" Lady Stabs whispered, loudly but hopefully not too loud that anyone else could hear. There was no reaction from Pantina's home, and no sight of the goddess.

Lady Stabs said it again, this time slightly louder, risking someone hearing her. "Pantina. Are you there?"

No sound, no movement. Lady Stabs felt disappointed, and a little silly. She'd built up all this great drama about sneaking over to see Pantina. Now if the goddess didn't show up, it would be all for nothing. She would simply have to live with her fantasies.

Suddenly the gold curtains behind Pantina's

throne moved! Lady Stab's heart rose with joy and emotion, for Pantina was coming! Why did the thought of seeing Pantina seem to make Lady Stab's heart throb so? Was it just because it was so forbidden? Or was there something else?

Pantina appeared. Her long, red hair shone in the light of the yellow eye. Her beautiful golden wings tucked on her back, looked soft and regal. Her green eyes seemed like a cat-beasties, glinting in the darkness. Pantina wore a red silk robe with black swirls on it, tied at the waist with a golden sash. Lady Stabs felt her breath catch, for she couldn't help but swoon at how beautiful Pantina was.

When Pantina saw Lady Stabs sitting across the void between the buildings, Pantina smiled with pleasure. Lady Stabs smiled back shyly and a little embarrassed.

"Hello again, Lady Stabs," Pantina said, her green eyes gazing at Lady Stabs. "I so hoped you'd return."

A lump formed in Lady Stabs' throat and she suddenly felt hot. She stood up clumsily and walked to the very edge of the opening. There she knelt down, so she could be as close as possible to Pantina. "Your holiness!" Lady Stabs said, giving Pantina the honor she knew the goddess expected.

"Please, don't call me that," Pantina said, as she smiled at Lady Stabs. "And don't bow to me. We are friends. Call me Pantina."

Surprised but delighted, Lady Stabs rose to her

feet. Then she stood awkwardly, not knowing what she should do. "How have you been, Pantina?"

Pantina frowned. "Let me fly you over here, so we can talk more freely."

Lady Stabs suddenly felt uneasy. "No, I shouldn't. I mean, if I were caught…"

Pantina frowned slightly, disappointed. Then she nodded. "I understand."

"Are you all right, Pantina? Do you need anything? I'll do anything for you."

Pantina smiled, happy to hear Lady Stabs say that. She sat on her throne, but not in a regal way, just like a lonely girl scrunched up in the middle, afraid and small. "Lord Flaggalon gives me have everything I need." She sounded sad. "Except friends, like you."

Her words sent a pang of sorrow shooting through Lady Stabs, and she felt tears come to her eyes. Then she felt cold fury thinking about Lord Flaggalon. How she'd love to throw him off the tallest building!

"Are you- lonely?" Lady Stabs asked, her eyes growing moist with sorrow, and her face twisting into a tortured mask of grief.

Pantina nodded. She bit her lip and gripped the arms of the throne and her eyes grew moist. "I have no one to talk to. Lord Flaggalon says I cannot leave, or I will make the people lose faith in me."

"Why can't you just fly away?" Lady Stabs asked.

"Where would I go? I know nothing but this room. I don't know anyone. I don't even know what is outside. I would surely die."

Anger once again filled Lady Stabs, and she vowed she would get back at Lord Flaggalon, if it was the last thing she ever did. And no matter what happened, she was going to help Pantina escape.

Pantina smiled. "Let's talk of more pleasant things. Tell me about your life. Tell me about the world. Tell me everything!"

Lady Stabs nodded and she sat cross-legged on the carpet. Her heart filled with joy, and she thought about how this moment was the happiest she could ever remember. To get to sit and gaze at the lovely goddess and talk to her, all night long! Look at Pantina's smile and gaze at her lovely face!

As Pantina listened, Lady Stabs told her everything, starting when she was a little scrabbler, to being in the Doomsday Prophecy, to meeting Johnny. And then she told her about their adventures in Ballmoor and how she had ended up with the Sky. Lady Stabs talked and talked all night, until the red eye began to rise in the sky. And Pantina listened. They began to be close, much closer than just friends.

CHAPTER II

As the red eye rose in the sky, it witnessed another bizarre sight in a world full of strange and bizarre sights. Three men holding three other men by the neck with long wooden poles and straps around their necks. The men holding the poles stood behind the others who shuffled and moaned, leading them towards an enclosed wagon. The men in front being held by the poles did not seem like men, however, but more like moving corpses, for that is really what they were.

The men holding the poles each wore expressions of fright, their eyes wide open and their faces white with fear. The men on the poles snarled and struggled, held their arms out and reached out for anything they could reach. They struggled and twisted their bodies, and the men behind them fought to keep them under control.

One of the dead men used to be Moxie. Still dressed in his pinstripe suit, blood and dirt covering himself, his eyes were red and wild. Next to Moxie stood an elegant, frail man in silk pajamas: the former king. The look on his face was one of surprise, as if he still didn't understand what had happened to him. The third man wore green pants and a black shirt, and looked like a common man. His brown hair was matted and his neck showed where it had been chewed.

Behind them stood an old, thin, tall man with long gray hair wearing a blue silk robe. He wore gold slippers and shiny gold necklaces, and gold rings with red stones in them on his fingers. This man seemed to be the only one who was enjoying himself, in fact his eyes were wild with pleasure and excitement.

"Hurry!" King Ferdinand barked. "Get them in the wagon and shut the doors before any of the people see them! I don't want to start a panic!"

"We're trying," one of the guards wailed. "They're strong and don't want to obey!"

"Hurry or you will be joining them!" King Ferdinand snarled.

Behind all of them stood ten other Nork soldiers, there to guard the wagon as it made its journey. And by the doors of the castle stood Alcapoon, watching with a look of utter disbelief and dark humor.

Finally, the men managed to force the three dead creatures up the steps of the wagon and inside. They dropped the poles, hurried back and slammed the doors shut. From inside, shuffled about, moaning and banging on the walls.

King Ferdinand walked back to his royal coach. This one was elegant, with golden wheels, curtains and soft velvet seats inside. Both vehicles had rattys harnessed to the front to pull them. Two of the king's guards helped King Ferdinand into the coach. They closed the door and King Ferdinand leaned out the window to give more instructions. He pointed to the three men who had held the poles.

"You three ride on the front of the wagon. Watch our cargo carefully. If they escape, you will be the first to be their victims."

The men nodded nervously and climbed onto the front of the wagon.

"The rest of you, keep the people away from the wagon and run alongside it. Tell the people that we have dangerous beasties inside. Beat them to keep them away if you have to. We aren't ready for them yet. We have quite a way to go, and we need to get there quickly! I have no idea what the fools guarding our prisoners are doing to them."

King Ferdinand turned to the soldier dressed in fine silk outfits who sat on the driver's bench of his coach. King Ferdinand waved his hand to him to signal for him to start moving. The soldier snapped his whip and the ratty tied to the coach screeched. It roared back its head and shook it, then reluctantly moved forward, pulling the royal coach behind it.

The wagon with the Lurkers fell in behind King Ferdinand's royal coach, and the strange and grisly caravan moved down the street away from the castle, heading south. As they moved through the streets, weaving around junk cars, weeds growing up through the concrete and piles of rubble, Norkers stood in the streets, staring at the strange and curious site. It was like nothing they'd seen before, a bit of excitement in their dull days. They pointed, laughed and talked amongst themselves, wondering if the king was in the royal coach, and what he could be hauling in the strange, sinister looking wagon. From inside the tall, wooden wagon came strange, horrible moans and banging. Everyone once in a while, the people would see eyes peering out from the cracks in the wood slats. Some people looked at the wagon with fright. Others grinned and followed the wagons, trying to get a peek inside. The guards walked along either side of the vehicles, pushing people away, threatening them and even pushing the ones who pressed in trying to get a look.

Inside the royal coach, King Ferdinand was in high spirits. He had found a young lady in the crowd and invited her in to join him. The coach had a small pocket by the seat filled with tasty dainties and wine, and Ferdinand made good use of it. He poured himself and the young woman a glass of wine and offered her some chocolates. He smiled at her with affection and desire.

"Hello, young maiden. What is your name?"

The girl, wearing a peasant frock and a cloth dress, had dirty blond hair and a long nose. Rather than answering, she simply glared at King Ferdinand and made a growling noise deep in her throat.

King Ferdinand opened his eyes in surprise and concern, wondering if somehow, she was a Lurker. But as he studied her, she didn't seem dead, just ill-tempered and of low intelligence.

"I am your king now. If you make me happy, things can go well for you, my dear."

She stared at him without replying, motionless. Then she spoke. "Cats! Devils! Dark caverns full of slimy worms!"

King Ferdinand began to grow very wroth. This girl reminded him of the silly wenches the king used to have all around himself, stupid mindless fools who were always laughing and spilling wine on the carpet.

"Listen to me, young woman. It would be good for you to change your attitude right now. Or I can put you in the wagon. There, you might find companions more suited to you."

The girl growled, and then she threw her wine at him!

"You stupid wench!" King Ferdinand screamed in fury. Then the girl tried to grab his arm and bite it! He pulled his arm back and yelled out the window.

"Soldier! Quickly!"

A soldier ran up and peered in the window. "Yes, My Lord?"

King Ferdinand, pressing himself against the side of the coach, pointed at the young woman, who clawed at him laughing eat him. "Remove this vile creature at once!"

The guard grinned. "That's Hasty. She's a little touched in the head, my lord. But she's real fun to be around, I hear, once you've tamed her." The guard ran around to the other side of the coach, opened the door and dragged Hasty out, kicking and screaming.

King Ferdinand was tempted to tell them to throw her in the wagon and let her become Lurker food, but at the last moment, he thought it might be fun to try and tame her. "Take her back to the castle and put her in chains in the dungeon. I will have a private talk with her later."

"Yes, Your Majesty," the soldier said. As he led the young woman away, King Ferdinand could hear him laughing. This irritated the king as well, for he'd looked like a fool and been embarrassed. He peered outside to try and remember the soldier's face so he could punish him later too. He sat back, feeling alone and disappointed. He would punish them all soon. No one would dare laugh at him, ever again.

The wagon and the coach trundled on down the road for what seemed like forever. As the red eye rose high in the noon sky, they finally reached their destination, the place called Madsom Skare Gardem, where they expected to find the prisoners of Pelpia.

As the huge round structure came into view, King Ferdinand chortled with evil glee and rubbed his hands together. "We are going to have some fun now!" He couldn't wait to see the death and horror that would soon occur as he watched people flee and get grabbed by his Lurkers. Then he would get to see them bitten and torn apart, all for his amusement.

As they entered the large gray stone area of street outside the structure, the coaches had to weave around old junk cars and piles of trash. King Ferdinand could hardly contain his impatience, like a little child about to open his gifts on his birthday.

Finally, they arrived at the main entrance and the vehicles came to a stop. The ratty, happy for a break, squealed and laid down. King Ferdinand banged open the door of the coach and ran to the wagon. The soldiers looked tired and nervous, having fought with the people of Nork the whole way and now dreading having to deal with their dead cargo again. They stood in circles, all staring at King Ferdinand, waiting for his orders.

"Well!" King Ferdinand spat out impatiently, waving at the wagon. "Get them out! Our guests are waiting to meet their new friends!"

With sad reluctance, the three soldiers who were tasked with leading the Lurkers waited, ready to grab the poles holding the Lurkers again. Another soldier slowly opened the door. As soon as the door was slightly open, the old king and the dead soldier burst out. The soldier holding the doors yelled and ran and the other three men stumbled backwards. Fortunately for them, the two Lurkers fell on the ground and writhed there for a moment, for the floor of the coach was a few feet up.

"Grab them, fools!" King Ferdinand yelled.

Quickly the men grabbed the poles. Once they had them, they wilted with relief. The third man who was supposed to grab the pole for Moxie looked on with fright, for his charge was still inside. The two guards holding the poles led the dead king and the soldier towards the entrance to the arena. The other man stood by the door of the coach, peering inside.

King Ferdinand grinned, knowing this was going to be entertaining. "Well? Go get him!"

The soldier, with a look of terror, crept towards the opening of the coach. From inside, a low moaning could be heard. The solder put a tentative foot on the step leading up to the opening. With a look of sad resignation, as if he knew he was facing his doom, he slowly walked inside. The other soldiers stood around laughing and pointing.

There was a moment of silence. King Ferdinand waited, holding his breath. What was happening inside? Suddenly he heard a loud scream and then a snarl as if from a savage beastie. The coach rocked back and forth, and King Ferdinand laughed again. They might have a fourth Lurker already, he thought.

Then there was silence again. Everyone waited and watched. It seemed like an eternity, but it was only a few seconds before a figure appeared at the door of the coach. It was Moxie! The skin of the lower half of his face was gone now, revealing the skull underneath. Bug-beasties crawled across his face and in and out of his mouth.

King Ferdinand's heart filled with dark joy. How wonderful it was to have monsters to use as his army! *But what of the soldier?* he thought.

As King Ferdinand and the soldiers watched, Moxie stumbled out. As he left the coach, they could see the pole attached to his neck was being held, and behind it, the soldier emerged, wearing a grin of victory. What the man didn't see, but King Ferdinand did, was the bite mark on his shoulder. King Ferdinand smiled with pleasure. Another Lurker for his army.

King Ferdinand hurried to the large entrance to the arena. The other soldiers holding the Lurkers were there, doing their best to keep the creatures under control. The soldier holding Moxie joined them. King Ferdinand walked over to a soldier and whispered to him, pointing at the soldier holding Moxie. The soldier listened and then looked at the soldier grinning. King Ferdinand whispered to him, "Make sure when he turns, he joins the others."

The soldier nodded to the new king, who then walked away, as they both gazed at the bitten soldier with grisly humor. King Ferdinand walked over to the front door of the arena and the Lurkers, staying far enough away to stay out of reach.

"Are my pets ready to have some delicious people to feast on?"

The Lurkers snarled and reached for him. King Ferdinand chuckled, turned and strode to the doors. He swung one of the doors open and gesturing for the soldiers to follow, hurried inside, eager for the fun to begin.

But as King Ferdinand entered the arena, surprise and dismay filled him, for as far as he could see, there was no one there! The place was empty and quiet as a tomb. He ran inside and gazed about in disappointed fury.

"Where are the prisoners!" He made a fist and shook it in the air, his mind numb with disappointment.

All the joy he had felt drained away, to be replaced with worry and anger.

The soldiers led the Lurkers inside, and the Lurkers gazed about, as if surprised themselves that there were no people to eat.

King Ferdinand grew even angrier. Someone would pay for this! He turned to the other soldiers who had entered behind them. "Find them! Find them or you will all be turned into Lurkers! You will be my Lurker army!" King Ferdinand had never been so disappointed in his life, and he desperately wanted to see someone die to make himself feel better.

As the king strode about in impotent fury, waiting for an explanation, he tried to imagine what could have happened to the prisoners. Could they have been killed by the people of Nork? Could they have escaped and went back home? Was Moxie lying all along, and were there really no prisoners at all? None of the explanations left King Ferdinand feeling good, for he couldn't come up with any scenario which seemed positive.

Finally, one of the soldiers ran up. The man looked frightened, his face a mask of worry. King Ferdinand suspected what the soldier was about to tell him would not make him happy.

"The prisoners are gone, Your Majesty."

The King's impatience reached a boiling point at the guard stating the obvious. He stomped over and slapped the soldier on the face, as hard as he could. Then he grabbed the man's green jacket.

"I can see that, stupid. Where are they?"

The soldier gulped. "We found the soldiers guarding them. They say the prisoners jumped them and tied them up. Then they said the prisoner went down the tunnel and disappeared. They went somewhere, they don't know where."

King Ferdinand couldn't remember feeling so frustrated and helpless before. He wanted to, had to kill something. He walked over to another soldier and grabbed his lance. As the first soldier watched in terror, King Ferdinand stabbed him in the chest. The man fell to the ground with a cry. King Ferdinand strode over his body in the direction the man had come from.

As one of the soldiers led him, King Ferdinand found the bound soldiers. They lay behind a wooden booth in the big open area outside of the arena, looking like trussed up chicken-beasties. One of the soldiers with the king pulled the gag out of one soldier's mouth.

"Lord Ferdinand! They jumped us in the middle of the night! It wasn't our fault!"

"I am King Ferdinand, you fool. And you failed me," King Ferdinand said. "I hate miserable, whining fools who can't even perform simple tasks."

As the soldiers laying on the ground and the ones with King Ferdinand watched, the king motioned to the ones holding the Lurkers.

"Come," the king said with a dark smile. The men with the Lurkers came forward. "Prepare some more poles, you're going to need them." King Ferdinand turned and glared at the soldiers on the floor, who stared back in fright. "Then let the Lurkers have their first meal. We will have our undead army, one way or another."

As the men on the ground screamed, the men holding the Lurkers led the dead king, Moxie and the dead soldier towards them. The Lurkers moaned with happiness, hands reaching out, ready to feast.

CHAPTER 12

Clancy and his men of the clan stood on an old, cracked, gray ribbon of road and stared at the remains of the Washton Brig. There were a hundred of the Clansmen there, all following behind Clancy. It was mid-morning and the red eye slowly made its way up into the sky from the distant hills. A rolling mist covered the ground, and the clansmen's furs were touched with dew. They had just arrived after spending the night bringing what little food and clothing, they could gather to their people back at Clanshame, their home. It was not much, and their people were very disappointed. Clancy had vowed that the next time they returned, they would be carrying more food than the people could eat, along with treasures and fine clothes.

Now they stood and stared at the remains of the brig, which extended out over the large water and ended in the middle, the center part of the brig gone and lying in the water. On the other side on the other side of the broken section the brig started again and kept going until it reached the large crude wall which surrounded Nork.

The men wore their heavy leather and fur war outfits, and carried their huge axes and spears. They were ready for war. Alasdair stopped looking at the brig and turned to Clancy.

Alasdair, with his short black hair, long face and pointed chin, put the head of his axe on the ground, leaned on it and studied Clancy's face. "Are we really going to walk on the brig, Clancy? It looks like it might fall down under our feet. And when we reach the end, we'll have to climb down and swim to the other half of the brig and climb back again. And when that is done, we'll have to find a way over the wall yonder."

"Would you rather swim the whole way, Alasdair? Or wait for a fairy to come and carry us over the water? We have to go now, while the king's army is busy with his wee little problems. If Dame Fortune gives us a kiss, we will occupy their castle and hold their king hostage before they know what is happening. Or we may just fight their army into surrender, and then they will have no choice but to make me king of Nork."

"And what if they still have more soldiers than us?" Gavin asked.

"We have a hundred brave souls here, and one of ours can take five of those pasty Norkers. Yet if that still not be enough, we will simply take their king and hold him hostage until they pay us a bounty."

"And then we leave this land for good," Alasdair said, looking back towards their home with a faraway gaze. "Go somewhere full of game and open spaces, where no one will fight us."

"Aye," Clancy said, his voice somber. "If we cannot be lords of this land, we will find a land where we can be. We will move inland and follow the path of the horned beasties. But we need supplies for that long a journey, and them in Nork are the ones who have it."

"And what of the yellow-haired lass?" Alasdair asked, grinning. "You can't leave without her. She put an arrow in Clancy's heart."

Clancy and Gavin laughed. Clancy stared at Alasdair and said, "You be reading my mind again. 'Tis true. I will be looking for the lass, and that Johnny bampot who stole her away from me better keep his sword handy. When I find him, you canna bet he'll rue the day he came up against Clancy."

Gavin's eyes suddenly filled with fear. "What if…" He looked at Clancy and Alasdair, and they looked back at him. "What if the Lurkers have already taken over the city?"

Alasdair looked at Clancy to see his reaction. Clancy nodded gravely. "Then the land is cursed. We turn and go back home, and find our supplies elsewhere. That will be a hard road, and let's hope it be not."

They all chuckled again. "Aye," Alasdair said. "If that be, then let them Lurkers have the Norkers. It twill serve them right."

"Let's get to it lads!" Clancy said. "Before this mist which hides us is no more."

Clancy strode forth and stepped onto the road

where the brig began rose from the ground. Alasdair and Gavin looked at each other and grinned, knowing they had some kind of adventure ahead. The fell in behind Clancy, and the other men followed. Soon they rose up into the sky, leaving the land far below. Ahead of them, the city of Nork beckoned.

Monsta, despite being a tough guy who wasn't afraid of anything, still felt his stomach drop out of his body as he rose in the air. The angel had rigged some sort of rope around Monsta's waist and around his shoulders. With an effort the young man flapped his wings and slowly, ever so slowly, rose off the ground.

"You are so big and heavy!" the young man cried. "I can't lift you!"

"You better," Monsta snarled, "or your girlfriend dies and you too! Hurry up!" In reality, Monsta was worried. If he was too heavy for the young winged freak, the boy might drop him. Monsta didn't like the idea of falling from the sky, plummeting to the ground only to be splattered on the hard stone below, in fact it terrified him. But he had no choice. This was his only way of getting up to where the winged freaks lived, and he had to take the chance.

Finally with an effort, Monsta rose up off the ground. The teen angel flapped his wings five feet off the ground for a while, and Monsta wondered if he really was too heavy. But then they rose, and the ground began to grow smaller and smaller.

Without intending to, Monsta held his breath. He watched the ground shrink away; his mind filled with fright. It wasn't long before he was so high, he knew he would die if the boy suddenly untied the ropes. Maybe that was the boy's intention all along, Monsta thought with panic. Get him up high enough to kill him. Monsta wondered whether if he felt the boy starting drop him, could he pull out the sharp steel he had hidden under his shirt and stab the boy in a last act of vengeance? Before he plummeted screaming to the ground?

Monsta shuddered, and hoped the boy was not that smart. For really, all the boy had to do was kill Monsta, then he could go back and search for his girlfriend himself. No, this teen didn't seem bright enough to think of that. Monsta sure hoped he wasn't.

Monsta had no choice but to breathe, and it came in ragged gasps, for the rope pressed against his chest. The world looked so small now, as they soared above it. Monsta could hear the young man grunt with each flap of his wings, and Monsta instantly hated the pathetic weakling. Why couldn't he have found a man among the angels to carry him?

Monsta gazed around. They were so high now, the gray strips that intersected the buildings looked tiny. Even most of the buildings looked small, like metal stacks of blocks. Monsta could see that Nork was a maze of buildings, going as far as he could see. Around the city on both sides, a big river flowed, and beyond the river on more land. As he gazed out at the world, it seemed to go on forever. The size of the city made Monsta dizzy. He'd never seen a place so huge, with so many buildings before. It gave him a secret feeling of fear, for this city was much bigger than where he and his gang had lived. But then it also gave him a feeling of elation, for there was so much area waiting to be explored, full of opportunity

They rose up, along the side of one of the tall buildings. Monsta had to admit, even though he was terrified, there was something exhilarating and exciting about flying in the sky. He envied the boy, which made him hate the boy even more.

As they flew, Monsta saw one tall building with a needle at the top. It was by itself and. In the far distance to the north, he saw another group of buildings huddled together, as if for protection.

The boy flew him towards a building, but it was not the one with the needle.

"That one with the needle? That looks important! Take me there!"

The boy gasped out breathlessly. He would have loved to take Monsta there, for it was one of their main dwelling places, sure to be filled with Sky. But he knew he couldn't make it.

"It is too high! I can't make it!"

"Take me there!" Monsta roared.

"Lord Flagallon does not live there!"

Monsta scowled, fear of the boy dropping him filling his mind. "Take me where he lives then!"

"I can't make it!" the boy yelled back in a tired, whiny voice.

Monsta knew he had better settle for anywhere now, for the boy seemed about to fall from the sky. "How much further?" Monsta yelled, worry in his voice.

The teen didn't answer, for he seemed to be struggling to stay aloft. Monsta tried to twist his head around to see the boy's face, and when he managed it, he wished he hadn't. The boy's face was red with exertion and covered with sweat. Was he going to make it to any building before they both plummeted from the sky?

"My wings are tired!" the boy wailed.

Monsta scowled darkly. "Keep going, or your girlfriend dies!" What you don't know, Monsta thought with an evil grin, is as soon as we arrive, I'm going to kill you!

They flew over shorter buildings, the boy dipping and rising in a most annoying and uncomfortable way.

"Take me somewhere quick, before you kill us!" Monsta snarled.

The boy turned and flew towards another skyscraper, one slightly shorter than the one with the needle but not too far away. In his mind, the boy picked this building because it was where the hero Johnny slept. If he brought this evil man there, the hero Johnny would take care of him!

Monsta could see inside the building, for part of the side of the building had broken off, leaving a jagged edge. It was almost like a giant beastie had taken a swipe at the building, leaving a large section of the shell gone and exposing the floors inside. Some of the floors inside had crumbled where the break was. Monsta saw some of the rooms were divided off with four-foot partitions, almost as if the people were beasties to be held each in their own pen. The floor right in front of them looked nice, full of rich red carpet and a nice, soft bed.

"It's right ahead!" the boy said, his voice high and frail and full of weariness.

"Then keep going, fool!" Monsta said, laughing for some reason, he didn't know why. He was beginning to enjoy this flying stuff, and really enjoy this teen's suffering.

They suddenly dropped five feet. Monsta felt his stomach lurch and he almost threw up. Bile filled his throat and he felt woozy. Then there was a second drop, and once again Monsta felt sick, but not as bad as the last time. Monsta saw an opening in the building ahead, a tall, white building with a triangle shaped top. On the side where they approached, the wall was gone.

Monsta also saw a giant spider-beastie clinging to the building ten feet below the opening. It looked furry and horrible. Monsta's head buzzed, but he shook it, knowing it was about time for him to act.

The teen wheezed and Monsta felt sweat from the boy fall on his neck. The boy better make it! They dropped again. Now they were below the level of the opening! They were close now though, only ten feet away. Was the boy going to get them there?

"I can't make it!" the teen cried out.

"Fly, fool!" Monsta yelled. "It's right in front of us!"

They reached the building and flew beside it. Monsta craned his neck and looked up. The opening was close, so close, just above them, but out of reach.

The boy didn't look like he was going to make it! He was slowly sinking! Monsta squirmed around, feeling totally helpless. He was so close to his goal, to die now because this stupid teen was so weak! The thought drove Monsta's mind mad with rage.

"Get up there! Now!" Monsta turned his head and glared at the boy with his fiercest, most angry scowl. The boy's eyes were closed and he labored. Monsta made fists with his hands, feeling frustrated and powerless. It was all up to this stupid angel!

Slowly, ever so slowly, they began to rise, one inch at a time. Monsta stared at the side of the building, rejoicing at each one, willing the boy to make it to the top. Monsta's palms itched to grab the ledge, as soon as it came into view.

After what seemed like an eternity, the ledge came into view. Monsta reached out for it desperately, but they were still a few feet away. The teen saw it too and let out a cry of effort.

Slowly, slowly they grew closer. Monsta grabbed the ledge! That was it. The teen passed out and fell. As he did, the boy's full weight, like a stone, jerked on the rope holding Monsta. Monsta yelled and gripped the edge of the building desperately. The boy's weight pulled him down, threatening to drag him from the building and plummet them both to the ground far below. Monsta held on by only his hands, his arms fully extended. His eyes opened wide with desperate fear. He turned and looked down. The boy hung there below him, fully unconscious, a dead weight pulling Monsta down.

Desperately Monsta reached into his shirt with one hand, holding on for dear life with the other. He pulled out his jagged steel. With a look of pure hatred, he hacked at the rope. "Die you worthless, weak fool! Die!"

Monsta hacked at the rope again and again. The fingers of his hand holding onto the ledge began to go numb. He knew he had seconds before he lost his grip.

And then, in one quick second, the rope parted. Monsta watched with pure, evil joy as the boy fell, turning over and over, his large white wings fluttering like those of a dead bird. With the weight of the boy gone, Monsta was suddenly lighter, and the feeling of falling lessened. He threw his jagged piece of steel over the edge and into the building. Then he turned to enjoy watching the boy die.

He watched until the boy was just a small dot. Then he watched the teen hit the ground far below. It was a wonderful dark moment, he knew he would always cherish.

With a chuckle, Monsta climbed up the ledge. He was in the angels' home. It was time to cause some mayhem.

CHAPTER 13

Morning came again and the red eye slowly rose into the sky. Deb could see its light from the openings around the drape covering the large hole in the wall. Deb lay in the four-poster bed under a thick animal fur with Deecee next to her. They were both warm and cozy. The last thing she wanted to do was to leave her warm bed, but hunger pangs and the need to go to the necessary room were giving her urgent signals.

She lay still and smiled, thinking of the first night with the Sky, and when Johnny lay in bed with her. She stopped thinking about it, for it only made her miss Johnny more. And sure enough, the mere thought of Johnny filled her mind with worry. She had to not think about what he was going through, or she knew she would go crazy. She decided she didn't have any choice but to get up and face the day, alone without Johnny.

Deb sat up. Deecee raised his head and looked at her. She smiled at him and grabbed his head. She snuggled against his face and petted him.

"I'm so lucky to have you to keep me company, Deecee!" she said. Deecee didn't answer, just wagged his tail under the covers.

Deb scrunched over to the edge of the bed and pulled back the covers. She instantly regretted it, for the fire in the fireplace had been reduced to embers and the room was cold. She hurried over and grabbed the silk robe the Sky had given her and put it on, but it was thin and fancy and didn't do much to reduce the chill.

She shivered and hurried over to the fireplace, walking on the cold, carpeted floor with her bare feet. She had to pee really bad, but she also had to put some wood on the fire before it went out, or she'd have a bigger problem. Kneeling down, she grabbed some small kindling from a pile next to the fireplace and tossed it on the embers. With satisfaction, she saw flames start to rise. Soon she could put bigger logs on the fire, and the room would get warm again.

She turned to Deecee. "You stay in bed where it's warm, fellow, at least until I get the fire going."

She walked towards the door to go to the necessary room, but stopped in surprise. A Sky girl of around twenty seasons walked in the door and stood, staring at her. The girl was slightly overweight with brown hair, dirty white wings and a cryptic smile that told Deb right away this girl was not very friendly.

"Morning, Deb stranger. I am Patto."

Deb frowned, grumpy that this girl had come into her room without so much as knocking or asking for permission.

"Can I help you with something?" Deb said.

Patto smiled wider, and Deb could tell Patto liked people who challenged her. Something told Deb they were not going to be friends.

"I'm here to collect you. You're to join us on our mission to find food today. You don't look like very strong or even too bright. Still, I do what I'm told."

Deb scowled at Patto with dislike, placing her hand on her hip. "I just woke up. I'm not even dressed."

Patto scowled and set her jaw. "Everybody's got to help out, or out they go. Even little cupcakes like you."

Deb wanted to continue the fight, but her need to pee was becoming really urgent. Still, Deb's mind burned with anger. She could show this Patto who the real cupcake was, she thought.

"Can I at least get dressed? Maybe have something to eat?"

Patto rolled her eyes. "You should have been up sixty dots of time ago, like everyone else, instead of lying in bed like a lazy Groundworm. I'll give you thirty dots, and that's being generous. Meet me in the hall, and don't keep me waiting."

Patto spun around and stomped out. Deb resisted the urge to kick her in her fat rump. How she'd like to pluck the annoying girl's wings!

Patto shut the door to the room with a slam. Deb felt a strange urge to lift her hand and show her middle finger to the door, but she didn't have any idea why. Was it something she'd seen once before? She couldn't remember.

Then she realized suddenly that if she didn't find the necessary room fast, there was going to be a puddle on the floor. She hurried out of the room before it was too late.

After finally relieving herself, Deb came back into the room and got dressed in tight leather jeans, a cotton top, a black leather jacket and black boots. The fire crackled merrily now, and the last thing she wanted to do was leave it. What she really wanted to do was crawl back in bed with Deecee. She petted Deecee, looking glum.

"You stay here, you lucky dog-beastie, and enjoy the bed. I have to go with this annoying, rude girl and maybe get killed."

Deecee didn't understand, but he licked her hand and smiled at her. She kissed him on the muzzle. Then she grabbed a hunk of bread and a piece of meat off the table in the room and reluctantly walked out.

What she didn't see was the young boy flying in the distance, carrying a heavy weight beneath him, heading right for her room.

Wheaties woke up first. His whole body was stiff, from lying on the cold, hard concrete. He looked over at Sephie. She lay there, with her head on her hands, eyes closed. She looked like an angel, with her long brown hair and soft, lovely face. He smiled inside, and a warm feeling of happiness filled him. He had gone on an adventure with her, and they had survived. Now they would always have something to bind them together. After they got back to the bus, maybe she would go on another adventure with him, and who knew, someday, she might actually kiss him!

Wheaties head swooned at the thought, and his mind filled with love for his new girlfriend, for that's what he hoped she was. Then he snapped out of it, and remembered the danger they had been in. If he wasn't careful, harm would come to Sephie, and then he'd look like an idiot to her!

Wheaties raised his head and looked around. The red eye was high in the sky, and the light from it shone into the main tunnel. Wheaties let Sephie go for a moment and walked up the steps to study the main tunnel. He didn't see any monsters, just the same old cars that were there the night before. Maybe whatever monsters that were there the night before had moved on. In the daylight, they should have no problem finding the bus again. Wheaties sighed with relief. It was time to wake Sephie and get back to the bus, fast! He walked back down to her and gently shook her shoulder.

"Sephie!" Wheaties said in a soft but urgent voice. "Sephie, are you alright?"

Sephie opened her eyes and looked at Wheaties. Wheaties smiled at her. She smiled back, filling his stomach with butterflies.

Sephie raised her head and then winced. She too

was sore from their uncomfortable bed. Wheaties reached out to her and touched her shoulder.

"Ow!" Sephie said. "This place is miserable!"

Wheaties grinned. "It sure is. At least it saved us from the monsters."

At the mention of the monsters, Sephie instantly remembered. She sat up and peered around.

"Don't worry," Wheaties said. "I think they're all gone. But we should get back to the bus."

Sephie looked at Wheaties, first with a look of concern, but one that quickly turned into a quirky smile of pleasure. Wheaties understood what she was thinking, that they had just enjoyed an adventure together.

Sephie stood up held out her hand. Wheaties took it with happiness, feeling joy Sephie now held his hand all the time. They walked up the steps and peered into the main tunnel. The light shining on the old, rusted cars made them look sinister and creepy. Everything looked decayed and deadly.

Suddenly they heard the horrible moans of the monsters again! They didn't seem close, but too close for comfort. There were other sounds as well, people shouting, explosions and the sound of fire crackling.

Wheatie towards the opening in the tunnel, seemingly miles away. Through the curved archway he saw something amazing. A man flew down into sight, heading towards the ground. The man had wings!

"Sephie, look!" Wheaties pointed at the man. Sephie looked.

"Wow!" she said with wonder. They looked at each other and shared a moment of amazement.

Then Wheaties remembered the sounds. "It sounds like our people are fighting the monsters! We have to hurry and get back to the buses!"

They ran into the main tunnel and hurried towards the sounds of battle. As they reached the opening, they saw an amazing sight. The sky was filled with flying men! The ground was filled with horrible monsters. And on the other side of the monsters, they saw the people of their tribe and the busses!

But on the other side! They were on the side with the monsters!

"How do we get around the monsters before they see us?" Sephie yelled.

Wheaties, his heart pounding, turned around, searching with his eyes. He saw an opening on the left where there were no monsters. He pointed. "Over there!"

Without even thinking about it, Wheaties and Sephie grabbed hands. They turned and ran towards the place without monsters.

But it was too late! The monsters spotted them. A monster walked right in front of them! It was hideous, with half the skin of its face gone on the right side, the right eye dangling down onto where the cheek should have been, and bony, shriveled hands. It wore a pair of purple pants, torn off at the knees and an unbuttoned white shirt, showing its shriveled and bony chest. It snarled, showing rotted, crooked teeth. It held out its hands, ready to grab Sephie and Wheaties and shuffled towards them.

Sephie screamed, a high-pitched sound that echoed into the sky. Soon more monsters saw them, and soon a whole group of them headed towards the children.

Wheaties turned and pulled Sephie back towards the tunnel as the monster in front of them shuffled towards them as fast as it could. The monsters were slow, however, for its feet were just bone and one foot was twisted sideways. Still, it was a terrifying visage that pursued them.

Sephie and Wheaties had no choice but to run back into the tunnel as monsters pursued them. Once again, they weaved around cars, zig-zagging back and forth.

As they rounded another car, they saw two more monsters! The two monsters knelt on the ground, and to the children's horror, they saw the monsters were feeding on one of the winged men, who lay on the ground dead.

Sephie screamed again, and this time, their minds full of terror, Sephie and Wheaties just ran, not even knowing where they were going.

"We have to go back to that door!" Sephie wailed. "We don't have a choice!"

"I know!" Wheaties said glumly. They both turned and looked back.

A sea of undead monsters lay between them and the buses. It looked impossible to make their way through it, and keep from getting eaten.

They saw more of the winged people in the air, still fighting the monsters. The strange, winged beings dropped fire on the monsters, and swung at them with swords.

"Why did we ever leave the bus?" Sephie said.

"We didn't know this was going to happen," Wheaties said.

They ran back towards the small side tunnel again, hoping they made it in time.

CHAPTER 14

Johnny, Mantayo, and the men and women of Sky continued their battle with the Lurkers. The Lurkers seemed to keep pouring out of the tunnel forever. Some of the Sky dropped flaming fire on them. Others landed on the ground and fought them in hand-to-hand combat. As the battle raged, it looked to Johnny as if he and the Sky would be quickly overrun. The Lurkers kept pouring out of the tunnels, as if they smelled food or a battle to join.

The men and woman of Sky only numbered forty, but there seemed to be hundreds and hundreds of Lurkers. More and more shuffled towards them.

"Johnny, what are we going to do?!" Mantayo yelled, as he hacked at another Lurker. Mantayo's face was covered in sweat and dirt, and he looked exhausted.

Johnny didn't answer, for he didn't know what to say. They had no choice but to keep fighting. Johnny wondered where his tribe was, for he saw the buses and vehicles when they arrived, but didn't have time to see if anyone was in them. The Lurkers didn't seem to tire, or even slow down. As they hacked one until its head fell off or its legs were gone, it kept crawling towards them. The only thing that seemed to stop them was to destroy their brains so they couldn't give commands to their bodies anymore or burn them with fire.

Then Johnny saw Starbucks! And Super ran right next to him, grinning cheerfully.

"Hey!" Starbucks yelled with a fierce smile and swinging his own sword. "Leave some for us!"

Johnny, even though he was battling a particularly horrible looking men with no jaw and bugs crawling out of his eye sockets, couldn't help but smile chuckle. Always the same old Starbucks.

Soon there were fifty more people helping Johnny and the Sky, men and women from Johnny's tribe. Many of them had guns, which they used to shoot the Lurkers in the head. Others had swords or hatchets, and they ran up and joined the fight with fury.

Still the battle raged on. The Lurkers crawled over and around the old cars, shuffling relentlessly towards Johnny and his army. Even with the new recruits, Johnny worried they might not be able to kill them all.

Suddenly a loud explosion rocked the ground ten feet in front and to the left of Johnny. Three Lurkers flew in the air in pieces, and two old cars rose up and came crashing down again.

"Take that, you denizens of the dead!" It was Misterwizard. He was throwing his special bombs at the

Lurkers!

"Back to the grave, you ghastly, grisly ghouls!" Misterwizard threw another bomb, and to Johnny's right, another explosion rocked the ground. Pieces of old cars flew through the air, steely missiles, which impaled other Lurkers in the head or cut their heads off entirely. Johnny grinned. This was becoming a fun battle!

Johnny looked over to see Super standing on the top of an old car. She wielded two swords, one in each hand. Her long, black hair flowed in the air, and she wore black pants, black boots and a long black jacket. Johnny thought how beautiful she looked, like a warrior princess. She swung her swords at passing Lurkers, slicing off their heads, dancing, almost as if she were performing a ritual. Then she would spin around, fall to her knees and slice off the head of another. It was amazing to see. She was confident and unafraid. Johnny sensed that all their experiences so far seemed to have turned her into a brave adventurer. She fit Starbucks well.

Johnny saw someone else he recognized, and wondered why he was there. It was a man of Asian descent dressed in elegant black silk robes. The man wore strange, shiny metal plates on his shoulders, chest and on both sides of himself below his waist. It was Lightpole! Johnny wondered why he was here, if that meant the people of Letfreedomring were here too? He didn't see them anywhere, and wondered how Lightpole got there by himself.

Lightpole seemed an expert with the sword he

wielded, a thin, long one with a white handle. The man spun and dodged, and sliced at Lurkers, jumping in the air and landing in front of them, slicing their legs off and then cutting off their heads. It was almost as if Lightpole were performing an ancient dance, and he looked elegant and deadly as he fought. No matter what the reason was, Johnny was glad to have the brave warrior fighting with them, though he made a mental note to ask Lightpole some questions if they ever got out of the battle alive.

Johnny heard a cry from somewhere. It was a little girl's voice, and Johnny swore it sounded like Sephie! It was a scream of fear, and Johnny's insides instantly were gripped by an unseen hand. More distressing than the scream was where it seemed to come from. It came from somewhere in the tunnel! Why would Sephie be there? Did the Lurkers have her?

Quickly Johnny sliced the leg of the Lurker he was fighting and it fell to the ground. It continued to reach out for him, but Johnny ran away, towards the tunnel in the direction of the sound he'd heard. Frantically he looked around, peering into the tunnel, trying to see Sephie anywhere, hopefully not being eaten by a grisly dead man.

He didn't see her anywhere, all he saw were old abandoned cars, Lurkers shuffling between them, their faces rotted and the hands out, looking for victims. Was he too late? Had one of the creatures grabbed Sephie? The thought was too terrible to think about. If anything happened to Sephie, Johnny would be shattered.

Johnny stepped into the middle tunnel where he'd heard the scream, slowly walking between cars. He peered into each one he passed, hoping he'd see Sephie hiding in one of them. A Lurker stumbled into Johnny's path, a short man with curly brown hair and no face left, only his skull showing. Johnny impatiently lopped off his head and left the body stumbling along, the left hand reaching out, as if wondering where its head went, before it fell to the ground and writhed around.

Finally, Johnny had no choice but to give up looking and rejoin the fight. He decided he'd run onto the buses and make sure Sephie was there. That way he'd know the scream didn't come from her. Johnny spun on his heels and quickly sprinted back to the buses.

When he reached the buses, he hurried up the steps and into the first one. He peered down the bus, his eyes scanning the huddled people inside for Sephie. All he saw were women and other scrabblers, hunched at the back, peering out the windows in fright, waiting for the battle to be over.

"Sephie?" Johnny called.

"She's not here, Johnny!" A woman in the back said in a scared, soft voice. "She was in the other bus, with her father Microsoft."

Johnny didn't reply, just turned and ran off the bus again. He looked around, and was encouraged to see less Lurkers on the horizon. Maybe they were finally making a dent in the number, and would be able to finish them all soon. Johnny ran to the second bus. The two long doors were closed, and Johnny had to slip his hand in between them and pry them open. As he climbed up the steps, the people inside screamed in fear, thinking he was a Lurker.

"It's just me!" Johnny yelled. "It's Johnny!" They all saw him and their screams turned to shouts of joy.

"Johnny!"

"Hurrah, Johnny's here!"

"We're safe now!"

Though the cries warmed Johnny's heart, he didn't care at that moment.

"Is Sephie here?"

The people on board looked around.

"No!" It was Cinnabon, the Latino woman with the long, coily black hair and long, solemn face, whose son was Wheaties. She spoke in a voice full of terror and dismay. "I don't see my son Wheaties either! Those things must have them!"

Everyone talked at once in frightened voices. It was as Johnny had feared most. It must have been Sephie who screamed! But why was she not on the bus? What made her run into the tunnel alone? Or had she gone with Wheaties? What had caused them to leave safety and venture so far away? Sick dread filled Johnny's stomach like a heavy metal weight. Worry and sadness filled his heart. He spun around again and ran towards the front of the bus.

"Save them, Johnny!" Cinnabon wailed. "Save my Wheaties!"

Johnny leapt off the bus and peered around. He was going to find Sephie and Wheaties, if he had to search forever. Even if all he found was what was left of them.

  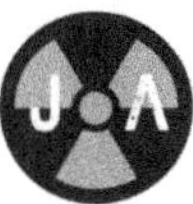

As soon as they were all past the metal turnstiles, Johnthebaptist led the whole group forward, into the darkness. There were so many of them, they filled the whole tunnel. They came to a place where there were upper landings on either side, and a lower area in the middle. They couldn't see much of what was below in the middle area because of the darkness, but in the near distance, they could just barely see a huge, long hulk of steel with windows and a long, vertical door at the end. Johnthebaptist knew it was an old vehicle people used to travel in down the long tunnel. He even recalled someone calling it a subwaycar.

Johnthebaptist stopped, and everyone stopped behind him. He raised his torch and peered ahead, trying to find the source of the moan. Then he saw it! On the landing on the other side, a lone man stood. A Lurker! He was thirty feet away, on the platform on the other side, looking the other direction.

"Oh no!" Starlite, the little scrabbler said, whispering in fright. "It's one of those things!"

The people all talked at once, their voices growing louder every second. Restaria hurried to shush them.

"Quiet, everyone! Listen to me!" she whispered.

"It is only one of the things. We have weapons, and torches. We will have to move silently, as fast as we can, to the next opening. If we see too many of those monsters, we'll turn back. But this is our only chance. So, stay quiet, and move when Johnthebaptist moves!"

The people all looked terrified and quieted down.

Johnthebaptist looked at the crowd. "I will lead the way. I will make sure there are no more monsters ahead before you follow. But you must be brave and ready to listen when I or Restaria speak. This will be over as soon as possible. Now follow me."

Johnthebaptist turned and walked slowly down the platform. He put his hand up to shield the light of the torch from the man on the other side, and the man at the back of the people did the same thing with his torch. Glancing at the strange man with fear, they all crept by, their faces white and their eyes open wide, trying to be as silent as possible.

As she passed by, Restaria watched the man closely. If the man saw them, he might make noise and signal others. And what if they walked down the passage right into a whole bunch of the creatures? What they were doing almost seemed like suicide, but she couldn't think of any other way.

The ground was wet and slippery. Slimy moss and grass covered the platform, and their feet seemed to want to slip out from under them. The crowd was so big, some had no choice but to climb down and walk in the lower passage. Here the going was even tougher, for there were wooden slats, metal rails which ran on the ground and sharp, uneven rocks. Grass and bushes grew up between the wet wooden planks, and they had to be careful not to slip and fall. Slowly, way too slowly, they all passed by where the man stood. The little scrabblers looked terrified, their eyes wide open, gripping their parents' hands in iron grips. Even the adults looked scared, for as they passed the strange man, they headed into the dark blackness, the only light from flickering torches which were now partially hidden.

They had almost all passed when a little scrabbler girl slipped on a wooden plank and fell on her bottom Without thinking she squeaked in fright. They all gasped, held their breath and turned to look at the man. Did he hear them?

It was hard to see him, for he was hidden in darkness again, and the main group were next to the old subwaycar now. They all peered into the darkness, which seemed like a living thing, swallowing up everything. They heard the moan again. It sounded closer!

"Hurry!" Johnthebaptist whispered intently. "Let's move!"

Restaria, though she couldn't see very well, stumbled back and helped the people by putting her hands on their arms and guiding them. It was so dark and cold, and the light from the torches never seemed to stay in the same place for more than a few seconds.

Slowly they stumbled down the tunnel. They had to stay on one side, for the giant hulk of an old subway train filled the middle of the path. As they passed it, they peered into the dirty, grimy windows, hoping they didn't see anyone inside.

The cold chill of their dark, underground prison filled each one of them with fear and kept anyone from speaking unless it was in soft, frightened tones. Restaria noticed the place had an evil smell, like things rotting. The ground was uneven and in some places the steel rails were broken and jutting up into the air as if to impale them if they didn't see them in time. In places, water filled the path and they had to tiptoe around it or simply walk through it, hoping it wasn't too deep.

The worst thing was not knowing where they were going, and having no idea when their journey would end. They had managed to avoid the strange man who groaned in the dark, for he seemed left behind in the blackness, but knowing that he was somewhere behind them only made their journey seem more frightening.

They made it past one subway car, and for a few minutes the going was easier. The old man who had asked Restaria the question stopped and glanced back at the old car. A face appeared in the window of the door at the end! It was a woman, a ghastly, ghostly apparition. Her face was totally white, but her eyes and teeth were black. Her hands splayed on the glass of the window, and her face wrinkled face pressed against the dirty, mold covered glass.

"Hey!" the old man yelled to alert the others. He looked towards the people of Pelpia, but they were already moving on, leaving him behind. The man with the torch at the back of the group had even passed by him. In a few seconds, the old man knew if he didn't hurry, he'd be alone in the dark. He glanced back, but lady seemed gone, and the car was quickly being swallowed up by darkness. He hurried and caught up with the man with the torch, then quickly passed him, wanting to get away from whatever was in that car as fast as possible. If the rest didn't want to know what he'd seen, well, he wouldn't bother telling them.

They came to another place on the raised landing on the left where it looked like stairs led up to another opening in the subway. Johnthebaptist stopped, and everyone stopped behind him. They stood around nervously, peering into the darkness, eager to move again.

"Yay! Another landing!" a woman yelled.

"We're saved!" a scrabbler in the crowd said.

Johnthebaptist peered through the darkness towards the opening, trying to decide whether they should venture up to the surface there. He couldn't see very far, for the torch only lit up a ten-foot area around it. Restaria walked up to him.

"Hey, I'm going to check out this exit," Johnthebaptist said to her.

"Hurry!" Restaria said, her voice tense and filled with nervous fear.

Johnthebaptist nodded. Slowly, he worked his way over to another set of the metal bar turnstiles. As he left, the people were left in darkness with only the man with the torch at the back, and panic gripped them. Their eyes peered into the darkness.

Johnthebaptist raised his torch and looked over at the other side of the bars. As the torch began to light up the area, Lurkers turned towards him, their faces ghastly and white. The landing on the other side of the bars was packed with wall-to-wall Lurkers! Alerted by the light, the Lurkers moaned loudly and reached out their hands. The shuffled to the metal bars and pressed against them. Johnthebaptist's eyes opened wide with fright and he ran back to the group. He raised the torch to illuminate their frightened faces. He hurried over to Restaria.

"We have to move, now!" he yelled. He leapt down onto the lower landing and motioned with the torch. "Forward!"

The people forgot to be silent and talked all at once in terror, moving forward as fast as they could.

Suddenly the air filled with the sounds of Lurkers moaning. Some had already climbed over the metal bars. They shuffled forward and fell down into the lower area, then lay on the ground as others fell on top of them. Other Lurkers walked down the raised platform. It wasn't long before the whole area was filled with Lurkers.

The people screamed in terror as Johnthebaptist hurried forward. Restaria stood at the edge of the crowd and pushed the terrified people forward. "Hurry!" she said in a loud, commanding voice. "Move! Be careful!"

The people of Letfreedomring stumbled forward and some fell, others running and landing on top of them. People panicked and pushed others out of their way. People began to be trampled and struggled to crawl along the wooden planks, crying in fright.

Behind them, the Lurkers slowly crawled, shuffled and walked after them. The people of Letfreedomring hurried down the tunnel following the torches, further into the darkness, as chaos erupted.

CHAPTER 15

Ticktock stared at the large wall of tempered steel raising up before him into the sky thirty-feet high. The wall, made of steel sheets fused together with heat and supported on the back side with wood, was much more beautiful than the crude walls the people of Nork put up. This one had designs of dragons and fighting men etched into it, creating a formidable but intricate piece of art. The wall was the border between Keens and Booklin where his people lived. The king of Nork and Ferdinand called them the Cursed, because of their different colored skin and other strange features, but the people of Booklin called themselves The Brethren.

Ticktock turned and looked at Keens, the part of the i-land which was occupied by the people of Nork. Here the people mostly kept to themselves, and though the king of Nork sent soldiers to make them pay tribute once in a while, he mostly left them alone. They in turn spent their days mostly foraging for food, and were even more ragged and dirty than the people on Mattan, the main i-land of Nork. Here on Keens, the buildings ran right up to the Booklin wall, with only a street separating them. The people of Keens never bothered the people of Booklin for they knew the people of Booklin to be fierce fighters who didn't like being bothered. And mostly the people of Booklin never ventured outside their land. The only one who cared about the people of Booklin was the king of Nork, and that was only because he wanted their land and to make them pay tribute. Ticktock knew Ferdinand hated the people of Booklin. He wanted only to kill them all.

Ticktock stared at the Booklin wall again. It surrounded all of Booklin, but at the water's edge the much more ragged and poorly constructed Nork wall took over followed the shoreline to surround Keens, just like the one around Mattan, the other part of the city of Nork.

The Booklin wall seemed to shimmer in the light of the red eye, the red eye's bright rays bouncing off the metal and creating blinding light. Ticktock was sure the men guarding the wall in Booklin were watching him now, as he stood only a few feet from the wall.

The door through the wall into Booklin was intricate and well hidden, and bolted on the back side with a heavy iron bar. Ticktock felt a quiet joy at being back home again, and looked forward to seeing his family and friends. He approached the wall where he knew the door was. Hidden behind a tall six-inch round wood panel which slid up, a tiny bell sat. Ticktock opened the panel and flicked the bell with his finger, making a tiny, melodious ring. Then he stepped back and waited.

Nothing happened for a few minutes, but Ticktock remained patient. He knew they were watching him and discussing what should be done. Ticktock stood still, staring at the wall, his hands folded in front of him.

Finally, a voice came from inside, muffled by the thickness of the door.

"Who seeks to enter the realm of The Brethren?"

"Ticktock. You know me. I have come to see my family."

A slot in the door slid open, and Ticktock saw a pair of Asian male eyes of about twenty seasons gazing intently at him.

"Ticktock," the man said. "It has been a long time. Did the king of Nork finally send you away?"

"No," Ticktock said, frowning. "I have come to see my family, and talk to the Wise Old Man about important things." The Wise Old Man was the leader of the people of Booklin. Picked by the Elders of the Good Council when the last Wise Old Man died, the Wise Old Man made the decisions for The Brethren, with input from the Elders of the Good Council.

The eyes disappeared, and another set of eyes appeared under busy white eyebrows. This appeared to be an older Asian man, almost ancient. He peered at Ticktock with a frown of suspicion.

The old man spoke in a wavering but commanding tone. "Ticktock. I remember you well. You walked away from The Brethren. You sold your loyalty to the king of Nork. Why do you come here now and expect to walk in to our land, as if you were still a friend? Have you come to spy on us? Is the king finally deciding to mount an attack on us and you are the bringer of death and destruction?"

Ticktock frowned glumly, for the old man, who Ticktock recognized, was not easily convinced. "Bingchang. I only joined them to seek my fortune. My loyalty was always to The Brethren. I come to warn you. Things have changed in Nork. The king of Nork is dead. Another man, even more evil, has taken his place. I have news the Wise Old Man and the Elders of the Good Council need to hear."

The current Wise Old Man was an old, black gentleman with white hair whose name was Neezer. He and the Elders of the Good Council made all the important decisions for the people of Booklin.

"News, you say?" the old man said. "Tell me the news."

"I will only speak to the Wise Old Man," Ticktock said, knowing that if he told Bingchang the news, Bingchang would simply close the window and go tell the Wise Old Man the news himself.

Bingchangs's eyes moved away, and intense whispering could be heard inside, arguing. Then Bingchang's eyes appeared again.

"How do I know the soldiers of Nork are not at this very moment hiding behind those buildings behind you, and this is a trap? If you have news, tell me. I will decide if it is worthy of the Wise Old Man's ears."

Ticktock grew angry. "If something happens to The Brethren because of your stubbornness, it will be on your head, Bingchang. I have news on which the fate of all of Booklin hangs. War is coming to you, but and new allies want to join Booklin and became friends. But I will only share the details with the Wise Old Man!"

Bingchang disappeared for a second, then came back. "I will tell what you've said so far to the Wise Old Man and the Elders. Come back in seven turns of the Red Eye, and I will tell you what they have decided."

Bingchang slid the panel closed. Ticktock's face fell with disappointment. What was he going to do now? He was all alone, with no friends, no family, with nothing. He had to survive for seven rotations, on his own.

Ticktock stared at the wall for a few minutes, not sure if he had anyplace else to go. Should he try to climb over the wall and get to the Wise Old Man on his own? No, it would surely make them think he really was a spy, and would most assuredly only end in his death. He couldn't go back to Nork, for they were looking for him. Then he thought of something; this new hero Johnny. What if he could find this Johnny and join him? If he showed Johnny his loyalty and helped free the people of Pelpia, then Johnny and his tribe might take Ticktock in. Even if Ticktock couldn't get back into Booklin, he might at least have a new place to be safe and warm.

Ticktock turned around and walked away from his home, not looking forward to trying to survive on his own, wondering just how he was going to find this Johnny, or convince Johnny that he was a friend when he did find him. Ticktock wasn't sure he would survive long enough to do either thing.

King Ferdinand watched with a dark twinkle in his eye as the soldiers fought to keep the new Lurkers under control. The undead pressed forward, trying to reach the living soldiers, whose faces showed panic and terror as they pushed the Lurkers back with poles.

"We can't hold them, Your Majesty!" one soldier said.

King Ferdinand chuckled. "Then use your brains, idiots. Find some rope and tie them around the necks. Then lash them together. If you can't manage it, I will have more Lurkers."

One of the men ran quickly to find something to tie the Lurkers with. The others led the Lurkers into one of the food booths, then leapt over and closed the gate. The Lurkers turned and tried to get out, but it was easier to control them, now that they were all trapped in one place.

The old king of Nork stared at King Ferdinand, almost as if he knew how the old man had betrayed him. King Ferdinand smiled back, enjoying the sad, decayed state the old king was in. If only the king hadn't been such a spoiled scrabbler, Ferdinand thought. They could have conquered lands together. But the old king was a fool, and left Ferdinand no choice.

Moxie, whose skin on his face sagged and looked like it was about to fall off, tried to climb over the short counter. Moxie's suit looked comical now, all rumpled and dirty, Moxie's thin ribs showing through his torn shirt. A soldier hit Moxie on the head with his stick and Moxie fell backward onto the floor.

Another soldier ran up with some rope he'd found.

"Rope them around the necks, long enough for us to get them into the wagon," King Ferdinand said.

The soldiers, looking terrified, did their best to tie the rope around the necks of the Lurkers, trying their best to stay out of reach.

The soldiers then dragged their larger group of Lurkers outside and forced them into the wagon.

One of the soldiers walked up to King Ferdinand. "What are we going to do now, Your Majesty?"

King Ferdinand looked towards the south. "We will take them to the gates and see if there is any evidence of this Johnny I keep hearing about. My guess is that fellow and his tribe have been killed by the Lurkers outside. If the world is now inhabited by Lurkers, then we will have the only truly safe haven left, and will be able to force the people to obey my will or die. But if there is no sign of this Johnny or the Lurkers outside, I have another plan."

Suddenly a soldier came running up from outside, out of breath and looking as if he was about to collapse. He breathed hard and was covered in sweat.

"Lord Ferdinand!" the man wheezed between breaths.

"King Ferdinand, fool!" King Ferdinand said.

The soldier looked confused, for he knew nothing about the recent events.

"What is it?" King Ferdinand asked, curious to know why the man had run so hard to reach him.

"I have some terrible news!" The man's face transformed into grief. "The Clan has attacked the castle! They have seized it and their leader, Clancy, sits on the throne! He is declaring himself king of Nork!"

King Ferdinand frowned deeply, digesting this news. Then he scowled. "I knew those clansmen were a threat, but our foolish king liked them, because of their outfits and hatchets. I urged him to kill them, but he refused. Now his foolishness had left the kingdom in mortal danger."

All the soldiers looked frightened and talked amongst themselves. The soldier who ran up with the news had finally recovered, and though he looked exhausted, he spoke in a somber voice. "What shall we do, Your Majesty? Do you think he has the king as hostage?"

King Ferdinand grinned and chuckled at the man's ignorance. "Yes," he said, "it is possible. Hurry back, and tell the leader of the army, Alcapoon, to surround the castle. I and the soldiers here will join them soon."

The soldier nodded wearily and ran out, heading

all the way back to the castle to do as King Ferdinand said.

"What are we going to do, Your Majesty?" Another soldier asked.

King Ferdinand smiled an evil smile. "It's time to put our undead army to use. Clancy wants to see the king, does he? We shall make sure and introduce him to the king then."

As the soldiers smiled, King Ferdinand laughed, a dark and evil sound.

Johnny and Mantayo surveyed the road where the battle had been fought. Everywhere, the bodies of Lurkers, burned or hacked into pieces, lay on the ground. Some lay on the hulks of old cars. Many still burned, filling the air with the horrible smell of burned flesh, and sending black smoke into the sky.

Around them, the other Sky, mixed with men and women from Johnny's tribe walked among the cars and hacked or burned Lurkers who appeared to be still dangerous.

Johnny had searched for hours, not joining in the fight anymore, just looking for Sephie and Wheaties. Finally, it seemed the battle was over and he still hadn't found them anywhere. He'd even ventured into all three of the tunnels by himself, fighting Lurkers in the dark, but saw no sign of them anywhere. Their loss was turning the victory into a bitter and sad one for Johnny.

Misterwizard walked up to them, a huge smile of triumph and curiosity on his face. He gazed at Mantayo as Johnny watched.

"Absolutely astonishing, stupefying and electrifying!" Misterwizard said, studying Mantayo intensely. "Men with wings! Truly the radiation which transformed our planet has created some amazing marvels, as well as terrifying physical aberrations."

Misterwizard gazed about. "I think, Johnny my boy, we have dispatched the aforementioned aberrations, at least for the time being. It's time for you to introduce me to your new companions!"

Johnny didn't do as Misterwizard asked, instead he posed a question to his long-time friend and mentor.

"Misterwizard, Sephie and Wheaties are missing. I've looked everywhere. No one can find them."

Misterwizard's smile faded away, to be replaced by a look of dismay. Misterwizard scratched his nearly bald head and pondered.

"Is it possible they became unnerved at the sight of the atrocious aberrations and took flight to what they presumed would be a suitable sanctuary?"

"I don't know," Johnny said, irritated this time at Misterwizard's big words he couldn't understand, because of his worry for the missing friends. "All I know is, I've looked everywhere. Even in the tunnels!"

Misterwizard nodded gravely. "Truly a lamentable occurrence, taking place during our battle with the dark denizens. But if we are to prevent another attack from the strange monsters which assailed, us, we must find the source of their origin and seal it up. Then we will be at our leisure to search for our missing companions, and you can introduce me to your new friends."

Johnny knew Misterwizard was right. They had to seal up the subway entrance where the Lurkers had escaped, and quickly. But what if in doing so, they sealed Sephie and Wheaties inside with the monsters? And how could they possibly know if they did? No course of action seemed to be ideal, and yet, Johnny knew they had little choice.

Johnny, despite his worry about Sephie and Wheaties, couldn't help but smile with joy when he saw Starbucks and Super run towards him. For a moment he even forgot about the children as Super ran up and gave him a big hug.

Johnny hugged her back. Starbucks walked up and slugged Johnny in the shoulder, making him laugh.

"Hey Johnny! Nice of you to join the party! And with such cool new friends too!"

Mantayo walked up with a smile. Starbucks and Super met him and shook his hand. "Wow," Starbucks said. "Those wings are cool!"

"Thanks!" Mantayo said, grinning. He glanced at Super with appreciation, which made Starbucks frown. Then Mantayo looked back at Starbucks. "You are friends of Johnny Apocalypse?"

"I'm his best friend," Starbucks said, sounding a little defensive and jealous. "Johnny and me have been friends since we were scrabblers."

"That is nice. It is good to have a real friend. I would like to be your friend too, Starbucks." Mantayo smiled at Starbucks, who looked less than convinced.

But then Starbucks relaxed and smiled. "Any friend of Johnny's is a friend of mine. And your people seem really nice."

Misterwizard joined them.

"Misterwizard, these are the people of the Sky. This is my good friend Mantayo."

Misterwizard gazed at Mantayo with unbridled fascination and excitement.

"You are truly an amazing and beautiful physical mutation, Mantayo. I would love to examine you and your friends to understand the mechanics of your ability to fly, and the transformation which has occurred in your DNA."

Mantayo looked perplexed, and Johnny laughed. "Don't worry Mantayo, Misterwizard is hard for anyone to understand. He likes to use big words."

Mantayo laughed, but then his smile faded. "Your friend Misterwizard is right on one thing; we need to find the opening to the subway and seal it quickly. We have no idea how many Lurkers there still are down there, and we will be lucky if we actually managed to kill all of them which escaped."

Misterwizard pointed towards Nork. "This grisly ambuscade by undead apparitions has waylaid us from our true objective, Johnny. We journeyed here at your request to help rescue your allies in distress."

"Yes, my people!" Lightpole said. "Who knows what terrible fate they are enduring at this very moment!"

"I know where they are!" Johnny said. "When Mantayo first took me to his home, I saw them being herded into a round building not far from the gate."

Super looked at Johnny. "But how will we get to them? We can't just walk in the front gate. There's got to be a whole army inside waiting for us."

Mantayo looked over at the crowd of Johnny's people. "We could fly you all to our home in the sky, but it would take us a lot of trips, and I'm sure Lord Flaggalon would not like it."

"We have a serious conundrum," Misterwizard said, wrinkling his brown and stroking his beard. "I knew when we arrived, we would have to come up with a battle plan. I was fairly certain it would be a monumental task, and it seems my fears were justified."

"I know this is not a plan that anyone here likes," Johnny said. "But maybe, instead of sealing up the entrance to the subway, we use it to sneak our way into the city."

Johnny turned to Matayo. "Have you ever been in the subways, Mantayo?"

Mantayo shook his head. "Never. We would have no reason, No one, not even the people of Nork, go there, if they ever did."

"I for one don't like the idea of going right where more of those monsters are," Super said. "We just finished killing a bunch, now you want to find more?"

They all looked at Johnny, who seemed to be pondering their choices. "Unless anyone can come up with a better plan, I have to think it's our only way inside. Mantayo, can you and your fellow warriors go back and organize your people? When you see us emerge from underground, you can help us fight, if you're willing."

"Of course we are," Mantayo said. "I don't care what Lord Flaggalon says. You are our friends, and we will fight beside you!"

Johnny looked at Mantayo for a moment, considering, before he turned to Misterwizard. "Misterwizard, do you think some of our people will be willing to risk fighting more of those monsters?"

"I will inquire, Johnny," Misterwizard said. "I am supremely confident they will be enthusiastic to do what must be done. We embarked on this journey to save your companions, and so we shall. No impediments, no matter how daunting, will prevent our success!"

"Then that's it," Starbucks said. "We travel down into a dark, creepy tunnel full of dead people, to come up in the middle of an army of enemies, not knowing what we are going to face, and rescue a whole city of prisoners. Then we smuggle them back out. Piece of cake!"

They all laughed.

"And hopefully," Johnny said, "find Sephie and Wheaties along the way."

CHAPTER 16

Deb went out into the hallway of the floor and checked every room. Lady Stabs had been assigned a much smaller room just down from Johnny and Deb, in a room Deb suspected was an old necessary room in the old days, for it had stalls with white chairs with raisable boards to sit on and holes in the middle. The room had an unpleasant odor as well. But Lady Stabs was not there.

Deb walked out of Lady Stabs' room and ran right into Patto. Patto glared at her in an authoritative way, hand on her hip.

"Well, you better be ready, because this ain't no scrabbler's party."

Deb's heart fluttered with apprehension, really not wanting to go anywhere with the annoying girl, and unsure what was going to happen.

"Where's Lady Stabs? Is she going with us?"

"I don't know where she is," Patto said with a disapproving frown. "She was supposed to meet us here, but she's off somewhere. She probably crawled off to hide and get out of work."

Deb frowned herself with anger. "Lady Stabs wouldn't do that. Maybe she just didn't want to be around you."

Patto stepped toward Deb in a threatening manner. "You looking for a fight, little girl? I'll be glad to oblige you. You're one of those pretty types, who thinks everybody's in love with you. Well, I'd love to smash that pretty face of yours."

Deb stood tall, showing Patto she was unafraid. "I'm not looking for a fight, but if you want one, I'll give you one. You many find I'm not so easy to take as you think."

Patto smiled, impressed with Deb's lack of fear. "Yeah, you're that Johnny's girl, I almost forgot. You may have had some adventures, and may be tougher than you look. Okay. Maybe later, after you've done your chores, we'll talk about it. We have a place where people go to fight for fun. Then I can show you who's the boss, and you'll regret being smart with me. For now, it will just be me, you and three of our other Sky girls. I'll report your friend when we get back, so don't think she's gonna get away with it. You better hope you're as good at foraging and keeping quiet as you look. Nobody's gonna feel bad if you get left behind among the Groundworms 'cause you were too slow."

Deb knew now she was going to be in danger the whole time she was with Patto, and she'd have to watch out for herself. She wished Johnny was there. At least then she could tell him where she was going.

Patto turned and walked, making it clear Deb was supposed to follow. Deb fell in behind. They walked down the hallway to where there was another hallway running parallel in front of them. Patto turned down the hallway to the right and Deb followed. At the far end of the hallway, another ragged opening let in the cold light of the red eye. There, three other Sky girls waited for them. The girls were all of average height. Two of them did not have wings, and seemed to be older women, thirty or forty seasons. The third one had wings, and she appeared to be younger, maybe twenty seasons, but there was something wrong with one of her wings. It seemed twisted and broken. Each girl held a large canvas bag, for collecting their treasures.

Patto stopped by the other girls. Deb walked over to see a metal arm jutting out from the building with a large basket hanging on a rope. The basket was pulled in so it sat on the floor, and was large enough for four or five people. On the floor next to the basket lay another canvas bag. Deb assumed that one was for her, so she picked it up.

"I'm not carrying you, Deb, so you will join the other Sky girls in the basket."

Patto pointed to the two girls without wings. "This is Borsa and Lenna. They're old, so they don't have wings. And Rellat here was born a freak, so her wings don't work."

The other girls glared at Patto, and Deb smiled inside. It was obvious nobody liked Patto, she was a bully and a blowhard.

Patto continued. "Once you get to the ground, get out of the basket fast and find a hiding place, before the Groundworms see you. If they see you, you're on your own, so remember that. You'll have lots of time to forage, but you better keep an eye on the spot where the basket comes down. I'm going to blow a noisemaker, and then lower the basket. You better run fast back, because when the basket comes down, I'm only going to give you a little time to get in before I raise it again. If you don't make it, guess what? You ain't coming back."

All three of the girls looked scared, and Deb couldn't help but look apprehensive as well.

"Last thing," Patto said, looking at all of them. "You better come back with some supplies, or Lord Flaggalon is going to hear about it. Even if you are Sky, that doesn't mean you can't be kicked out for not contributing. So, I better see some pretty cool stuff when you come back up here."

The girl named Borsa, a large woman with black hair and about thirty seasons said, "Someday, someone is going to pay you back, Patto. You don't have any friends. Remember that."

Patto's eyes filled with fear, which made Deb feel good. It was nice to see her get a little back for the way she was treating them. It also showed Deb that Patto wasn't liked very much, and Deb possibly had some allies in her hunting party.

"You just remember that I'm like this with Lord Flaggalon!" Patto snarled, crossing two of her fingers together. "Someday, I'm going to be in charge, so you better remember to kiss my toes."

"Unless something happens to you before that," Rellat, the one with the disfigured wing said.

Patto glared at Rellat, but she didn't respond. Fear showed on Patto's face, and Deb could tell Patto knew she was outnumbered.

"Just get in the basket. I'll give you plenty of time to get back in when I return. Just don't wander off too far."

The girls and Deb climbed into the basket, which had a door made of the same material as the basket. The door opened and then was shut and secured with a rope.

"You better, or if I ever get back up here, I'll come looking for you," Borsa said.

Patto closed the door. The she grabbed the rope holding the basket and pushed the basket out over open space with her foot. The basket dangled in midair, swaying back and forth. Deb grabbed the side and felt her stomach churn. For a moment she felt light-headed.

"Hide, run, and find stuff," Patto said as she began lowering the basket down. "And do it fast!"

In Deb's room, Deecee tried to lay his head down and sleep again, but he missed her too much. All he could do was wonder where she'd gone, and when she would return. And he missed his master as well. It had been a long time since his master left. Deecee wished they could go back home and stay there.

A young boy of six seasons walked in the door. He had short white wings and curly golden hair. Deecee watched him as he walked over, sat on the edge of the bed and looked at Deecee.

"You're a pretty doggie," the young boy said. "You're Johnny's doggie, aren't you? May I pet you?"

The boy moved his hand slowly towards Deecee. Deecee looked at it warily at first, but then realizing the boy meant no harm, he licked the boy's hand. The boy smiled with pleasure and stroked Deecee's head. "My, I wish I had a doggie like you. My name is Sandl. What's yours?"

Suddenly Sandl saw someone climbing up from the ragged opening in the wall! An evil, dark-looking man with a black beard and scar stood there. Monsta smiled at him. Deecee growled.

The royal coach carrying King Ferdinand rolled up to a block away from the castle and stopped. As King Ferdinand stepped out, he saw the Nork army encamped around the outside of the castle on all sides. He smiled, for he knew the ones who were really trapped were Clancy and his clan. They had come thinking to kidnap the king and somehow take control. What they had found instead was an empty castle, and an army surrounding them. The situation was perfect for King Ferdinand. He couldn't have asked for a more perfect scenario to begin to grow his undead army.

As he walked towards the soldiers surrounding

the castle, Genral Alcapoon walked up to him. He wore an old green jacket with strange colored ribbons on the upper left side. It was the jacket like Moxie had owned, and one worn by all genrals of the Nork army as a symbol of their importance. It was like one they saw in old pictures of men in battle from the time before the mushroom monsters and when the jackets were found, they were saved for the genrals. The jacket looked silly with the striped pants of his old suit and the ragged tennis shoes he wore, and yet Alcapoon wore it with pride in his new position as head of the army.

"We have them surrounded, Your Majesty," Alcapoon said. "We've sealed the doors so they can't escape. They are trapped, just like birdies in a cage."

"Excellent!" King Ferdinand said, chuckling with dark joy. "Have they attempted to fight or escape?"

"They did at first, but then they gave up. Now if anyone tries to get close to the castle," Alcapoon said, "they shoot arrows at them out the windows. But they're trapped alright. We've got all entrances guarded. Give the word and we'll storm the castle."

"Yes, but I only want a small group to go in," King Ferdinand said, smiling. He strode over to the wagon full of Lurkers and addressed the soldiers guarding it.

"We need to bring the wagon as close as possible to the doors of the castle."

"Yes, Your Majesty," the lead soldier said.

The soldier turned and barked orders, and they prodded the ratty pulling the wagon. The ratty moved forward, pulling the wagon along towards the front doors.

"Is what's inside that wagon what I think it is Your Majesty?" Alcapoon asked. "Is the king in there?"

King Ferdinand put an arm around Alcapoon's shoulders and led him a little way away. Then he spoke to him in a low voice.

"You must understand, Genral, that I couldn't prevent what happened to our old king. He moved too close to Moxie, and was bitten. I had no choice but to include him in with the other Lurkers."

Alcapoon's face filled with sorrow, and he gazed at the wagon. "It's a terrible way for our king to die."

"Yes. But at least he can still be of some use to his people. He will help us rid the city of the invaders."

Alcapoon looked at King Ferdinand. "After that, you will have a big enough army. Can you put him out of his misery and bury him proper?"

King Ferdinand realized that this was an excellent plan. A city funeral, full of pomp and pageantry, would be just the thing to make the people accept him as the new king.

"I promise you, General Alcapoon, once we have vanquished all our enemies, we will honor the old king and bury him next to his ancestors in the most glorious of funerals. In fact, I will even throw some his ladies and loyal followers into the grave with him, to keep him company for eternity."

Alcapoon frowned at the last idea, but stopped thinking about it and thought of the funeral honoring the old king. "It's what the king deserves."

"Exactly what he deserves. As soon as all our enemies are dead, it will be our first priority. For now, I want you to unseal the front door. I want a small group of soldiers to enter, say ten or twelve. They shall lead my undead army into battle."

Alcapoon nodded and hurried to carry out the king's orders. King Ferdinand smiled. Another fun entertainment was about to begin.

CHAPTER 17

Screams filled the darkness as the people of Letfreedomring ran down the tunnel, arms held out in front, eyes wide open, trying to see in the pitch black. Restaria peered through the darkness in the flickering light of the few torches and ran towards those who stumbled and fell. She helped them up and pushed them forward. They ran all alongside the next old, steel carcass of the subwaycar, some putting their hands on it for balance, others grabbing the ground in front of them and crawling on all fours, trying to keep going without falling on their faces.

More evil twisted faces appeared in the windows of the subwaycar. Restaria saw Johnthebaptist far ahead. The people were becoming too scattered, some running far ahead and others stumbling along. Restaria looked back behind them, and saw the man with the trailing torch held aloft. By its flickering yellow light, she saw a horrible visage, something out of a nightmare. Twisted, ragged faces, eaten away by rot and death, on the bodies of men and women in crumbling clothes stumbling towards them, like a crawling, shuffling horde of death.

She heard Johnthebaptist yelling in the darkness ahead. "Slow down! Stop! You're missing exits!"

But Restaria could see the people were not listening, just stumbling along as fast as they could. She hurried to follow them, as they limped down the tunnel, for what seemed like forever, lost in a dark, twisted nightmare. How would they ever get all the people to stop so they could escape?

Restaria stumbled along, for it was very hard walking, since in the dark none of them could see where the openings between the rails were, and they were constantly slipping and risking twisting an ankle, or falling.

People kept falling, landing on their elbows or sides. Then someone would stumble into them and both would end up on the ground. Still, they worked their way down the dark passage, though it seemed like they were inching along at a snail-beastie's pace.

The darkness seemed like an alive thing, coating them, touching them. The tunnel was cold and damp, and there seemed to be no end. Restaria could tell the people were starting to panic, and some were even looking like they were losing touch with reality. Some wandered off towards the right and the landing, looking as if they were in a dream. Others, even more dangerously, tried to open the door of the subwaycar. Didn't they see the Lurkers inside? If one managed to open the door, they would let more Lurkers out!

Restaria hurried to grab a man whose hand was on the brass knob of the door at the end of one car. He twisted the knob and pulled, and it wouldn't be long before he managed to open the door.

"Stop!" Restaria said as she grabbed his arm.

"Let me go!" the man yelled, pulling his arm away. "We'll be safe inside!"

"No, you won't!" Restaria said. "There are Lurkers in the subwaycars!"

"Not as many as out here!" the man said. "Get away from me!"

The man put both his hands on Restaria's chest and pushed her hard. She fell backwards with a yelp and landed on the ground on her rump. A sharp pain shot through her back where it hit on a wooden rail.

"You die if you want, stupid! I'm going where it's safe!" The man glared at her with anger. As Restaria watched, the man got the door open. She watched with horror as the man climbed up into the train car and pulled the door shut. The thought of what was waiting for the man inside the car made her shudder. There was nothing else she could do. She had to go back to helping the others. She put her hands on the railing and forced herself up. She took one more glance through the glass of the car door, but it was so dirty she couldn't see much. All she could see was the man's form, working his way down the train car.

Restaria stood up and looked ahead. What she saw made her heart flutter. She was very far behind now! The light of the torches was far away, and dwindling fast! She used the train car's side as a guide and hurried along as fast as she could, stepping gingerly so she didn't twist her ankle.

She looked up and saw the man's face in a window. His face twisted with terror. He stared at her, his eyes pleading for help, his mouth opening and saying words she couldn't hear. And then she saw ragged, wrinkled hands grab the man's shoulders and pull him back into the darkness of the subway car. Restaria stared at the window and tears came to her eyes. A feeling of helplessness washed over her and a sick feeling in the pit of her stomach at what was happening to the man right then. She hurried along, hoping in a grim way his death would keep the Lurkers in the train occupied and give the rest more time to escape.

They hurried past more subway trains, some seemingly empty, others with faces peering out, faces with rotting flesh and horrible yellow teeth.

She reached some other stragglers, a woman and her little girl. Forgetting about herself, Restaria grabbed the woman's arm and helped steady her. The little girl moved slowly, afraid of the dark.

"Take my hand!" Restaria called out, and then she felt the little girl's hand touching hers. Restaria grabbed it, and holding the little girl's hand and the woman's arm she helped them inch along.

Restaria saw another landing far ahead, and this time it seemed as if Johnthebaptist had managed to get the people to stop. As Restaria tried to hurry, holding the little girl's hand and the woman's arm, she saw Johnthebaptist helping people up onto the landing.

Restaria turned and looked back, and screamed. Hundreds of Lurkers were heading right for them!

Suddenly she saw the old man who had asked her questions. He bolted past her, waving his arms, running right towards the mob of dead Lurkers.

"Hey! You creepies! Come here!"

As Restaria watched with shock and amazement, the old man ran right towards the undead. He stopped just in front of them and waved his arms.

"You want to eat someone? Eat me!"

As Restaria watched, the old man ran off to the left between two subway trains, waving his arms. Restaria realized with sorrow and gratitude the old man was sacrificing himself to draw the Lurkers away.

"Stop!" she yelled at him, but it was too late. His efforts were working, as all the Lurkers turned as one and started chasing after him. Tears came to Restaria's eyes. Her heart filled with grief for the kind, old man, who would soon be torn apart by the monsters, but did it for the love of his people.

The last of her people ran past Restaria, and the man with the trailing torch ran back to her, holding the torch aloft.

"He may have just saved us!" the man said.

Restaria nodded. "Let's not make his sacrifice in vain. Hurry, we have to get onto the landing!"

The man nodded and ran back towards the landing. Restaria wiped the tears from her cheeks, took one grieving look towards where the man disappeared, and said a silent thank you to him. She willed him to somehow escape and rejoin them. Then she turned, knowing she had to go back to helping her people escape.

In the darkness she heard the excited voice of the woman she was still helping. "Hurry, let's get out of here!"

Restaria tried to move faster, but the girl and her mother slowed her down. Her heart fluttered with new hope, but also mild panic at being left behind. It seemed like they were still a mile away. She cursed the stupid railings and the way her foot kept landing in between them, threatening to twist with each step. Her forehead grew hot, and she felt faint. Don't pass out now, she screamed at herself. You'll die if you fall here, and no one will ever find you!

Then they made it! Some of the people were already climbing over the metals bars and hurrying up the steps. Johnthebaptist was trying to maintain order, but the people were terrified and pushing and shoving. The tunnel filled with yelling and curses. It made Restaria's heart flutter, for surely the Lurkers would hear it. It was dark, for there was only one torch left, but fortunately the man holding it stood on the landing and held it high.

Restaria's heart lifted with hope and relief. Maybe they would make it out of the dark, horrible nightmare after all! She helped the little girl up onto the landing, then turned and helped the woman up. As he climbed up herself and sighed with relief, she looked back down where they'd come, wishing and hoping the old man would suddenly join them. The thought of him dying to save them still filled Restaria with sorrow.

Finally, she had no choice but to forget about him and concentrate on making sure everyone made it up onto the landing and to safety. She busied herself helping others up and pointing them towards the stairs.

The dark, cold tunnel felt even more oppressive with the feeling they would escape at any moment and the panic seemed to grow more intense, as if the fear of being caught now was worse than before. Restaria knew it was just her imagination, but she felt like the tunnel was unhappy, disappointed it hadn't swallowed them in death. For that was what the tunnel was filled with now, death and horror. Restaria would be so happy to leave it for good. She just hoped someday she could forget the grisly images etched in her memory.

There were only a few left below now. Restaria smiled. Then she turned and saw the old man! He stood not far away on the landing, just standing there, looking at her.

"You survived!" Restaria shouted. She climbed down and ran over to the man.

But then she stopped. The man had a dark frown on his face, and his right ear was covered in blood. A large bite, ugly and bleeding was on his neck. His clothes were covered in blood. And his dead eyes stared at her with malice.

"Oh, no!" Restaria said, realizing the man hadn't

made it after all, but was now one of the Lurkers. "I'm so sorry, good man. We will always honor you as one of our heroes!"

The man stared at her for another moment. Then he frowned. "Get the people safe! I'll stay here with my new friends."

Tears filled Restaria's eyes as she nodded. Then she took a risk and kissed the man on the cheek. "We will always remember you."

The man with the trailing torch ran up to her again. He yelled, "Let's go!"

Restaria watched as the old man waved at her, then wandered off into the darkness.

Then she turned and joined the man with the torch. They both climbed over the metal rails and ran up the steps. The tunnel was left in darkness again, full of monsters.

Sephie and Wheaties managed to make it back to the steps which led down into the darkness and the hidden door. They ran down the steps holding each other's hand, their hearts beating wildly. They ran to the door and scrunched down, hidden in the darkness.

"We'll wait until the battle is over, and those winged people kill all the monsters," Wheaties said.

With surprise, Wheaties felt Sephie's lips on his cheek. He grinned with joy and forgot all about the monsters. He could just see Sephie grinning at him.

"I love you, Sephie," Wheaties said shyly, hoping he wouldn't be embarrassed.

Sephie kissed him on the cheek again, and Wheaties felt his heart thump and swoon.

"I love you too, Johnny."

Her words made Wheaties' heart swell with pride and happiness. "And you're my Deb," Wheaties said. Then Sephie kissed him, right on the lips! It was everything he'd hoped for.

"Will you be my girlfriend?" Wheaties asked, gazing at her lovely face in the semi-darkness.

"I already am, silly," Sephie said, and she gave his hand a squeeze. Wheaties didn't care if they were mobbed by monsters at that moment, he would die a happy person.

Then, as if listening to Wheaties' thoughts, a dark shadow passed in front of the stairs. An evil visage of a rotting old man shuffled past, moaning in a horrible way. Wheaties put an arm around Sephie and held her tight.

The monster passed by, but then it came back! It looked like it was heading down the stairs!

Wheaties knew he had no choice but to fight it this time. He picked up a jagged piece of steel about the size of his hand and holding it high, let go of Sephie walked towards the monster

"Don't!" Sephie yelled, but Wheaties knew he had no choice.

The Lurker walked down the first step. Wheaties ran up and slashed the monster's leg with the steel. The monster stumbled and his leg twisted, but it didn't go down. It stumbled down the next step.

Sephie joined in the fight. She ran up and kicked the Lurker in the leg viciously. The monster's leg twisted and this time it fell backwards onto the steps. Wheaties and Sephie attacked it, Sephie kicking it and Wheaties stabbing at its legs as it squirmed and moaned. Then Wheaties hit the monster in the head with the piece of steel. It was like hitting a rotten watermelon, and the head caved in.

"Ooh, yuk!" Sephie winced with disgust, but then she stomped on the monster's head, crushing it in.

The monster struggled weakly, its arms out, as Wheaties continued to step on its head. Soon there was nothing left of it, and the monster lay still.

Sephie and Wheaties smiled at each other. Then they peered down the tunnel.

All they could see were a sea of old cars. In the far distance through the tunnel entrance, they could see the buses far away. They didn't see any more flying people, and it seemed quiet.

"I don't see any more monsters, or flying people. Maybe it's over. Should we try to get back to the buses?"

"Yeah, I guess so," Wheaties said, sounding unsure.

Suddenly monsters were everywhere, behind every car, walking towards them.

"Hurry, back to the door!" Wheaties yelled.

They ran back down the steps. As Sephie watched behind them nervously, Wheaties pulled the door with all his might. It swung slowly, scratching a groove on the concrete floor, groaning in protest. Finally, it was open far enough for them to squeeze through.

They looked back, and all they could see were monsters heading for the steps.

Reluctantly they went through the door. Slowly the door groaned again, as it was pulled closed from inside. It sealed with a snap.

CHAPTER 18

Monsta climbed up into the Johnny's room, sticking his jagged piece of steel in his pants behind his back and covering it with his black leather jacket. As soon as Deecee saw him, the dog-beastie sensed the evil and malice in Monsta and growled deep in is throat. Monsta stared at Deecee with unhidden dislike.

Sandl looked up at Monsta with fear, for he didn't recognize Monsta, and he'd never seen such a scary looking man before. Monsta's black hair and black beard, along with the scars all over his face filled the boy with dread. Sandl could tell right away this stranger was evil and mean.

"You're not allowed in here!" Sandl said. "This is Johnny and Deb's room!"

Monsta stopped a few from the bed and put on a jaunty grin. He felt the warmth from the fire on his cheek. "Johnny and Deb's room, is it?" Monsta looked around and his face filled with anger. "A fine room it is.

Fitting for a 'hero' like Johnny. And for a man like me."

Sandl felt his heart beating hard. This big man could easily grab Sandl before he could get away, and Sandl was too afraid to fly for he'd not practiced much. He knew he had to be very careful if he wanted to escape.

"I'm a good friend of Johnny, and Deb," Monsta said, not trying very hard to sound convincing. "They call me Monsta. We both come from the same city far, far away, and I've come all this way to find him. Johnny will be so happy to see me! And Deb too! Do you know where he is?"

Deecee continued to growl. Sandl put an arm around Deecee and his hands over Deecee's snout. Sandl decided to play along, knowing if Monsta suspected Sandl didn't believe him, things would get dangerous very fast. Deecee stopped growling, and Sandl stroked Deecee's head. Sandl smiled at Monsta as best as he could with his mind full of fear. Sandl thought that if he could only get outside the door, he could run and tell Lord Flaggalon. Then the stranger would get what he really deserved, that was for sure! Men of Sky would kill the evil man and throw him out the hole in the wall. If only he could get to the door...

"Johnny's not here right now, but I can show you where to find him!"

Monsta could tell the boy wasn't being honest as well, for he knew liars when he heard them. It was a game of cat-beastie and mouse-beastie between them, and Monsta was worried the boy might outsmart him, for Monsta had never been good at winning contests that took a lot of thinking.

Monsta decided he would have to forget about Johnny and concentrate on the real reason he was there, no matter how painful it was. The boy would take him to Pantina, or he'd rip the boy's wings off. He might do it anyway, for it sounded like fun.

Monsta walked closer, and now he didn't appear as friendly, for he wasn't good at pretending. "I'm really here to see your goddess, Pantina, just like Johnny is. We've both heard how wonderful and mighty she is, and I've come to worship her too. Do you know where she is?"

"Pantina?" Sandl said, surprised and alarmed. He was dismayed to think this evil man had plans to hurt their goddess. He could see the piece of steel in Monsta's pants, despite Monsta's attempt to hide it, and Sandl saw how sharp and scary the weapon was. He wondered if this scary, huge man with the scar, black hair and beard was really an evil god, come to attack their goddess. Was he conjured up by the Groundworms to kill Pantina and destroy the Sky? Sandl realized this was his time to be a hero and fight for his goddess and his people, even if he died doing it.

"I'll show you where she is," Sandl, putting on the best smile he could, though he suspected it was pretty pathetic because of his fright.

"You are a good boy. Pantina will bless you, and I will give you a very special reward when we're done."

Sandl's stomach twisted at Monsta's last words,

for he could hear the malice in them, and he knew just what kind of reward the man had in mind. Sandl looked at Deecee and spoke in a soft voice. "Deecee, will you come with me?"

Deecee wagged his furry black tail. The boy walked towards Monsta and Deecee hopped off the bed and followed.

As Sandl and Deecee walked by him, Monsta stared coldly at Deecee. "Is that Johnny's dog-beastie?"

"No, it's mine," Sandl lied, not wanting Monsta to hurt Deecee either.

Sandl's heart beat wildly for he was almost at the door. He could feel Deecee's fur rubbing against his leg, for Deecee walked right beside him.

Suddenly, a rough hand grabbed Sandl's arm and he cried out in pain.

"You're not going to try anything, are you boy?"

Sandl looked at Monsta's face, for Monsta leaned down and glared at him. There was no more pretending to be nice now, the man scowled at Sandl with pure hatred and cruelty.

Sandl shook his head, terrified. The man's grip hurt his arm. Deecee growled again, this time deeper, baring his fangs.

"Get him, Deecee!" Sandl yelled, and Deecee responded. Leaping up, Deecee bit Monsta's arm in a vise-like grip and clamped down with his sharp teeth.

Monsta yelled in pain and his hand opened, letting Sandl go. Sandl took off running out the door and down the hallway, hearing Deecee's snarls mixing with

Monsta's shouts.

Sandl's heart filled with sadness, for he was sure Monsta would kill Deecee, but he had no choice. He had to get away and tell Lord Flaggalon about the horrible intruder. He just hoped Deecee could hold out until Sandl could bring help.

Clancy, Gavin, Alasdair and the rest of the men of the Clan walked up the road, weary from their long journey. Straight ahead of them, they saw the beautiful white spires of the king of Nork's castle.

"There it be, Clancy!" Alasdair smiled, his eyes sparkling with excitement. "We'll be in for it soon. A bonnie battle to determine our fate, and that of the king of Nork."

"Aye," Clancy said, gazing about. He studied the streets and buildings around. He saw people of Nork milling about, wandering up and down the streets. He didn't see any soldiers, which made him happy. But most important of all, he didn't see any Lurkers.

"Whatever happened to Moxie and his men hasn't reached this far yet," Clancy said. "It be quiet as a church mouse, and the castle be ripe for the picking."

Gavin grinned and walked up to stand by Clancy. "Yee! They be off fighting this Johnny character, or maybe dancing with the undead. Let's plunder while the time is right!"

Clancy grinned at Gavin and Alasdair and they grinned back. All three men hurried towards the castle, the rest of the clansmen following close behind. They fell into a trot, keeping their eyes open for any soldiers, but surprisingly, they didn't see one anywhere.

As the entered the grounds of the castle, Clancy looked around, sure someone would challenge them, but no one, not even the people milling about on the streets seem to pay them any mind. A thread of worry tickled Clancy's mind, for something didn't seem right, and he was a good enough warrior to sense such things and have alarms go off in his mind. He didn't see anything amiss, however, so he just filed the feeling away, planning to keep it close and refer to it from time to time, if anything happened that might bring the feeling back.

The people of Nork watched and pointed at the strange men in their beastie-fur coats with heavy boots, long beards and heavy hatchets. Always eager for something new to entertain them, the people stood around and laughed at the strange sight. No one thought to tell a soldier, for the people of Nork cared little for their king or their government. They busied themselves with trying to find food and clothing, and if they did think of the king of Nork, it was only to curse his name. Some of them watching had a notion these strange men might be attacking the castle, but to them it only meant a moment of exciting entertainment.

Clancy and his men ran as fast as they could, but still managed to watch the crowd around them. They saw the people smiling and pointing. Clancy saw a little scrabbler girl smile at him, and he thought of how she reminded him of his own sweet child at home. He grinned at her and raised his hatchet in the air, shaking it for her entertainment. The little girl's eyes opened wide and she smiled wider, showing a missing tooth.

Clancy and his mean reached the tall, heavy, ornate doors at the backside of the castle. They hid as best as they could under the shadows of the archways above, catching their breath. Once again, Clancy thought how it seemed almost too easy, but he dismissed it, sure the army of Nork was busy elsewhere. They had timed their attack at just the right moment.

Clancy walked up to the doors. He grabbed one of them with his left hand, holding his hatchet high in his right. Alasdair and Gavin stood right behind him, and the other men readied themselves.

"Here we go men. Remember, no peep from any inside. Kill them fast, before they can sing. Then it's up to the king to say good morning!"

The men all nodded and grinned. Clancy pulled the door handle, and the door swung open ponderously. A draft of cool air blew their hair back, and a faint smell of roses filled their heads. Clancy rushed in, and the rest all followed. When the last man had entered, they pulled the door shut with a bang.

As they poured into the large, elegant hallway inside, they gazed around at the beautiful paintings on the walls, the elegant white statues and the lush red carpet. The hallway stretched in both directions, circling the inner rooms. In front of them a set of stone stairs with a red carpet in the middle led up to a second floor. Next to the stairs, an inner set of doors led to an inner chamber.

Clancy spotted two guards by the doors to the inner chamber, and so did all his men. They all rushed at the guards at once. The guards, totally outnumbered, dropped their tommy guns and raised their hands in surrender, but it didn't help them. The men of Clancy's clan were full of the bloodlust of war and before Clancy could say a thing, the guards' heads lay on the floor next to their bodies. They had been hacked off with hatchets before they could utter a sound.

The killing energized the clansmen, and they let out a cheer.

"Quiet that noise!" Clancy thundered. "Circle the hallway here and find any other guards. Do the same to them. Then we shall have a bonnie chat with the Nork king!"

The clansmen ran in both directions to comply. Clancy signaled to Alasdair and Gavin to stay and follow him. Clancy started up the stairs, his hatchet held in front of him. Alasdair and Gavin leapt up the stairs right behind him, their hatchets held ready to strike in both hands.

In the distance below, Clancy heard the screams of Nork guards which were swiftly cut off. He smiled grimly, knowing the guards met the same fate as the others. Clancy, Alasdair and Gavin reached the second floor. Here, another smaller hall led to a series of doors.

Clancy suspected one of them was the king's sleeping chamber. In front of them, doors led into a circular interior room. This was the balcony, overlooking the king's throne room.

Clancy walked up to the doors to the inner balcony. Quietly he opened one of the doors and peered inside. He saw a circular pathway overlooking the throne room below. Glancing at Alasdair and Gavin, Clancy crept inside. The other men followed him. He looked around but didn't see anyone anywhere. Carefully and quietly, he walked over to the edge and gazed down at the throne room.

The throne room had a dark wooden floor covered with rich rugs. Just below where Clancy and his men stood, the throne sat empty. The whole room seemed empty! There was no king!

Clancy frowned. Something was wrong, very wrong. The worry which had tickled his mind now banged on it with a heavy hammer. Why was no one there? Did the king of Nork somehow know they were coming and set a trap?

Alasdair and Gavin sensed something was wrong as well. Their faces transformed with worry and fear.

"Clancy, where be the king?" Alasdair whispered, his voice tense.

"Could he be with his men, fighting Johnny and the Lurkers?" Gavin asked as he peered down at the throne room.

Something inside Clancy told him it was time to leave, and fast. It whispered to him, 'hurry, before it's too late!' Clancy turned and hurried back towards the door to the hallway.

Clancy, Alasdair and Gavin ran back outside and down the stairs, all bravado and thoughts of war disappearing to be replaced with a single desire to flee.

They reached the bottom of the stairs to be met by the rest of the men. One of the men walked up.

"There's none here but a few guards, Clancy!" The man said. "We killed them, and now it's empty as tomb in here!"

Alasdair turned to Clancy. "We need to leave! This place is cursed or bewitched!"

"Aye!" Clancy said. He strode over to the large doors leading back outside. Then he stopped when he heard a sickening sound. From outside came the sound of pounding. It sounded just like someone nailed something to the doors!

Clancy and his men all heard it at the same time and they all rushed to the doors. Clancy pushed on them, but they wouldn't budge! Someone was sealing them inside!

"Hurry!" Clancy said, all semblance of bravery gone to be replaced by panic. He ran down the hallway, followed by Alasdair, Gavin and the rest of the men. Clancy found another set of doors, but just like the first, pounding sounded outside.

"Clancy!" Alasdair yelled, no pretense of quiet anymore. "They're sealing us in!"

Clancy reached the other doors and with a roar of fury threw his shoulder into them. They didn't budge!

They were sealed tight!

The men gathered around Clancy, Alasdair and Gavin.

"We're trapped!" one man yelled. "They knew we were coming!"

"Blarney," Clancy said "'Tis no way they could have known. They must have been watching us from afar. I knew seemed too quiet and easy getting in here."

"What are we going to do, Clancy?" Gavin asked, gripping his hatchet with both hands tightly.

"To the back way. We've got hatchets, don't we? We'll chop our way out!"

Clancy led the men back around to the other side of the hallway where they'd come in. Without another word, the men fell in to chopping at the doors, and the air filled with the sound of splintering wood and heavy blows.

They turned the doors into splinters, but to their dismay, a metal wall had been placed behind the doors, solid and firm.

"Now what?" Gavin said, his face wet with sweat from the effort, and out of breath.

Clancy turned to Alasdair. "Let's go upstairs and see what we can from the windows."

Alasdair nodded and quickly Clancy and his men ran back up the stairs to the second floor. They ran around until they were near the front of the castle again and peered out one of the small windows.

Below they could see their worst fears. It looked like the whole Nork army camped just outside. As Clancy watched, an old wagon rolled up. The Nork army parted to let it pass. It was pulled by a horrible looking rat-beastie and it moved right up to beneath them, near the front entrance.

"What do you think is in that wagon, Clancy?" Gavin said nervously.

"Nothing good, that I'll wager," Clancy said. "Hurry, lets to the other side and see if we can get one of these windows open."

The whole clan ran down the second-floor hallway, back to the other side. As they raised their axes to strike the glass, they looked outside and stopped. This side of the castle was filled with Nork soldiers as well!

"If we climb out, they'll just kill us!" Alasdair said.

They heard the front door below on the other side of the castle creak open. Clancy raised his axe. "This is it, mates! Fight for our freedom and our land!"

Clancy let out a roar and ran down the stairs. The rest of his men yelled too and raised their hatchets, ready to fight. They reached the first floor. Soldiers of Nork came rushing at them, and the battle was on.

The Nork soldiers had swords and long spears, and the men of the Clan had their hatchets. They crashed into each other, swinging their weapons in deadly arcs and yelling war cries.

Clancy cleaved a soldier's head in two, and the man fell to the ground. Clancy's axe was stuck in the man's skull and he had to wrestle to get it free. He wrenched at it back and forth, and finally it came loose. He looked with surprise and saw is men slaughtered the men of Nork, who barely seemed to fighting back. It was like they came to let themselves be killed. More alarms started sounding deep in Clancy's belly. Something was wrong. He was missing something. What could it be?

Clancy turned around. His eyes opened wide with shock. Standing in front of him was none other than the leader of the Nork army, Moxie!

CHAPTER 19

Another strange event occurred in the Wasteland, in a world of bizarre and odd happenings. On the street, surrounded by old cars and vegetation growing up between the concrete and down just a small way from three dark tunnels, two different tribes met. One of the tribes looked like what used to be called human, just men and women with two arms, two legs and a normal body. The other tribe looked very different, for it was made up of men and women with huge white or gray wings. And surrounding them lay dead bodies, some decayed and rotting, others with wings like the strange tribe, and a few like the men and women of the normal human tribe.

Johnny was greeted with shouts of joy and happiness as he joined his tribe. Many of the women, and some of the men, came over and hugged him, their faces beaming at seeing him alive. Misterwizard spent his time talking to the people of the Sky, for he was still fascinated by what he called, their "physical metamorphosis.”

Finally, Johnny walked over to Misterwizard and Mantayo, who talked a few feet away from the group.

“Let’s go, Misterwizard. I think a small group of us should proceed into the subway and scout it out. We can find a way into Nork and then a place inside the city where we can hide, until we make our move. Then we’ll come back and lead the rest of the tribe there.”

“A respectable plan, Johnny. While we wait, the rest of our contingent will need a place of concealment. I suggest we find suitable camouflage for our modes of transportation. Then I and the other members of—oh, did I forget to mention Johnny? The tribe took a vote while you were gone. We have a name now!”

Johnny, curious, grinned. Starbucks and Super heard and walked over to listen as well.

“You didn’t tell us about it, Misterwizard,” Super said.

“I’m afraid in all the excitement and adventure, my mind failed to set the revelation as a priority.”

“Well,” Johnny asked. “What is it?”

Misterwizard beamed, his mouth turning upwards into a proud grin. “We are now the USA.”

“USA?” Starbucks said. “What does it mean?”

“They are what’s referred to in the old vernacular as initials, my dear Starbucks,” Misterwizard said. “Three letters which refer to three distinct words. In this case, United States of America.”

“But that’s four words,” Super said.

They all laughed.

"Yes, I know it is," Misterwizard said. "I'm not sure why one of the words is not considered part of the initials, but that is simply the way it is written."

"You mean there's something you don't know?" Johnny asked. They all laughed again.

Misterwizard patted Johnny on the shoulder. "There are many vaults of knowledge I have yet to open, Johnny, despite my appearance as a fountain of knowledge."

"USA," Super said. "I don't know what the words mean, but I like them! USA! USA! USA!."

"Well, Super, you see in the old days before the mushroom monsters, the country was divided into what were called states..."

"Uh, Misterwizard, we really don't have time. We need to get going." Johnny said.

"Of course! Onward to victory!" Misterwizard turned and walked back to the people of the USA to discuss their part in the plan. Johnny turned to the others.

"Starbucks, do you want to come with me? And you too Super, if you want. Mantayo, you're going to fly home and alert your people, correct?"

"No Johnny. I want to stay with you. I've asked my fellow Sky, Lever to fly back. He will organize our people, and when they see you and your people approach the building you speak of, they will fly down and join us. Tendaza, my fellow Sky is also staying with us." Mantayo pointed to two young, strong looking teens with big white wings. "This is Tendaza and Lever.

They are both very good fighters, and not afraid of anything."

Johnny walked over and shook the two men's hands. Tendaza was tall, but muscular, with black hair and gray wings. Lever was shorter and stocky, but looked like he was all muscle.

"Glad to join you, Johnny," Tendaza said. "Together, we will find our way to Nork."

Lever nodded then flapped his wings and took off, back towards Nork, quickly rising high in the sky.

"We're going to join you as well, Johnny," a voice spoke from behind them in the direction of the buses.

Johnny and everyone else turned to see who was talking. It was Microsoft! And next to him stood a brown-skinned man named Baskinrobins. Johnny knew he was Cinnabon's mate, and Wheaties' father. He was of average height, with black hair, a thin mustache and a wiry, muscular frame.

"Our children are missing," Baskinrobins said. "We want to go with you. Hopefully, we can find them."

Johnny's heart felt a twinge of sympathy for them. "You know it's going to be dangerous. And if we find them…"

Microsoft nodded. "We know. We are prepared for the worst. We just want to know."

"All right. Let's get going, before we lose the red eye. We'll make up some torches and get some good weapons." Johnny said. "We have no idea how long this is going to take, or what we're going to face along the way. It' may be a long time before we're back."

"As I walk through the valley of death, I will not fear, for you are with me," Super said.

"What does that mean?" Starbucks said, looking at Super with a confused frown.

Super grinned at him. "I don't know, ask Misterwizard."

They all laughed, and gathered weapons.

King Ferdinand stood in front of the Nork soldiers. Now most of the army had gathered in the streets, having been called by King Ferdinand from their base at Sental Par. The soldiers surrounded the King's Castle, standing in the street and on the sidewalks around the giant, white spired castle.

King Ferdinand and his men stood motionless, all staring at the large front doors of the castle. A few moments before, a small group of soldiers, sacrifices, had entered, and right after them, King Ferdinand's small undead army. Now they waited to see what would happen.

King Ferdinand's heart beat wildly, and he almost couldn't contain the dark glee he felt inside. He imagined what was happening inside the castle. The Clansmen would see the soldiers, and start to fight, thinking they were in for a swift victory. They wouldn't be expecting what was coming behind the soldiers, and with any luck, they would be caught off guard. It would be the last mistake they ever made.

Behind King Ferdinand, the soldiers murmured, talking quietly, joking, laughing. Behind them, the people of Nork watched the strange, bizarre spectacle, men, women and scrabblers all wondering why the army stood outside castle, waiting for something. Was the king going to emerge and make an announcement? Was there going to be a battle? The people stood back and hid behind old rusted cars or inside the ruined buildings, just in case things grew bad and they had to run.

King Ferdinand had brought more wagons, twenty of them, and men with nets, in the hope of having a larger Lurker army to corral. He waited impatiently. It had been what seemed like an eternity since the soldiers and Lurkers had entered. At first, the sounds of shouting and fighting was heard inside, but now there was only silence. Had Clancy and his men defeated King Ferdinand's Lurkers? Were they about to open the doors and unleash the Lurkers on King Ferdinand and his men? The waiting was dampening King Ferdinand's spirit, and making him feel anxious.

Suddenly all the talking ceased behind King Ferdinand, and he realized why. One of the doors to the castle cracked open.

"Be ready with the nets!" King Ferdinand yelled over his shoulder. The men with nets reluctantly shuffled forward, looks of fright and unhappiness on their faces.

"Ready the ropes and the wagons!" King Ferdinand yelled, and the doors to the wagons were opened. Men with ropes moved forward as well. Other Nork soldiers with tommy guns and other weapons raised them, ready to fire. The soldiers near the castle on the sides ran back towards the large group behind King Ferdinand in a panic. Everyone stared at the door.

The door remained slightly open, and nothing happened. King Ferdinand cursed under his breath, so eager for the mystery to be over. Finally, he couldn't stop himself, he advanced past the soldiers towards the doors. As the soldiers watched with open mouths and looks of dread, King Ferdinand walked all the way up to the doors. He crept forward and peered in.

Suddenly the partially open door burst fully open. King Ferdinand backed up as fast as he could and fell on his back with a cry.

As he watched from the ground, a figure stumbled out. It was Clancy. He was covered in blood and held his axe in his right hand, dangling towards the ground.

With a supreme burst of elation, King Ferdinand realized he had won. Clancy's eyes were dead, and the right side of his face was chewed. His left hand was missing, and his leg was bloody.

Even though he lay on the ground in imminent danger, King Ferdinand burst into dark laughter, evil joy filling his heart. Clancy stumbled out, right towards the king. The soldiers around backed up, terrified.

King Ferdinand scooted backward, having a hard time because he was laughing so hard. Finally, he was able to spit out, "Capture him, fools!"

The soldiers ran forward and one of them threw a net over Clancy. Clancy howled and struggled against it. Behind Clancy, more clansmen and dead soldiers poured out. King Ferdinand realized he'd better get up and fast. He turned over and crawled away on his hands and knees

"Grab them! Capture them! Don't let one escape!" he yelled as he quickly crawled back to his royal coach.

Panic ensued then, as the soldiers in the streets all yelled and the man with the nets and the ropes hurried to grab the Lurkers, being careful to stay out of their clutches. More Lurkers poured out, ten, twenty, thirty. The men trying to capture them yelled to the other soldiers behind them, and soon more soldiers joined them.

They started leading the Lurkers they had caught to the wagons and pushing them inside. When the first one was captured, there were over a hundred, including the old king and Moxie. The crowd let out a yell of excitement. The Lurkers stared out the slits in the side of the wagon, glaring at the soldiers and the people.

When the people of Nork saw the Lurkers, some screamed and took off running. Other watched in scared excitement, smiling and pointing. It was the most exciting thing most had seen in a long while, a day they would remember forever.

One of the soldiers with a net was not swift enough, and a clansmen Lurker came at him, knocking him to the ground. As everyone watched in fascinated horror the Lurker bent down and bit the soldier on the neck as the soldier screamed. The soldiers around the pair pointed and laughed, waiting until the Lurker was done. Then grinning at each other, they threw a net over both of them.

King Ferdinand had reached the safety of his royal coach and he managed to get to his feet. He watched the horrible spectacle with a smile of happiness, rubbing his hands together. It was just as he'd dreamed it would be, a wonderful macabre scene he would cherish all his life. He had his Lurker army. Let this Johnny character come now. King Ferdinand would love to feed him to his Lurker army. And King Ferdinand would find the people of Pelpia who had escaped, and they would join his army too.

King Ferdinand began to feel it; he was now invincible. He would create an empire of Lurkers, and Nork would be his dark fortress. He turned and looked at the skyscrapers behind him. He scowled with disgust, looking at the hideous spiders clinging to the sides of the buildings. He knew how to get rid of those disgusting monsters; he knew just what he was going to do. And then, it would be his pleasure to feed the angels to his Lurker army, one by one.

Restaria joined Johnthebaptist and together they ran up the cold, marble steps from the subway station.

Johnthebaptist still held his torch, though it contained only orange embers at the end. It gave off an orange glow, which only lit up the steps in front of him about three feet. Together, Restaria and Johnthebaptist stumbled up, feeling their way. Ahead and above them they heard voices, people of Letfreedomring talking. The voices echoed off the marble walls, sounding a million miles away.

"What are we going to find above us?" Restaria asked, as she felt with her hand in front of her, taking one step at a time and feeling as if she was floating in the air. Her voice sounded disembodied, as if it didn't even come from her.

"Another barred gate, filled with debris, no doubt," Johnthebapstist replied, his words floating out of the darkness next to her. "I just hope we can find a way to get out, before…"

He didn't have to finish the sentence. Restaria knew what he would have said. Before the Lurkers discovered them. If that happened, they would be trapped at the top of the stairs, helpless before the undead horde.

The voices above them grew louder, closer. The voices were full of fear and panic, for the people ahead of them stumbled around in the dark.

Restaria and Johnthebaptist reached the top of the stairs. In the meager light of the dying torch, they saw a large group of people, the whites of their frightened eyes like little white circles. They stood before another set of short metal turnstiles, and beyond them, a huge set of yellow doors, closed tight. The people huddled in front of the bars, their hands out, searching in the darkness. Some of them cried, others simply stared out at the darkness, looking as if they were about to go waksy.

Restaria and Johnthebaptist stopped in front of the metal bars and the people. Restaria looked with alarm at the torch Johnthebaptist held. It had only two orange embers left, and they appeared about to wink out.

"We're here, everyone. Don't panic," Johnthebaptist said.

"We can't see!" a woman wailed. "What do we do?"

"We wait until the man with the torch arrives," Restaria said, her heart pounding in her ears. "Then we will open the doors and escape."

"Hurry!" a man said. "I have to get out!"

More people stumbled up, running into the others already there. Shouts of anger and fright filled the small space. The sound of fighting broke out.

"Stop!" Restaria yelled, hoping desperately, not only for the others but for her own sake, the man with the torch arrived soon.

Finally, to her relief, she saw a yellow light glowing on the walls below. The man with the torch was coming! They had to get out of there, before they all started panicking and went waksy in the dark. Or worse.

The man with the torch had trouble getting up the stairs, for they were packed with people. Some tried to grab the torch away from him, and he had to stop and fight them back.

"Let that man through!" Johnthebaptist yelled, and people stopped and moved out of the way as best as they could in the dark. The man finally made it to Restaria and Johnthebaptist. Restaria almost wept with relief. She didn't realize the sight of a light could be so important, almost like the choice between life and death.

Now that they could see a little better, Johnthebaptist climbed over the metal bars. Restaria followed him, clumsily making her way over them, trying not to fall on her face in the darkness.

They reached the yellow doors, Restaria, Johnthebaptist and the man with the torch. The man with the torch held it high. The yellow torchlight glowed on the yellow doors, which were made of some kind of dull metal like gold, but not as shiny.

"Do you think we can get them open?" Restaria asked.

"It depends," Johnthebaptist said.

"On what?" Restaria asked, not wanting another problem.

Johnthebaptist looked at the doors. "On whether they open inward, or outward. If they open outward…"

He looked at her. "Then whatever is barring them will not let them open."

Restaria nodded, understanding. They had a fifty-fifty chance. If they lost, they might never make it out of the subway, for all the other doors on all the other platforms would probably open the same way. It would mean their doom, for she was certain the people would never have the courage to go back down the stairs and try another entrance. And the Lurkers waited below as well.

With her heart thudding and a feeling of dread, Restaria looked at Johnthebaptist. She found it almost impossible, she didn't want to do it, but finally she did. She nodded. He understood. He walked towards one of the large doors. Behind him, a hundred anxious faces peered at him from behind the railing.

Restaria felt as if she might throw up. She closed her eyes, the tension too much for her. She couldn't watch.

Johnthebaptist grabbed the handle of the door. There was a thumb latch and he depressed it. Then he pulled on the door. At first, the door didn't budge. He set his feet and pulled harder. The door hadn't been opened in years, and it was covered in dirt and rust. The man with the torch handed it to Restaria, who had to open her eyes to take it. Then she stared, her mouth a grim line, her eyes full of worry.

They both pulled as hard as they could on the door. Finally, with an ear-piercing shriek, the door began to move... inward!

Restaria almost collapsed from relief. She silently cried, tears filling her eyes. The rest of the people behind her cheered and shouted. Restaria put a hand on the wall, for she felt suddenly weak. They were not out yet!

Johnthebaptist grinned with joy, and the man who had held the torch smiled back. They pulled hard and now enjoyed the effort, for the door came easier as the hinges grew more used again.

They swung the door wide. Restaria walked up and handed the torch back to the man who'd held it. The man held it up high, while Restaria and Johnthebaptist gazed at what lay on the other side.

There in front of the doors they saw large wooden beams mixed in with old trash cans and piles of old concrete. As they watched, a piece of concrete not against the door anymore, fell at their feet.

"Can we clear it?" Restaria asked.

Johnthebaptist grinned. "Yes, I think we can!"

The people behind them all heard and cheered again, some wailing with relief.

Restaria, happiness filling her for the first time in what seemed like ages, turned to the people behind them. "Everyone, come up here and help us clear this passage!"

People began climbing over the metal bars to comply. Their nightmare in the subway appeared to be over. But ahead of them lay the city of Nork. And they had no idea what faced them when they walked out onto the streets.

CHAPTER 20

andl ran down the hallway, his heart thumping wildly in his chest. "Don't hurt Deecee!" he yelled at Monsta silently to himself. Panic filled his mind and made it hard to think. Where would Lord Flaggalon be? In his own mansion in a special skyscraper, he kept for himself, probably. It was down the street from the one Sandl was in now, about a half block away. Sandl could run across the web bridges to get to it, but it would be faster for him to fly.

Sandl didn't fly much, for he was still afraid of it. He had practiced in his room, and flown as high as the ceiling, but that was it. He had never crossed between buildings so high up, but he knew he had to do it to save Deecee. Sandl reached the large opening in the wall which looked outside. Across the open space, he could see the building where the Sky held court, and to his left the tall building Lord Flaggalon kept as his private mansion. It looked so far away. Sandl peered over the edge, and wished he hadn't. The ground looked tiny!

Could his small wings keep him in the air, all the way over to the other building?

He looked outside and down at the webbing. It was strong and wouldn't collapse, even it swayed back and forth in the wind.

Just use the webbing, the scared part of him said. But Sandl thought about Deecee, and the danger the evil man meant for his people. It would take too long! Wearing a determined frown, he flapped his wings and rose from the ground. Closing his eyes, he floated out over open space. Then he hovered there for a second, making sure he wasn't going to fall. He didn't! He looked down, and saw he was perfectly safe, floating in the air. The effort of flapping his wings was hard, but the longer he did it, the easier it seemed. He grinned with happiness. He was flying!

He took off towards Lord Flaggalon's building, laughing with pleasure and enjoying his first real flight. As he flew, he looked down on the world below. It seemed to small and far away, but he was safe from it, up in the air.

Before he knew it, he was at the other building. He flapped around and until he found a window with no glass in it. For a brief moment he thought how much trouble he could get into, entering Lord Flaggalon's mansion without permission. But no one could be mad at him now, for he had to warn Lord Flaggalon of the danger, right? He sure hoped that was the case.

Landing on the edge of the window, he dropped inside. The room was dark, and musty smelling. It looked like no one had used this room for a long time, for the bed and furniture were moldy and covered in dust. A thrill of fear went through Sandl, as he wondered if he was just walking himself into trouble.

He hurried across the room and opened the door. Bright light stung his eyes, for the hallway was lit with lamps on the walls. He saw that the doors to all the other rooms were removed. He crept carefully into the hallway, his face wet with perspiration from his first flight.

He peered into one of the other rooms, and saw that for most of the other rooms, the interior walls had been removed, making all the rooms connected on either side of the hallway. He peered into a space filled with luxury. Everywhere he looked there were silk couches, pillows and chairs. And food! There were tables everywhere filled with all kinds of delicious things to eat. The walls were covered with beautiful paintings in rich colors. Lord Flaggalon sure knew how to live!

Sandl carefully tiptoed into the large space on the right through the first doorway. He didn't see Lord Flaggalon anywhere! Ignoring all the beauty around him, he ran through the space, searching. Where was their leader?

Then he heard something! It was Lord Flaggalon singing to himself somewhere ahead. Sandl ran towards the sound. Then he saw Lord Flaggalon. He was in a huge, golden bathtub. Sandl approached him timidly, waiting to be seen.

Finally, Lord Flaggalon looked up and saw him. A

look of pure fury came to Lord Flaggalon's face, and Sandl shook with fright.

"What are you doing in my private quarters?" Lord Flaggalon thundered, his face twisted in anger. "I'll punish you and your family for this!"

Sandl frowned, and he felt as if he might cry. "I had to, Lord Flaggalon! There is a bad man here! He hurt Deecee!"

Lord Flaggalon frowned differently this time, with interest. His anger seemed to subside slightly. "A bad man? Where is he?"

Sandl pointed towards the building where he'd come from. "In the building where Johnny and his friends are staying. "He told me to get you. He says he wants to worship Pantina. But I think he only means to do mean things!"

Lord Flaggalon forgot all about his anger at Sandl, his mind now consumed with worry over what he'd just heard. "Quick, fetch me my robe. Then tell me where this evil man is."

"He's right here."

Lord Flaggalon and Sandl both turned towards the voice. There standing next to the nearest door stood Monsta. He wore an evil grin, and he held his jagged steel in front of himself in a menacing way.

Sandl screamed in fear and ran around behind the bathtub. Lord Flaggalon blanched, and shook with fright, totally helpless and naked in the bathtub and at Monsta's mercy.

"I saw where the boy flew, and followed over

those rope bridges. He led me right to you."

"What do you want?" Lord Flaggalon said in a frightened voice.

Monsta chuckled. He casually strolled over and stood next to the bathtub. Lord Flaggalon moved as far away as he could in the tub and tried to shrink down. Finally, only his face was out of the water. He lay there and stared with frightened eyes.

"Why, only to worship your goddess, Pantina," Monsta said. "I've come from a long way away to pay my respects. Surely you know her fame has spread all over the world?"

"What did you do to Deecee?" Sandl asked, his voice sad.

Monsta turned toward the boy. "I killed him and skinned him. He'll make good eating later."

Sandl cried, and Lord Flaggalon looked like he wanted to cry too. He spoke in a whiny voice. "Pantina doesn't see outsiders. If you don't leave, I'll get my guards and have you thrown out of the building!"

Monsta scowled and looked fierce. He moved the tip of his jagged piece of steel until it was right under Lord Flaggalon's throat. "What you'll do, old man, if you want to live, is take me to Pantina now. Or the one who will be thrown out of the building will be you. After I've carved out your heart!"

Lord Flaggalon gulped hard then nodded. Monsta walked over, grabbed Lord Flaggalon's robe and threw it to him in the tub. It fell into the soapy water and floated there.

"Get dressed. And be quick about it. Meanwhile, I think I'll enjoy some of your hospitality."

Monsta walked over to a table of food and began helping himself. Lord Flaggalon turned to Sandl. In a whisper he said, "Go get help!"

Sandl nodded, his eyes open and full of fear. Watching Monsta carefully, Sandl crept away. Then when he was far enough away, he ran for the nearest door.

Lord Flaggalon climbed out of the tub and put on his soaking wet robe. He stared at Monsta, just hoping he escaped the horrible encounter with his life.

As soon as Sephie walked through the door, it closed behind her and she was plunged into total darkness. She spun around and tried to find the door again, but all she could feel was cold wall, with no sign of the doorknob or even the outline of the door.

Sephie's heart dropped in her, and she instantly felt sick, for she'd never been in such complete darkness before. It seemed to not only take away her sight, but lay on her body like a blanket, a living thing which hugged her with its horrible presence.

"Wheaties!" Sephie yelled, her eyes wide open and unseeing.

"I'm over here!" Wheaties' voice floated out of the darkness to Sephie's right. Sephie turned her head towards the sound, but she could see nothing.

"Come over here!" Sephie yelled. "I'm by the door. We need to get out!"

Wheaties' voice, like a strange creature without a body, floated in the air. "I'll try!"

Sephie moved her hands in front of herself, waving them around, trying to feel anything. Panic filled her, for even though she couldn't have been more than a few inches away from the door, she wasn't sure she would be able to find it again.

She turned back to the wall and felt it, trying to find the door again. She was afraid to move too far, for fear she would be moving further away from the door instead of closer to it.

"Sephie, where are you?" Wheaties' disembodied voice came from the darkness again, but it sounded further away! He was moving down the tunnel, not closer to her!

"I'm over here!" Sephie said, her voice rising in panic and filling with fright and desperation. "Come towards my voice!"

Suddenly another sound came from the darkness. A moan, like someone in pain. Sephie's heart leapt in terror. A Lurker was inside with them! It was impossible to tell where the moan came from, whether it was close or far away. Was the Lurker near Wheaties? Would it grab him? The thought of a Lurker attacking Wheaties, biting him, killing him, was too horrible for Sephie to think about. And even worse, then she would be alone in the darkness!

"Wheaties!" Sephie wailed. "Come here, quick!"

The darkness began to make Sephie feel weird. Suddenly it was like her body floated in the darkness. She stood still, but she had the sensation of lifting off the ground. Strange thoughts came to her mind. She felt like crying. They had to get out of there!

"Wheaties!" she yelled again, and then realized it wasn't the smartest thing to do, for the Lurker would hear and come towards her. She felt even more vulnerable then, and she shrank back against the wall, her skin tingling, waiting for the feeling of being grabbed by a shriveled bony hand any second.

A hand did grab her shoulder! She screamed in terror and beat at it.

"Stop! It's me!'

With relief and joy, Sephie saw it was Wheaties. She grabbed him and they hugged each other, both weeping silent tears.

In the darkness, Sephie pressed her cheek against Wheaties' and he pressed his back against hers. The he kissed her, and for a brief moment she forgot everything.

Finally, with tears in her eyes Sephie said, "I thought I lost you!"

In the darkness, Sephie could just make out Wheaties's smile. "I thought I lost you, too!"

"There's a Lurker in here!" Sephie said.

"Let's find the door!" Wheaties replied.

"Don't let go of my hand!" Sephie said.

"I won't, ever again," Wheaties relied.

That made Sephie smile, despite their danger. Sephie's left hand held tightly to Wheaties' right. With their other hands they felt the wall, looking for the door.

The moan came again, making them both jump. It sounded close! Or was it? It was so hard to tell.

"We have to hurry," Sephie said, this time remembering to whisper.

"It's got to be right here," Wheaties replied.

The moan came again, and this time they knew it was close. Sephie imagined she could feel the horrible dead man's breath on her skin. She couldn't help but yelp.

Suddenly an explosion of light filled the space. Both Sephie and Wheaties covered their eyes with their hands, for the sudden light hurt them.

When they were able to open their eyes again, they both looked towards the light. It was coming from the open door! Somehow, they had moved more than thirty feet away from it down the wall.

As the light shone in the tunnel, they could see that they were not in a subway at all, but a long narrow tunnel which ran down the side of the larger tunnel. And there, not ten feet away was the Lurker!

It was a man. He had matted gray hair, black eyes and rotted, yellow teeth. He wore an old gray suit which was torn and covered in dirt and mold. The man's right arm was missing from the elbow down, and he wore only one black shoe on his right foot. His bare left foot was twisted and pointing sideways.

As the light shone into the tunnel, the Lurker

saw them too! It turned and started to stumble towards them.

"Hurry! Let's get to the door!" Wheaties yelled. Sephie didn't need any more encouragement. Still keeping hold of each other's hand, they ran towards the opening.

And then something happened which filled Sephie's heart with joy and excitement. Johnny walked through the door!

The light came from a torch Johnny held high in the air. The dancing flames seemed cheery and wonderful after the darkness.

Behind him came a strange man with large white wings. And after that, Starbucks walked in! Then Super! Then five more people, and another stranger with big, white wings.

Sephie laughed and half cried with relief. "It's Johnny!" she cried. "Johnny!"

Wheaties, overcome with emotion as well, said, "Yeah! Hurry!"

Johnny didn't hear them, for he was too far away. They ran towards the door and their friends. As Sephie and Wheaties watched, Sephie's father Microsoft walked in and joined Johnny!

The sight of her father made Sephie's heart fill with joy and relief. If they could only get to him! Then Wheaties said, "Look! It's my father!" He pointed at another man walking in and joining the group

Johnny and the others with him took off down the tunnel, moving fast.

Suddenly Sephie and Wheaties stopped and Sephie screamed. The horrible Lurker was right in front of them! They were forced to back up. As they did, they saw with dismay that Johnny and his group, and the light from the torch, were moving farther and farther away down the tunnel.

Sephie and Wheaties had no choice but to run backwards a for a few feet as the Lurker shuffled towards them.

"Hurry!" Sephie said. "We have to get around him! We can't lose them! It's going to be dark again!"

They had no choice but to risk running around the Lurker, and just hope he didn't grab them. Quickly they ran around it to the right. The Lurker spun and came within inches of grabbing Sephie's arm, but just missed.

As fast as they could, Sephie and Wheaties chased after the retreating torch light. It bobbed and weaved in front of them, getting smaller and smaller. The darkness closed in again, threatening to plunge them once again into darkness. They ran, holding each other's hand, hoping they didn't run right into another Lurker.

CHAPTER 21

As the basket lowered down on the side of the building, it swayed back and forth and banged into the building because of the wind. Deb hung onto the side, feeling as if at any moment she was going to be pitched out, and fall screaming to the ground far below. Her stomach twisted, and she felt sick.

Deb looked over at the other girls, Borsa, Lenna and Relatt. They didn't look any better, each with white faces full of worry, just like Deb. The clung to the sides as well, peering over the edge at the world far below. Deb felt a pang of sympathy for them, and a sense of comradery. They were in it together, all three forced into dangerous labor by the mean, bossy Patto.

"When we reach the ground," Relatt said, speaking loudly to be heard over the wind, "Run and hide in a building, quick. The groundworms will see the basket coming down, and they some of them will run towards us, looking to attack. And find something on the ground to defend yourself with."

Deb's mind filled with apprehension. This trip was even more dangerous than she's suspected. She began to wonder if it was a way for Patto to get rid of her rival. But why include Deb? What did Deb ever do to her? Unless Patto was doing it at Lord Flaggalon's command, which Deb thought might be very likely. Either way, Deb knew she was in a fight for her life. She had to survive, no matter what it took.

As the basket dropped further and further from the opening in the building and closer and closer to the ground, Deb felt more and more apprehensive. Her heart began to pound in her chest, and the ground seemed to be getting closer much too fast. She could see the street below now, a gray straight line running in front of the building until it ran into cross streets at the corners of the building.

Deb scanned for people below. She saw a few, walking down the sidewalks and crossing the streets. They didn't look dangerous, and yet they still gave her the chills. She didn't see any of them looking up yet, which gave her some comfort, but she knew it wouldn't be long before they noticed the basket. Would Deb and the other girls have time to jump out before they were surrounded?

As if reading Deb's thoughts Rellat said, "Get ready! We're almost there!"

Borsa said, "As soon as we hit the ground, climb out and take off in different directions. With any luck, we can blend in before the groundworms even realize we're there!"

The basket was only ten feet off the ground now, and with dismay, Deb saw the people on the streets pointing at them and talking excitedly. The bottom of the basket hit the ground! All three girls were momentarily knocked off their feet. Then before Deb could even react, Borsa leapt over the side and took off running.

Lenna struggled, one leg over the side, the other still in the basket. Deb stood up and quickly glanced around, trying to decide where to run. They were right in front of the entrance to their building, on a big concrete patio. The street was fifty feet away, and no one seemed to be on the patio, so it looked as if they had a little time until the people could reach them.

Deb leapt out of the basket and landed on the concrete. In front of her on the patio a huge fountain stood, dry and empty of water. Deb ran to hide behind it, crouching down. She heard excited voices raised in anger from the street. How did she ever get into this mess, she thought, and how was she going to survive long enough to get back in the basket?

Holding tightly onto her bag for collecting supplies, she stood up and ran towards the building they had come from. She could see the entrance had once sported glass walls and a revolving door, like the one at Misterwizard's old castle, but now the glass was all shattered and only the skeleton of the revolving door remained. Behind the remnants of the door, she saw a bank of closed double doors in a wall. She recalled those were elvatrs, like the ones she saw in Pelpia in the building where they escaped the Krakn. They probably didn't work, just like all the others she'd seen. But next to them there was another door. She recognized it, for it was like the one in Misterwizard's castle. It led to stairs that went up. Should she go inside it? She might be trapped there, with no way out.

She took off running towards the building, just to have someplace to go to get away from the basket. She glanced back and saw Lenna running to the right. The people of Nork seemed to be concentrating on her, for she was slow. A large crowd ran towards Lenna, and Deb felt sorry for her. It didn't look like Lenna was going to escape. That horrible Patto, sending them to their death! In Deb's mind, she thought of ways to pay Patto back, but then made herself stop thinking like that. It wasn't like her, or Johnny to get revenge. If Patto threatened her directly and Deb had to defend herself, well, that was a different matter. For now, she just had to concentrate on staying alive!

Deb ran past the remnants of the old door and up to the bank of elvatrs. She looked both ways, her mind racing, trying to think what to do next. She decided she'd run down the hallway to the left, and out the other side of the building. Then she could find a hiding spot to start looting.

Deb ran around the left side of the wall down the hallway. Ahead she saw the remnants of the glass wall on the other side. Here and there, dangerous panes of dark glass still clung to the frame, seemingly ready to fall on someone at any moment.

Deb's breath came in sharp gasps as she ran out the building on the other side. Then she stopped and screamed. The whole street and patio on this side was filled with people! They all turned and saw her and yelled. A loud explosion of voices filled the air. Deb stopped, but it was too late, there was no way she was going to escape them.

The crowd, knowing she was trapped, ran over and surrounded her. Deb's mind filled with fear and sadness, for she was sure she was going to die at any moment. And sure enough, the people all smiled darkly and raised their hands, looking like a pack of hungry wolves. Deb made fists, and tried not to cry.

Suddenly the crowd stopped. Deb heard a strong male voice behind the crowd, and the people all seemed to turn and look behind them. Then as Deb watched in curiosity, she saw the crowd parting to let someone through.

Who could it be, Deb wondered? Was it the King of Nork? Moxie and his men? Or, she thought with humor, could it be Johnny? Had he already won the people over and was now their friend? Deb didn't doubt that could have happened. She doubted she could be that lucky, though. Deb waited, her heart pounding, to see who it was.

When the person emerged, Deb was surprised, and not sure what to think.

"Hello. You are Johnny's girl, aren't you? The one they call Deb?"

It was one of the Nork soldiers! She remembered

sitting on that horrid rat beastie as Moxie ordered this black man to take Lady Stabs and that rotten Monsta to Nork. His name was Ticktock. She also remembered he was no friend, and surely was planning on taking her back to Moxie. She thought about turning and running, but that would be impossible, for the people of Nork now surrounded her on all sides. It looked like after all her efforts she was going to be a prisoner again after all. She glared at Ticktock with barely concealed fury.

Ticktock walked over to stand next to her. He had a strange smile on his face, and it almost looked friendly. "You're lucky I happened to see the basket and ran to meet it. Otherwise…" Ticktock gestured to the crowd, "you'd be their next meal. Most of these people only eat once a day, if they're lucky."

"I won't let you take me back to Moxie," Deb said, knowing she really didn't have a lot of choice.

Ticktock frowned with seriousness. "This may be hard for you to believe, but I have no intention of doing that. Besides, Moxie is in no condition now to do anything but drool and moan. He's a Lurker now."

Deb's mouth opened in surprise, then she closed it. She remembered the tunnel, and suspected Ticktock was telling her the truth.

"Then what are you going to do with me?"

"I want to be you and Johnny's friend. I am no longer a member of the Nork army. I am realigned with my own people now, in Booklin. We call ourselves The Brethren. We are made up of people King Ferdinand despises, because our skin color and faces do not look like the people of Nork. But my people are good people, and even though they don't like white people any more than the white people of Nork like them, I think I can reason with them.

"I want you to take me to Johnny, so together can talk to my people about an alliance. Together, we can kill King Ferdinand and set Nork free."

Deb put a hand to her chin, interested. Her long, blond hair blew in the breeze and she stared at him with her bright blue eyes, pondering. This was a new and totally unexpected turn of events. If Ticktock was telling the truth, he was offering Johnny and the tribe something that could greatly help their chances to help save the people of Pelpia. And even possibly change the city of Nork and the whole region for the better. It was definitely something Johnny should hear about, if it was real and not a trap.

"How do I know you're telling the truth? That this isn't just a trick to get me to trust you?"

Ticktock walked closer, so only Deb could hear. Then he spoke in a low tone. "I don't think you have a lot of choice. You see these people? They are very hungry. The only reason they aren't tearing you apart, is because they think I'm a soldier of Nork and in charge. I wouldn't wait too long, because I don't know when their hunger will overcome their loyalty."

Deb glanced at the people around her, and she felt sick. Their faces all showed a hunger. She realized Ticktock was telling the truth.

She turned to Ticktock. "Take me somewhere we

can hide out until the basket returns. Then I'll take you up to the Sky. That's where you can meet Johnny."

"Will the Sky let me into the basket?"

"That's something we'll have to work on."

"And once we get up to the angels? Won't they just kill me?"

"That's the other thing we'll have to work on. You said you wanted to meet Johnny."

Ticktock nodded. He took Deb's hand and led her through the crowd. Deb held her breath, hoping the people held off until they could get away. Her heart beat wildly and her skin felt hot.

They made it through the crowd to an open space, but as they walked, the crowd followed them. Suddenly Ticktock pulled her and took off running.

"Run! Now!"

Deb ran too, and holding each other's hand they took off as fast as they could. The people of Nork screamed and took off after them. Could they escape before they were both eaten alive?

The royal coach, the strange wagons full of moaning sounds and the army marching on foot reached the huge gate which led to the three tunnels where supposedly this Johnny Apocalypse waited. The tunnels were known as the Lincoom tunnels, nobody knew why. It was what they were always called, since anyone could remember.

The royal coach stopped and King Ferdinand climbed out. He peered up at the red eye. It was a warm day, though he knew the cold time was approaching, when water and white powder would fall from the sky. It was best to be inside when that happened, in a nice warm place. People died during the cold time, lots of them. This was good, King Ferdinand always reasoned, for it provided food for the others, and they complained less. Also, during the cold time, the threat of rebellion lessened greatly, for everyone was too cold to do anything but huddle next to fires and try to stay alive.

King Ferdinand walked over to one of the wagons and peeked in the long, narrow slot on the side. He smiled as he watched what had been Clancy, moaning and bumping into walls. Then he turned and looked at dead Moxie. Moxie had been dead for a while, now, and his flesh was starting to rot. His left eye was now black, and his lips had curled back, showing his yellow teeth.

And there with them was the former king. He still wore a surprised expression, as if he was not sure what was happening. His flesh had begun to turn white as well, and his hair was falling out.

"Who would ever think the three of you would be such close friends someday? Even if it was only after you died." King Ferdinand laughed heartily with dark pleasure. So many things were going so well, it was almost scary. To think that he would get to see the arrogant Clancy and his clan turned into Lurkers, and watch them stumble around, dead men walking. Life was beginning to be so wonderful and full of pleasant horror. King Ferdinand couldn't wait to see what pleasures he would experience next. He was not just a king anymore; he was a god. Soon he would be master of the whole city, and then the world, and all would bow down in terror before him and his army of undead. Soon he would have many more Lurkers, hundreds, maybe thousands, and anyone who didn't obey him would be food for the monsters. He imagined the intense pleasure of watching people being eaten alive, those who didn't bow to his wishes. He couldn't wait for that to happen!

King Ferdinand leisurely strolled back to his royal coach in his long, purple silk robe, feeling powerful. Surrounding his coach, the wagons and the army, the people of Nork stared and pointed, enjoying the strange spectacle.

Alcapoon, leader of the Nork army, walked up to him. King Ferdinand turned to him. Alcopoon's curly black hair was mussed up and his face was covered in sweat. King Ferdinand gazed with contempt at the stubble on Alcapoon's chin and his sloppy look with his green genral jacket open. Someday, King Ferdinand vowed, he would feed Alcapoon to the Lurkers and find a real leader for the army. For now, he would have to endure the stupid man.

"Where are we going to do now, Your Majesty?" Alcapoon asked.

King Ferdinand walked casually back towards his royal coach. "You, my imbecilic friend, are going to take some of your men to the top of the gate and look for this

Johnny Apocalypse fellow, if he even exists. Then report back to me. Meanwhile, I will be eating a very pleasant lunch that your men will set up for me next to my royal coach."

"Yes, Your Majesty," Alcapoon said, blinking, feeling as if he was just insulted but not really sure. He turned and barked orders at some of the other soldiers. Five broke off and joined Alcapoon. Ten others moved to the back of the royal coach and began taking out supplies for the king's meal.

Alcapoon and his five men ran up the ramps towards the top of the gate. When they reached the top, they gazed out at the concrete road below. In the distance, they could see the entrances to the three tunnels.

Alcapoon gazed around. He saw some dead bodies lying far below on the road, and some near the entrance to the gate. The bodies were torn apart, arms and legs everywhere, heads separated from bodies, and all the bodies looked as if they'd been chewed on and half eaten. But he didn't see Lurkers anywhere, or any sign of life.

Alcapoon turned to the soldier next to him. "Go down and tell the king there's nothing here. Only dead bodies. I'm going to keep looking for a little while."

The soldier nodded, turned and ran back down the ramp. Alcapoon peered out at the landscape some more. Off in the distance to the left, he saw the weird statue of the lady with the spiky crown on the little i-land where it stood. The statue's arm had broken off, and some of the spikes on the crown had broken too. Nobody bothered to visit the i-land, for there was nothing on it worth going there for. Not even the wildies went there, for it was a long swim to get to it and there was no food anywhere.

Alcapoon looked further to the left, and saw the huge i-land called Statn I-land. That's where the Gants lived, huge men twenty or thirty feet tall, slow-witted and peaceful, but still dangerous when provoked. The old king used to secretly give them people to eat, just to keep relations with them on a peaceful level. Alcapoon wondered if King Ferdinand would do the same thing.

Almost as if reading Alcapoon's mind, the soldier he'd sent to talk to King Ferdinand returned from running down the ramp and back, out of breath.

"King Ferdinand says we're supposed to send most of the soldiers back to the castle to prepare for his return. He wants only you and a small group of soldiers left here to watch the Lurkers in the wagons and keep guard. He's taking a few soldiers and Lurkers with him over to Statn I-land."

The thought of anyone talking to the Gants made Alcapoon nervous. "What is he doing that for?"

The soldier shrugged. "I don't know. Maybe he is going to try and talk them into joining us."

Alcapoon snorted with laughter. "I thought King Ferdinand was smarter than that. He should know those Gants don't want nothing to do with anybody. He don't want to make them angry. They are best left alone."

"Well, King Ferdinand says he wants everything

ready by the time he finishes his lunch."

Alcapoon turned and gave orders to two soldiers to stay and keep an eye out. Then he headed back down the ramp. Just what did King Ferdinand have in mind?

CHAPTER 22

Restaria and the people of Letfreedomring waited in the cold, dark entrance to the subway. As most of them stood on the cold marble floor, huddled together, they stared at the entrance with hope mixed with fear, waiting for Johnthebaptist to return. Johnthebaptist went out to find a safe place in Nork for them to hide, but he'd been gone a long time now. The people whispered and every few minutes grew louder, and Restaria had to shush them again. Everyone was hungry and exhausted from their ordeal with the Lurkers. Those at the back of the crowd, the most vulnerable, gazed down the steps leading back down to the tunnel with wide-open eyes and beating hearts, listening for Lurkers, terrified the monsters would appear at any second.

One of the women with long, stringy brown hair and a thin, gaunt face in the front clutching the hand of a scrabbler girl of four seasons said what everyone was thinking. "What if he doesn't return? What are we going to do?”

Restaria turned to her and smiled. “He will return. He is just taking his time to make sure and find us a hiding place big enough for all of us that we can defend. It takes time.”

“And what if he doesn’t?” a man in the middle of the crowd said.

Restaria glanced at him. “Then I will find us a place. Have faith!”

Just then Johnthebaptist did return, and a cheer went up from everyone. Restaria shushed them with a smile of relief and turned to Johnthebaptist. He walked up to her.

“We are very near the place where we were imprisoned. It seems we didn’t go very far in the subway. Something is going on outside, however. A large parade of wagons and soldiers is passing by, heading towards the gate by the tunnels. A large crowd is following them. I see what looks like a royal coach, the king’s coach, being pulled by those horrible rat-beasties. I suggest we wait until they pass by.”

“No!” a lady in the crowd said. “The monsters could come at any time!”

Another man yelled, “And we’re starving!”

“And thirsty!” another voice piped in.

Another woman said, “If I don’t get out of this darkness, I’m going to go waksy!”

Restaria raised her hands, palms towards them. “We will get out. But it will do us no good to leave here if we are just captured again.”

"I can't wait any longer!" one man said, his voice rising in panic. "I'll leave on my own, and you can all stay here!" The man's words set off a loud babble of talking and he moved towards the doors.

"Stop!" Johnthebaptist said blocking the man's way.

"You let us leave, or we're going anyway," the thin woman with the scrabbler said.

"Those Lurkers will be here at any moment!" Another man in the back said. "I heard moaning!"

Restaria turned to Johnthebaptist. "Did you find a building we can go to?"

Johnthebaptist nodded. "Yes. It is a tall building with yellow sides. It is very tall. It appears deserted, probably because it has no food or supplies in it. The only problem is, the street in front of it is very narrow, and there are a lot of people from Nork there."

Restaria thought for a moment. "Maybe if we go in ones or twos, try to blend in with the crowd, no one will notice us."

She looked at Johnthebaptist. "Do we look like the people of Nork?"

Johnthebaptist chuckled. "After being in that subway, we are dirty enough. Some of the men are wearing weird suits with stripes, like the soldiers wore, and the woman are in dresses with small round hats. But there are just as many people wearing nothing but rags. I don't think we will be noticed, if we make sure to not look at anyone too closely."

Restaria nodded. "Then that's our plan. You can

lead the people across, in small groups. Try to vary your route, so it doesn't look like you are walking to the building."

Restaria turned to the people huddled in the dark behind her. "Listen. You will go in small groups, two or three. When you are outside, do not talk. Do not look at anyone, and try not to look as if you don't belong. Don't gaze around like you've never been here before. Follow Johnthebaptist closely and do everything he tells you to do. Keep silent, and keep your wits about you."

The people whispered amongst themselves with excitement, smiling about the new adventure they were about to undertake and the fact they were finally going to get out of the dark subway. Restaria's stomach tensed, for she could see so many ways things could go wrong. If only the people were willing to wait!

Restaria walked forward and pointed to the woman with her scrabbler. The woman smiled with pleasure at having been picked to leave first. Restaria turned and pointed at another middle-aged man in a ragged trenchcoat nearby.

"Why them?" another man complained. "We should draw lots to see who goes first."

"Because I am your Mayr, that's why, and I make the decisions," Restaria responded. "We don't have time to play games."

The woman, her scrabbler, and the man in the ragged coat chosen to be the first joined Johnthebaptist. Together they all moved to the opening. The woman with the scrabbler looked back and smiled at the crowd, and they smiled back at her. "Wish us luck," she said.

"Just don't do anything stupid to draw attention to yourselves!" a man yelled. "We all have to get out too!"

The woman scowled back at him. Then they walked out. Restaria watched them with a mixture of hope and worry. She felt so helpless, wishing it was her doing something instead of just sitting around and waiting. But she knew it was the same way her people felt, and she had to stay and keep them calm.

"Don't worry," she said. "It won't be long before he's back for the rest of us."

Sandl ran to the opening in the building and leapt out, not even thinking about his ability to fly. He had to get back to Deecee and find out if he was okay. Surely that evil Monsta was only joking when he said he'd eaten Deecee, wasn't he? Flapping his wings faster than he'd ever before, Sandl pushed himself towards Johnny and Deb's building. He flapped his wings so hard he began to tire quickly, and mentally scolded himself. It wouldn't do any good if he made himself so tired he didn't make it!

Breathing hard and sweating, he finally reached the opening in the wall to Johnny's room. He landed and had to stop for a moment to catch his breath. Then he looked up with a look of misery and yelled, "Deecee!"

The room was quiet. Folding his wings, he

hurried around the room, looking for Johnny's doggie. Then he saw paws sticking out, right next to the bed! He ran over, knelt down and looked at Deecee, and tears came to his eyes. Deecee was covered in blood!

Sandl stroked Deecee's head. "Deecee, please don't be dead!"

Deecee opened his eyes, but didn't raise his head. He was alive! But hurt.

Sandle looked Deecee over, and saw that Deecee had a stab in his side. Blood oozed out of the wound.

"Poor doggy! That horrible man!" Sandle leapt up and grabbed a sheet off the bed. He carried it over and swabbed the blood from Deecee's fur. Then he tried to tie the wound.

He heard a sound outside. Was that terrible man back? No, it was a woman's voice. Sandl recognized it with joy. It was Lady Stabs!

"Lady Stabs! Lady Stabs!"

Lady Stabs walked in the door, looking curious.

"Help me! Deecee's hurt!"

Lady Stabs ran over to Sandl and Deecee and knelt beside them, her face grave.

She looked at the wound and scowled with anger. "He's been stabbed!" She turned to Sandl. "Who did this?"

"An evil man! He's here to hurt Pantina!"

Lady Stabs put her hands under Deecee. "Let's get him on the bed."

Together they lifted Deecee and laid him on the bed.

"Is Deecee going to die?" Sandl sobbed, backing up and letting Lady Stabs work on Deecee.

"I don't know," Lady Stabs said. "I've fixed a lot of knife wounds, when I was in the gang. As long as none of his important parts inside were hit, he should survive, if we bind the wound very tight."

Lady Stabs twisted the sheet into a tight roll then wrapped it tightly around Deecee. Then she cinched it tight and tied it.

As she continued to work on Deecee, she looked at Sandl. "What did this man look like?" Lady Stabs asked.

Sandl, tears running down his cheeks said, "He was big and strong, and had a black beard. He said his name was Monsta."

Lady Stabs stopped moving and looked at Sandl. "Oh, no," she said. "How did he survive? And get up here?"

Lady Stabs thought for a moment, her mind full of dark thoughts. She looked at Sandl again. "He said he was here to hurt Pantina?"

Sandl nodded. "He followed me over to Lord Flaggalon's place. He kidnapped him! He's going to force Lord Flaggalon to take him to Pantina so he can kill her!"

Lady Stabs turned to Sandl. "We have to do something. We have to help Pantina."

"But she's a god. Surely, she can destroy Monsta with just a look of her eyes."

Lady Stabs replied, "Listen, sometimes even gods need help from ordinary people. You're going to have to help me get to Pantina before Monsta does."

"How can I help?" Sandl said, looking confused and afraid. "And what about Deecee? We can't let him die!"

"We both care about Deecee, but what he needs now is rest. We have to help Pantina, do you understand?"

"What can we do?" Sandl said, raising his hands palm up. "I can't fly you there, I'm too small."

Lady Stabs stood up. She walked over to an old wooden box with drawers and opened the bottom drawer. She knew this was where Johnny and Deb hid their weapons. She pulled out a sword and a sheath, and put it on. Then she grabbed a small knife and stuck it in her belt. She turned back to Sandl.

"We'll have to find someone else to help. I have to get to Pantina before Monsta does. Or Pantina will be helpless and defenseless. You will help me, won't you?"

Sandl stroked Deecee's fur. Then he nodded slowly. "I'll do whatever I can. I want to see that Monsta get what he deserves!"

"Good." Lady Stabs put out her hand and Sandl walked over and took it.

"We have to hurry," Sandl said. "That evil man is on his way to Pantina with Lord Flaggalon right now!"

Johnny and his group walked swiftly down the tunnel, for it was smooth and narrow, with a curved ceiling and a flat floor. Every once in an awhile they would pass a door which led into the big tunnel. The doors all had boards across them or iron bars wedged tight so Lurkers couldn't escape.

"This isn't a subway," Johnny said. "What is it?" His words seemed to be swallowed up immediately by the close walls and lack of air.

"I believe it's a tunnel where workers came to work on the big tunnel," Mantayo said, his voice also sounding strange and without any echo. He glanced around, feeling weird having to walk instead of using his wings. The space seemed so tight and confining. He was used to soaring in the sky. Panic made his heart beat faster, and he began to think negative thoughts, such as they only had one torch, and if they hit a pack of Lurkers, they would be trapped. Mantayo dismissed the thoughts as cowardly and stubbornly ignored the feeling of being buried alive.

"We have to hurry, as fast as we can," Johnny said. Johnny picked up his pace. The other men followed close behind Johnny and Mantayo. Microsoft watched the torch nervously, hoping there was enough air to keep it lit. The flame flickered and sputtered. The last thing they needed was to be plunged into total darkness in the tight, airless tunnel.

Microsoft heard something, or was it just his imagination? It sounded like Sephie's voice, but it was so faint. He wondered if it was only in his head. He stopped and looked back towards where they'd come from, listening. There was nothing but silence. He suspected he'd only made it up in his mind, because he was so desperate to hear her. He turned back and saw with panic the others were moving away fast. What was their hurry? Young men, trying to show how tough and unafraid they were. Microsoft scowled and hurried to catch up, before he lost them in the dark.

Suddenly he heard shouting up ahead. Johnny and the others must have found some Lurkers!

In the darkness behind Johnny and his group, Sephie and Wheaties ran as fast as they could, panting from the exertion and also the lack of air in the tunnel. It was so hot and stuffy. Sweat covered them both. It was like being in an oven and running for the door.

"They're getting further away!" Sephie panted, her voice muffled in the darkness. "I can barely see the torch now!"

"How far are they going?" Wheaties said irritably. "Why don't they stop, just for a second."

Sephie wanted to yell, but she was so out of breath. Her mind began to go woozy, and the dark tunnel began to look strange, like a horrible dream. Finally, she gathered what strength she had and yelled, "Daddy! Stop! It's me, Sephie!"

The sound seemed to be swallowed up right away by the tunnel, and didn't seem to travel more than ten feet.

"It's no good," Wheaties said. "We're going to lose them!"

Sephie scowled with anger and determination, mad at Wheaties for looking weak and afraid. They had to stay strong, like Johnny and Deb. "No, we're not! Run faster!"

CHAPTER 23

Microsoft joined the other men to see he was right. There on the floor of the tunnel lay two Lurkers. Their bodies had been chopped to pieces and their heads lay beside them. Johnny and the other stood over the Lurkers staring at them, as if they had just killed a wild beastie and were proudly looking at their kill.

Johnny and Mantayo grinned at each other as Microsoft stopped and leaned over, trying to catch his breath.

"I think most of the Lurkers in this tunnel must have walked out, and we killed them in our big battle. We need to find where this tunnel connects to the subway, so we can block it off."

Then they were off again! Moving again at a swift pace.

"Wait!" Microsoft said. "Can't we take a breather?"

Johnny stopped and the rest stopped too. "We don't dare, Microsoft. The torch is almost out."

Johnny turned to Mantayo. "Mantayo, do you think we're near the city yet? And do you think this tunnel goes underneath the wall?"

"I don't know, Johnny. We must be close," Mantayo said. "We should try to open the next door to see where we are and try to strengthen the torch." And give me some air, Mantayo thought to himself.

"Okay," Johnny said. They continued on, everyone hot and sweaty and having trouble breathing. The torch seemed to suck up what air there was in the tunnel, and it filled the tunnel with acrid smoke.

"There's another doorway," Johnny said, pointing ahead. They all hurried over to it. It was barred with wooden planks held to the tunnel wall with crude spikes. Together they pried the spikes loose and dropped the boards. Then they pried open the door. Bright sunlight streamed into the tunnel, bouncing off the opposite wall, temporarily blinding them.

"I never thought I'd be so happy to feel air again," Baskinrobins said. In a rush, they all poured outside and breathed deep of the fresh air. They gazed around. They discovered they were near the end of the tunnel near the gate to Nork.

Johnny gazed around, remember the last time he and Deb had been in that very spot, fighting to escape the Lurkers. They did it with Deecee's help. Now looking around, Johnny didn't see any Lurkers anywhere.

"The Lurkers must have all came after us, and we killed them," Johnny said.

Mantayo pointed to the open door. "We'd better

close that door, so no more Lurkers get out." He walked over and closed the gate, then made sure it was latched. He joined Johnny and the others and looked up at the huge wall leading to the city of Nork. "We have to be careful. We're exposed here, and any guards will see us."

"Let's all take cover behind the cars," Johnny said.

They all walked over to the old rusted piles of cars which filled the tunnel and knelt down.

"The small tunnel looks like it keeps running under the gate," Johnny said, keeping an eye on the huge Nork wall. "I think we can get inside a little way, at least. Then we may have to take to the streets."

"Do you know where your missing friends are, Johnny?" Mantayo asked.

Johnny nodded. "I saw them when you first flew me to your home. They're in a big, round place not far from where we are right now. But they're sure to be heavily guarded."

"If we can just find where they are, we can signal my people. Together we can free them," Mantayo said.

"Can we stay out here for a little while?" Microsoft asked. "I don't like the thought of going back into that tunnel again. And I don't see any sign of Sephie or Wheaties. Do you think they might be out here somewhere?"

"I don't know," Johnny said, looking at Microsoft with sadness. "I wouldn't give up hope, just yet. We'll find them."

"They couldn't have wandered this far away,

could they?" Baskinrobins said. "Surely they wouldn't go through this dark tunnel by themselves."

"Let's look around for some supplies, maybe a rag to add to the torch," Mantayo said. "If you want Microsoft and Baskinrobins, you can stay up here and keep looking for your missing children. The rest of us should keep going."

"I don't know what to do," Microsoft said, rubbing his gray hair and looking sad with his big ears and long nose. "I don't see anyone out here."

Everyone spread out, looking for supplies and material to add to the torch, and for any sight of the missing children.

Sephie and Wheaties kept running, feeling as if at any moment they might collapse. Sephie kept her eyes on the torch far ahead. The torch bobbed and swayed, a beacon of hope in the darkness, and their only hope.

"I wish they'd stop for a moment," Wheaties said, his voice a mixture of anger and worry.

Suddenly, Sephie stopped, her mouth open in terror. The torch disappeared! They were plunged again into total darkness.

"Where'd they go?" Wheaties yelled, in full panic mode.

Luckily, they still had hold of each other's hand.

"Hurry!" Sephie said, her heart thumping in her

chest and her legs wobbly. "They must have gone around a corner!"

"Maybe we should give up and go back!" Wheaties yelled.

"That Lurker is back there!" Sephie said. "They've got to be right ahead."

In the darkness they continued to run. Fortunately, the ground was level and the tunnel continued straight ahead. As Sephie ran, she began to feel as if she was floating outside her body. She knew if they didn't get out soon, they would go waksy, and spend the rest of their life wandering through the dark tunnel.

King Ferdinand and the wagons reached the southern end of Nork. They had been careful to take side roads away from the large skyscrapers, so the Angels wouldn't spy them from above. King Ferdinand wasn't too worried, though, for unless the Angels decided to attack at that moment, they would only see his royal coach, some wagons and his army moving around, and have no clue what was really happening.

At the very southern end of Mattan, the I-land they were on, was another gate. This one was small and well hidden, and for only one purpose. There was now a total of one-hundred and forty Lurkers in total, including Clancy and his former men. The king had been forced to add more wagons and old buses to hold all the Lurkers. The buses didn't drive, but were dragged along by rattys like the wagons. It was a strange and bizarre troupe which traveled down the empty streets of the crumbling city.

King Ferdinand had left most of the wagons and buses back with Alcapoon, and only taken one wagon of Lurkers with him. Still, it was a bizarre troupe which traveled down the empty streets of the crumbling city.

King Ferdinand ordered the gate opened. Then he told the men to take out three of the Lurkers. The soldiers complied, and soon three soldiers led three Lurkers with rings around their necks and poles to keep them under control. King Ferdinand ordered the men with the Lurkers and five more of his men to follow him.

King Ferdinand walked through the gate. On the other side, there was nothing but a rocky wall next to the water of the bay, and a small path through the rocks.

King Ferdinand and the men and Lurkers with him traveled down the rocky path to the water's edge. Here they found a large wooden ship, with a crew of soldiers and a captain. The ship was always at the ready for when the former king wanted to take it to Statn I-land and talk to the Gants. King Ferdinand and his group boarded the ship and he ordered the captain to sail it to the northern tip of Statn I-land, to a spot where the king would always meet with the Gants.

When they arrived at the shore of Statn I-land after a short trip, King Ferdinand and the men with him got out. They walked up to another wall, this one more massive than the one surrounding Nork. This wall was made of sticks and mud and cars and buses. Huge pieces of buildings were in the wall, and large boulders. This wall was built by the Gants to keep everyone out so they could live in peace.

A massive gate with two huge doors was part of the wall. King Ferdinand and his men approached it. On the side of the wall there was a ramp which led to the top of the wall. King Ferdinand, his soldiers and the Lurkers walked up the ramp to a small flat area on the top of the wall. There, a huge bell hung.

King Ferdinand turned to look at his men. They all wore frightened expressions and gazed out past the wall. They saw an empty wasteland, with the bases of buildings which had been removed. The vegetation had been allowed to grow back, and the whole landscape was filled with trees and bushes. Beyond the trees in the distance, they could see a strange square building, made up of buildings smashed together, like they were building blocks. The site scared the men and they glanced at each other with eyes open in fear, for they knew only the huge creatures living here could pick up buildings and smash them together like that. And the king was about to summon them!

The Lurkers moaned loudly and reached out their hands to try and grab anyone close. The soldiers holding them had to constantly push and twist the poles to keep them under control. They glanced at the king for help, hoping he'd see how difficult it was to control the monsters, but the king ignored them.

King Ferdinand turned and looked at the bell

with a smile. As his men watched nervously, King Ferdinand grabbed the bell's rope and swung it, ringing the bell. With an ear-shattering sound that echoed over the land, the bell rang. The sound bounced off the wall and drifted over the new forest. The hearts of all the soldiers jumped, and they waited to see what would respond.

King Ferdinand and his men waited, watching the forest. The air was still and quiet, the only sound the moaning of the Lurkers. After what seemed like an eternity, they saw the leaves in the trees in the far distance moving.

"They're coming!" one soldier yelled in frightened excitement. King Ferdinand just smiled. He had only been there once with the former king, and the site of the Gants amazed him. Now he was king. The former king had been terrified of the Gants, and offered them people to eat to keep them happy. Ferdinand had always scoffed at this and saw it as another sign of how cowardly and weak the old king was, for the Gants never even asked for the people to eat. The Gant were simple-minded and gentle, and just wanted to be left alone. Now, King Ferdinand planned to do just the opposite. If he could make the Gants his slaves, they would prove to be a powerful tool in his quest for power.

A loud breaking sound echoed through the forest below, as whatever came broke branches on its way towards them. King Ferdinand felt a thrill course through him.

Then they saw it. Towering as high as the trees,

the Gant walked out of the forest. He was twenty-five-feet tall and wore green clothes made out of tree bark and leaves. His wild, brown hair stood up in all directions, and he his whole body and face were dirty and unwashed. He wore no shoes, and his feet were large and cached with mud. He frowned and looked grim, but there was a child-like look in his eyes that showed he was simple-minded and slow.

The Gant stopped ten feet from the gate and gazed up at King Ferdinand, his men and the Lurkers.

"Men for eat?" the Gant asked, its voice loud and strong, like quiet thunder.

King Ferdinand smiled.

Johnthebaptist walked outside into the cold, brisk morning air. He glanced around to see how many people were about. The streets in this area of the city had been cleared of rubble and old cars by the people. Still, grass and trees grew up from the cracked concrete. The buildings on all sides of the streets were empty shells, most with holes where they had been hit by the blast from the mushroom monsters which landed to the north of the city.

Johnthebaptist looked down the street in both directions to the intersections on either side. He saw people everywhere, moving about aimlessly, looking at nothing, simply existing. He felt sorry for them. He got the feeling their king really didn't care about them, and they were mostly left to fend for themselves. They all wore dirty, torn clothing and their faces and hair was dirty and matted. Little scrabblers ran around, playing. They seemed to be the only ones having fun.

Johnthebaptist turned and motioned with his hand. The woman with her scrabbler and the man with the ragged coat came outside. They gazed about fearfully.

Johnthebaptist pointed to his right. "That's the building we are going to. Once we get inside, we need to go up as high and as far away from the street as we can. Just follow me and don't talk. Don't look at anyone. Just act like you're weak and miserable, like everyone here."

The woman nodded, fear in her eyes. She grabbed tightly to her little girl's hand. Johnthebaptist walked slowly towards their destination, and the others followed him. The entrance to the subway was in the middle of the block, so they walked down the sidewalk past old deserted shops with brick storefronts.

Johnthebaptist kept his eye on the people around them. No one seemed to look at them when they first appeared, and now no one seemed to be noticing them as they walked. They hadn't been discovered, yet, it seemed.

They passed a man in ragged clothes laying on the sidewalk up against a building. His leg looked shriveled and his right eye was red and swollen. He put out his hands. "Food? Give me food!"

Johnthebaptist felt for him, but they didn't even

have any for themselves. The woman with Johnthebaptist scowled at the man, and the man with them just ran past as quickly as he could.

The beggar turned to watch them after they passed him. Johnthebaptist glanced back at him. He was alarmed to see the man staring intently at them. Did the beggar suspect something?

Johnthebaptist hurried along the sidewalk. They reached the street and crossed it. Though the woman, her scrabbler and the man with them kept their eyes looking at the ground, Johnthebaptist glanced around, making sure they were safe. He was alarmed to see more people seemed to be looking at them now. Some wore confused looks, as if they didn't recognize Johnthebaptist and his group. One woman stopped and stared at them. A man pointed at them! Johnthebaptist held his breath, hoping they wouldn't be recognized as outsiders.

They reached the concrete area in front of the entrance to the building. Johnthebaptist hurried to get in front of the others. "

"Hurry! As fast as you can without running!" he whispered.

They made it to the glass wall which made up the front of the building. All of the glass was gone, leaving only a black metal frame where the glass walls had stood. On the ground, glass shards, covered with dirt and dust, lay all over. They stepped over the bottom of the metal frame. They entered a large open area with a white stone floor and a huge stone desk in front of a stone wall. Johnthebaptist led them around the corner to the left. There they found three sets of double closed double doors with number dials above them. Johnthebaptist hurried past them to a door with small sign next to it which said "Stairs."

Johnthebaptist looked back to see if anyone had seen them come in or was watching. With the glass front wall gone, they were exposed to the street. With dismay he saw a small group of five people, two women and three men, all in ragged clothes talking and pointing at them.

Johnthebaptist opened the door to the stairs and led them inside. As soon as they entered the small room, they felt the chill. The area was dark and hidden from any heat of the red eye, and a smell of mold filled the air.

The woman with her scrabbler spoke in a frightened voice. "They were watching us!"

"I saw it too!" the man said. "What if they tell the soldiers?"

"We'll deal with that when it comes," Johnthebaptist said. "Go up these stairs all the way until you see the door that is open. I've already checked it out. That is the fifth floor. Go inside the room there, close the door and find a corner to hide and wait."

"You're going to leave us here?!" the woman wailed.

"I have to go back for the others. Just push something in front of the door, and don't let anyone in unless they give you the special word."

"What word is that?" the man asked.

"Letfreedomring," Johnthebaptist said.

The man, woman, and her scrabbler smiled and nodded.

Johnthebaptist opened the door and peeked out again. He looked out at the street, but the crowd who had been watching them was gone. Not knowing if it was a good sign or bad, he walked out and closed the door.

Only two hundred or so more people to get across, and all without anyone getting suspicious. Easy!

CHAPTER 24

Sephie and Wheaties ran on, their eyes wide open but seeing nothing. They both dreaded the feeling of a slimy, dead hand on their shoulders or running into a Lurker in front of them, but there was nothing they could do. They just had to hope they caught up to the torchlight before something terrible happened,

Finally, Wheaties slowed down and stopped, forcing Sephie to stop too. He bent over and panted, a scary sound in the dark. Sephie's heart quailed and tears stung her eyes. "We can't give up!"

"I just need a second," Wheaties said. After a pause he added, "I think my eyes are adjusting to the darkness. Look!" He pointed with his free hand in the dark, though Sephie couldn't see it. "Is that a light up ahead?"

Sephie peered ahead, and she could just barely see the faint hint of a light, just a crack in the wall to their right. "It's not the torchlight," Sephie said, her voice wavery.

"But it might be a way out!" Wheaties started walking again, pulling Sephie along with him. They grew closer and closer to the faint light. Then they were next to it.

"Don't let go of my hand!" Sephie yelled.

"I won't," Wheaties said. He walked up and felt the wall. "It's a door!"

Sephie's heart thumped hard with hope. "Can we open it?"

"I don't know," Wheaties said. "Listen. I'm going to let go of your hand, but I'm going to be right here. Touch the wall right in front of you, and don't move."

Sephie nodded, and with reluctance felt Wheaties take his hand away. She quickly pressed both hands against the tunnel wall and turned to watch him. She could barely see his outline now, from the faint light of the door.

Sephie watched as Wheaties moved his hands around the door. "There's a small set of steps and a door. The light is coming from around the door. But the door is sealed by two pieces of wood!" he said, his voice sounding happy and hopeful. "I think I can pull the boards off!"

Sephie felt frightened joy fill her and she smiled tentatively, not sure if she should hope just yet. "Good!" Was all she said, not able to say more.

She heard Wheaties grunting and the sound of creaking. Then she heard a loud *chunk* and a yell.

"What happened?" she yelled.

Wheaties laughed in the darkness. "I got the first

one off, but I fell!"

Sephie laughed too. "Well, be careful, silly."

They both laughed for a moment, a wonderful feeling after all the fear and darkness.

She heard Wheaties working on the second board. "This one is tough!"

"Let me help!" Sephie said, then felt her way to the steps and then the door with her hands. Her hands landed on Wheaties back. She felt a warm and comforting feeling at touching him. She felt around until she found the board. She grabbed it next to where Wheaties held it and pulled with all her might. It didn't budge!

"It's not moving!" she yelled.

Suddenly she heard a sound from somewhere in the tunnel. It was so faint, she wasn't sure if it was a Lurker, or something else. It instantly brought back the fright, and dispelled the happiness she'd been feeling a moment before.

"Something's coming!" she yelled.

"Pull!" Wheaties yelled back.

Then with a pop, the board came free! They both fell to the floor. But now they could see, for the door creaked open on its own, letting in wonderful, welcome light.

Sephie looked over at Wheaties and they grinned at each other. At that moment, she loved him so much. He had saved them!

Wheaties helped her up and she grabbed him around the waist. Then she kissed him again. Wheaties didn't do anything, just let her, and they gazed into each other's eyes.

"Didn't I tell you I would protect you?" Wheaties said, looking at her with affection.

Sephie let him go and walked to the door, trying to act nonchalant. "I know. Just like I protected you."

Wheaties grinned as Sephie pulled the door open. It gave way slowly with a loud groan. They gazed out at the world beyond. They were now on the other side of the wall! They were in Nork!

They stepped outside onto the street and looked around. The buildings close to the wall had all been knocked down. The door they emerged from was in a small, concrete building, the only one still standing. After a few city blocks, they could the small buildings where the city began again and beyond them in the near distance, tall skyscrapers.

Sephie turned around and gazed at the giant wall that surrounded the city. It looked high and scary. They were in the city now!

Wheaties looked at Sephie. "Now what do we do?"

Sephie shrugged. She didn't have a clue.

King Ferdinand made one of his soldiers get on his hands and knees and King Ferdinand sat on his back for a chair. Then he smiled at the Gant. The Gant stood still arms at its sides, gazing up at King Ferdinand and his men with a placid expression, like a cow-beastie.

"What is your name, mighty Gant?" King Ferdinand asked.

"NAME?" The Gant repeated stupidly in a thunderous voice which echoed off the wall and seemed to make the trees shake.

"What do they call you?" King Ferdinand said, grinning humorously. "When they want you to come?"

The Gant blinked for a second, trying to think, then it said, "GEE."

"Gee," King Ferdinand said, laughing. His men, even the one being used as a bench, laughed. "Gee, I do have eats for you. We are your friends. But we need your help!"

Gee blinked again, trying to grasp what King Ferdinand was saying. "HELP?"

"Help. You know what it means to help, don't you?"

Gee scowled and said, "NOT DUMB."

"I know you're not," King Ferdinand said. "You are the smartest Gant on Statn I-land. That's why I'm glad you were the one to come help me."

Gee shifted on his feet, feeling uncomfortable. He frowned and scratched one leg with the other foot. Then he stuck a finger up his nose and rooted around. "HELP?"

"I have a spider problem." King Ferdinand turned his head and pointed at the skyscrapers in Nork, then looked back at Gee.

"PIDER?" The Gant asked in a loud, thunderous voice, patiently waiting for King Ferdinand to explain.

King Ferdinand rolled his eyes, irritated and not expecting the conversation to be so difficult. He pointed at Nork. "Do you see those tall buildings? That is where we live. But if you look closely, you'll see black things on the side of the buildings. Those are spiders. They are annoying, but nothing to be scared of. We can't go up in the buildings because of the spiders because we are too small. But you and the Gants are big and brave. We need you to be our friends. We need you to kill them for us!"

The soldiers all grinned, talking amongst themselves. The men holding the Lurker chains and poles jabbed the Lurkers with sticks to keep them from shuffling forward and attacking them. They were the only ones not smiling, for they were constantly in a fight to keep themselves from being grabbed and eaten.

Gee scratched his head. "KILL? PIDERS?"

King Ferdinand nodded vigorously. "Yes, kill piders—I mean, spiders. Just go over there." King Ferdinand pointed to the skyscrapers. "Kill the spiders, and then you will get wonderful, yummy people to eat!"

Gee looked upset. He turned around, cupped his hand to his mouth and shouted. The sound shook the wall and echoed off the trees.

"PO! HA! MUK! PO! HA! MUK!"

The soldiers looked nervous and afraid. They pointed at the forest, for it was obvious Gee was calling more Gants to come. Only King Ferdinand didn't seem worried. The face of the man he sat on twisted in a grimace of pain, for his back was beginning to bow and ache.

Once again, the trees shook, but this time in three different places. The soldiers stepped back and almost fell over the back side of the wall. Even the man who King Ferdinand sat on forgot the ache in his back in his interest to see who came.

From behind the trees they came, all tall as the trees. From the left one man came, wearing a simple yellow cotton shirt and ragged pants cut off at the knees. His hair was brown and plastered to his round head. From behind Gee a giant woman came. Her hair was brown too and went down to her shoulders. She had a big nose and a long face and was very homely and plain. She wore a brown dress made out of rough potato sacks, with words written on the sacks all over her. The third one came from the right. He was older with gray hair. His giant face was full of wrinkles, and his dark eyes looked like raisins poking out of old dough. He wore a multicolored shirt and pants, made up of many smaller garments sewn together in a mishmash of colors.

The three new Gants stomped up, each step making the ground shake. They gathered around Gee and looked at King Ferdinand and his men with bored curiosity.

"WHAT DO THESE TINY PEOPLE WANT?" the old man, who was Muk, said. He seemed to be a little more intelligent than Gee, and able to make full sentences.

Gee turned to look at Muk. "ME KILL PIDERS."

King Ferdinand, seeing that this Gant seemed to

have a little bit more on the ball than his companion, hastily explained things again.

"I see you are the leader. Hello, I am King Ferdinand, king of Nork. You are our friends. We need your help. In return, we will give you lots and lots of yummy people to eat. We need you simply to kill the annoying spiders on our buildings. An easy task, for a great reward."

Po, Ha, Muk and Gee gathered together and argued with each other. Muk raised a giant hand and they stopped.

Muk turned to look at King Ferdinand. He frowned, and his face wrinkled up even more. "YOU TALK TOO MUCH. I NOT TRUST. WHY WE LEAVE OUR HOME AND KILL SPIDERS FOR YOU? WHAT HAVE TINY MEN EVER DONE FOR GANTS?"

"We've fed you, often," King Ferdinand said, sounded as if he was the wounded party. "We bring you food, all the time," King Ferdinand added. "Lots of tiny men and women to eat. And we've never asked for anything in return. Surely, one small request of our friends. And…"

King Ferdinand turned and pointed at his men. "We will give you many, many more men and women to eat, as many as you want!"

King Ferdinand turned to two of his soldiers. He pointed at another soldier. "Throw that man over the wall."

The face of the man about to be sacrificed filled with terror and his eyes opened wide. As he screamed, two of the other soldiers grabbed him, one around the waist and the other around the legs. Then they threw him over the wall.

The man fell screaming, but he didn't hit the soft dirt below, for before he could reach it, Gee grabbed him from midair. As the man continued to scream, Gee popped the man in his mouth and chewed with relish. The sound of the man's bones snapping and breaking took over as the man's screams suddenly stopped. Gee chewed the man happily, enjoying the little snack. The others watched Gee with hungry envy. Gee rubbed his belly and burped, the sound echoing off the trees, and the smell of it making the king and his soldiers wince.

Muk turned back to King Ferdinand.

"TASTY MEN GOOD, BUT GANT NEVER LEAVE HOME. WE FIND OWN FOOD."

King Ferdinand shook his head with mild disappointment. "I had a feeling you might say that. And so, I another way to persuade you, one I hoped I wouldn't have to use."

King Ferdinand motioned to one of the men holding the Lurkers to bring the creature forward.

"You see these tiny men?"

The Gants peered at the Lurker, who snarled and moaned and looked rotten and horrible.

"These tiny men are dead. But they still move about," King Ferdinand said dramatically. "Do you want to know why? You remember the mushroom monsters from long, long ago which filled the sky? The mushroom monsters gave these men a horrible disease which killed them and made them walking dead men. But the worst part of it is, if they bite you, you will die and become just like them!"

The Gants stared at the Lurker with wide eyes full of fear. King Ferdinand smiled, for he saw the Gants were taking it in, believing every word he said.

"If you do not help us, I will let these monsters free in your forest. Then one night while you're sleeping, they will sneak up and bite you, and you will become the walking dead!"

The Gants' faces filled with fear. They backed a step away and huddled together.

Gee said, "NO!"

Ha said, "UNDEAD!"

Po yelled, "YOU BAD TINY MAN!"

King Ferdinand, seeing his point had been made, motioned for the man with the Lurker take him back to join the others.

"I don't want to do this. But we need your help with the spiders. If you help us, we will never let the monsters into your forest, and we will feed you lots and lots of yummy people to eat! The choice is up to you."

The Gants turned and argued with each other. Then Muk turned to King Ferdinand.

"WE HELP, NO DEAD MEN? LOTS MEN TO EAT?"

"I give you my solemn promise!" King Ferdinand said. "All the men you can ever want, enough to fill your giant, fat bellies."

The Gants talked again. Then the others pointed at Gee, and he looked scared. He raised his voice even louder and stomped his foot, making the ground shake, but Ha and Muk talked back to him in stern tones. Finally Gee, looking glum, dropped his chin in defeat.

Muk turned to King Ferdinand. "GEE GO. HE KILL SPIDERS. YOU TAKE DEAD MEN AWAY. BRING US MEN TO EAT!"

King Ferdinand grinned in triumph. "It is a deal, my giant, slow-witted friend."

Johnthebaptist led the fourth group of men and women across the street to the building. Tense and on edge, he was slightly encouraged by the fact it seemed the people of Nork had begun to ignore them. The people they passed now seemed to simply watch them with dull eyes, standing still, with little interest.

Johnthebaptist was with two men and three women. He had told them not to look in either direction, but to continue staring straight ahead. They did as he said, but he could tell because of the tension and fear racing through them, they didn't look normal. He was pleasantly surprised the Norkers didn't seem to notice anything.

Johnthebaptist reached the broken glass wall of the building. As the men and women walked over the broken steel frame, Johnthebaptist turned one more time and studied the crowd. Then he saw the little scrabbler girl. She stood watching him intently, standing still, her eyes fastened on him. And she looked hungry. Her eyes held the look of a beastie, and her mouth was held in a hard, firm line. Their eyes met, and Johnthebaptist felt a chill run down his spine. She was thinking of how tasty he looked. And then Johnthebaptist knew there was something very wrong.

He looked around at the other people wandering the streets, and he saw what he didn't before. They walked, but their eyes glanced at him and then looked away. They knew perfectly well he wasn't one of them, and they were planning on having them all for dinner. They were just waiting, until all their prey was in the trap.

Johnthebaptist turned and hurried to the men and women with him.

"Go to the door down the hallway. Tell them the secret password. Then tell them to be ready. We're going to have to move fast."

The men and women nodded and hurried down the hallway. Johnthebaptist turned and walked quickly back across the street. He had to get the rest of the people of Pelpia inside the new building, before the people of Nork attacked. They were trapped in the subway, and their only hope was to go up inside the new building until they could come up with a plan.

The people of Nork watched him nonchalantly as he walked back across the street. He reached the subway entrance and hurried inside.

Restaria met him. She saw the look of concern on his face and frowned. "What is it?"

Johnthebaptist spoke to her in grave tones. "We have to move everyone right now."

The remaining members of Letfreedomring gathered around them with worried looks.

"Won't that draw suspicion?" Restaria asked.

Johnthebaptist glanced at the people then turned back to Restaria. In a low voice, hopefully so only she could hear he said, "It doesn't matter anymore. The people of Nork are waiting for us to all be inside the building. Then they think they'll have us surrounded."

Restaria's eyes opened wide with alarm. "They will! Maybe was should stay here, go back down, and…"

Johnthebaptist smiled grimly, and Restaria understood.

"We have no choice. We can't go back down inside that subway, and some of our people are already over there." Johnthebaptist said. Restaria nodded grimly.

"We'll just have to defend ourselves there and hope Johnny and his friends can come help us, before it's too late."

Johnthebaptist walked to the door and glanced out, then he looked back at Restaria and the people.

"We have to all get safely inside the new building. It is the one to the right across the street with the broken glass. Once you get inside, lead them to the right down the hall to a door there. The password is "Letfreedomring." Get them all inside. Then we'll climb as high as we can, and set up a defense. I just hope we can get all of us over there before they attack."

Restaria nodded. She turned to the remaining people. "Listen, please. We're out of time. I need you all to follow Johnthebaptist and me. We are going to all go as a group to the new building. Everyone stay close, and move as fast as you can."

The people murmured with fear, their faces showing fright.

Johnthebaptist turned to Restaria. "You lead; I'll take up the rear. That way, if they attack, I can fight them off. Hopefully."

Restaria nodded. She motioned with her hand to the crowd. "Let's go!"

Restaria walked to the door and flung it open. The people, talking loudly and in frightened voices, crowded up to follow her.

"Don't panic!" Johnthebaptist said, but nobody listened.

Then they were all outside. There were over one hundred fifty of them, a whole crowd huddled together. There was no way they wouldn't be noticed, but it was too late anyway. Restaria turned and saw the building. She blinked from the sudden light of the red eye and shaded her eyes with her hand. She looked around and saw the people of Nork. They were not too close, most at least twenty feet away.

Restaria turned and motioned and started moving, as fast as she could. There was no point in trying to be quiet now, there only hope was to get to the building as fast as they could.

The people of Pelpia ran after her. Some women

picked up their scrabblers and held them tightly as they ran. Others ran so fast they passed Restaria.

The people of Nork saw what was happening. Yells and shouts of anger filled the air. Restaria felt her heart in her throat as she ran. They made it to the street and crossed as fast as they could. The people of Nork reacted. They forgot trying to appear casual and ran towards the group.

A woman in the group from Pelpia screamed in terror as she watched the Norkers run towards them. They all made it across the street, but then the people of Nork were on them!

Johnthebaptist appeared. With a sword in his hand, he swung at the nearest Norker. The man backed away, snarling like a beastie. Johnthebaptist saw the little girl. She stood five feet away, her lips curled back in a snarl, her yellow teeth showing. She held up her hands in claws and walked towards him.

People from Nork closed in on both sides. The people of Letfreedomring reached the building and poured down the hallway, filling it quickly. Restaria stopped at the metal frame and helped get people inside. Johnthebaptist ran and swung his sword at the people of Nork on one side and then the other, forcing them back. They snarled at him like a pack of wolf-beasties, circling, looking for an opening.

The crowd of Norkers grew. Johnthebaptist saw people coming from every direction. There was no way they could fight them all off.

The last of the people of Pelpia made it inside

the building, but now the whole area in front was full of Norkers.

"Johnthebaptist!" Restaria yelled from the building.

"Go!" Johnthebaptist yelled. "Get them inside!"

Restaria didn't hesitate. She ran inside to lead the people to the door.

Johnthebaptist stood at the entrance to the building just inside the metal frame. In front of him a huge crowd of Norkers pressed in, their eyes full of hunger and ferocity.

"Stay back, you monsters, or I'll cut you to ribbons!" Johnthebaptist yelled, but his eyes showed resignation. He knew he was going to die, but he would do it to save his people.

The people of Nork rushed him. Johnthebaptist sliced and downed one, two, three, but then they were all on him. He disappeared under a mass of snarling Norkers.

Inside the building, Restaria they got the door open and the people crowded up the stairway. It was agonizingly slow, for they all crowded and pushed, but slowly, ever so slowly, they made it up the stairs. Restaria ran back to look outside. The crowd was busy tearing Johnthebaptist apart, buying them precious time. Restaria's face filled with sorrow, and tears fell from her eyes. She reluctantly turned and pushed the last people towards the door. When they were finally inside, she shut the door. The bolt slid in place with a loud click.

CHAPTER 25

Sephie and Wheaties, without a word, took each other's hand and walked out into the city. There didn't seem to be any people around, so they didn't worry about being seen. The whole area seemed totally deserted.

Wheaties looked serious. "We may not find our people for a long time. We had better find some food and water, and then look for a place to sleep for the night."

Sephie nodded. She liked the way Wheaties was taking charge and coming up with a plan, just like Johnny would have. "Let's go towards where the buildings start. Maybe we can find some food there."

"Let's hurry," Wheaties said. "I don't see anyone, but somebody may be watching us."

They ran, staying on the street between where the buildings had been. They ran fast, but as they did, Sephie looked back at the doorway they had just left. She felt a pang of regret leaving it. It was the only real connection they had with their tribe, even if it was a scary and dark place full of Lurkers. Leaving it made her feel like they were leaving any chance of finding their family and friends again.

After what seemed like forever, they finally made it to the buildings. They ran inside the first one and hid in the doorway, panting. Sephie looked around the inside. The building was two stories and full of old rotten clothing, dirty and ripped. The place smelled of mold and decay.

Both Sephie and Wheaties looked unhappy. Wheaties gazed outside and down the street. It looked deserted. He began to relax, for it seemed like none of the people of Nork came this far down the city.

Wheaties took Sephie's hand again, and they walked outside again. This time they walked more leisurely down the street, looking at each building for one which seemed to hold some promise of food or water.

They walked a block, and then two. Then they saw someone! A lone man in ragged clothes. He was short but his face and body was dirty and he had wild, gray hair. He looked scary.

"Inside, quick!" Wheaties said. They darted into the closest building and peered outside.

"That was close," Sephie said. "We'd better be more careful now."

Then they heard something else. A woman's voice! She cried out weakly, seeming to be in pain. It was a soft, melodic voice, and sounded like someone in trouble.

"Who's that?" Sephie asked.

"I don't know, but it's none of our business!"

Sephie looked at Wheaties. "She sounds like she's in pain!"

"Somebody's probably attacking her and eating her!" Wheaties said. "We can't do anything to help her."

The cry came again, a sad, pitiful sound. "Help me, please! Somebody!"

The cry sent an arrow of sadness and fear shooting through Sephie's heart.

"We can't just leave without finding out who it is," Sephie said. Johnny would find out, she thought. He'd never leave somebody who needed help.

"It's probably a trap!" Wheaties said, frowning at her. "To get wary travelers to investigate, and then kill them!"

Sephie looked annoyed. "Why would they expect travelers here? They would have no way of knowing we were coming. I want to take a peek and see who it is. We can be careful and make sure they don't see us."

Wheaties said, "All right. But we may end up wishing we hadn't."

Sephie smiled at winning the argument. Together they crept to the door and listened for the cry again. It came, but weaker! It was from a building across the street.

"What about that man?" Wheaties said.

"Keep an eye out for him. If we see him,

we'll run!"

Reluctantly, Wheaties followed Sephie as she crouched and ran as fast as she could towards the other building. They ran inside and stopped by the wall, making sure no one saw them.

The cry came again, louder. It was clear whomever it was crying out was in a lot of pain. It came from the room past a doorway inside.

Sephie and Wheaties glanced at each other and tiptoed towards the door. Wheaties picked up a piece of concrete and held it as a weapon.

They entered the next doorway, and gazed around. Then they saw the source of the cries and stared, mouths open in amazement. It was a girl with golden hair, but she had wings! She lay on a metal bed frame but was pinned under a huge rock, and it looked as if she was hurt. Her side was bloody, and it looked like she had a bullet wound.

As they came in, the girl saw them. Her eyes showed hope. "Please!" she said weakly. "Please help me get free! If you help me, I'll see you have a great reward from my people!"

Sephie said, "You're not from this city?"

The girl looked at them curiously and smiled despite her discomfort. "You aren't from here either, are you? Are you friends of Johnny Apocalypse?"

At the mention of Johnny's name, both Sephie and Wheaties grinned with joy and happiness. She knew Johnny! She must be a friend!

They ran over to the girl.

"Hurry, please free me. There is an evil man who trapped me here. He might be back any minute!"

"If you're a friend of Johnny, of course we'll help you!" Wheaties said. Sephie and Wheaties looked around for a way to move the rock.

"May I please get something dry to wear, at least?" Lord Flaggalon asked in a whiny voice. He stood shivering in front of Monsta in his soaking wet robe. Monsta stared at him with deadly eyes and held his jagged piece of steel a few inches from Lord Flaggalon's throat, making it very clear he would have no qualms at all about stabbing Lord Flaggalon to death with it.

Monsta glanced around, anxious to get going before more angels showed up. Then he snarled, "Get moving, before cut your eyes out."

Lord Flaggalon shook with fear, knowing full well the tall, muscle-bound man with the black beard and scars wouldn't hesitate to do exactly what he said he'd do. He regretted having a building all to himself now, for there was no one around to call to or to help him.

As Lord Flaggalon walked across the room dripping water, Monsta followed closely behind, the jagged steel poking Lord Flaggalon in the back.

"Ow!" Lord Flaggalon yelled. Monsta only laughed and poked Lord Flaggalon again, liking the reaction he was getting from the weak, cowardly man. It was great entertainment.

Lord Flaggalon finally was able to think clearly, though his heart beat so hard it was painful and he felt as if he might pass out at any moment. Lead the evil man back to the main building, tell him it was the only way to get to Pantina. Then he could get help.

"We have to go across the web pathway," Lord Flaggalon said, "back to the building there." Lord Flaggalon pointed. "It's the only way to Pantina."

"I know where Pantina is," Monsta said. "Don't try any tricks. If I so much as see one other angel, you're dead, do you understand me?"

"How can we get there without seeing anyone?" Lord Flaggalon said. They reached the hallway and Lord Flaggalon led them to the web bridge to the next building.

"You'd better find a way," Monsta said. They reached the opening in the building.

"Stop." Monsta said, and Lord Flaggalon complied. "That there," Monsta pointed. "That's where Pantina's throne is, right?"

Lord Flaggalon nodded. "Yes, but as you can see, there's no way to get there. There are no web bridges which can reach it. The only way is to fly there. What you want is impossible."

Monsta grabbed Lord Flaggalon's robe and pulled him close. Lord Flaggalon gasped. Monsta stared coldly at Lord Flaggalon's face. "Find me the nearest building near your goddess, one that is empty. Then you'll call Pantina there. If you don't want me to throw you out of one of these buildings."

Lord Flaggalon nodded glumly. This evil man had thought of everything and any mistake on Lord Flaggalon's part meant his certain death. Lord Flaggalon didn't see any way he was going to survive much longer, unless he was very, very lucky. His only hope was to sacrifice Pantina in exchange for his own life. Maybe if he helped Monsta, the horrible man would let him go. His life depended on getting Pantina to Monsta, without her having a clue what was going to happen. He began to think up a plan, knowing it had to be a good one, if he wanted to live.

Johnny and his group finished gathering supplies and remaking the torches. They didn't find any sign of Sephie and Wheaties anywhere. Reluctantly they entered the dark tunnel again and continued their journey. Their torches were brighter now, the tunnel lit up well. They could see it was a long straight square tunnel with nothing inside except old lettering on the wall.

"I don't think we're going to find our scrabblers," Baskinrobbins said sadly. "I doubt they came this far."

Johnny looked at him and nodded. "The good news is, we haven't seen a lot of Lurkers. I think they must have all exited into the main tunnel. I'm sure there's more in the subways of Nork, but hopefully we stopped them escaping at least."

As if on signal at Johnny's words, they heard moaning from the tunnel behind them. They all turned, lifted their torches and looked behind them. There in the darkness, one, rotted corpse walked towards them.

"I'll get this one!" Tendanza, the winged member of the Sky said with confidence. As the others watched, Tendanza ran towards the Lurker. As the other watched with grim smiles, Tendanza quickly cut off the Lurker's head with his sword in a swift and efficient manner. The head of the Lurker fell to the ground and rolled around, staring at them. The body wandered about for a few seconds then fell on the ground and writhed around.

"So, there were more Lurkers!" Microsoft said worriedly.

"I think he was the only one," Mantayo said. "We didn't see any more in the tunnel."

Johnny turned to Microsoft and Baskinrobbins. "I think the best thing for us to do is to get into Nork, open the gate and let people of USA in, and then we can make new plans. With any luck, when they meet up with us again, Sephie and Wheaties will have rejoined them."

Microsoft nodded. "I don't see much choice. I just hope-well, you know what I hope."

Johnny put a hand on Microsoft's shoulder in sympathy. Then he looked at the others and headed back up the tunnel towards Nork. The rest followed, each feeling Microsoft and Baskinrobbin's pain.

They didn't encounter any more Lurkers as they

went. But suddenly up ahead, they saw light!

"Look! Johnny!" Mantayo said. "An open door! I wonder if we're inside the gate now!"

They all began to run and soon reached the door. As they reached the door, they saw two boards on the ground. They looked like they had been torn off the door.

"Look, Johnny," Mantayo said. "It looks like someone has been here and opened this door."

"Maybe it was Sephie and Wheaties!" Microsoft said, his voice full of hope and excitement.

Johnny smiled and nodded. "Maybe, but I wouldn't get your hopes up. It could have been Lurkers too, or anyone. We should be careful looking out, for if it wasn't Sepie and Wheaties, it could be anyone outside, waiting for us."

The others nodded gravely. As they waited, Johnny peeked outside. In front of the door, three small steps led up to it. The door was open and creaked in the wind. Johnny slowly crept up the steps and peered out.

What he saw was nothing but rubble around him. And then he saw the wall! It was behind them. They were on the other side!

"We're inside Nork!" Johnny said with happiness. The others smiled at each other. Johnny looked around, but didn't see anyone. Then he looked at the gate. He saw two lone soldiers at the very top, gazing away at the wasteland outside Nork.

Johnny turned back to the others. "There are only two guards at the gate. We should be able to take them easily!"

"We'll have to do it quietly," Mantayo said. "Then get your people in quickly and hide them. Someone will surely come to check on the guards."

"Let's do it!" Johnny said, walking out of the door. The others walked out as well. Then Tendaza of the Sky worked on closing and resealing the door.

Together they hurried through the rubble, keeping low and watching the guards. Soon Johnny's tribe would be inside Nork. Then the real fight would begin.

Deb and Ticktock ran as fast as they could. The crowd of Norkers chasing them began to grow, the shouts and excitement of those in pursuit causing others to join the chase.

As they ran down the street, Deb's only thought was how they were getting further and further away from the basket and her chance to get back to safety. They didn't have any choice, however, for they had no time to stop. The crowd was only a half a block behind them.

They passed by old broken-down buildings and rusted cars. Deb grew winded and afraid she'd have to stop soon.

"What are we going to do?" Deb said breathlessly.

"If we can just get ahead of them long enough to be out of sight, we can duck into a building," Ticktock said.

"I'm not going to make it!" Deb panted, panic making her heart beat fast.

Ticktock stopped and grabbed her. He threw her over his shoulder. Then he ran as fast as he could. Deb's upper body faced the Nork people chasing them. She could see the looks of hunger on the faces, and it sent a chill up her spine. They had to get away. The thought of what the people would do if they caught them filled Deb's mind with horrible images.

Ticktock ran around a corner. He was fast, now that he didn't have to slow down for Deb, and he covered half a block in a few seconds. Then he darted into an old building and ran behind a counter in the front. He set Deb down and scrunched down himself. Then he waited.

They heard the crowd before they saw them, the excited voices yelling with eager anticipation. Deb got up and joined Ticktock peering over the counter, just their eyes visible.

The crowd rushed around the corner of the street, looking for Deb and Ticktock everywhere. Deb could see the anger and disappointment in the eyes when they could see them.

"If they spot us, we got to take off, fast," Ticktock said quietly.

"I thought you said they obeyed you," Deb replied.

"If I had more soldiers with me, they would have." Ticktock kept his eyes on the crowd as he spoke. "But the king ain't gave them food in a while. They're all starvin' and ready to act waksy."

Deb was about to reply, when she saw something that made shocked her to her core and made her mouth drop open in surprise. There across the street, half a block away from the roving crowd, she swore she saw Sephie! With Sephie was a brown boy. Deb remembered his name was Wheaties. And with them was a girl, a member of the Sky. The girl looked hurt, holding her side. The three came out of a door and stood on the sidewalk, looking around.

"Ticktock!" Deb pointed. "Those are scrabblers from our tribe! And there's a member of the Sky with them! If the crowd sees her…"

"Ain't nothing we can do," Ticktock said, shaking his head. "If we go out there, they'll see us."

Deb worked her way around the counter, staying low. Ticktock looked at her with alarm.

"You ain't goin' out there, are you?"

"I have to. I can't let those people get them."

Ticktock looked resigned. "Then I guess I got to help you. I'll create a distraction; you go get your friends."

Deb said, "Thank you, Ticktock. I won't forget this."

"Listen, we gonna get split up. You get your friends and hide somewhere while I lead the people away."

"I will," Deb said. "Listen! We'll try to hide near where Patto is going to lower the basket," Deb pointed to the building where she'd been lowered down. "When you get away, join us there, as soon as you can!"

"Okay," Ticktock said.

Deb smiled gratefully at Ticktock. They both moved to the door.

"When I take off yelling, you go get your friends. Then high-tail it to your hiding place."

Deb nodded. At an unspoken signal, they both darted out the door. Ticktock took off to the left, yelling. Deb ran as fast as she could across the street, her heart pounding in her ears. She had to get Sephie and Wheaties before they were discovered.

CHAPTER 26

Sephie and Wheaties had managed to move the rock and help the girl from Sky, whose name was Dallanda, to stand. Wheaties had impressed Sephie by finding a big, long beam and pressing it under the rock. Then he put a chair under the beam and pried the rock up. It rolled off as Sephie looked on in surprise and admiration. Wheaties smiled at her and shrugged. "It was something my father taught me. He like to teach me lots of cool tricks."

They helped Dallanda bind her wound as best as they could with old rags. Now all three stood peeking out the door at the city.

"If we can find a way to contact my people, I'll take you with me to Sky," Dallanda said. "You will like it there. We are nice people, and we'll reward you well for helping me."

"Just give us something to eat," Wheaties said.

"And help us find Johnny," Sephie added.

"We'll do both," Dallanda said. "If we can only

find a way to let my people know we're here."

With alarm they all saw a huge crowd of Norkers in the street. The Norkers looked agitated. They yelled and carried weapons. Quickly the three moved back inside.

"There's a lot of people here now," Wheaties said. "And they look really scary!"

"Let's get away from here, before they spot us!" Sephie said.

But just as they turned to retreat back inside, Sephie saw something that filled her with joyful surprise. Her face lit up with happiness. She grabbed Wheaties' arm and pointed out at the street.

"Look!" she said, joy filling her voice. "It's Deb!"

"It can't be!" Wheaties said, but then he looked and his face filled with happiness and relief too.

"How did she find us?" Wheaties said with a bright smile.

"She hasn't!" Sephie said. "We have to let her know we're here!"

Dallanda recognized Deb as well. "It's Johnny's mate! Maybe Johnny is nearby as well!"

That thought made Sephie and Wheaties giddy with hope. They kept just far enough to be hidden from the crowd but still, hopefully, signal to Deb. But they didn't have to! In excitement, they saw Deb smiling at them.

"She sees us!" Sephie yelled, her voice thick with emotion.

As the weary travelers watched with joy, Deb ran

to the building and ran inside. Sephie ran over to her and gave her a big hug, sobbing with relief, and Deb hugged her back. Then she smiled at Wheaties, who was trying to look unemotional, but failing. Deb hugged him too. Sephie's throat grew tight and tears of joyful relief dripped from the corners of her eyes. They weren't alone anymore!

Deb looked at them. "What are you two doing here? Are you here with our tribe?"

Sephie shook her head. "No, we did something foolish. We went exploring at night, and monsters attacked us. We had to run away. We were following Johnny through a tunnel, but we lost him!"

"Then we came into the city looking for food, and found her," Wheaties said, pointing at Dallanda.

Deb put on a mock reproving look. "You did do something foolish." Then she smiled at them and hugged them again. "But now you're safe, with me." Deb turned to Dallanda. "You look hurt."

Dallanda smiled at her. "I am, but thanks to these children, I think I'm going to be all right. But we have to find a way to get back to our home!"

Deb said, "I have a way. I was supposed to be out gathering supplies. Patto, one of your people, is going to lower a basket to pick me back up. We have to get to the spot fast, before she thinks I'm not coming back!"

"What about that crowd?" Dallanda said, peering out at the street. It seemed less crowded now, only a few Norkers milling about.

"A man named Ticktock is leading them away," Deb said. "He's going to join us at the basket after he's able to escape. Hurry, we don't have much time!"

They all crept to the door, and then at a signal from Deb, they snuck out and ran across the street, keeping an eye on the crowd. Deb led them to another building and then another. It seemed to take forever, but finally they made it back to the spot where the basket would be lowered. They found a place nearby in a doorway to hide and waited.

It seemed as if they waited forever. Deb began to worry Patto had already given up on her and the basket wasn't going to come down. As they watched, two of the other girls, Borsa, and Rellat appeared from two different directions, carrying things in their bags. Panic instantly jumped into Deb's mind, for she had forgotten about them. There wouldn't be room for the girls and all of them.

"I know those girls," Dallanda said.

And just then, Ticktock crept around the corner. Deb waved to him, and he joined her. He smiled at her and glanced at Sephie, Wheaties and Dallanda.

"Who is this?" Dallanda asked, pointing at him and looking suspicious.

"He's a friend," Deb said. "He's going to help Johnny and your people contact the Brethren, who live in Booklin. Hopefully, they will be willing to join us in our fight."

"Is he coming in the basket with us?" Dallanda said. "Lord Flaggalon sure isn't going to approve."

Just then, Deb saw the basket high in the air. It was coming down!"

"Hurry!" Deb said. "We have to get to the basket before those girls do!"

They all took off running towards the spot where the basket would drop. The other girls saw them. They recognized Deb and Dallanda, but not the others.

"Who are they?" Borsa said as Deb and her group reached her. "You were supposed to be getting supplies, not strangers!"

Deb knew she might have to get tough with the girls from Sky. She glared at them and tensed up, ready for a fight.

"This girl is one of your own, and she's wounded. And these are my friends. They all have to be lifted up to your home too."

"Well, they're not going before we do!" Borsa said, scowling.

"What happened to Lenna?"

"She was eaten," Borsa said. "Just like you will be, because we're going up in that basket."

"We're all going up," Deb said, frowning. "Dallanda is hurt. And I'm not leaving Sephie and Wheaties here any longer than I have to, so we're all just going to have to fit."

Borsa stepped forward in a threatening manner. "And just how do you think you're going to make that happen?"

Ticktock stepped in front of Deb. Rellat's eyes opened wide with fear and she stepped back. "Guess how." Rellat and Borsa looked frightened and dismayed.

"Well, what's going to happen to us? We can't all fit," Rellat asked.

"Don't worry," Deb said. "As soon as we get up there safe, I'll send the basket down for you."

"What if Patto won't let you?" Borsa said.

Deb smiled, and they all chuckled, understanding. Borsa pointed at Ticktock. "He'll make sure she does."

Deb nodded. The basket arrived. Deb, Dallanda, Sephie, Wheaties and Ticktock climbed inside. The basket rose on its way up to the home of the Sky, as Rellat and Borsa found a place to hide, and wait.

Monsta and Lord Flaggalon reached the opening in the building they were in which faced Pantina's throne. Lord Flaggalon's heart beat hard with fear. They hadn't passed any of the Sky on their trip, other than some scrabblers playing in one of the hallways a few buildings back. They stopped playing when they saw Lord Flaggalon and watched him, knowing he was the leader, and also that he was generally unpleasant. Lord Flaggalon realized they were afraid he would scold them or frown at him and scare them. If they only knew the man with Lord Flaggalon was the real person to be afraid of. He didn't dare even look at them as they passed, though they stared at Monsta with curiosity. Lord

Flaggalon knew one false move might mean Monsta would kill the scrabblers, or himself. For a moment, Lord Flaggalon wondered if he could find a way to get Monsta interested in the children long enough for him to escape, but he dismissed the idea as only wishful thinking.

As they stood now at the opening in the wall, just the two of them, a breeze blew, cooling Lord Flaggalon's face. It didn't ease the lines of worry etched there, or the fear radiating from his eyes. Monsta, on the other hand, wore a huge, evil grin. Monsta was edgy though, nervous, glancing around for anyone who might raise the alarm.

"Call her. Tell her you have urgent news to discuss with her, and tell her to fly over here. Do it now!"

"That's not how it works!" Lord Flaggalon wailed. "We fly over there and kneel before her throne. She will not come, for she never leaves her holy place."

Monsta pushed the jagged steel against Lord Flaggalon's neck harder, causing a drip of blood to ooze down Lord Flaggalon's neck.

"She'd better this time, or you're going to learn what pain is like. You'll be screaming. I'll torture you for hours, and then cut off your head and throw it over this ledge." Monsta's words dripped with venom, and Lord Flaggalon knew he meant every word.

Monsta hid around the corner his jagged steel pointed at Lord Flaggalon. "Call her! And make it convincing."

"Pantina!" Lord Flaggalon yelled in a wavery, melancholy voice. "Pantina! Are you there?"

Nothing happened. Lord Flaggalon glanced at Monsta, who looked angry.

Lord Flaggalon called again, louder. *"Pantina! Help us!"* Finally, with relief, he saw Pantina appear from behind the curtains of her throne room.

Monsta gazed for the first time at Pantina. A beautiful woman with long, kinky red hair and huge golden wings. Monsta could understand why they thought she was a goddess. For a moment, he wondered if she really was one, and if she could strike him dead. Then he laughed at himself. Still, it seemed a pity he had to kill such a beautiful girl. Monsta for a moment dreamt of having the goddess as his mate, a fitting queen for him when he was a king. He had no illusions about her, though, knowing she would surely not love a tough, scarred, ugly man as himself. No, he was there to end her life, so he could gain the king of Nork's favor. And bring her head back as proof. Still, it was a shame.

"Is that you, Lady Stabs?" Pantina asked.

At the mention of Lady Stabs' name, Monsta's ears perked up. So, Lady Stabs was here somewhere! Surely pretending to be a friend of the angels so she could do something crooked later, like stealing or helping Monsta conquer them. Smart girl!

Lord Flaggalon was interested to hear Pantina mention Lady Stabs as well. What had that stranger been up to? It was too late for Lord Flaggalon to do anything about it at the moment, but he vowed if he survived, he would investigate.

"It's me, Pantina, Lord Flaggalon! There is a

crisis! The Sky need your help!" Lord Flaggalon looked over at Monsta unhappily. He hated the deception, and knew what Monsta planned to do, but he had no choice if he wanted to save his skin. "I can't get over there right now. Please fly over here so we can talk!"

Pantina walked to the edge of the opening in her building, and frowned with confusion. "But I'm never to leave my throne room, you have said. You said everyone is to come over here and worship me. You said my leaving will cause the people to lose faith."

"I know what I said," Lord Flaggalon replied grumpily. "But I am in charge of the people, and I need you over here today. No one else is here, it is only you and I." Lord Flaggalon glanced over at Monsta, who grinned evilly. Sadness and fear gripped Lord Flaggalon, and his face twisted into a picture of misery.

Lord Flaggalon glanced outside at the buildings around them, and in amazement, saw something bizarre. A giant man, bigger than the tallest tree, was hanging from the side of a building nearby. He held a long wooden spear. He was stabbing at the giant spiders!

Without realizing he said it out loud, Lord Flaggalon said, "Someone is killing the spiders!"

Pantina glanced out and saw what Lord Flaggalon had seen. A look of pure horror came to her face. She turned and began concentrating, her brow creasing with the effort.

"Get her over here!" Monsta whispered fiercely.

"Pantina, you must come over here to help the

spiders. I need you to fly over and join me!"

Pantina stopped concentrating and looked at Lord Flaggalon. "But I must help them! They will die if I don't tell them to flee!"

"Come over here!" Lord Flaggalon thundered, losing patience. "I must tell you where to send the spiders, so they will survive. Hurry!"

Reluctantly, Pantina flapped her golden wings and rose into the air. She flew out the opening. With grace and gentleness, she floated across the open void and landed next to Lord Flaggalon.

"Hurry!" Pantina said. "Tell me what to do to save them!"

Monsta stepped out of the shadows. Pantina saw him and frowned. "Who are you?"

Monsta smiled. "I thought you were a goddess. Don't you know everything?"

Pantina looked at Lord Flaggalon with a confusion, waiting for him to explain.

Lord Flaggalon's lip quivered and he looked terrified. "I'm sorry, Pantina. I will miss you."

Monsta raised his jagged steel and strode forward. "I don't need you anymore."

With a mighty shove on Lord Flaggalon's shoulder, Monsta pushed him out the opening. Lord Flaggalon screamed in terror as he fell to his death outside. Pantina screamed as well, her eyes open wide in horror. She backed up, turned around and flapped her wings to escape, but Monsta quickly grabbed her wrist in a painful iron grip.

Pantina screamed in pain and went limp, trying to get Monsta to stop. Monsta dragged her over to an old chair. Pantina flapped her wings like a trapped bird-beastie and kicked him, but he was too strong for her and just laughed. He forced her to sit, then put the jagged steel at her throat. As she glared at him in fright, he grabbed a dirty piece of rope he'd found and brought with him.

"Don't move, or I'll cut your throat," Monsta said. As Pantina sat unhappily, Monsta tied her to the chair. The he stood back, smiling with pleasure. It was going to work! He was going to get to enjoy killing her!

"It's too bad, what I have to do to you. You are very beautiful. I'd love to take you somewhere where you and I could get to know each other better. But no telling how much time I have, so I guess I'm just going to have to do what I came for."

"Who are you?" Pantina said, her voice strained with fear.

Monsta grinned with evil delight. "I'm Monsta. I came to worship you. But now that I see what a pathetic excuse of a goddess you are, I've changed my mind. Now I'm going to see how much pain a goddess can endure. Then when I grow bored, I will cut off your head and bring it to the king of Nork as a prize, so he can put it on his table for a trophy."

"Leave her alone, you sick, twisted piece of garbage."

Monsta looked to see who it was who spoke. There in the doorway stood Lady Stabs and the little boy

Monsta had met earlier.

Lady Stabs held a sword in her hand, pointed right at Monsta.

Monsta frowned, confused. So, she had joined the angels now! There was nothing Monsta hated more than traitors. He scowled in hatred and stomped towards Lady Stabs ready to kill her first.

King Ferdinand entered Nork again through the small gate with the remaining soldiers and the Lurkers. In the rubble near the wall, he saw the soldiers of his army milling about, bored. Alcapoon had left a small group of forty soldiers with him to guard the Lurkers. The rest had returned to their base at Sental Par, to await the King Ferdinand's return. There was nothing but rubble for a city block blocks until the buildings began again, and no food or water anywhere, but the men had brought meat and water in their own packs and munched on it. As King Ferdinand and his group entered, Alcapoon hurried towards him.

Suddenly everyone saw something and turned to watch with excitement. Gee the Gant climbed over the wall a few hundred feet away. As they all stared at him in amazement the Gant headed for the tall buildings in the distance, holding a giant wooden spear. The horrible black spiders, as if sensing he was coming for them, crawled around to the sides of the buildings where they couldn't be seen.

The soldiers shouted and pointed at the sight. King Ferdinand smiled. The Gant was actually going to do it! As they all watched with interest, Gee reached the first building. He scaled it easily. Then he moved out of sight. After a few minutes, they saw a giant spider fall from the building and land on the ground, its legs twitching. They all cheered and raised their fists. King Ferdinand felt a dark joy and a feeling of victory swell inside.

Soon King Ferdinand and the soldiers saw angels flying around the Gant like moth-beasties, trying to distract it and fight it, but the Gant just ignored them.

"He's really going to do it, Your Majesty!" one of the men who had been with him at the Gant wall said to King Ferdinand with amazement.

King Ferdinand smiled. "Of course he is. And when he's done, I'll have other tasks for his slow-witted people as well. And look at those angels trying to stop him." King Ferdinand laughed. "Watch this well, my friends. It is a sight you will want to remember forever."

King Ferdinand gazed around at the deserted rubble next to the wall, and then into the distance at the tall skyscrapers. It was a cool day, for the cold and wet time of the year was approaching. A mist surrounded the buildings, and the air was cold.

King Ferdinand ignored the approaching Alcapoon and headed back towards his royal coach. As he walked, he muttered to himself. "What a depressing place this is," King Ferdinand muttered to himself.

"These people are nothing but filthy animals. I deserve better people to lead; a kingdom of intelligent, sophisticated people, like me."

Alcapoon reached King Ferdinand before he could reach the comfort of his coach. "Your Majesty! I have some exciting news!"

King Ferdinand, though tired and wanting only to sit in his royal coach and make plans, couldn't help but be curious. He turned to Alcapoon to listen.

Alcapoon spoke in an excited voice, his eye lit up with excitement. "We have found the missing prisoners!" Alcapoon pointed to the buildings in the distance.

"They are a tall building with yellow skin, not far from Madson Skar Gardem, where they were imprisoned. The people have surrounded them! They are trapped like ratties!"

King Ferdinand smiled. "Good. But we have a problem, General Alcapoon."

Alcapoon frowned in confusion. "What is that, Your Majesty?"

King Ferdinand looked beyond Alcapoon at the city in the distance. "My Lurker army is still too small to fight them. We need an undead army that is formidable, and terrifying. We have only a few hundred now, and this is not enough to intimidate anyone! We need thousands!"

"Where are we going to get them, Your Majesty?" Alcapoon said. "And how would be control that many of the monsters?"

King Ferdinand put an arm around Alcapoon in a friendly way and led him over to the wagons full of Lurkers.

"Easy questions, easy solutions. Some of the rabble living in this city will be our source. They do nothing but complain, and there are too many of them. We can't possibly provide for all of them, genral. When some of them are Lurkers, we can control the rest of the people much more easily. Then we will create an elite class, one made up only the best people, to rule."

"But the people," Alcapoon said, frowning, rubbing his black hair with his hand. "They are just simple folk, trying to survive, and they trust us to take care of them."

"Nonsense," King Ferdinand said, taking his arm from around Alcapoon and walking back towards his coach with Alcapoon following. "They are greedy, self-centered fools, who do nothing but complain. I know, genral. I have been at the king's side for a long time, you know."

They reached the coach and King Ferdinand opened the door to get in. Alcapoon stopped and looked at King Ferdinand with concern.

"But how will you control them?"

The king stepped up into the coach, closed the door and looked out the window.

"With fire and soldiers with sharp sticks. We will lead them with sound, and light. They will go where I want them to go, and attack who I choose. And those loyal to me..." he looked at Alcapoon with meaning,

"...will rule the city by my side."

Alcapoon smiled, but then when King Ferdinand looked away, he frowned again.

King Ferdinand pointed to the city ahead. "I want you to take the rest of the soldiers and go back to Sental Par. Leave the Lurkers here and a small group of say twenty soldiers. Then be prepared when the Lurkers reach you to control them. I want you to build a new wall, just in front of the castle. Then be ready for my Lurker army to arrive. You will need to be ready to control them."

Alcapoon frowned this time and didn't try to hide it. His eyes showed he didn't agree with King Ferdinand's plans, and in fact he might find a way to secretly stop it. "What about the families of the soldiers? Are they to be turned into Lurkers too?"

King Ferdinand waved a hand impatiently. "If your families are on this side of the castle, tell the soldiers to take them with them, but don't tell anyone what is happening."

Alcapoon looked upset. He glanced at his soldiers, then at the wagons full of Lurkers. "Are you really going to set the Lurkers on our own people?"

King Ferdinand smiled. "Not all of them. Just enough. Now go, quickly! I want the fun to begin."

Alcapoon frowned and looked at the king with concern. He began to suspect the king was waksy, dangerously so. The king didn't care about the people he was king over, only seeing more death and destruction. Alcapoon knew there could only be one outcome from the king's plan, and that was total disaster. But he nodded and acted obedient. "I will do what you order, Your Majesty."

Alcapoon turned and hurried over to his soldiers. Soon he was barking orders in a loud voice, and the soldiers hurried to comply.

King Ferdinand watched Alcapoon and the soldiers march away towards the city. He grinned with an evil, twisted smile. Maybe he wouldn't be king of the city. Maybe he would simply watch it burn, and die, as the Lurkers killed everyone in it. They would kill the angels, and then the Bretheren, and then when they were finished, King Ferdinand would be the king of the undead.

The thought had almost as much appeal as being king. Why did the thought of seeing people die please him so much? He didn't know, all he knew was that thinking about it filled him with such dark excitement he almost couldn't wait to see it happen.

When the last of the soldiers of the army had walked away to where they were out of sight, King Ferdinand turned to the men watching the wagons and buses. There were twenty of them. They stood, awaiting his orders.

King Ferdinand climbed out again and walked up to the lead soldier.

"Open the wagons and the buses," King Ferdinand said in a level, emotionless voice.

"Which ones, Your Majesty?" the soldier asked.

"All of them," the king said, grinning with malice.

"We can't, Your Majesty!" the soldier wailed. "They will kill everyone!"

King Ferdinand walked over to another soldier. He took the man's tommy gun. Going back to the other soldier he shot him dead. The man fell to the ground, full of holes.

"Anyone else want to argue with me?" King Ferdinand yelled. The soldiers all moved to comply with his wishes. They opened the doors of the wagons and the buses, and then stood back watching in fear.

As King Ferdinand and the soldiers watched, the Lurkers, including the old king, Moxie and Clancy stumbled out of the wagons and gazed around.

"Feast, my friends. Set out and eat everyone you see!" The king laughed with waksyness, his eyes full of a wild gleam.

"He's waksy!" one of the soldiers yelled. He turned to run. The Lurkers shuffled towards the soldiers, and they turned to run. But they didn't get far. King Ferdinand opened fire on them, shooting them in the legs so they fell. The Lurkers were upon them in seconds. Screams filled the air as the Lurkers bit into the fallen soldiers.

King Ferdinand walked casually back to his coach. The ratty pulling the wagon squeaked in fright. The soldier sitting on top of the coach stared at the king in terror, wondering if he was going to be next.

"Follow them, slowly," King Ferdinand said. He climbed up to the seat at the front of the coach with the soldier. "I will ride up here with you. I don't want to miss a thing."

As the king and the last remaining soldier watched, the Lurkers finished their meal of soldiers and turned towards the city. They shuffled towards it on dead, twisted feet. When the last Lurker had moved off, the king motioned, and the soldier whipped the ratty. The coach began to follow the Lurkers. Slowly the grim procession of death moved towards the city.

CHAPTER 28

Johnny and his group of explorers stood at the gate leading to the tunnels. After quickly disposing of the guards on the top of the gate they waited at the bottom for their tribe, the people of the newly christened USA, to arrive. Tendanza had flown back over the tunnels to let the tribe know it was now safe, and then came back to let Johnny and Mantayo know the people of USA were coming.

Now as Johnny and the others watched with pleasure, they saw the USA emerge from the middle tunnel and head their way, with Misterwizard leading them.

"Just like Mosa and the people of Isral," Starbucks said, making Johnny look at him.

Starbucks looked back and grinned. "A story Misterwizard told me once."

Johnny grinned and shrugged. Microsoft glanced backwards at the city. Beyond the rubble of broken buildings, he saw the shorter buildings and beyond them the skyscrapers in the distance. Microsoft saw the huge black spider-beasties sitting on the sides of the buildings, and it gave him a shudder. He turned back to Johnny.

"Are you sure we're safe to just walk in, Johnny? This city looks scary."

Johnny glanced at him. "We don't have a lot of choice, Microsoft. We told the Sky we would meet them at the big round building, where the people of Letfreedomring are being held. When we get there, we'll fight the soldiers of Nork and rescue them, and then get out of here as fast as we can."

Microsoft nodded. Baskinrobins lowered his head in sorrow. "Where do you think Wheaties and Sephie are? Do you really think they're somewhere in the city alone?"

Johnny glanced at him with sympathy. "Don't give up hope, just yet. This is a big city, and there are a lot of places where they could be hiding."

Baskinrobins nodded woodenly.

Misterwizard and the other members of the tribe arrived. Super gave Misterwizard a hug and he hugged her back.

As they gathered at the gate on the Nork side, Starbucks looked back at the city. "Man, this place is a dump. It's worse than our old city."

Super pointed up at the skyscrapers. "Look at how tall the buildings are, and how many!"

Misterwizard, with a jovial smile, walked up and gave Johnny a pat on the back. "Here we are united in purpose and good fortune once again. The extraordinary and fascinating city of New York, or Nork, as the citizens now call it. Even after a nuclear war, it is still an impressive display."

The others from the tribe all hurried inside, and Johnny and the others closed the gate. There were more than one hundred of them now, and they milled about, pointing at the sights and talking.

"Shouldn't we find a more suitable place of concealment before the curious populace of this metropolis discover our presence?" Misterwizard said.

"Sure," Johnny replied. "Our plan is to head south just a little way, to the round building where they are holding the people of Letfreedomring. Then we will free them then head back here and escape."

Lightpole strode forth and walked in front of them, his sword held ready to fight. "Let's hurry! Who know what horrible indignities and torture my people endure?"

Mantayo, spoke. "Your plan will save your people, but still leave my people with the problem of the king of Nork and his people."

"When we're all safe outside again, we'll find a good spot to plan," Johnny said. "Then we'll come up with a strategy to deal with the king of Nork. But I think that's a battle which will take some time and thought to pull off successfully."

Mantayo nodded. "I understand. Good plan."

"Well, let's get going!" Super said. "I want to see all the sights!"

They all laughed and began their trek south and

to the right, towards the round building. They passed down the streets past the blocks full of nothing but broken buildings and concrete rubble, and soon came to the first one-story and two-buildings where the buildings had not been leveled.

Moving up cautiously, they looked for residents of the city.

Starbucks asked, "If we see some people, what do we do, Johnny?"

"Just ignore them if we can," Johnny replied. "We're too big to hide, but if we pass by them quickly, hopefully thew will mind their own business. But if they start yelling, we'll probably have to take them prisoner."

Tendanza spoke. "The people of Nork shouldn't bother us. They will find us curious, but they spend most of their days looking for something to eat. The only problem will be if we run into a crowd large enough that they think they can take us. Then they will think we are a good source of food."

They walked down the street, and Johnny thought it was good there was no one around, for being so many there was no real way to hide.

They passed the dead body of a ratty. There was not much left of it, for any meat on it had been picked clean. It was nothing but bones and the head.

"Eew!" Super said. "Those things are so disgusting. How could anyone eat it?"

"When one has a voracious enough appetite, my dear," Misterwizard said. "Any provender, no matter how unappetizing, will become suitable to sustain life."

Then Johnny saw someone! A lone man in ragged clothes with a craggy beard stood in a doorway. He stared at them with wide eyes of surprise, just staring, his mouth open. Johnny and his tribe watched the man as they passed silently. The man didn't move, almost as if he was a statue.

Then they saw another person, a woman, standing in the street to their left. Then a small group of people, two women, a man and a scrabbler. All the people of Nork watched them silently.

"What if they tell the soldiers we're here?" Starbucks asked.

"We'd better pick up the pace," Johnny said. He started walking faster, and soon everyone else followed. Johnny turned to Mantayo. "I don't see your people yet, Mantayo."

"I'm sure they are watching. They will come when they see us approach the building."

Soon they could see Madson Skar Gardem in the distance. Johnny pointed. That's where we're going!"

"We should be ready for strong resistance," Misterwizard said. "A formidable structure such as that will not be easily breached."

"Johnny," Mantayo said. "Let me and my fellow Sky fly over it and see how well fortified it is, before we all attack."

Johnny nodded. "A good idea, Mantayo. You can tell us where the people of Letfreedomring are inside as well. Then we'll now just where to attack. Meanwhile, we'll find a place to conceal ourselves until you return."

"I'll do it," Tendaza said the Sky with the large body and gray wings. He flapped his wings and took off, soaring high into the sky towards the round building.

"Let us find a suitable structure which will give us adequate concealment from the indigenous population," Misterwizard said.

"Yeah," Super said. "Let's hide."

Quickly Johnny and the large group ran to a ten-story high brick building across the street labeled, "The Paramount Building". They ran inside and moved towards the back, so the others could enter. Then Johnny, Misterwizard, Lightpole, Starbucks and Mantayo peeked out of the glassless windows towards Madson Skar Gardem.

Two things happened then which filled all of them with surprise and dismay, and also made them glad they had hidden when they did. As the three men watched, a large army marched down the street on their left, past Madson Skar Gardem and the Paramount Building. Johnny turned and shushed all the people inside, and the four of them watched with concern as the army passed by.

Super joined them. "That looks like the whole Nork army!" She whispered with concern.

"They're on their way somewhere. It's a good thing we hid when we did." Mantayo said. "I only hope they don't see Tendaza flying about the round building"

"Could they have been watching over the people of Letfreedomring?" Johnny asked in a worried tone. "And if they're leaving, what happened to the people?"

"They better not have killed them!" Lightpole spat, his voice full of pain and anger. "I will make sure to kill every one if that is the case!"

Misterwizard patted Lightpole on the shoulder. "I can say with relative certainty that will not be the situation. Your people would be too useful a commodity for them to squander in such a manner."

Then they all saw something even more amazing and frightening. Johnny pointed at the nearest skyscraper, his mouth open in surprise. "Look at that giant man! He has a spear, and he's attacking the spider-beasties!"

"Oh, no!" Mantayo said. "If he kills all of our spiders, we will be much more vulnerable to attack. There will be nothing to stop the army of Nork from climbing the buildings and breaking through our barriers. But Pantina should tell the spiders to flee so they are not hurt!"

"Look!" Starbucks said, pointing at the horrible scene unfolding on the building. "Your people are trying to fight it!"

"That's why the Sky haven't come to help us, Johnny," Mantayo said, in a voice full of sorrow.

"It doesn't look like any signal is coming from your Pantina, whoever she is," Lightpole said. "That big man is killing your spider-beasties one by one!"

Mantayo turned to Johnny. "I have to leave, Johnny, and join them in the fight."

"Go!" Johnny said. "We'll free the people of Letfreedomring alone. Then we'll wait for you outside the gate. Be safe!"

Mantayo took Johnny's hand, and they shook. Mantayo hurried outside and took off towards the grisly fight to save the spider-beasties.

Just as Mantayo took off, Tendaza landed. Tendaza turned and watched Mantayo fly off. Then he hurried inside the building and found Johnny.

"Johnny, what's going on? Where's Mantayo going?"

"A giant man is attacking the spider-beasties on your buildings. Mantayo flew away to help save them."

"What of my people?" Lightpole asked.

Tendaza turned to him. "There's no one inside the building. It is completely empty!"

Johnny realized things had just gotten way more complicated and much more dangerous.

Alcapoon walked over to his men waiting in the piles of rubble. Some ate food they'd brought with them, hard biscuits and questionable meat they'd kept in their backpacks. He stood in front of them, and they all turned to listen.

"What's going on, Genral?" a soldier asked, curious.

As the men gathered around, Alcapoon cast a glance back at the king. King Ferdinand stood next to his coach, watching them, but he was too far away to hear.

Alcapoon turned back to his men and talked to them in a soft whisper.

"King Ferdinand wants us to go back to Sental Par. When we get there, we're to put up a big wall in front of the castle for when is Lurker army arrives."

The men glanced at each other, and then back at Alcapoon. Another asked, "What Lurker army?"

Alcapoon glanced at them all again. "The one he's going to make from our people."

The soldiers all glanced at each other in amazement and dismay, then back at Alcapoon.

"Our people!" another soldier said. "Our families, our children?"

"Not ours. On our way back yer supposed to grab your people and take them back to Sental Par with us. It's everybody else who's foobered."

"This is bolluk," a soldier said, using an old slang term. "This new king is waksy!"

Alcapoon turned and glared at the soldier with a dark scowl. "I know some of you don't agree with what he's doing, but remember, he's king. Watch how you talk, or you will be a Lurker too. Believe me."

Grumbling and complaining, the men reluctantly turned and walked away, towards the city. One soldier, another genral named Eliotness, walked up and whispered in a low voice.

"Alcapoon, our new king is smart, isn't he? He's going to be king of the world?"

Alcapoon glanced back at the king's coach and then at the genral. "He's going to get everyone killed.

Can you keep a secret?"

Eliotness nodded.

"I'm going to try and find this Johnny fellow. Maybe he and his friends can help us stop the king before it's too late."

Eliotness nodded again with a somber grin.

"Go with the others," Alcapoon said. "If I find this Johnny and he's willing to help us, I'll tell you. Then together, we'll stop this waksy king before he kills everybody."

Eliotness nodded and ran to join the others. Alcapoon followed slowly, wondering where he was going to find this Johnny, and if it was going to be in time to stop the whole city from turning into undead monsters.

Deb, Ticktock, Dallanda, Sephie and Wheaties rose up into the sky in the basket. The basket barely fit them all, and they crowded together. Sephie and Wheaties gazed over the edge of the basket with joy, even though the basket tipped and swayed dangerously, pointing at the city around.

Deb looked worried, wondering what kind of a reception they were going to get. Ticktock wore a frown, looking ready for a fight.

They reached the opening of the building, forty stories up in the air. As they drew close, Patto stood just inside, looking hot and tired from pulling the crank which raised the basket. She peered out the opening at the basket, interested to see who made it back alive and if they actually found any loot. When Patto saw who was in the basket, she stopped cranking, leaving the basket a few feet below the opening.

"Who are these people?" Patto thundered, her puffy face screwed up in anger and surprise. "Even children? What do you think you were supposed to be doing out there? You were supposed to bring back food!"

Patto scowled at them and started lowering the basket again.

"Oh no you don't, Patto!" Dallanda yelled. Patto saw her in the basket.

"What are you doing in there, Dallanda?" Patto noticed Dallanda was wounded. "You can fly. Did these thugs hurt you and force you to bring them up here?"

"They rescued me," Dallanda said. "And they are our friends! Now let us up, or when I can fly again, I'll beat you until you are even uglier than normal!"

The others laughed. Patto looked scared and unhappy, and Deb grinned behind her hand. Ticktock, Sephie and Wheaties smiled too.

"All right," Patto said, for she knew Dallanda could definitely do what she'd threatened. "I'm just trying to protect our home from invaders."

Patto raised the basket again. When it was level with the opening, they all climbed out. Patto looked with concern at Dallanda. "What happened to you?"

"I was shot during a raid." Dallanda pointed to the others. "This is Ticktock. He's Deb's friend, and a member of The Brethren from that area on the other i-land. This is Sephie and Wheaties. They are in Johnny and Deb's tribe." On the trip up in the basket, Deb introduced Dallanda to Ticktock and told her their situation.

"Hello," Sephie said to Patto cheerfully. "Hello!" Wheaties said, playfully mimicking Sephie.

Patto looked them all over. "The Brethren? Aren't they the ones who hate everybody?"

"Yes, they are," Deb said. "But it's just a misunderstanding. They're only that way because of the way they've been treated by the people of Nork and their king. Ticktock is going to help arrange a meeting so Johnny can talk to them. Together, they're going to try and make The Brethren realize we are their friends and want them to join us. Then we can get The Brethren to rid the city of the king of Nork."

"Well, that's all good and fine and sounds real noble, but Lord Flaggalon…"

Patto's words stopped as she saw something out the opening in the distance, something amazing and terrifying. She pointed. "Look! A giant man is coming down the street!"

They all crowded around the opening and watched in amazement as Gee, a spear in his hand, strode over the land, stepping on short buildings and crushing them, passing by skyscrapers and heading right for them.

"What does he want?" Dallanda asked. "He looks fierce and terrifying!"

As they watched with concern, they watched Gee stride up to the building they were in. Then he started climbing up it!

"He's attacking us!" Patto screamed, her hands on her head. "We have to tell everyone!" She turned and ran to the door, screaming.

"She's right for once, we have to warn everyone!" Dallanda said, though she looked weak and pale.

Deb turned to Ticktock. "Get your sword ready. We may have to fight it first, to keep it at bay until others can arrive." Ticktock nodded and readied his weapon.

They stood, weapons at the ready, peering out the opening as the Gant climbed up the side. But as they watched, the Gant stopped. It turned sideways and looked. Deb and the others followed its gaze, and they saw it was looking at one of the giant spider-beasties.

"He's going to attack the spider-beasties!" Sephie said.

"What can we do to stop him?" Wheaties asked, looking at Deb.

"Nothing," Deb said, sadly. "We can't fly, and he's too big to fight."

As they watched in grisly horror, the Gant lifted his spear and stabbed the spider-beastie. It flinched and all its legs shook. As they watched in horror, it plummeted off the building to fall far below.

"He was sent to kill them," Ticktock said. "The king of Nork must have done it."

From behind them, a crowd of Sky men and women ran in, all carrying swords, torches, and sharp sticks. Deb and the others moved back from the opening. Patto ran in as well.

"Look out! We have to defend our home!"

As Deb and the others watched with excitement, they saw one of the Sky after another leap out of the opening and fly towards the giant man. The battle was on.

CHAPTER 29

Johnny and the people of USA stood waiting in the building. Johnny, Misterwizard, Starbucks, Lightpole and Tendaza stood near the front window openings and peered out at the abandoned buildings of the city in front of them, wondering what they were going to do next.

"This is truly a conundrum, Johnny my boy," Misterwizard said, sitting his round body down on an old broken office chair and stroking his beard. "We have the wherewithal to rescue our imprisoned compatriots, but have no way to ascertain their current whereabouts."

"We don't know where they are, either," Super said, walking up and putting her arms around Starbucks. Despite their predicament, Johnny smiled, seeing Starbucks and Super together again. He couldn't wait to get back to Deb as well.

Lightpole chuckled. He was beginning to really like the people of the USA. He only hoped one day they would have peace, and be able to really get to know each other.

Tendaza turned to Johnny. "Johnny, I really should go help my people fight this giant man who is attacking our spiders."

Johnny nodded. "I understand if you feel like you have to leave, Tendaza. Though it would be nice to have one member of the Sky with us to keep your people informed on what happens to us."

Tendaza nodded somberly. "Yes, I see the need for that as well. I will stay with you until I'm sure you are safe with your friends. Mantayo would want me to do that."

Johnny smiled at Tendaza in gratitude. Then he saw someone approaching the building from the left in front of them and he frowned. It was a man dressed in a green jacket and pinstripe pants. He held one of the Nork army's tommy guns in his hands. He looked odd, but Johnny suspected he had to be a soldier from the Nork army!

"Oh, oh, I think we've been spotted," Johnny said. The others saw the person then as well.

"Our decision on which course of action to take my soon be decided for us," Misterwizard said. "I suggest we find an alternate egress from this building perform a disappearing act."

Johnny turned to his old friend. "Misterwizard, do you mind looking for that, if you mean another door out, while the rest of us deal with this soldier? Try to get the people to move towards the other way out as fast as you can!"

But before Misterwizard could comply, the soldier was at the door of the building and peering inside. Lightpole put his hand on his sword, and so did Johnny. Starbucks made fists of his hands, and even Super tensed, ready to fight.

The soldier peered around inside, and his eyes rested on Johnny. "You are Johnny Apocalypse, is that correct? I remember you from the tunnels."

Johnny realized this soldier was familiar as well, but couldn't remember his name. The soldier didn't appear to be ready to fight them, so Johnny relaxed just a little, but kept on his guard.

"Who are you, and what do you want?" Johnny replied. "You were with Moxie and his army when they attacked Pelpia. You're a soldier of Nork."

In surprise, Johnny watched the man place his tommy gun on the ground. Then he raised his hands. Alcapoon nodded. "I am Alcapoon. I am now genral of the Nork army. I know we were enemies before, Johnny. And I can understand if you don't want to trust me. I hope you understand that our army was only following orders, and we were trying to bring food home for our people."

"So, you killed my people!" Lightpole snarled, raising his sword and advancing on Alcapoon.

Johnny raised his hand to stop Lightpole. Reluctantly, Lightpole stopped, his sword still raised above his head. He stood still and glared at Alcapoon, waiting for any sign that would justify his killing the Nork soldier.

Alcapoon didn't even look at Lightpole, but kept his eyes on Johnny. "I think you are a good man Johnny, and so are your people, and the people of this man," he pointed at Lightpole. "I think the time has come when we need to join together, or we will all perish."

Misterwizard returned, having heard the conversation, curious to see what Alcapoon had to say.

"We're listening," Johnny said. He turned to Lightpole and Starbucks and whispered to them, "check the other windows. Make sure we are not being ambushed."

Starbucks and Lightpole nodded and hurried away. Johnny turned back to Alcapoon.

Alcapoon walked forward and looked at Johnny with eyes full of worry. "Johnny, Moxie is dead. And so is our real king. Moxie was bitten and turned into a Lurker. And Lord Ferdinand used Moxie to infect our king and take our king's place."

Johnny glanced at Misterwizard in concern, but Misterwizard was intent on gazing at Alcapoon. Johnny looked back at Alcapoon.

"We simply want to get our friends from Pelpia back, Alcapoon, and protect our friends the Sky. If your people would only be willing to join us, we could all live in peace."

Alcapoon nodded. "There are some of us who would love that, Johnny, not only the people but in the army as well. The people of Nork only want food and clothing. The king has used the army to keep us all enslaved. But right now, there is a much more serious matter I need to tell you about."

Johnny and the others gathered around Alcapoon. Starbucks and Lightpole returned. Johnny wondered what Alcapoon could think was more important than what he'd already told them.

"There's no one approaching, Johnny, no one at all," Starbucks said.

"Okay, Alcapoon, we're listening," Johnny said.

Alcapoon looked frightened. "King Ferdinand, as he now calls himself, has gone waksy. He has over a hundred Lurkers now and he's creating an undead army. As we speak, he is releasing is Lurkers at the south end of the city. He's going to let them infect everyone they run into. The army is building a barricade next to the castle and we're supposed to be ready to capture the Lurkers when they reach it. Johnny, Ferdinand is going to kill half the city to make his Lurker army. He thinks he's going to use it to take over the whole world!"

"Releasing Lurkers intentionally?" Johnny said. "That is waksy. He'll never be able to control them. They'll infect everyone!"

"Johnny," Starbucks, said, "if he's releasing them at the south end of the city, that means they are heading this way!"

Alcapoon nodded quickly. "Our army has gone to Sental Par to organize and build a wall to keep the Lurkers in. But before then, the Lurkers will have infected half of the city!"

Johnny grabbed Alcapoon's jacket and pulled him close, scowling at him. "Where are the people of Pelpia?"

Trying his best to turn with Johnny holding him, Alcapoon pointed out the window. "They are all trapped in a tall, yellow building not far from here. The people of Nork have them surrounded."

Johnny pushed Alcapoon back and released him. "So why are you telling us all this, Alcapoon? It doesn't sound like your army is planning on helping us."

"But they will, Johnny, if you go with me and we talk to them. Once they realize Ferdinand is going to kill everyone in the city, they will agree to join you and your friends. I will show them Ferdinand is waksy."

"Our first priority has to be to save my people!" Lightpole said.

"And you don't have any of the army to help us do that, do you, Alcapoon?" Johnny asked.

Alcapoon shook his head. "No, but Johnny, the Lurkers are coming."

"Which means the people of Letfreedomring are right in their path, and trapped," Johnny said. "Give us a moment to talk, Genral Alcapoon. Alcapoon nodded and walked a little way away so Johnny and his friend could talk.

Johnny, Starbucks, Lightpole, Tendaza and Misterwizard huddled together a little way away where Alcapoon couldn't hear.

"Misterwizard," Johnny asked, "what do you think we should do?"

Misterwizard stroked his beard and looked at the floor thinking, his brow creased with concern. "We have multiple different strategies on the chess board of reality to ponder, Johnny. If you go with this Alcapoon alone, you may be putting yourself in a most precarious position. If, on the alternative hand, we ignore him and concentrate on saving our beleaguered companions, we risk the chance Alcapoon will relinquish his offer of cooperation. If, on the third hand, we all join this soldier of Nork, and ignore our wayward friends…"

Lightpole interrupted impatiently. "Please, Misterwizard, tell us what we should do, before we all grow old and die on this spot!"

Misterwizard chuckled. "This is what I would consider the wisest alternative." Misterwizard bent over and they all moved in as he whispered his plan to them. They nodded and smiled in agreement.

Johnny and the others walked back over to Alcapoon.

"This is what we've decided, Alcapoon," Johnny said. "We're going to go break through to our friends and protect them from the people of Nork, for that is our first priority.

"You join your army in building a wall against the Lurkers, and try to get as many people of Nork as you can on the other side. Then you, Alcapoon, find us in the yellow building. Me, Misterwizard, Lightpole and someone from the Sky will meet with your army and we will discuss joining forces with you to defeat King Ferdinand and his Lurker army."

"I just hope we can do all this before the Lurker army reaches the castle," Alcapoon said. He picked up his tommy gun again, walked to the door and stopped. "What if we lose, Johnny?"

"Then we're all Lurkers," Johnny said. "Just get your wall ready, and save as many of the people of Nork as you can. And hope we can get to our friends. Don't worry. If we work together, we're going to win."

Alcapoon nodded and smiled. He hurried away, running across the street and disappearing around a corner.

Super smiled. "How hard can it be to save our friends from an angry mob, kill one giant attacking spider-beasties and defeat one undead army?"

Restaria and the people of Letfreedomring hurried to block the door to the stairway. Then they ran up to the fifth floor and looked for other entrances. Then they blocked them as well.

Restaria looked out the empty window frames at the street below. With dismay, she saw the whole street was filled with people, all looking up at the and shouting. The crowd surged and poured inside the building, looking for a way to get to them. They looked like wild animals, all carrying clubs and sharp sticks and rocks. Restaria wondered how long they could hold out.

Arrex, the medicine man for Letfreedomring walked up behind Restaria. "There are many people with small wounds. Are we going to be able to stay here long enough for me to treat them?"

"I hope so. We need to barricade every entrance and stay away from the windows. Hopefully, they will lose interest if they can't find a way in."

Starlite, the little Brown girl, walked up and Restaria took her into her arms.

"I'm scared, Restaria. What if they get in and get us?"

Restaria smiled at her. "They won't. I promise. Why don't you help Arrex? That will give you something useful to do."

Starlite nodded with a smile. Restaria set her down and Starlite ran to follow Arrex.

Restaria looked out the window, hoping her words to Starlite would prove true.

CHAPTER 30

Johnny and his group slowly worked their way down the streets towards the tall, yellow building. Now that they had a plan, the moved swiftly, knowing that the army of Nork was not going to fight them and the only resistance they may face would be that of people on the streets.

Johnny, the people of USA and the others with them made a large crowd of their own. They ran down a street towards their destination, trying to stay on one side or the other next to the empty, broken buildings to be less noticeable. Still, anyone seeing them would be able to tell right away they were a large group of strangers.

There was nothing they could do about it, however, and Johnny thought to himself how soon, being hidden wouldn't be possible anyway. When they reached the yellow building, they were going to have to fight the crowd. Johnny just hoped the people would be scared and run away, rather than attack them, for he dreaded the idea of having to hurt anyone.

Having left their vehicles back on the other side of the tunnel because of all the rusted cars blocking the way, they were now all on foot. Johnny's Harley was somewhere back by the tunnels as well, for Johnny had left it there what seemed like years ago. He hoped that when this battle was over, he could find it again.

As they hurried along, people in their group peered in the windows of the buildings, or stared up at the tall skyscrapers in the sky. Some smiled with pleasure and amazement, as if they were on some kind of pleasure trip. Others were more serious, frowning and looking around for trouble.

Misterwizard was like the first group, grinning widely and walking slowly, gazing around and talking about the city to anyone who would listen. Wearing his ever-present sandals, flowery shirt and shorts, he looked like anything but a soldier in an army.

"What an amazing and fascinating city this was once, Johnny! A kaleidoscope of culture and industry. The Big Apple! The home of the Yankees! The place where King Kong was defeated!"

Johnny grinned at Misterwizard, despite the danger. "Who was King Kong?"

"In the old stories, he was a giant ape-beastie, taller than the buildings. It seems he was absconded from some i-land far away and brought here, without his consent and to his considerable displeasure. According to the story, he had an infatuation with a young blond girl, who ultimately caused his downfall."

Johnny didn't know when to take Misterwizard seriously and when his round, bearded friend was making something up simply to impress Johnny and his friends. Johnny supposed it didn't really matter. If it made Misterwizard happy to tell stories, there was no harm. Johnny knew when the time came, Misterwizard was the best person to have by your side in a fight.

They drew close to the yellow building, and Johnny could see the large crowd milling about in front of it. Johnny signaled with a wave of his hand, and all the people with Johnny stopped and crouched by the buildings they were next to. The yellow building was across the street in front of them, a street packed with Nork citizens.

The people of Nork were excited and shouting. The ones in the back looked at the ones in front, who pressed in, trying to get inside the building, but the whole area was packed. Johnny could see there was already a crowd packed wall to wall inside. He suspected somewhere in the interior they were fighting to break down the barriers the people of Pelpia had put up and get to them.

Lightpole grabbed Johnny's arm in excitement. He pointed with his other hand at the second floor. "Johnny, look!"

Johnny looked where Lightpole pointed and he smiled. There, standing at the window on the fifth floor gazing down at the crowds was Restaria! She looked worried. Johnny knew they had only a very short time before the people of Nork broke in.

"Misterwizard," Johnny asked, "Do you have any of your special bombs we could throw to scare the people away?"

Misterwizard nodded. "But I have a better solution, Johnny. We know this King Ferdinand is planning to unleash Lurkers on these people. These people need to get behind the barriers the Nork army is going to construct. I suggest we try to reason with them intelligently and appeal to their self-preservation and desire to survive."

"What if they decide to eat us too?" Super said, crouching next to Starbucks behind Johnny, Misterwizard and Lightpole.

"Then we resort to the unpleasant use of physical deterrence," Misterwizard replied. "After all, we are armed, they are not."

"Let me try first," Johnny said. "If they refuse to listen, then I'll signal to you."

Misterwizard patted Johnny on the shoulder. "Good fortunes, Johnny."

Johnny stood up and with his heart beating wildly, walked out onto the street where the people could see him. At first, they didn't notice him. Then one man did. His eyes opened wide and he grinned with hunger. He grabbed the person next to him and when the person turned around, the man pointed at Johnny. Soon the news spread through the crowd, and they all turned to look at Johnny. They didn't move at first, curious.

Here goes nothing, Johnny thought, another

expression of Misterwizard's. "People of Nork! Listen to me! My name is Johnny Apocalypse. I come from a city to the south called Washington Deecee. My friends inside this building are from Pelpia, the city just a little way away from here. We are your friends, and we need to tell you something. You are in danger, and we need you to listen to us."

The crowd moved towards Johnny, and he stepped back a step, nervous. The crowd didn't attack him, though, which Johnny found encouraging. The crowd stopped four feet in front of Johnny, and Johnny knew if they tried to rush him, he could never get back to his friends in time. He just had to hope for the best.

Johnny gazed over the crowd. "I know you are all starving. Your king doesn't help you but leaves you to fend for yourselves. But killing my friends and I is not the answer. Your king has been killed by the evil man Ferdinand. I know you know him. He has seized the throne and has gone waksy. He is at this moment unleashing an army of Lurkers to the south on the city. They are coming this way, infecting everyone in their path."

One man, a thin, tall man with a long, hooked nose and thin black hair who looked like a string of poles tied together grinned and walked towards Johnny. He seemed to be some kind of leader, for the rest of the crowd watched him.

"So you say, so you say, Johnny. We have no proof. No proof of what you say. But you will make a tasty meal, that we do know."

The people laughed and yelled in agreement. They put on dark, hungry looks. Johnny knew it was time to reinforce his position. He waved behind himself, and Misterwizard and the rest of the people of USA walked out and stood behind Johnny. Some raised their weapons and pointed them at the crowd. Misterwizard walked up to stand right next to Johnny, and some of the people of Nork pointed at him and laughed.

"We are many, and we have weapons," Johnny said, staring at the thin man. "But we don't want to hurt you. We want you to join us and our friends from Pelpia. Together, we can create one people who live by the rules of freedom and 'mocracy.'"

"Freedom? 'Mocracy?'" The man said, smiling slyly. "We don't know these words. We do know the words hungry, and feed."

Another woman, tired of the man's bantering about, stepped forward. "Be quiet Lim. What would you have us do, Johnny?"

Johnny turned to her, grateful for someone who seemed willing to listen. "Your army is setting up a wall in front of your king's castle. There they plan to make a stand against the Lurkers Ferdinand is sending. You need to take all of your people there quickly, while you have time. Then when we have helped your army defeat the Lurkers and Ferdinand, we will all talk again about joining together."

"We are starving!" a woman in the crowd said, her arms around a dirty scrabbler girl. "What can you do to help us?"

Johnny looked at her with compassion. "Once we have defeated the Lurker army, our people and the people you call the angels," Johnny pointed to Tendaza, who walked up to join him, "will help find food for you. But first, you have to get to the wall, before it's too late."

The crowd of Norkers talked amongst themselves, arguing and debating. The thin man with the long, hooked nose rubbed his chin, thinking. "And what if this is just a way to save your own skin from being eaten?"

Johnny turned to the man. "Did you see the giant man killing the giant spider-beasties on the buildings?"

They all talked to each other and nodded at Johnny.

"Ferdinand sent that giant there. He wants to kill Tendanza's people as well. Go to the castle and see. If the army is not there building a wall, you'll know I'm lying. Then you can come back and eat us. We won't even put up a fight, I promise."

The crowd laughed at that. The thin man smiled. He turned to the crowd and raised his hands. "We will do what this Johnny says, for now. We all know how rotten Ferdinand is, and what this Johnny is saying may have some truth."

The thin man glanced back at Johnny and then back at the crowd. "If he is lying, we will be back to feast on their bones!"

The crowd all laughed and murmured. The thin

man pointed towards the castle. "For now, let's hurry. If a Lurker army is coming, I don't want to be its dinner!"

The crowd nodded in agreement. Slowly they started shuffling north down the street, talking. Then they picked up the pace and soon people ran down the streets, heading for the soldiers and the new wall. The thin man joined the end of the crowd, as moved. Those inside the building had been listening as well, and they poured out and followed the rest.

Johnny returned to Misterwizard with a look of victory. "Well played, my boy. Let's get inside to your friends from Pelpia, before the Norkers reconsider their cooperation due to the rumbling of their empty stomachs."

Johnny nodded. Quickly Johnny, his companions and the rest of USA ran across the street to join the people of Letfreedomring.

King Ferdinand's mind burned with a strange fire, elation mixed with evil joy, and mixed in with a dose of unreality. He couldn't remember being so happy before, and yet it was strange, he felt almost as if he wasn't in control of his actions. He almost felt like something deep inside drove him, a desire to see death and horror. He wondered if it was this new world, where everything was dead and destroyed. Did it somehow make him want to see everything gone, and only himself left? He'd always thought he wanted to be king, but now it was almost as if seeing the world burn was more wonderful than anything he could imagine.

He sat on a cushion on top of the coach, which slowly rolled along, staying behind the Lurkers. He gazed at the Lurkers shuffling down the street. The first death had been the most exciting. A man had come out of a building and walked right into Moxie. Before the man could do anything but scream, Moxie was on him, knocking the man down and tearing him apart. Then there were others, some even more grisly, men, women and even scrabblers. It was like a horror show, put on just for King Ferdinand.

King Ferdinand and the coachmen moved slowly, so as not to attract the Lurkers' attention. The coach passed by Moxie and his meal and kept going. Moxie didn't look up.

Once a whole family, a man, woman and two scrabblers walked out into the street. Three Lurkers moaned and hurried towards them. The man tried to fight them while his family ran away, but unfortunately for them, they stumbled right into two other Lurkers. One of the scrabblers got away, but King Ferdinand was sure it wouldn't last long on its own.

As the people were bitten, they lay on the ground, but eventually they became Lurkers too. It soon seemed dangerous for King Ferdinand and his driver, for it wasn't long until there were Lurkers all around them. The driver kept looking up at King Ferdinand with pleading eyes, as if asking when they were going to speed up and get away. King Ferdinand ignored him. They could always put the whip to the ratty and speed off if they had to, as long as the road ahead seemed clear. The Lurkers didn't seem to see them up on their coach, so intent on finding people around them. And King Ferdinand was not going to miss seeing any deaths, if he could help it.

King Ferdinand watched the former king, now a mindless Lurker, stumble along the road, looking pale and pathetic. His skin was turning black now, and his hair had begun to fall out. His clothes were nothing but bloody rags, and his left foot looked as if it had gotten twisted somewhere. Seeing him made King Ferdinand almost cry with delight. How long he'd wanted to see the old king like this, as he had to bow before him and scrape on the floor to the pathetic, spineless idiot! Now he finally had his revenge.

They were reaching larger crowds now, and the people ran away screaming from the Lurkers. It was glorious! Kill them all, King Ferdinand thought. Turn the whole city into an undead kingdom, and he would be the king of the undead.

The Lurker nightmare rolled on, as Lurkers caught the unaware or slow, and the rest of the people ran for their lives.

Mantayo flew up to see the battle against the giant man was already in full force. Men and women of Sky flitted around the twenty-five-foot-tall giant, some around its head, trying to distract it, others stabbing it in the arms and legs. But they seemed like flies to the giant, who batted them away and continued on his task of killing the spiders.

Lever flew up to Mantayo and hovered, flapping is wings. "Mantayo, he's killing all the spiders! Why hasn't Pantina responded and told the spider to fight back?"

Mantayo hovered next to Lever, flapping his wings. "I don't know. We can't wait until she does, we have to kill it!"

Gee the Gant clung to the building with one hand in a window frame and his two feet in other windows and alternately stabbed at the spiders or swung his spear in a deadly arc to swat the flying attackers. The simple look on Gee's face showed fright, for he never expected to be attacked when he did the job that little evil man told him to do. Now it seemed as if he might get hurt! He had to hurry and do the task, and get back, for the little flying creatures were stabbing him and it hurt a lot. In anger, he hit one member of the Sky, and the man plummeted to the ground, knocked out. Gant watched it fall sadly, for he didn't really want to hurt anyone, but he had no choice.

A gnat-beastie-girl stabbed Gee in the cheek, and he howled in pain and grabbed for her, but she flew just out of reach.

"STOP!" Gee yelled in anger and fright, but the little annoying gnat-beastie-people kept attacking him.

Mantayo flew next to Lever. "We have to use fire. It may be the only thing which will stop it!"

Lever nodded and flew towards the building. As Mantayo watched, the giant man leapt from the building it was on to the next one and grabbed hold, for it had killed all the spiders on the first building. As Mantayo watched in dismay, he saw the giant men move towards the next spider. Mantayo flew inside the building to help get fire to fight with.

As he landed inside, Mantayo saw Deb, Johnny's mate, a black man he didn't know and two young children standing in the corner. On the bed next to them, Mantayo saw the strange furry dog Johnny had brought with him. He had never seen a dog-beastie before he met Johnny, but it looked friendly. It looked as if it had recently been wounded, for there was a bandage on its side.

Mantayo's mother Layla ran up to him, looking panicked, her eyes wild. "Mantayo, we can't find Lord Flaggalon anywhere! And Pantina is not answering our prayers!"

"Has anyone gone to her throne room to call on her?" Mantayo asked, grabbing her by the shoulders. "Maybe she is under attack by the giant men as well!"

"We haven't had time!"

Lever ran up, carrying two torches. "We're making more, but here are two for us!"

Mantayo grabbed one and together they flew back out the window to rejoin the fight.

Gee waved his free hand, trying to get the annoying gnat-beastie-people to go away. His cheek bled where the flying girl had stabbed it, and another had poked him in the eye, making it hurt and his vision in it blurry. Fear filled Gee's heart, making his heart beat hard. What did this evil man get him into? The man said nothing about gnat-beastie-people attacking him. He thought about giving up and climbing down, then running back home. But if he did, what would Po, Ha and Muk say? And then the evil man would sic the undead monsters on all of them, and Po, Ha and Muk would blame Gee. He decided he'd better just finish the task fast.

He moved faster, climbing along the building, grabbing handholds on the open windowless window frames. Sometimes the brick would crumble and fall to the ground when he tried to grab it, making him almost fall, but he just found another opening and got a new grip.

He noticed with relief that when he jumped from one building to the next, the little gnat-beastie-people lost him for a few seconds. If he could just kill the spiders really fast, then jump to the next building before they could catch up, he might survive! He had to be careful though, for it was a long way down to the ground, and a fall would hurt!

At a new building, he saw two spiders! How many of the things were there? Suddenly his head felt hot. He realized with terror the little gnat-beastie-people had set his hair on fire!

He yelled and patted on his head until the fire was out. He had to get done fast! Fire terrified him! He quickly scampered over and stabbed the two spiders and watched them fall. He looked to his right and saw a terrifying sight. Many of the gnat-beastie-people had fire! What did they want? Why were they attacking him?

He was at the last building with a spider! All he had to do was kill this last one, and he could go home. He sobbed in relief. Hurry, he told himself. Hurry, before they catch you on fire! In anger, Gee let go of his spear and grabbed the spider-beastie in is hand. He bit on it hard. Black blood oozed out and down Gee's chin. The spider shivered in its death throes as Gee tore its body in half. Then he threw it to the ground far below. There! He was done!

But it was too late! As Gee screamed, the little gnat-beastie-people all put their torches against his clothing! Fire sprang up all over him! He frantically fought to put out the flames, but it grew fast, his green clothing made from tree bark dry as tinder and ready to burn. Without thinking, Gee let go of the building with both hands and slapped at the fire burning all over his body. And then he fell.

Gee fell forty stories down, tumbling through the air. He crashed on the hard concrete street below. Pain shot through his body and his head slammed backwards onto the concrete. Instantly blackness filled his vision, coming from the outer edges of his sight and quickly moving in, until he could barely see. His head hurt bad, and his clothes still burned. Pain from the fire burning his body pierced through his groggy state, and he rolled back and forth in pain, howling.

In his last moment before passing out, he saw little men coming towards him. They looked different than the gnat-people. He wondered if they were going to eat him, for they all had open mouths. Then he saw there was something else strange about the little men. They all looked sick, shuffling towards him with arms outstretched, dead eyes and rotting flesh. They looked like they were dead already! Was Gee already in the afterlife? Had he already died?

As everything went black, Gee watched the little dead men climb on his body. Some caught fire, but others crawled under his clothes and he could feel them biting him. Gee thought with sorrow how he wished he'd never left home. Then everything turned dark.

CHAPTER 31

So, you've joined these winged freaks, is that it, Lady Stabs? What do you think Ripper would say?"

Lady Stabs grinned with anger in her eyes. "Ripper's dead. Didn't Johnny and his tribe teach you anything?"

Monsta put on a look of disgust and fury. "So, you've been a traitor to the Doomsday Prophecy all along. I should have known. You were always weak. I'll teach you to betray Ripper and the gang. I'll cut your head off too, and that little scrabbler's as well."

Monsta ran towards Lady Stabs and swung his piece of jagged steel in a deadly arc. Lady Stabs screamed and fell backwards, dropping her sword. Monsta, with a roar of rage, advanced on her as Lady Stabs crawled away on all crab-beastie-like on all fours. In the chair, Pantina, struggled against the ropes.

Lady Stabs passed another red silk chair and picked it up, holding it in front of herself like a shield. Monsta's piece of steel descended on it, crashing into it with such force the chair almost slid out of Lady Stab's hand. Then Monsta, with a scowl of pure hatred, tried to stab around the chair but Lady Stabs shifted it at the last moment. The blade imbedded itself in cloth seat and was stuck.

Sandl watched in terror, not knowing what he could do to help. He tried to work his way around to get to Pantina, but every time he tried, he was cut off by the combatants. He knew he had to help Lady Stabs before Monsta killed her, or they were all dead.

Lady Stabs let go of the chair as Monsta grabbed it and worked on getting his steel free. Lady Stabs stumbled backwards and ran for her sword.

Sandl saw something. On an old desk sat a pair of scissors. Sandl ran over and grabbed them. With a scowl of courage, Sandl jumped on Monsta's back and stabbed him with the scissors, like one of the wild scrabbler children of Nork.

With a snarl of fury, Monsta reached, trying to grab Sandl. But Sandl kept stabbing Monsta in the back, then he started stabbing Monsta in the side of the throat. Finally, Monsta managed to grab Sandl and pry him off. With a scream of animal fury, he flung the boy at the wall. Sandl hit the wall and fell to the floor, knocked out. But Monsta's throat dripped blood, and his back ached from the stab wounds.

Lady Stabs reached her sword and picked it up. She knew Monsta was going to be a tough opponent, but didn't count on how strong and evil he was. She worried she wasn't going to be able to defeat him.

Monsta ran at her. Before she could swing the sword, he grabbed her arm. Then he put his other arm around her and dragged her towards the opening in the wall.

Before Lady Stabs could stop him, Monsta threw her out the opening. She screamed and fell but managed to grab onto a ragged piece of concrete. Her sword flew into open space. She struggled, eyes wide open in fright, trying to keep her grim and not fall forty stories to the hard concrete below.

"Do you have wings like these other freaks, Lady Stabs? It's time to find out!" Monsta yelled with dark humor.

Monsta reached down to pry her fingers loose. But as he did, she reached her hand up and grabbed his leg. She pulled it forward and Monsta fell onto his back with a cry. Lady Stabs wrapped her arm around his leg, and together they slid out into open space.

They fell, tumbling over and over, but then they landed on a jutting finger of round bars which had once been inside one of the floors, but were now exposed and hanging out in mid space. They landed with a crash, and the metal bars bounced. Lady Stabs cried out and desperately grabbed at the bars for a hold. Monsta did the same thing.

Lady Stabs slid, but at the last moment she was able to grab two metal bars. Her feet dangled in open space. She held on for dear life, trembling.

Monsta hung down. He was underneath the round bars, both hands holding onto a bar. He looked dazed for a moment, but only briefly. He swung his leg up to get it on the top of the bars so he could scramble back up.

Lady Stabs knew she was about to die, but she was going to make sure she took Monsta with her. She was close enough to kick him, so she did, as hard as she could. Her kick made his leg fall back down. He looked at her with hatred. Then he kicked at her, landing a blow in her side.

Lady Stabs screamed out, as much in frustration as in pain. She twisted and kicked at him again and again.

Monsta laughed, a shaky but cruel sound. "I'm stronger than you. I can hold out here forever. You're gonna fall any second now. Then I'm gonna finish off your pretty angel up there. I'm going to cut her into little pieces and throw them down, so they land on your dead body."

Lady Stabs clenched her teeth in anger, but with fear, for he suspected there was no way to keep Monsta from winning. Then with excitement she saw her sword. It had fallen on the metal bars, just above her. With a supreme effort, she reached up and grabbed it.

Dangling by one hand, she swung herself over and stabbed Monsta in the stomach. He screamed in pain, and then made a mistake. He reached a hand down to grab her sword. That was all it took. He lost his grip with the other hand. He fell.

Lady Stabs laughed with relief and joy as she watched Monsta drop, twisting in the air, until he hit the ground and splattered like a ripe tomato. He was dead!

Then she lost her grip, and knew she was going to join him. She felt the sick sensation of falling, and knowing she was going to die.

Suddenly she felt an arm wrap around her waist. With joy and immense relief, she realized it was Pantina! Quickly she stopped falling and floated in the air. Then they were rising up!

Lady Stab's eyes filled with tears of relief, as she realized she wasn't going to die, that Pantina had saved her. And Monsta was dead!

Pantina landed back in the room where they'd done battle. Pantina let go of Lady Stabs, who turned towards her with a look of triumph.

"You're safe now, Your Majesty," Lady Stabs said.

Then something totally unexpected happened. Pantina put her arms around Lady Stabs and kissed her. Lady Stabs immediately felt a rush of pleasure and joy course through her, and she realized what she'd only wondered about before. She loved Pantina madly, and had since the moment she first saw her.

Lady Stabs couldn't help herself. She leaned forward and kissed Pantina back, hard. The two shared a lover's kiss and held each other, lost in passion.

Then Lady Stabs pulled back. "Your Majesty, I love you. I always have."

"Call me Pantina. I love you, too, Lady Stabs."

"But how do you know what you're saying, Pantina? You haven't had much of a chance to meet anyone, or get to know anyone, really."

Pantina took Lady Stab's hand and stroked it. "I may be inexperienced and spent most of my life trapped in my home, but I'm not a child, Lady Stabs. I have met many men, and women. You're not the only one to come and talk to me. And I know when I love someone."

Lady Stabs nodded happily. They sat down on a blue velvet couch, kissed and held each other, enjoying their new found romance.

Johnny reached the stairway which led up to where the people of Restaria waited. Most of the people of Nork had left now, only a few watching them from the street. Behind Johnny, Misterwizard, Lightpole and the people of USA waited. Johnny tried the door but it wouldn't budge.

"Hello! Restaria! Are you there? It's Johnny!

"And Lightpole!" Lightpole said, standing next to Johnny.

"And Starbucks and Super!" Starbucks yelled, grinning at Johnny.

From behind the door, they heard excited voices. Then one man's voice said, "Is it really you, Johnny? And Lightpole?"

"Yes," Lightpole said, looking impatient. "Hurry and let us in! We have important business to discuss with the mayr!"

"All right," the muffled voice said, "it will take a

few times, we have to remove all the junk in front of the door.”

"Well, hurry!" Lightpole said. He turned and sat on the floor, as Johnny and Starbucks chuckled and relaxed.

Misterwizard paced up and down the hallway, as the people of USA made a path for him. "Time is of the essence, friends. We have no indication when our undead enemies will arrive."

Finally, after what seemed like forever, the door finally opened. The people of USA cheered. Johnny, Lightpole and Starbucks and the others filed in the door after them.

As they arrived at the fifth floor, they were greeted with cheers and smiling faces. Men and women grabbed them and hugged them and patted them on the back.

Restaria walked up and saw Johnny. Her face lit up with joy and relief. She walked over and went to shake his hand, but had too much emotion. Instead, she put her arms around him and hugged him. Johnny happily hugged her back. When they separated, Restaria said, "I knew you would come for us, Johnny. I never lost hope."

Johnny smiled at her. Then Restaria saw Lightpole and her face lit up with pleasure. She let go of Johnny and hurried over and gave Lightpole a warm hug too.

"Our city's real hero and champion. I'm so glad you are safe, my friend."

Lightpole hugged her back and smiled with stiff pride. "I am pleased to see you have protected our people all this time, Mayr Restaria. You are truly the one who is the hero."

Restaria turned and gazed at Starbucks and Super. "And our wonderful Starbucks and Super. You have truly been saviors of our people. Thank you!"

Starbucks and Super, grinned, slightly embarrassed.

Misterwizard walked up, and Restaria gazed at him with pleased curiosity.

"Restaria, I'd like you to meet my good friend and mentor, Misterwizard," Johnny said. "He is the really smart one amongst us, and he's our real leader."

Misterwizard, who was preoccupied looking at Restaria with more than a little interest, replied, "Nonsense, my boy. You are the born leader. I am just the old man who gives you advice, from time to time."

They all laughed for a moment, enjoying each other's company. Then Tendaza walked up looking concerned. "Johnny, I need to go back and see what has happened to my people."

Johnny nodded serious again. "Can you take me with you, Tendaza? I have to make sure Deb is all right. We should also coordinate our plan with your people as well, so we can fight these monsters together."

"Of course. Let's go quickly!"

Johnny turned to the others. "I'll be back, as soon as I can. Misterwizard and Restaria, can you keep an eye on everything until I get back?"

"Of course, my boy!" Misterwizard said. "But don't dawdle. I feel certain our time is very limited!"

Johnny nodded. Then he and Tendaza went to find a window for Tendaza to fly out of.

Once they were gone, the people of USA and Pelpia spent the time getting to know each other. Misterwizard and Restaria gazed out a glassless window at the city below.

Tendaza landed softly on the floor after flying in the window of the skyscraper where the Sky were gathered. As soon as they landed and Johnny was free, Deb ran up to him and grabbed him in a big hug. Johnny hugged her back with rapture, so glad to be back into her arms and see she was safe. Deecee, overjoyed to see Johnny, barked and wagged his tail. He gingerly hopped off the bed and limped over to Johnny, who hugged Deecee with happiness.

When Johnny stood up again, he was greeted with a passionate kiss from his lady love Deb. Everyone around them laughed, and then grew embarrassed when it seemed like Johnny and Deb kissed for a long time. When they finally parted, Deb put on a mock reproving look. "Where have you been, silly?"

"Oh, just fighting monsters," Johnny replied, smiling. "It looks like you've been having some adventures of your own!"

"We sure have! And so has Deecee! Johnny, someone hurt him."

Johnny knelt down and grabbed Deecee's face, his own full of sadness and concern. "Are you all right, Deecee?" Johnny stroked Deecee's fur, and Deecee licked Johnny's hand.

Deb knelt down next to them and petted Deecee too. "It looks like someone tried to fix his wound, Johnny. I think he's going to be all right. I just wish I knew who hurt him. I'd love to do the same thing to them!"

Mantayo walked over and joined them. He was bloody and sweaty, and looked exhausted. Johnny stood up and turned to him. "We killed the giant man, but not before he managed to kill all the spiders."

Johnny was about to reply, when he saw something that filled him with such happiness he couldn't help but smile in pure joy. As he stood still, gazing at them, Sephie and Wheaties walked up, grinning.

"You too have been having adventures of your own, I guess!" Johnny said. Then he knelt down and they ran into his arms for a hug.

Sephie wiped the tears from her eyes with the back of her hand. "We snuck out, Johnny, and almost died, but then Deb found us. Now we're safe!"

Johnny mopped Sephie's hair with his hand. "I know some people who are going to be very happy to see you again."

Sephie nodded and Wheaties grinned, for they

knew who Johnny was talking about.

Ticktock walked up to Johnny, and Johnny stood up, looking at him with a curious frown.

"Johnny, I know what you're thinking," Ticktock said. "But I'm no longer with the Nork army. I realize now that the king of Nork is evil, and only wants to enslave his people. I have a way to help you and your friends."

Johnny looked at everyone in the room. "The king of Nork is dead. A man named Ferdinand has seized power, and he is totally waksy. He's creating a Lurker army and sending it to kill everyone in the city."

Mantayo and his mother Layla looked at each other, then back at Johnny. "Why would he do that, Johnny?" Mantayo said. "He'll have no one to rule!"

"I don't think he cares, Mantayo. I think all he wants is to cause death and misery for his own amusement. Like I said, he's out of his mind."

Tendaza said, "Where is Pantina? Why didn't she save the spiders?"

Mantayo shook his head. "No one knows."

Ticktock said, "Johnny, if you and Mantayo go with me and talk to The Brethren, I think we might be able to convince them to join us in an alliance. The Brethren, though fiercely independent and untrusting, know they are all alone. I think if they know there are people they can trust, they will join us."

"Where are your people, Johnny?" Mantayo asked.

Johnny brought Mantayo, Layla, Deb and the

rest of the Sky up-to-date on everything that had happened so far, including his meeting with Alcapoon.

Johnny looked somberly at the others. "We have to stop the Lurker army, before they find a way to escape this i-land. If they do, there will be no stopping them."

They all talked for a moment about the situation, then Mantayo spoke. "Johnny, let's go meet with The Brethren. Meanwhile, Tendaza will try to make contact with the Nork army, who you say is willing to help fight the Lurkers. My people will try to bring your people up here where they will be safer. Then we can come up with a plan of attack."

"There's only one thing, Johnny," Ticktock said. "The Brethren don't trust people of your color. They say they hate you, but it's really that the king of Nork and his people have always treated anyone not like them as cursed. You're going to have to convince them to trust you."

"Then maybe we should take Lightpole and Starbucks with us. If they see that we have people of all colors and types with us, it might help convince them."

"A good idea," Ticktock said.

"Where's Lord Flaggalon?" Mantayo asked.

"No one knows," one of the Sky men said. "We haven't heard from him all day. He's probably in his mansion, sleeping."

CHAPTER 32

Johnny, Mantayo, Starbucks, Ticktock, Lightpole and Super walked over to the hole in the wall of the building. They reached the opening and all gazed out at the city far below and the buildings everywhere. It was a cold, chilly day and the world seemed bathed in a white coat of frost.

"Do you think the cold will slow down the Lurkers?" Mantayo asked.

"I doubt it," Johnny said. "I think they're beyond feeling any sensation of cold or heat. Mantayo, are your people going to be able to carry so many of us over to Booklin to see The Brethren?"

Mantayo smiled. "We have a surprise for you, Johnny."

Just as Mantayo finished speaking, Johnny and the others marveled at what they saw being lowered down in front of the building. It was a large basket, big enough for ten people inside. Johnny looked and saw it was being carried by four strong Sky men on ropes.

Johnny smiled at Mantayo and he smiled back. "If we are going to become allies, we will surely have to have many more meetings between us. It makes sense for us to come up with a more efficient method of transporting our new friends."

Johnny, Starbucks, Lightpole, Ticktock and Super jumped into the transport basket, which was a few feet below the opening. Deecee came to the opening and was about to jump in, but Johnny put up a hand to Deb. "Deb, please keep Deecee here. I know he wants to go, but it looks like he needs more rest."

Deb said, "Deecee's staying, but I'm not. I'm not losing you again!"

Johnny chuckled as Deb handed Deecee over to Sephie. Then she jumped into the basket too. When all of the travelers were inside, the Sky men holding the basket flapped their wings and slowly flew in the direction of Booklin. Mantayo flew next to them, gazing down at the city to try and spot the Lurker horde.

For the passengers it was a pleasant and exhilarating ride. They stared down at the world below talking and pointing out sights. They were high enough they could see the whole city, and as they flew over the river, they marveled at it. Starbucks and Super acted like little scrabblers on a fun walk, pointing at everything and grinning. Deb held onto Johnny, and the gazed at each other, wishing they were alone so they could enjoy a proper reunion.

They soon grew close to Booklin, passing over Keens. Mantayo flew next to the basket and talked to

Johnny. "Johnny, what about the people of Nork in Keens?"

Wind whistling through his hair and making it hard to talk, Johnny shouted, "They should be safe for now, Mantayo, being on the other side of the river. Hopefully we will be able to stop the Lurkers before they can get across the water."

"Johnny, look!" Starbucks pointed at Nork to the South. They all crowded on that side of the basket and looked where Starbucks pointed. There they saw them, the horde of Lurkers between the buildings, lurching their way north, towards the yellow building and their friends. The Lurker horde was still far away, but moving swiftly. There were already what looked like hundreds of them. Johnny saw men, women and scrabblers amongst them. Johnny felt pangs of sadness for the people of Nork who had been turned into Lurkers. This King Ferdinand was a monster, and totally evil. If they did nothing else, they had to make sure and make him pay for all the people he'd let die.

"We have to hurry, Starbucks!" Johnny yelled over the whistling of the wind.

"We sure do, Johnny," Starbucks said.

Genral Alcapoon watched as the soldiers drug wood, pieces of steel and chunks of concrete through the street. A makeshift wall began to form on the street in front of the king's castle, stretching in both directions as far as he could see.

The wall had to be tall enough to stop the Lurkers, and it had to reach from one side of the island to the other. Could they possibly get it built in time?

A small section of the wall was left open, and through it, the people of Nork poured in, running and yelling, their faces full of fright. What kind of a world was King Ferdinand creating? Alcapoon wondered if the city would survive the next few days.

Alcapoon ran back and forth behind the wall, looking for pieces of rubble which could be used. A few of the smaller old cars were even being dragged over to support the wall. Once the cars were by the wall, they were flipped over onto their sides so they made a solid steel structure. Then crude ropes and wires were used to connect them to the existing wall.

One of the Nork soldiers ran up to Alcapoon. The man was out of breath and wet with sweat. He looked exhausted.

"Genral, we have finished this section and are moving down to try and finish the section next to the water by Keens."

"Good," Alcapoon said. "Hurry, we don't have much time."

Alcapoon climbed onto the makeshift wall and stood at the top. He peered down the streets, looking for the first sign of Lurkers. So far, he didn't see anything, but he knew it would be that way for long. What if they didn't finish the wall in time?

"What an interesting place Nork is," Restaria said as she gazed out the fifth-floor windows at the city. "I only hope we are able to stop this evil king and his undead army. Then we can form some sort of alliance with the people of Nork and create a harmony between all our tribes. I would love to have a moment of time before we return to explore this fascinating city, with all its interesting structures."

"I agree indubitably!" Misterwizard said. He found himself not looking at the view, but gazing at Restaria. Without consciously thinking it, he noticed how beautiful she was, regal and intelligent. She seemed learned and cultured, someone who appreciated learning and knowledge, much like himself. He also remembered how earlier he was wishing he could find a romantic interest of his own, just like Johnny and Starbucks. It was almost as if the fates had heard him, and provided a possible candidate.

She turned and noticed him looking at her. She smiled at him with what appeared to be interest of her own. "I'm so grateful your people were willing to risk so much to come to our aid."

"How could we refrain from assisting such a benevolent and worthy people as yours, Restaria? You appear to engender the same acclivity for freedom and democracy as us, and have the same ambitions for reforming our once great nation."

Restaria walked closer to Misterwizard, standing only a few inches away, and something strange happened to Misterwizard which had never happened to him before. Suddenly his mind went blank, and he couldn't think.

"Johnny told me what an amazing man you are," Restaria said, her eyes twinkling. "So wise and full of knowledge. Now that I've met you, I can see everything he said was true."

Three thoughts sped through Misterwizard's brain, like speeding trains, all at once. The first was how attractive Restaria was. The second was how alike him she seemed to be, intelligent and wise, and eager to fill her mind with knowledge. The third thought was, what are you waiting for, old man? Time and opportunity wait for no man!

"And I can see everything Johnny told me about you was accurate, though not nearly descriptive enough," Misterwizard said. "He didn't elucidate how attractive and pleasant you are."

Restaria laughed, sensing just what Misterwizard was thinking, and thinking herself along the same lines. "Johnny didn't tell me how handsome and funny you are, either." She reached out and took Misterwizard's hand. "Maybe after our conflicts have been resolved, we might get a chance to explore a more meaningful interaction."

Misterwizard laughed with pleasure, and Restaria joined him.

"I was thinking along the same avenues of thought, my dear."

Restaria leaned towards Misterwizard, and moved her face close to his. Misterwizard looked slightly terrified, as she moved her lips towards his lips. Restaria closed her eyes, and Misterwizard watched her with quiet excitement. He pursed his lips, waiting for her kiss.

Up in Johnny's room with the Sky, the people of Sky had a big surprise. As they stood amazed, Lady Stabs and Sandl stood in the room. And behind them walked Pantina!

All the people of Sky immediately fell to their knees. Layla, Mantayo's mother, hurried over and knelt in front of Pantina, her head bowed.

"Oh, holy goddess, we are not worthy of your presence!" Layla said.

Pantina's lip quivered, and she placed a hand under Layla's arm. She lifted Layla up. Layla looked at her with surprise and confusion.

Pantina gazed at all the people of Sky. "Please, my dear friends, stand and listen to what I have to tell you."

As the people slowly rose and looked at Pantina with curious looks, the people of USA and Restaria stood back, waiting to see what Pantina was going to say.

Pantina smiled at them with sad eyes and

sorrow. "I love all of you. You are my people, and I have always tried to do everything for you I can. But you must accept the truth. I am not a goddess. I am only an ordinary girl, just like any other."

The people of Sky looked dismayed, and they glanced at each other, not liking what they were hearing.

"It was Lord Flaggalon who told you I was a goddess. He wanted you to believe that, so he could keep you under his control."

"Where is Lord Flaggalon?" Layla asked.

Pantina turned to look at her. "He is dead. An evil man who attacked me pushed him out a hole in the building by my throne room. Lord Flaggalon fell to his death. The evil man named Monsta then tried to kill me, but my friend Lady Stabs helped me defeat him."

The people all murmured, looking at each other with fear. Layla looked at the people, then at Pantina.

"We don't understand. You have special powers and abilities. You have the red hair, and the golden wings. You control the spiders."

"I have special abilities, it's true. I've always had the ability to control animals, and some less intelligent people. And my hair is red, and my wings golden. But I am not a goddess, any more than any of you are. I am a member of the Sky, just like you. And as long as you still want me, I will always do what I can to help our people."

Layla smiled and took Pantaya's hand. "Of course we will, Pantina. It will take some time for us to accept you are not our goddess, but we will love you even more than ever before."

The people of Sky smiled and rushed over to crowd around Pantina. All talking at once in happy voices, they hugged Pantina and Lady Stabs, who hugged them back with joy.

The four Sky men lowered the basket down to the ground on the street in front of the wall of Booklin. Johnny and his friends stepped out, and the four Sky men lifted the basket again, flew a small distance away and lowered the basket back to the ground. Then they landed and sat down, waiting. Johnny and the others gazed at the giant wall and looked at each other with a smile which showed they were impressed. Ticktock once again walked up, opened the little panel and flicked the bell, making the tinkling sound again.

He stood back, and they all waited. After a few minutes, the small panel slid open again. This time, a pair of eyes in the brown face of a young man. The man spoke in a strong but suspicious voice.

"Who seeks to enter the realm of The Brethren?"

"It is I, Ticktock. I have returned as I was told to, longer than seven suns, with the friends I spoke of. I have Johnny Apocalypse here, and Mantayo of the Sky. I also have other friends with us. We need to speak to the Old Wise Man right away!"

The brown man stared at Ticktock for a few

seconds. Then he slid the panel closed. Johnny and his friends could the man talking behind the wall to someone. Then the panel slid open and Bingchang appeared again.

"Ticktock, I spoke to the Wise Old Man. He was not convinced, or interested in what you had to say."

Johnny walked forward. Bingchang shifted his gaze to look at Johnny.

"I am Johnny Apocalypse. I am of the tribe called USA. Along with the people called Sky and the people of Letfreedomring, we are making an alliance of men who want to return freedom and 'mocracy to this land, the way it was before the mushroom monsters came. We came to see if your people would like to join us and be our friends, and normally we would have more time to get to know you. But the man who took over Nork and killed their king, an evil man who calls himself King Ferdinand, is creating a Lurker army, and it is infecting everyone in its path. We need to warn your people, and we need your help to fight King Ferdinand and the monsters. The Lurkers will infect everyone in Nork, and then they will be at your gate. If you don't help us, we may all be defeated, and the world will be filled with Lurkers. Please, just let us talk to your leader, and he will be able to see we are good people who only want to be your friends."

Bingchang looked at Ticktock and then back again at Johnny. "You are a white man. We don't trust white men. They are nothing but trouble!"

Johnny was prepared for this. He motioned to

Starbucks and Lightpole, and the two walked forward. Johnny pointed to them.

"These men are members of our tribes. As you can see, they are not white. We treat all men the same, regardless of their color or looks. Please, let us show you that we come as friends."

Bingchang peered at Starbucks and Lightpole with a frown. Then he smiled and burst into laughter. Everyone smiled too. "All right. We will let Ticktock and your small band enter and speak to the Wise Man. Know you will be surrounded by our soldiers the whole time. One false move, and we will all die. We will let the Wise Old Man decide if what you're speaking is true."

Johnny smiled. "That is totally acceptable. We want you to know we are your friends and you can trust us."

Bingchang studied them for a few more seconds. Then he nodded. The panel slid closed. After a few more seconds, the giant door creaked and swung slowly open. Ticktock, Johnny and the others smiled at each other in relief. Then Johnny, Ticktock, Mantayo, Starbucks, Super, Deb and Lightpole walked into Booklin. The giant door closed with a loud bang.

CHAPTER 33

Alcapoon waited, watching the streets. The soldiers of Nork stood all along the wall, watching, their guns pointed at the wall.

"Soon men, Johnny and his men will join us, along with the angels," Alcapoon said in a loud voice. "They will help us stem this terrible tide of death and destruction."

Behind him, Elliotness listened with contempt. Elliotness had listened to Alcapoon talk about overthrowing the king, and while Alcapoon was gone, he made a pact with some of the soldiers to kill Alcapoon and save their new king. Keeping one eye on Alcapoon, Elliotness turned and talked to a small group of soldiers in a quiet voice only they could hear.

"This waksy traitor really thinks we're gonna hand over this city to his new friends."

"We ain't gonna, are we, Elliotness?" another man named Tommy, after tommy gun, whispered back with a dark grin.

"'Course not. King Ferdinand is coming with his new Lurker army. He's gonna expect us to help him, and we ain't gonna let him down. Pass the word along to the men. When we see the Lurkers come, we attack Alcapoon and all his new "friends." We throw 'em over the wall into the Lurkers. Then we kill any that's left. This is King Ferdinand's city, and ours. We ain't giving it up to no one."

The men all nodded, glancing furtively at Alcapoon. Then they left in different directions to spread the word.

Johnny and his small group of friends entered Booklin. What they saw was a beautiful city full of color and magic. The streets were lined with golden statues of dragons and lions, and paper lanterns hung over them in bright, cheerful colors. The transformation from the drab, empty streets of Nork to the beauty of Booklin surprised and delighted them.

As they followed Bingchang down the street, men who all dressed like Lightpole, in silk jackets and leather coats and adorned with thin, elegant swords surrounded them.

Johnny and his friends smiled and pointed at the sights. Lightpole seemed even more excited than the others, for it almost seemed like he was coming home to a place he'd never been to before.

As they walked down the streets, people of all different colors and races surrounded them, all except for white people. Little Asian children ran around them in brightly colored silk robes and slippers, laughing and playing games. Black men and women in exotic dress strolled down the streets. And they saw brown people sitting on the curb and at different shops, selling different bits of clothes and food.

"Why would you ever leave here, Ticktock?" Lightpole asked, his voice full of marvel.

Ticktock looked regretful. "Booklin is truly a wonderful place, but very crowded. Food and other things are very hard to get, and there is a constant battle to find supplies for such a large group of people, especially when surrounded by enemies on all sides. I thought I could join the army of Nork and have more opportunity to gain riches and fame. I met Moxie, and we became friends. He spoke for me to the king, but I knew Ferdinand always hated me because I was what he calls cursed."

Johnny, who was listening in, smiled. "With your help Ticktock, we can all become friends, and together, we will make sure every city prospers and has enough."

Ticktock looked at Johnny. "You see things in a very positive way, Johnny Apocalypse. I hope the future you see comes to pass."

"Look!" Starbucks said, pointing in the distance with eyes full of wonder.

They all looked to see a golden castle in front of them, nestled between giant skyscrapers on a large plot of land.

"The Temple of Booklin," Bingchang said. "It is where the Wise Old Man holds court. He will decide if we will join you on your quest."

Johnny and his friends looked at each other, smiling. "Let's hope you are as good at convincing him as you are so many others, Johnny Apocalypse," Lightpole said. They walked towards the temple.

Gathered in front of the king's castle in Nork behind the crude makeshift wall, Johnny and his ragtag army waited. After Johnny and his friends had met with the Wise Old Man and convinced him of their friendship, a council was held in the Temple of Booklin with the leaders of all the different groups. Misterwizard and Restaria were there, as well as Pantina and Layla who came to represent the Sky. The only one who was not there was Alcapoon, to represent the people of Nork, but it seemed like that would have to wait until King Ferdinand was defeated.

Together it was decided they would all fight the Lurker threat, and then make an alliance. They would collectively call themselves America, for that was the name of the country before the mushroom monsters fell.

Now the armies from all the groups stood together, ready to fight. They had fashioned crude walkways behind the ragged wall so they could see out beyond it at the streets where the Lurkers would come from.

Armed with bows and arrows, torches, tommy guns and other rifles, soldiers of Nork, men and women of Johnny's tribe USA, men and women of Pelpia and men and women from Booklin all stood shoulder to shoulder. Behind them, men and women of Sky waited, ready to fly, holding buckets full of oil and torches. When the Lurkers arrived the people of Sky would take off and pour the oil on the Lurkers and then set them on fire. It was a large army, united and strong, but would it be enough to stop the Lurker horde?

The people of USA and Letfreedomring had been flown up to the skyscrapers of the Sky while Johnny and his group met with the Wise Old Man. The people of Nork waited in Sental Par with the soldiers from the Nork army. They were armed with makeshift weapons, ready to fight if the first line of defense didn't hold. The truth was, if the Lurkers breached the wall, everyone would all fall back towards Keens and try to escape across the water in boats and across the broken bridges. Then the battle would have to be fought from Keens and Booklin, and the i-land of Mattan would be considered lost.

Johnny, Starbucks, Mantayo, Lightpole and Mistewizard stood together on a stand at a spot right in front of the castle. Bargainbin and Jewelrydept had joined them. They all peered out silently. Everyone was quiet, and it seemed as if the world was on hold, waiting for the action to begin.

As they waited, Johnny thought with happiness about the moment Microsoft and Baskinrobbins were reunited with Sephie and Wheaties. He hadn't been there, but Misterwizard had told him about it later. Johnny heard there were lots of tears of joy and happy smiles when it happened. He just hoped they could all have a happy ending soon.

Behind the main army in Sental Par, Elliotness walked amongst the soldiers, secretly talking to them. He would wait until the battle was fully raging with the Lurkers, then his men would attack the invaders from all the other lands. He hoped the moment of surprise would be enough to help him and his men defeat them.

At the wall, Johnny heard something in the distance and tensed. Deb walked up behind him. He turned to her. "Any sign?"

Deb nodded. "I can see them from the windows of the castle. They are only a few blocks away now. It won't be long."

Johnny nodded. "Go back and watch, Deb. You and Super be ready to tell the women and scrabblers to hurry to Sental Par once the fighting starts."

Deb nodded and hurried away.

Suddenly Johnny heard screams. They came from around the buildings in front of him. Everyone on the wall tensed and looked to see what was happening.

A woman came running towards them down the street to the left, her hand holding the hand of a little girl. They both looked terrified and the ran swiftly, their mouths and eyes wide open. Then another joined them, and soon there was a huge crowd of people heading for them.

"It's the residents of Nork!" Misterwizard said. "Attempting to elude the undead horde!"

"We have to let them in, Johnny!" Alcapoon said.

Johnny nodded, but he knew if they opened a hole in the wall, they would be leaving a place for the Lurkers to get in as well.

"Hurry!" Johnny said, climbing down the wall "We have to let them in fast, before the Lurkers arrive!"

Together, Johnny, Starbucks, Mantayo, Alcapoon and Lightpole worked feverishly to disassemble the wall in one spot. The people escaping reached the wall and banged on it, desperate to get inside.

Johnny and the others finally managed to get an opening large enough for people to get through. Lightpole wormed his way out and yelled at the people to come towards him. The all ran towards him, and soon a large group of people formed in front of the opening, all pushing and shoving to get in.

Deb opened a window in the castle and yelled down. "They're here, Johnny!"

Johnny hurried back up to the wall, to see with dismay Deb was right. Not a block away behind the people, Lurkers came. Lurching and shuffling, their faces dead and deformed, they slobbered and chomped their teeth, their hands out, reaching, grabbing.

"We have to hold them off!" Johnny yelled

"Mantayo!"

Mantayo nodded and he motioned to the men of Sky. They took off and flew over the crowd of people towards the Lurker horde. As the rest of the army watched, the Sky soldiers reigned fire and arrows down on the approaching Lurkers. Lurkers burst into fire and stopped, writhing and falling. Others fell to the ground, their legs and bodies full of arrows. The battle had begun.

Slowly, too slowly, the terrified people of Nork worked their way through the wall. Johnny ran back to the top of the wall and looked out. The Lurkers were close! As he watched in horror and dismay, he saw a Lurker grab a man who ran towards the wall. As Johnny watched helpless, the Lurker dragged the man to the ground and bit him.

"We have to close the wall!" Lightpole said, after he fought his own way back in. But not everyone was through! The Lurkers were only a half a block away now, and moving fast. Johnny wondered where the evil King Ferdinand was. He was the one Johnny really wanted to kill. King Ferdinand was the cause of all this death and destruction, and he was the one who deserved to pay.

The Lurkers reached the wall! There were still some people outside and the Lurkers shuffled towards them. The people had no choice but to run away.

Johnny yelled, "Fight!" The fight was on.

Bullets and arrows whizzed over the wall. Buckets of oil were poured on the Lurkers, and flaming torches dropped, turning Lurkers into undead torches.

The undead torches stumbled into others, setting them on fire as well.

Johnny and Starbucks hurried to the wall and tried to pull the last few people inside. They had to fight back Lurkers, one who had hold of a woman's coat. They managed to beat it off and pull the woman inside.

They had no choice but to close the opening. Many of the people of Nork didn't make it through. They ran down the wall on the outside, trying to escape, but the Lurkers were everywhere now and most didn't make it very far before being surrounded and attacked.

The soldiers of Sky shot arrows and fire from above, and now all the soldiers of all the armies stood at the wall, reigning destruction on the undead horde.

But the horde was massive, and more and more poured down the streets towards the wall all the time. Soon the streets were clogged with Lurkers. Some piled on top of others, and the ones on fire spread the flame throughout the crowd, but the fire didn't stop most of them, they just kept stumbling ahead until their legs finally burned enough, they couldn't walk anymore. Then they fell and crawled along, using their arms, as their bodies continued to burn.

Elliiotness knew it was time. From behind the battle in Semper Par, he turned to his men. "Now men! Kill the intruders!"

The soldiers of Nork shouted and rushed forward, their guns aimed not at the Lurkers, but at Johnny and his friends.

Johnny and his army were so busy fighting the

Lurkers, they didn't see the men of Nork at first. Then the first members of Johnny's army began to fall from bullets and arrows, and slowly Johnny and his men realized they were under attack from behind.

Johnny turned and looked at the new threat. Then he turned to Alcapoon. Alcapoon looked at Johnny with regret. "I'm sorry Johnny. This was not my idea. I've been betrayed as well as you. This is not all of the army, only a small group."

Johnny didn't have time to worry about it. He turned to the men of Booklin and Letfreedomring. "The soldiers of Nork are betraying us!" he yelled. "Fight them!"

Slowly the men of America responded. The soldiers of Nork attacked them with swords and clubs, and now the fighting was inside as well as outside.

Johnny turned to Misterwizard, asking, "Misterwizard, what can we do?"

"You fight inside the traitorous vermin inside, Johnny, I will try to even the odds outside." With that, Misterwizard opened a bag which sat next to him. As Johnny watched, Misterwizard took out one of his special bombs. Johnny grinned and nodded. He ran to help the men fighting the soldiers of Nork.

Misterwizard lit his special bomb with his square piece of steel with the small flame. The bomb hissed and sparks flew from its top. With a smile of childish joy, Misterwizard threw the bomb out over the wall, as far as he could. The bomb flew in a lazy arc. The Lurkers saw it and watched it fly. It landed in the middle of a block to the left. With an ear shattering boom, it exploded, sending Lurkers flying. The rest of the Lurkers, attracted by the sound and light, turned and shuffled towards the site of the explosion.

"A most satisfactory display!" Misterwizard said chuckling. He prepared another bomb.

The soldiers of Nork had used the element of surprise to try and get an advantage on the people of America, but they didn't count on what good fighters the people of Booklin would be. Using their swords and with ferocity, the men of Booklin leapt on the traitorous soldiers of Nork and cut them down. The soldiers of Nork were outnumbered, and soon those who weren't killed turned and fled. The soldiers of Booklin ran after them as the rest of the army turned back to fight the horde of Lurkers again.

Alcapoon caught Elliotness by the doors of the castle. Elliotness stood defiantly, holding a sword high, ready to fight. Alcapoon held a tommy gun, aimed at Elliotness's heart.

"Why did you betray us, Elliotness?" Alcapoon asked. "I trusted you."

"It was you who betrayed your own people, fool," Elliotness said, scowling with hatred. "You let outsiders take over our home. You betrayed King Ferdinand, who trusted you to protect his kingdom."

"King Ferdinand is waksy. He wants to turn the whole world into a world of Lurkers, can't you see that?"

"He is going to make Nork the ruler of the world."

"Not if we can prevent it." Alcapoon aimed and fired, but his tommy gun just made a coughing sound and jammed.

Elliotness saw his chance and attacked Alcapoon. Roaring with rage he leapt forward, swinging his sword down in a deadly arc. Alcapoon stepped aside, and Elliotness rushed past him. Alcapoon smiled, for he was a much better fighter than Elliotness. He waited for Elliotness to turn back around, then he used the butt of his rifle to bash Elliotness in the chin. Elliotness fell down with a crash on the ground and his sword flew away, clattering on the ground.

Alcapoon put his tommy gun down. He picked up the unconscious Elliotness and flung him over his shoulder. As the battle raged around him, Alcapoon carried Elliotness to the wall. Climbing to the top, he threw Elliotness over the side, into the arms of the waiting Lurkers. "If you want to be in King Ferdinand's undead army, I'll help you!" Alcapoon yelled, as he watched the Lurkers tear Elliotness apart.

Another one of Misterwizard's bombs went off, this time closer, right in the middle of the crowd right in front of the wall. Lurkers flew everywhere. The rest shuffled towards the sound and commotion, and soon a pile of Lurkers lay at the spot, Lurkers climbing on top of each other.

With the full power of the combined army of America, the Lurker numbers began to dwindle, as more and more of them were burned or hacked to pieces. Johnny began to think they would win after all!

Then Johnny saw what he was looking for. At the very back of the street on the right, a lone coach sat, and sitting on top of the coach was none other than the evil King Ferdinand!

"There he is!" Johnny said, pointing, his face full of fury. Alcapoon saw him and nodded.

"Let me take him, Johnny. After all, he betrayed my people first."

Johnny nodded at Alcapoon in understanding. As Johnny watched, Alcapoon jumped off the wall on the other side. He held a sword in his hand. When he hit the ground, Alcapoon took off running. Heedless of the Lurkers around him, Alcapoon ran towards King Ferdinand. It was almost as if Alcapoon didn't care if he died, as long as he got his revenge first.

Johnny knew somehow that Alcapoon would make it, for the man was determined and fearless. Starbucks, Misterwizard, Lightpole and Ticktock joined Johnny and together they watched Alcapoon.

King Ferdinand looked on the battle with an evil grin. His eyes seemed lit up with an unnatural fire. His hands were bloody, and as Johnny and his friends watched, they saw why. King Ferdinand kept biting his fingers, as if eating himself. It appeared he was truly out of his mind.

Alcapoon reached a spot right in front of the coach. King Ferdinand gazed down at him.

"King Ferdinand!" Alcapoon yelled. "Look what you've done to our people! You are going to die for this!"

King Ferdinand smiled at Alcapoon, then

chuckled. As Johnny and the others watched with surprise and sorrow, King Ferdinand pointed to his coachman. The coachman raised his gun and shot Alcapoon in the shoulder. Alcapoon fell to the ground, wounded.

King Ferdinand looked over the sea of undead and burning Lurkers at Johnny and his friends. "I am the king of the undead, and soon you will all bow to me! You will never destroy my undead army!"

Johnny and the others looked at each other and then back at King Ferdinand. Then Johnny saw something even more terrifying and amazing than anything they'd seen so far.

Behind King Ferdinand, a giant figure shuffled forward. As it came into view, Johnny and the others could see it was not alive. He was a giant Lurker!

As Johnny and his friends watched, Gee grabbed King Ferdinand in his hand. As King Ferdinand screamed in terror, Gee lifted King Ferdinand up to his mouth and swallowed him whole!

Johnny and his friends grinned in triumph.

"That will teach him!" Lightpole said.

"We have to kill that giant Lurker!" Johnny said, pointing at Gee.

"Leave that to us!" Mantayo said. "We killed him once; we can do it again!"

As Johnny and the others watched, the men of Sky flew off to fight Gee the Gant once more. It was an amazing battle, as Gee, his eyes dead, tried once again to swat the small men away in the air. He was slower this time, though, and the men of Sky filled him with fire and arrows. Others landed on the ground and hacked at his legs. A small group found ropes and tied his legs together. As everyone watched, Gee fell forward, landing on the ground with a mighty crash, crushing all the Lurkers beneath him.

It was all over soon after that. The army of America was able to defeat the remaining Lurkers. When the main horde was destroyed, men and women went from block to block, dispatching any which were left. Then a giant bonfire was lit right in front of the wall, with Gee being the main fuel. All the Lurkers were burned, causing as smoke and a stench which rose from the ground for days.

THE VICTORY
AND A NEW BEGINNING

When it was all over, the leaders of all the different groups met in the old king's throne room. Present were Johnny, Deb, Alcapoon, who had survived his wound, Restaria, Lightpole, Misterwizard, Pantina and Layla, Lady Stabs, the Wise Old Man, Starbucks and Super.

They discussed the future and made a pact to join together as the people of America. Each city would have their own sovereignty, but each would work together to make laws and rules so the old ways of democracy would be preserved.

Johnny watched with pleasure as they all talked when the meeting was over. Then in surprise, Johnny watched as they all turned to him, smiling.

Restaria spoke for them all. "Johnny, Misterwizard has convinced us to be under a presdent, just like before, and to keep Washington Deecee as the captol. We have all discussed the matter, and would like you to be the first present."

Johnny's mouth opened wide in surprise. He looked at Deb, who simply smiled and shrugged. Johnny turned back to them.

"My father is presdent. He is in Washington Deecee right now, helping the people learn all the old rules and laws."

"We know your father is what Misterwizard calls, protemp," Lightpole said. "Whatever that means. But you are our true leader, Johnny. It was you who helped bring us all together. Please accept this position. We need you. You will cause all peoples we meet to stand with us!"

"After all," Restaria said, "I understand the presdent is elected by popular vote. And we all vote for you."

Johnny didn't know what to say. Deb put an arm around his waist and laid her head on his chest. Starbucks and Super walked up to him.

"It's up to you, Johnny," Starbucks said.

Johnny looked at everyone, and they all waited for his answer. "I'll think about it," Johnny said, not sounding very sure of his answer.

Johnny and Starbucks found their Harleys, and for a month as the different tribes and leaders talked and grew close, Johnny and his friends spent their days riding around Nork, looking at the sites. Deecee had healed up nicely and was his old self again. He ran next to them and explored the old buildings, occasionally scaring up a rabbit-beastie or a raccoon-beastie and then chasing it until it found a hole to hide in. Alcapoon was elected mayr of Nork. Pantina became the co-leader of the Sky, along with Layla.

All the bodies of the Lurkers were taken and placed in the old subways, which were searched for more Lurkers. The source of the "radiation" which caused the Lurkers was found to be in a site north of the city, where a mushroom monster had fallen into a lake which fed the rivers and streams in the subways. The mushroom monster had exploded, causing the destruction of many of the buildings in Nork, and the lake become tainted. The area for a long distance around the lake was roped off and posted as a no entry zone.

Soon, it was time for the members of USA and Letfreedomring to return home. Everyone was excited to get back to their own cities, and truly start the new nation with Johnny as their new presdent.

One day Johnny met with Lady Stabs. Her face seemed to radiate with a happy glow.

"So, what are you going to do, Lady Stabs? Are you coming back with us?"

Lady Stabs looked slightly embarrassed, and she played with the knife in her hand, twirling the blade against her palm. "I'm staying here, Johnny. Pantina is going to make me genral of her army. And not only for the Sky, but Alcapoon, now that he is going to be leader of the Nork people, wants me to genral of the Nork army as well."

"That's great, Lady Stabs!"

Lady Stabs looked embarrassed for a moment. "And Johnny…"

Johnny smiled wryly. "You and Pantina are a thing, aren't you?"

Lady Stabs smiled, her face full of emotion.

"That's great, Lady Stabs. I'm so happy you've found someone, just like me and Deb and Starbucks and Super."

Lady Stabs looked at the sky and then back at Johnny. "You know Johnny, all my life, I've never felt like I fit in. I always felt like an outsider. But here, for the first time, I feel like I've found where I belong."

Johnny walked over and gave Lady Stabs a hug. Tears came to her eyes, and she hugged him back. "I'll always love you, Johnny. I'll never forget you, as long as I live. You'll always be my hero."

"And you're mine, Lady Stabs," Johnny said, gazing into her eyes with conviction and warmth. "I owe you so much. Remember, you saved our lives back in Ballmor."

As they pulled away, Lady Stabs wiped the tears away with the back of her hand and sniffed. She tried to look tough again, but Johnny didn't buy it for a second. "So, watch yourself, if you come to Nork from now on. There's a new sheriff in town."

They both laughed, a relief after the strong

emotions. "Well, the nice thing is, it gives us a reason to come visit Nork," Johnny said.

Then came the day Johnny held Deb's hands as they gazed into each other's eyes. They stood in the open courtyard behind the king of Nork's castle. Next to Johnny and Deb sat Johnny's Harley. Not far away, Deecee lay on the ground and gnawed on a bone.

"So, you're going to be presdent, Johnny!" Deb said smiling brightly. "You'll be in charge of a whole new world and help shape it for 'Mocracy!"

Johnny smiled and nodded, but there was an unhappiness playing at the corners of his eyes.

"You'll have to learn all the rules, and tell the people what to do. Misterwizard will teach about all the stuff he's always talking about, the Constuton, and the Billrights, and the Declation of Inpendens. And you'll sit in the big white building in that fancy room where the presdent sits, in that big, smelly chair, just like Foodcourt does now!"

Johnny studied Deb's eyes and her tone of voice. It gave him hope, because he heard some reluctance in her voice.

Deb noticed the strange look in Johnny's eyes. "Johnny, what's the matter?"

Johnny hesitated. Then he frowned and gazed at Deb with a worried look.

"What if I said I don't want to be presdent, Deb? Would you be disappointed? If we didn't go back to the nice, peaceful Washington Deecee?"

Deb grinned, for she had suspected Johnny felt this way all along.

"I know you said you were tired of adventures…" Johnny said.

Deb put a finger on his lips. "So instead, you think I want to go back and watch you become an old man, and me turn into an old maid?"

Johnny grinned. Deb kissed Johnny, and put her head on his chest. "What do you want to do, Johnny?" Johnny turned and looked west, past the river at the distant hills. Deb looked at where Johnny was looking then put her head on his chest again. "Well, you know what I always say. Where Johnny goes, I go."

At that moment, Super walked around the corner, munching on an apple. She looked at Johnny and Deb and saw the way they looked so serious.

"What going on, guys?"

Deb turned to Super with a tight smile. "We're leaving, Super."

Super grinned. "'Bout time!" She turned her head and yelled towards the other room. "Starbucks, get over here!"

Starbucks walked into the room, smiling. "What's up?"

"We're leaving!" Super said.

Starbucks looked at Johnny. "Where are we going, Johnny?"

Johnny pointed west.

"All right! This place was getting so quiet!" Starbucks walked over and hopped on his Harley. Super yipped with glee and hopped on behind him.

Johnny looked at Deb and they laughed. They walked over and climbed on Johnny's Harley. "Deecee!" Deecee looked up and then leapt up. He ran for the Harley and jumped in his side seat. They all laughed.

They started up the Harleys and the air filled with the familiar and comforting roar. Johnny turned and smiled at Deb, then kissed her. Then he turned around and started rolling. The roar of the Harley filled the air.

Starbucks fell in behind Johnny. Soon they were flying down the road, past the old, deserted skyscrapers, weaving around the old, rusted cars towards the tunnels, leaving Nork behind, heading for new adventures and dangers in the Nuclear Wasteland.

MARK ROBIJN is an author, screenwriter and filmmaker. He lives in Tacoma Washington where he loves to hike Mt. Rainier, read science fiction and write. He is also the author of the horror anthology Midnight Terrors, the thriller Dead by Midnight, and three children's picture books.

Contact Mark either by email at: johnnyapocalypsenow@gmail.com or on his website at www.markrobijn.com, where you can buy all of Mark's books and sign up for his newsletter.

If you like this book, please review it on Amazon or Goodreads.com. Thank you!